Black as Death

A Collection of Café Cozy Mysteries

Kate Swenson, Brenda Beem, Martina Dalton, Maren Higbee, Robin Russell

Write as Rain Books

BLACK AS DEATH

A Collection of Café Cozy Mysteries

Cover design by Mariah Sinclair, https://www.thecovervault.com/

First Edition: February 2022

ISBN: 978-1-7331168-7-9

A STEAMY CUP OF MURDER

by Kate Swenson

CHAPTER 1 - CAFFEINE DIVA

Why must every single day come with a morning? Noon is the only appropriate time for waking. I grimaced against the relentless light, pushing my Italian sunglasses closer to my face as I stumbled down the sidewalk. The ten-minute trek from my riverfront condo to the coffeehouse in historic downtown Cedar River felt like a marathon. It is possible that I moaned dramatically.

"Are you going to make it, Auntie Babe?" my usually adorable niece asked, skipping along beside me.

Part of me admired the dry derision of Lavender's tone —such talent in one so young. But mockery at that level should be gifted from the top down, a weapon reserved for true divas, like myself. Unlike those who claim diva status for fun, I'd actually earned the title by clawing my way up the gilded ladder of the opera world. I'm the soprano you call when you want the chandeliers to swing. My instrument is startlingly large considering the tiny package. And at this ungodly hour, I was every inch the grumpy prima donna.

"Hush, darling. We're almost there." I flung my silk pashmina over my chilly shoulder. June-uary in the Pacific

Northwest requires strategic layering; at 11 a.m. the air was a bit cool for my leopard-print jumpsuit.

I was desperate for my caffeine hit and looking forward to showing off my new project to eleven-year-old Lavender, who'd arrived the night before from Minnesota for a long visit. Her goth-baby ensemble was flawless. Dress, tights, combat boots, purse, headphones—all black —contrasting her peach-blush hair. Very ghost-whisperer. And my darling niece had earned her title too.

In the Cuckoo family, strong fashion sense and paranormal talents get passed down like dimples. Most of us have a bit of sensitivity for everything from ghosts to precog, along with a specialty area. I'm an empath. If I let my psychic shields down, I experience the emotions of anyone in the vicinity. So I keep my shields activated and caffeinated the best I can. Lavender's a medium, chatting with ghosts since the crib.

An irritating repetitive sound beat against my skull. "What is that terrible racket?"

"Birds? Singing?" Lavender grinned, enjoying my misery.

Luckily for both of us, we'd reached the ironclad doors of my new project and the blessed coffee inside.

"This is it, niecling." I gestured to the brick façade. "Auntie is a business owner!"

Lavender applauded and I curtseyed deeply. The Metal Grind was a coffeehouse/art gallery/bar/concert venue dedicated to Heavy Metal and started by an old friend. I'd jumped at the chance to invest as a (mostly) silent partner. The location, in my own Seattle suburb, cinched the deal. Cedar River's burgeoning art scene and charming neighborhood was the perfect location for our hybrid venue—a converted theatre. The café had been open for a week for coffee and lunch. Tonight, we'd scheduled an invited event to kick-off our bar and concert venue before the grand opening tomorrow evening. And the headliner? You guessed it.

"Whoa." Lavender spotted the life-sized poster of me under the "Now Playing" sign next to the front door, her eyes growing wide. "Brionne LeFave's looking pretty badass."

My stage name is Brionne LeFave—Wagnerian Soprano. My real name is Brionne Cuckoo—quirky, but hardly opera appropriate. And my friends and family call me Babe. Part of legit diva status includes enjoying multiple names.

"I'm going heavy metal," I announced. On the enormous poster, my alter ego posed, a dangerous goddess, clad in leather and smoke, flaming red hair streaming about her head like Medusa. Pale skin and enormous blue eyes added to the otherworldly vibe, I was very pleased with the results and the possibilities.

My voice may have been built for opera, but my personality leans more towards rock and roll. And as much as I loved my classical career, it was a grueling circuit of touring and training. Plenty of glamour, but not much pay, and I was ready for a new adventure. Not giving up opera totally—diversifying. At the tender age of thirty-nine again (again), change felt healthy. And putting new creative pursuits together with a caffeine-related business investment equaled win-win. The whole combination really got my blood pumping. My opera following would likely not make the transition to metal with me, so I was courting a very different audience. A new vocal challenge. A new business. My life's savings. Summer 2015 was going to be one to remember. I suddenly felt a bit faint.

Coooooooffeeeeeee.

"You know I don't drink coffee, right?" Lavender asked, reading my mind (or perhaps I said it aloud.) "I'm eleven."

"Of course." I made a face, smoothing a crimson curl back into my enormous messy-bun. "What kind of Auntie doesn't know that her niecling doesn't like coffee? Or that she eats breakfast before noon? C'mon, kid. You'll get your whiskey."

That got a giggle out of her. Lavender tended to linger on the dark side. I knew firsthand that managing paranormal gifts was rough even for adults, and pre-teen Lavender was managing a rare combination of genetics.

I grabbed the silver handle and pulled open the door to the coffeehouse. "Behold—The Metal Grind." I gestured grandly, ushering her inside.

"Oooo, skulls!" Lavender clapped in delight at the reoccurring decorative theme. The original brick walls of the historic building showcased a collection of skulls: metal, glass, genuine, and guitars: electric. Lavvy loves skulls. While most kids treasure a stuffed animal as a comfort item growing up, Lavender loved a walnut-sized skull made of purple amethyst. His name was Stanley. As far as I knew, he was currently tucked away in her pocket.

The Metal Grind was surprisingly bright—or would've been if I were foolish enough to remove my sunglasses— thanks to a bank of high windows bracketing the space. The morning playlist focused on acoustic covers of hard rock, but the only music I heard was the gorgeous sound of the industrial coffee grinder. I let the holy elixir fill my senses, dragging the perfume into my lungs like oxygen, and paused long enough to enjoy Lavender's reaction.

"Wow!" Lavender looked perfectly at home in the heavy metal wonderland.

The café area spread out in front of us, and I was pleased to see almost a dozen customers enjoying themselves. Our daytime service appeared to be a success as we reached the end of our first week. Next up—the evening side of The Metal Grind.

Vintage burgundy theatre curtains, salvaged from the theater's original stage, backed the space dividing the performance area and café. The bar spread out on our left; from the far-right corner rose the painfully expensive, circular metal staircase leading the eye up to the artwork hanging from the black ceiling.

"The metal work is Xenith's," I said. Xenith Morgan, my friend and business partner in this little venture, was an incredible visual artist. "The big one's called *Infinite Jest*." I gestured to the enormous metal sculpture dominating the center of the room. A representation of Hamlet and Yorick ensconced in a cyclone of skulls and twisted electric guitars, the piece was a tribute to Xenith's mentor, who'd been the previous owner of the space.

"There are more up there." I smiled as Lavender tipped her head back like a Pez dispenser to take in the ceiling. "And those glass pieces are authentic Chihuly."

"Chi-hoo-lee?" Lavender said. "Is that a Wookiee?"

"I'm sure your father would be proud," I laughed, referring to my twin brother. "But sounds like we need to add Seattle Art Excursion on our list of fun stuff to do." I slung my arm around Lavender's narrow shoulders and squeezed, steering her towards the coffee. "I knew you'd love it. The Metal Grind is just your kind of place."

The black and steel bar dominated the left side of the space and was currently filled with buzzing barista bees. The mirrored wall behind them displayed coffee and gleaming alcohol bottles. At the register, two men in business suits admired Xenith's legendary curated whiskey collection as they moved down the bar to pick up their drinks.

"Good morning, Ms. LeFave. You're up early!" Darien, the slender, pierced cashier called. Xenith's nephew, a recent college grad, was a whiz with customers and just as handsome as his uncle. "Here's your starter." With graceful flair, he presented a doppio shot in a custom Metal Grind black ceramic demicup.

My heart sang.

"Bless you, Darien." I dropped a perfect curtsey and tossed back the shot. I could feel the magic dancing through my veins as I set the cup on the counter with a click.

"I think you may have an addiction problem, Auntie Babe," Lavender said.

"Duh, darling, duh."

"The usual?" Darien asked.

"Yes, please." I savored the opening jolt.

"Got it, Al?" Darien called over the symphony of the espresso machine.

"One Venti Diva's Delight," she called back. Al Mendoza our third partner in the business. A high school friend of Xenith's, she'd moved back to the States from the Philippines, where she'd been living with relatives, to help open The Metal Grind. Al was a coffee virtuoso—and I don't use that term lightly. She made the magic and managed the café with military precision. I was still getting to know the private woman but was a mega-fan of her barista and business talents.

"You are my favorite people," I announced. "We're having breakfast, too. Highway to Hell Hash for me, and whatever my niecling, Lavender, wants."

"I'm starving," Lavender admitted.

"Not for long, sweetie." Darien handed her a laminated menu.

"And while Lavender's deciding, Darien, you must tell me everything about this new lipstick." The caffeine began to loosen my natural charm.

Darien grinned and pouted his metallic purple lips. The color popped beautifully against his dark brown skin. His tight cap of black curls highlighted enviable bone structure —he was born photo-ready. "Isn't it fab? And you want to hear something hilarious? It's called Electric Lavender."

Lavender looked up in surprise.

"I totally wore this color to celebrate your arrival." Darien leaned across the counter toward my niece, feathered earring swinging. "You should get some too. Electric Lavender—this lipstick literally has your name on it! I bought it at Ink Blot, right across the street."

"It does look really cool," Lavender said.

"Thank you!" Darien stole a quick millennial glance at himself in the mirrored wall behind him before returning his attentions to my delighted niece. "I'm a HUGE fan of you and your show, BTW. I can't wait to ask you a million questions."

Lavender and her mother starred in a reality web-series featuring my brother's unusual family business— renovating haunted houses. The show was quickly gaining popularity, and Darien was a sincere fan.

"Thanks." Lavender was dazzled. "And I guess I'll try the Skullsmasher Breakfast Burrito?"

"Absolutely." Darien rang up the order. "What do you want to drink?"

Lavender stared at the endless list above the bar. "I—"

"Oh!" Darien clapped with excitement. "You should totally have Al read you."

"Read me?" Lavender frowned.

"Yeah, she's our drink whisperer," Darien said. "One look —she knows your drink, even if you don't."

"Okay." Lavender gave me a smirk. "That'll be a switch."

"Al's never wrong. Go let her get a good look at you." Darien fluttered a hand in the barista's direction. "Al, time for your party trick."

Al's dark, buzzcut head was bent over the milk she was steaming. She made a noise that could have been an affirmation or a denial. Her golden-brown arms, sleeved with colorful tattoos, moved with surety as she completed numerous tasks at once. Lavender walked to the end of the bar, peering around the espresso machine at the stoic barista. Al handed off two drinks to waiting customers then leaned across to Lavender, studying her with hazel eyes.

"Mexican."

"Mexican?" Lavender echoed.

"Hot chocolate." Al ended the conversation, returning to her mysterious work hammering, grinding, and steaming potions.

"Ummm," Lavender said, returning to the register. "Is Mexican Hot Chocolate a thing?"

"Oooo, interesting choice," Darien said. "A little spicy. Sophisticated. You'll love it."

"Okaaaaaay."

"We're going for a Mug o' Montezuma, Al," Darien called.

"I know," Al called from the end of the bar. "Diva's Delight is ready."

"Thank the goddess," I sang, snagging my enormous mug and escorting Lavender to one of the high-top tables near the entrance with a view of the charming street. I was nearly functional, but my sunglasses were still firmly in place—the butterfly emerges slowly.

Lavender gazed out to the street. "This is a cool neighborhood."

"It is." I climbed up into the tall stool and sipped deeply. "Thirty years ago, this block was a handful of struggling businesses. Now, Cedar River has a bit of everything. Book store, salon, cupcakes, yoga, and a preschool going in next to the park. And of course, one old theatre turned into a perfect coffeehouse/art gallery/bar/concert venue."

"You know this place is haunted, right?" she asked.

"Quite," I said with a nod. "All theatres require a ghost, after all. And we've got a definite trickster in residence. Loves to leave surprises, like precarious stacks of dishes, turning the guitars on the walls backward, cranking the music, unraveling the TP in the bathrooms and randomly changing the music to show tunes—my personal favorite. Nothing mean or malicious, just unnerving. Although there have been complaints from our terrible neighbor about after-hours music when we know everything was shut down."

Lavender grinned. "Sounds fun. Want me to...?" She waved her fingers around, indicating an exorcism—not a word you want to use in front of nosy spirits who can manipulate matter. "Help with an eviction?"

"Maybe. I was mostly hoping you could tell me more about our friend," I said. "But only if you want to. I would totally understand if you needed your vacation to be a break from woo-woo business."

"No big deal. I only need a break from the cameras—I never get a break from spirits," Lavender said, twisting back and forth on her stool. My heart squeezed at her matter-of-fact description of her life. "Maybe tonight. Spirits like the dark. I don't sense anything malevolent, but you'd feel that before me, probably."

I spotted Al headed our way. "Here comes your drink. How cool is that skull mug? Xenith's wife, Lana, made them."

"Very cool. Thank you." Lavender's legs swung as she admired the vessel and the tower of whipped cream floating on top.

"You'll like it." The barista stated without inflection, and solemnly winking with one eye. Al rubbed a hand over her stubbled head and departed.

"*Will* I like it?" Lavender sniffed suspiciously at the cup.

"Only one way to find out," I said. "Let me record for posterity." I took out my phone, capturing a shot of Lavender taking a teeny, testing sip of the hot chocolate, and getting whipped cream all over her nose. I laughed, handing her a napkin.

"Yum," she declared, diving back into her disturbingly named Mug o' Montezuma, this time avoiding the whipped cream mustache. "Back to spirits. I see a dude hanging out near Al. Looks like her, maybe a relative? He's younger, around Darien's age. Collegey? Tattoos, pierced ear—I guess that's everybody in this place, isn't it?

The spirit guy's wearing the same Soundgarden shirt Dad has, but it looks new. He keeps moving Al's cups just slightly, so she reaches without looking and they're gone. Totally cracking himself up—could be your TP artist."

"Interesting." I watched Al at the machine. "I wonder if she knows she's got a Casper?"

"Maybe," Lavender said. "She's probably some kind of sensitive. I've never heard of a drink whisperer, but she totally nailed it."

I smiled, nearing comfortably caffeinated. Leaning back, I spotted Xenith emerging from the second story catwalk that connected the spiral staircase to the office area, our dressing room/green room combo, and the apartment where he and Lana lived. I waved up at him. "Here comes Xenith."

His broad frame rose well over six feet and his dreadlocks were pulled on top of his head, making him seem even taller. Performer, metal-sculptor, and occasional model, Xenith was a work of art all on his own. In a recent Seattle Times feature on black-owned businesses, a besotted reporter had called Xenith "the Lenny Kravitz of modern art."

Years ago, Xenith and I were briefly an item. Unfortunately, we held different exclusivity requirements. I don't share. Now we're just good friends—but I still enjoyed the view. His sleeveless Metal Grind T-shirt nicely displayed his muscular, sepia-brown arms as he waved before winding down the stairs.

As he reached the floor, the front doors slammed open, a beam of morning light cutting like a laser across the floor. A backlit figure entered the coffeeshop, heading toward Xenith like a bullet.

"You MONSTER!" the figure cried, jabbing a finger at Xenith. "This has GOT TO STOP!"

CHAPTER 2 - NOT SO ZEN DIVA

The natural din of The Metal Grind screeched to a halt as we all stared at the shrill woman confronting Xenith.

"I will shut this place down!!" The enraged woman was dressed in aggressively orange yoga attire, standing toe-to-toe with Xenith by the central sculpture. I jumped off my stool, putting myself between Lavender and possible danger. You didn't need to be an empath to feel the threat and I felt it like a Tasmanian Devil attacking my guts.

The blonde intruder wore an orange yoga mat slung across her back like a quiver, and gestured wildly with orangely tanned arms. Ah, a theme. Xenith recovered quickly, ushering the woman away from *Infinite Jest* in the direction of the door. He glanced up the circular stairs, toward his apartment. He appeared calm, though I could sense he was rattled.

The woman's arms showed impressive, carved muscles. I wouldn't win in a purely physical altercation—but I fight dirty.

"Auntie Babe," Lavender said in the tone one uses to calm a dangerous animal. "It's okay." I felt her small hand on my tense forearm. "No weapons necessary."

The steak knife in my fist was held low against my leg, the blade hidden from view by the flowy fabric of my jumpsuit. Stylish and practical. I put the knife back on the table and kissed Lavender's shiny ginger hair.

Calm restored, I strengthened my psychic shields and assessed the situation without anyone's unexpected emotions clouding my judgment. Xenith maneuvered the enraged woman toward the front door, facing-off with her near the empty hostess station.

"Ah," I said as I put it together. "It's Yoga Banshee."

"What?" Lavender asked in a whisper.

"The Grind's terrible neighbor. She's been making Xenith's life hell. He told me about her, but I've yet to witness her in all her glory. I'm not usually up this early."

"You're welcome," Lavender said smartly.

I side-eyed my niece and picked up my coffee, closing the distance to Xenith and Yoga Banshee. Up close, I could see his unease. The customers and staff were clearly enjoying the show, even as he tried to use the Infinite Jest sculpture as a barrier. He glanced upstairs again, and I realized he was worried about Lana. Although his wife was a dozen years younger than him, she was going through a challenging pregnancy. Lana might be chronologically young, but her old soul was Xenith's true north. His love for the gorgeous ceramic artist had settled him into the happy man he was today, and his concern for her was incredibly sweet. My protective instincts unfurled their well-manicured claws.

"What have we here?" I said, meeting Xenith's gaze over the raging blonde's head. "Sheena, is it? I've heard so much about you."

"It's Shayla." She whirled around, giving me a full glare. Well, as much as she could manage with a high ponytail pulled so tight it was an eyelift. She had the body of a twentysomething, but up-close she was clearly closer to my age. I'd been so focused on Shayla, I'd overlooked the other woman standing at her elbow. The two visitors shared the same face, but wildly different styles: brassy vs. mousy. They must be sisters. The other woman shifted nervously, pale and unhappy in a zombie gray tracksuit. Who wouldn't be?

"Oh, perfect, the washed-up opera singer," Shayla sniped.

I threw back my head and laughed with sincere delight. This could be fun.

"If you're going to sling insults, darling, they should at least be accurate," I said with a raised brow. "But I imagine you don't know much about the opera world—it is rather exclusive."

Xenith tried to pretend the situation was civil. "Let me make some introductions. Brionne LeFave, our neighbor from the Endless Zen Yoga studio, Shayla Starr, and Missy Jo James."

"It's not THE Endless Zen," Shayla burst out. "It's Endless Zen!"

"Clearly." Taking Xenith's cue to the high road, I added, "Nice to meet *you*, Missy Jo." I shook the gray-clad woman's icy hand and she smiled at me beneath her unfortunate beige bangs.

Shayla barreled on, undeterred by social graces. "And I am not *from* the yoga studio, I *own* it. And *you're* ruining my business. This horrible place is a blight on the neighborhood. Peddling poisons, endless caterwauling, truly tasteless art." She gestured angrily at *Infinite Jest*. "What even is this pile of metal crap? And the kind of people you attract? This has got to stop."

"Art *and* coffee hater? That's so sad." I placed a mournful hand on my heart. "What's in the travel mug then?" Missy Jo held two mugs, one a virulent orange container with "Shayla" etched up the side in gold script. "Green tea? You may want to check the caffeine levels."

"It's mushroom tea, thanks," Shayla hissed. "I don't drink toxins. Now, I am warning you." She moved in very close to Xenith, leaving just a sliver of air between them. "Put an end to this madness or else!"

"Shayla," Xenith said with a sigh and a deliberate step back. "Always with the threats. What exactly is the problem this time? I'd offer to discuss it calmly, but that does not seem to be an option."

"Don't take that tone with me!" Shayla's breathing was rapid, her cheeks flushed. She was enjoying this confrontation with my handsome partner. Iiiiinteresting. "Turn down this music, or I'm calling the cops."

"Darien," Xenith called. "Is the music set to the levels that we mutually our lawyers negotiated for morning hours?"

"Yes, indeed, Uncle Zee."

"This is not MUSIC," Shayla blared. "This is SCREAMING!"

"The only thing screaming at the moment is you, Shayla," I pointed out helpfully.

"Let's g-g-go, Shayla," Missy Jo, the mouse piped, up. "C-c-class is starting—"

"God, Missy Jo!" Shayla screeched at the shy woman. "You are the WORST!"

Suddenly, a pile of napkins stacked on the hostess station took flight, as if blown by a strong wind. The recycled paper products hit Shayla in the face like the fluttering wings of angry bats. Our resident poltergeist wanted Yoga Banshee banished too.

"That is assault!" Shayla yelled. "You'll be hearing from my lawyer. I will own you."

Her rage pinged like bullets against my psychic shields— something more than just noise complaints was going on here. Yoga Banshee departed in a cloud of sandalwood and rose, ponytail whipping behind her. As the heavy door swung closed, a smattering of applause filled the room.

"I'm very sorry about that," Missy Jo said. "My sister's been having a tough time lately."

"A tough time not transforming into a werewolf?" I asked.

"Um, Zee, I hate to ask," Missy Jo continued, ignoring my quip, "but I have to, or, well, you know. May I hang this flyer on the c-c-c-community board?"

I couldn't get over her tragic hair. She needed a curl mentor or possibly an intervention. Her pretty face was nearly identical to her sister's, but Missy Jo appeared to be making an effort to be unattractive, to fade into the background. Sad.

"Community. That's how it works." Xenith continued with the graciousness. "Are you coming to the event tonight, Missy Jo?"

We'd invited friends and local merchants to a soft open of our night service. They would attend my rehearsal, getting free whiskey and song, while giving the staff a casual, friendly audience to practice on before the grand opening tomorrow. Genius!

"Oh, I c-c-c-can't. I—thanks. Sorry. Nice to meet you, Ms. LeFave." The nervous woman hurried to pin up her flyer. Her phone rang, and she pulled it from her pocket.

"Yes. Right behind you, Shayla. Sorry. Sorry." Still apologizing, Missy Jo disappeared out the door.

"Wow," I said, shaking my head. Leading Xenith back to our table, I gently guided him to my seat across from Lavender. Al appeared, setting a mug of coffee in front of Xenith. They exchanged silent shoulder punches in a love-ritual I'd often seen—a holdover from their teen years. Reserved around almost everyone else, Al shared the easy affection of siblings with Xenith.

As she returned to her post, I released my shields and read Xenith's emotions. Outwardly calm. Underneath, I read anger, frustration and, oddly, a current of guilt. What was that about? I was missing something and feeling a little guilty myself for reading without permission. I clamped down on the woo-woo and I gave his arm a friendly pat. "Those two are sisters? Talk about contrast."

"Yoga Banshee is intense," Lavender said.

"She is," I agreed. "I thought you might be exaggerating, Xenith. Clearly you weren't, but maybe we should call her something else? I feel bad for the banshees."

Xenith shook his head. "She's a legend," Xenith said. "So angry. Pretty much everyone around here has been her target."

"I'm sorry she threw shade at your sculpture," Lavender said. "I really like it. The skulls are awesome."

"Thanks, Lavender." Xenith gave her a dazzling smile. "It's an homage to *Hamlet*. But mostly to Elliot James. He used to own this place, back when it was the Starrlight Theatre." Xenith put on an affected air and gestured dramatically, channeling his mentor. "*That's Starrlight with TWO Rs, so it won't be confused with the bloody cinema.*" Xenith broke character and smiled with affection. "Whatever that meant. He was a drama queen. And a groundbreaker in this neighborhood. In the late 80s this was a rough place to be gay, but Elliot didn't give a sh—" He looked guiltily at Lavender. "—a *shiny* penny about what people thought."

"Shiny penny." Lavender giggled and I hid a smile. Her dad swore like a sailor. Lavender's sister's first word had been *shiny*, Xenith's language adjustment was years too late.

Xenith shook his head at us and continued. "Elliot always treated everything like a grand joke—hence *Infinite Jest*—

and he lived to the fullest. Owned the whole block—literally. Created a semi-professional theatre here through the sheer force of his will. The Starrlight turned things around for the neighborhood. It was basically our home. Things really fell apart the year Elliot died, but eventually, I came back home, and I think he'd be proud of what we've done here."

"Sounds like quite the character," I said, pulling another stool around so I could pick at the remains of my breakfast. "I remember you telling me he changed your life."

"Saved it." Xenith leaned back impressive arms crossed behind his head. Several café patrons swooned. "When I found out he left the theatre to me—I freaked. But I'd probably be dead without this place; I was headed down a bad path in high school." He pointed at Lavender with mock gravity. "Stay in school, young lady."

"I homeschool," Lavender said, matter-of-factly. "Easier that way. I can work on the show and make money being myself, rather than try to survive thirteen years of being beat-up for being myself."

Xenith and I exchanged a look.

"Lavender is more grown-up than we'll ever be," I said. "She has much to teach us."

"Obviously," Xenith said with a warm laugh. He drank some coffee and, finally, appeared to relax.

Lavender finished her hot chocolate off with a slurping flourish. "Your place here is really cool, even with Yoga Banshee dropping in to Mean Girl you."

"Yeah, she's been pain in the... artichoke." Xenith censored himself adorably. "She loves calling the cops on us. Our buildings share a wall and a common entrance in the back, so Shayla's hard to avoid. She filed noise complaints the whole time we were under construction. And since morning operations started last week, it's music complaints." Xenith sighed. "We installed sound baffling. Offered to do her side too—she refused. I had Deimos work out an agreement with her lawyer."

I smiled thinking of Xenith's suave younger brother. Deimos leaned heavily on the corporate lawyer vibe. Darien had far more in common with his uncle than his straightlaced father.

"Not that stops Shayla's complaining," Xenith sighed. "Luckily, Endless Zen only operates mornings and afternoons—"

"OHMYGOD!" Darien was staring at the flyer Missy Jo had posted on the community board. "Bosspeople, you're going to want to see this." He ripped down the paper, waving it in the air.

"What is it?" Lavender asked.

"There's a new class at Endless Zen Studios," Darien announced. "Sunset Zen. And guess when it starts?"

"Tonight," Xenith and I said in unison.

"Yes! Fridays and Saturdays at 8 pm," Darien said. "Y'all are psychic."

Oh, darling, you have no idea.

CHAPTER 3 - DING! CUPCAKES!

"And that was Ink Blot," I said in my best tour-guide cadence as we exited the boutique. "Where you can get pierced, tattooed, *and* fill all your goth-boutique shopping needs."

Lavender and I were doing some shopping and reminding the neighbor merchants to attend The Metal Grind's soft opening that night. My niecling was delighted with her too-cute-to -pass-up-auntie-presents and, of course, her new lipstick. Darien would be thrilled they were Electric Lavender twinsies. I continued the grand tour.

"This area is part of historic downtown Cedar River, been around since the early 1900s,"

Lavender obligingly looked up from her oversize Ink Blot bag. "So much brick."

No denying that. Brick buildings lined either side of the one-way street, nestled cheek-to-jowl. Some painted their façades, others kept the natural variations of brownish red. Decorative metal streetlights, adorned with flower baskets, lined the sidewalks. And the public art was fantastic. Murals, unique fire-hydrants, and revolving window displays were everywhere and proudly maintained. A-dor-able.

"Xenith grew up around here, a theatre kid. Even after graduation he stayed around working at the Starrlight, and eventually inherited the building as a reward for his loyalty." I gestured across the street to where the Metal

Grind and Endless Zen took up the block. The bricks ran seamlessly across the exterior of both facades—they'd once been a single structure—the smaller building on the corner had apartments on the second story, and Endless Zen Yoga Studios filled the ground level.

The studio featured a picture window with a lotus flower painted in gold; the lower sill aggressively lined with candles, crystals, and Himalayan salt rocks like jagged teeth. Missy Jo seemed to be teaching a class inside a monster's mouth. I felt a shiver and pulled my pashmina tighter.

Something about the morning's conflict between Xenith and Shayla kept scratching at the back of my mind. The truth would come clear soon enough; it always did.

"Cupcake time," I announced, gesturing to the pink and white entrance of the bakery owned by the Dings with the unforgettable name—Ding! Cupcakes!

"Are you trying to kill the child?" Yoga Banshee was standing next to a tiny electric car parked in the bakery's loading zone.

"Like a bad penny," I said, hackles rising. What was with this woman? I wrinkled my nose; she smelled like an essential oil factory. "That much sandalwood cannot be good for the soul, Sheera, darling. You may want to cut back on the oil and focus on unblocking your third eye chakra. You are clearly not picking up the 'unwelcomed' vibe."

I whirled away, planning to escort Lavender inside the shop to buy her 57 cupcakes, but had to jump out of the way of a tiny tornado wielding a broom. The baker's icing-white dancer's bun featured a charming streak of pink. I seldom can see the top of people's heads. Mrs. Ding was a positively pocket-sized grandma.

"Get out of here. Leave my customers alone!" Mrs. Ding jabbed the bristly end of the broom at Shayla.

"It's a public street. I'll do what I want, you sugar-pedaling witch." Shayla's fighting words lost their impact as she scrambled to get inside her car and escape the broom.

"You are violating the restraining order." Mrs. Ding gestured to the video camera above her store's window. "On camera."

Shayla's electric car ticked on, and she pulled out into the street, cranking at the wheel. The car was utterly silent and accelerated with comedic lethargy. She made a slow left through the intersection, pulling into a newly opened spot on the side street, directly across from her studio. Nose in the air, the angry yogi shot us the upward-facing finger as she started toward the entrance to Endless Zen, just out of sight around the side of the building. At the curb, karma intervened, and Shayla tripped, her dramatic exit destroyed by our laughter.

"You okay, Mrs. Ding?" the owner of Ink Blot called out her door, where she'd been filming Shayla's drama with her metallic iPhone.

"Yes, Cassy-honey, thank you."

The broad woman flexed her inked muscles. "Let me know if you want me to report anything official for your restraining order. Yoga Banshee must be stopped."

"She will be," Mrs. Ding proclaimed. "By the way, I am loving my new boots." The bakery owner kicked out a tiny, hot-pink Doc Martin. "Thanks for the recommendation. My back feels way better. Gonna get Mr. Ding a pair too. I'll be over later."

"Rad." Cassy exchanged a thumbs-up with Mrs. Ding. "See you guys tonight. Looking forward to the party." The boutique owner smiled, multiple face-piercings glittering in the sun, before reentering her shop, the chimes on her door ringing merrily.

"You have a restraining order against Shayla?" I asked, raising a brow at Lavender. Sounded like a good idea.

Mrs. Ding nodded. "I used to feel sorry for the girl. Her sister is a sweetheart; I'm trying to fix her up with my grandson. But Shayla was always too full of herself. She was going to be a famous actress and leave us all behind."

"Shayla is from here originally?" I asked. For some reason, I'd assumed she was a transplant.

"She used to come here in the summers, visiting her uncle and putting on airs." The baker snorted. "And when she didn't achieve her dreams, she moved back here to make us all suffer with her."

"What did she do?" Lavender asked, wide-eyed.

"She stood in front of the shop with signs saying we poison children. Terrible, disturbing photos. Harassing customers, scaring little kids. Made my blood boil. Now, she mostly just glares out her window at us." Mrs. Ding poked in the direction of the studio with her broom. "Mr. Ding and I moved to this neighborhood in 1990. Twenty-five years, and Yoga Banshee is by far the biggest pain in the patootie we've had to deal with. And they own the building, so no chance she's leaving anytime soon." She patted her cheeks charmingly. "But enough about sour; let's talk sweet! Why don't you two come inside—cupcakes are on me."

"I. Will. Kill. Her!" a voice roared from across the street.

The three of us whipped around to see Xenith charging out of The Metal Grind like the Minotaur escaping the labyrinth and charging in the direction of Endless Zen. A moment later, Darien and Al ran out of the coffeehouse after him.

"Oh dear!" Mrs. Ding dashed across the street, and we followed.

"Which way did he go?" Darien asked. I pointed in the direction of Endless Zen as we all hurriedly moved after Xenith.

"What happened?" I asked.

"Someone destroyed the sound system," Darien panted, hand on his chest. "Poured some kind of oil into the equipment—smells like a perfume shop exploded. Uncle Zee flipped."

Indeed, the scent of sandalwood and rose wafted from the two coffeehouse workers.

"Yoga Banshee." Lavender immediately placed the signature scent.

"She's nuts," Al said.

We reached the end of the block and spotted a crowd, mostly in yoga gear, gathered at the entrance to Endless Zen, where Xenith was beating on the glass doors. Shayla, visible on the other side, waved her oiled arms and screamed.

"Whoo-hoo! Go, Xenith!" Mrs. Ding elbowed her way to the front, applauding Xenith into making a huge mistake.

I staggered against the sudden onslaught of emotions from Xenith, Shayla, and the onlookers. For an empath, too many powerful emotions at once feels like being unexpectedly caught in a strong current, struggling to keep your head above the waves.

"Can you help him?" Lavender touched my hand, voice pitched for my ears only. She knew I was more than your garden-variety empath. I don't just experience other people's emotions; I can influence them with my touch. Not a talent that one advertises. I worked on my shields, imagining emotion-proof plexiglass surrounding me.

"What do we do? Maybe I should tackle him?" Darien cracked his knuckles and loosened his skinny shoulders, contemplating a physical altercation with his (profoundly buffer) uncle.

"No tackling. I'll handle this," I declared, with a confidence I was mostly faking. "We stop this before it goes any further. I'll take Xenith. Lavender, you protect Darien and Al."

Issuing orders helped me achieve full diva. I couldn't just walk up to my raging friend and suck his emotions out like a vampire; I needed to cause a distraction—something I excel at. I stepped into the space between parked cars and prepared my instrument as best I could on short notice.

Xenith continued to pound and pull on the doors of Endless Zen. Glass and metal rattled loudly. The crystals and Buddhas lining the transom window above the door shuffled ominously. They were going to fall. As much as Shayla needed a bean in the head with a healing crystal, Xenith's temper was about to make a bad situation worse. I needed to act fast.

Drawing in a deep supportive breath, I let loose with a high C, the note famous for being able to shatter fine crystal. I'm a small woman, but my diaphragm is naturally powerful and highly trained. With apologies to my voice teacher, Monsieur Garbes, I cranked up the volume. The razor-sharp note bounced off the bricks with the force of a bullhorn. As I intended (and prefer), all eyes were on me.

CHAPTER 4 - LISTEN TO YOUR WIFE

Using my weaponized voice to stun the neighborhood into silence worked like a charm. Xenith stopped pounding on the doors to Endless Zen and turned to stare at me. Lookie-loos dropped their jaws in identical expressions of confusion and surprise.

Hopefully, no one caught my mini concert on video; Monsieur Garbes would murder me for not warming up properly, thus producing a less than stellar quality. Plus, I was in no way camera ready—thank the goddess for sunglasses.

"Xenith!" I called, glad to see his eyes clear. He backed his way down the steps, as if surprised to find himself there. Relieved, I met him at the bottom of the stoop, putting my hand on his impressive bicep and subtly channeling additional calm into him. He didn't need much. His artistic temperament could burn hot and fast, but his gentle nature was close to the surface.

"Oh man, I totally lost it there," he said, dazed. "Why do I let her get under my skin?"

"You are a menace!" Yoga Banshee shrieked as she opened the door. Missy Jo hovered behind, draping a towel over Shayla's shoulders like she'd just completed a round in the ring. Shayla took an angry swig from her travel mug.

"I WILL be calling the police," Shayla announced from the top of the steps, playing the crowd for sympathy. "This is harassment, and destruction of property."

"What destruction of property?" I asked coolly. "Nothing is damaged here. Unlike our sound system, which is covered in Endless Zen signature oil. Actually, Ms. Starr, please do call the police. I have plenty to say. And I'm sure The Metal Grind's security video will too."

Shayla's tan visibly faded. Unfortunately, we didn't have any security video, just dummy cameras meant to deter thieves—the real stuff is expensive.

"I don't know what you're talking about." She gestured aggressively to the yoga-clad crowd. "Let's go ladies, time for class."

"Sorry for interrupting, neighbors," Xenith said, finally regaining himself. "Free coffee for everyone. Come on over after your session."

Excited chatter burst out as Shayla's students discussed the offer. She turned six shades of red, glaring at Xenith with death in her eyes.

"Aaaaand, graceful exit," I whispered. Pulling his arm, I kept a trickle of calm flowing as we sashayed with Darien back toward The Metal Grind. Mrs. Ding returned to her side of the street. Lavender and Al were already ahead of us, deep in conversation.

"Yoga Banshee is guilt-tee," Darien announced. "And she's got some kind of sorceress hold over that poor Missy Jo. It's a real Patty Hearst vibe."

Distracted by Darien's surprising historical reference, I was unprepared for the sudden burst of guilt from Xenith when he saw his wife standing in the doorway of the coffeehouse. Lana's hands rubbed restlessly over her very pregnant belly. Her glossy-black curls, held back by a jewel-toned scarf, created a bouncing frame for her startlingly pale eyes and lightly freckled face. A match for Xenith in height and looks, Lana was the kind of person who radiated good health—their baby would be too beautiful for anyone to handle. At the moment, she looked flushed and tense. The pregnancy had been delicate, and she was ready to pop any day.

"Thanks for pulling me back," Xenith said to me in a low voice. "I'm glad those doors held. I'm not sure what I would have done. Shayla just—" He squeezed my hand and released himself, jogging up the steps to Lana. "Sorry, Hot Stuff," he said, kissing her check. "Let's go sit down."

"What's going on?" Lana's gray-blue eyes were deep with worry. "What were you doing?"

Back inside The Metal Grind, the place was empty of customers, but still held the scent of lingering sandalwood polluting roasting coffee aroma. Lavender huddled next to Al at the espresso machine. Xenith helped Lana lower into a chair at one of the café tables and knelt by her side.

I collapsed onto the chair next to her, rubbing my temples. The headache I'd been pretending not to have crashed into the back of my skull—empath exhaustion is similar to a hangover. Guilt, greasy and sickening, poured off Xenith like smoke, feeding my nausea.

"Lost my temper," Xenith said to Lana in a low voice. "But I'm better now, I promise. I'm so sorry to stress out you and the baby, my love."

Lana put her elegant hands on either side of his face. "What are we going to do with you?"

They were a great pair; like champagne and beef jerky, they went together surprisingly well. "What happened, exactly?"

"Someone poured oil all over the sound equipment. As soon as I smelled it, I knew Shayla was responsible. She wanted me to know," Xenith mused.

"That woman is psychotic!" Lana said, throwing her hands in the air.

"Everything went blank for a while," Xenith continued. "I don't even remember what happened until I was pounding Shayla's door, and Babe brought me to my senses by singing opera in the streets."

Xenith filled in all the details. I'd rather expected him to gloss the extent of his actions, but he told Lana the truth. So why did I feel like he wasn't being completely honest?

Lavender appeared at the table, carefully watching her own hands as she set two mugs on the metal tabletop. Only a little liquid spilled over the rims. Her face filled with pride and concentration.

"Diva's Delight, for Auntie Babe's headache." She slid one mug my direction, slopping a bit more down the side "Hi, I'm Lavender and this calming herbal tea is for Lana. Al says it's good for stress and okay for your baby so you should drink."

"I always do what Al says." Lana picked up her cup. "Thank you, and nice to meet you, Lavender."

"You're welcome." Lavender pointed at Xenith. "And Al says that you're next. Whiskey neat—whatever that means." She grinned and then skipped over to the bar to retrieve his drink.

"My niece, the eleven-year-old barmaid," I mused, glancing around in case the authorities were lurking. "Her parents will be impressed with the skills she learned while visiting me." I took a fortifying gulp. The drink-whisperer had included extra sugar, which I probably needed. "Al is a true treasure. We must never lose her."

"Agreed." Lana smiled and sipped her tea.

"That sound system is a total loss," Xenith said, deep in misery. "Thousands of dollars that we do not have. And even if we did, we'd never get it replaced by tonight. I'm so sorry, Babe."

"Don't apologize for what that troll did," Lana said before I could respond. "Remember, you're not in this alone. It's not all on your shoulders, my love." She patted his hand sharply. "Next step, we call our insurance agent, and make a plan for tonight."

"Your brilliant wife is right as usual, darling. We may have no money, but we're rich in connections," I said, pausing for a dramatic sip. "As they say in the opera world, Yoga Banshee will not win."

CHAPTER 5 - DEATH BY KARMA-MEL

Hours after Xenith's meltdown, Lavender and I emerged from the dressing room onto the second-floor catwalk of The Metal Grind. We called it the dressing room, but it really served as the all-purpose talent holding area with an attached restroom. I'd been the first diva to use the space and could readily declare it a success.

My niece and I were fabulously ready for the soft open, dressed in head-to-toe black. This was Lavender's go-to look, but a sharp contrast to my usual vibrant palate. I'd compensated somewhat with a pair of killer red boots, which looked spectacular against my insanely tight leather leggings. Hopefully, I'd still be able to breath—singing heavy metal requires as much breath-control as opera. Leaning on Lavender for balance, I tiptoed across the grid of the catwalk to the spiral stairs. I didn't want to risk getting my needle-thin heels trapped.

Thumping music filled the space. The event was continuing as planned, despite attempted sabotage. Borrowing sound equipment had been as easy as a few phone calls.

The niecling and I paused at the top of the staircase, observing the invited guests mingling below—only about twenty people. The following night, we'd be hoping for at least a hundred. This soft open might be just a dress rehearsal, but my performance nerves were jangling. I knew it meant so much to Xenith to bring live performance back to the Starrlight. I'd do my best to make him and Elliot James' memory proud.

Glancing at my watch, I knew I needed to head backstage soon. I didn't see Lana or Xenith anywhere—he was supposed to be working the floor. Time for a hostess schmooze while I figured out where my partner was; I started down the stairs.

"Sunset Zen starts soon," Lavender said, nodding toward the shared wall with the yoga studio. "Why would the angry orange purposely schedule a class when she knows our music is going to be loud?"

"Some people love to make themselves miserable," I said as we wound our way down. "Maybe it's the path to true nirvana?"

Lavender giggled. "Darien and his boyfriend are going to attend the class to scope it out. Darien was super excited about his 'athletics costume.' He just posted this picture." She showed me her phone as we reached the first floor. "Yoga Spies."

I laughed at the image of Darien and his sweetie, Javier. They were posed back to back, Charlie's Angels style, both wearing garish vintage Lycra. Must have been a fun thrift store experience.

"Look, Mrs. Ding just got here," Lavender said, slipping her phone back into her skull purse. The tiny baker stood near the door, slightly out of breath. Next to her was Mr. Ding holding a large pink box. He was tall and thin, with silver hair pulled back in a ponytail—I wondered if he knew that pink Doc Martins were in his future.

"Welcome!" I opened my arms and approached the newcomers, slipping into hostess mode. "We're so glad you're here."

"This is Mr. Ding," Mrs. Ding said to my niece with a wicked gleam. "Isn't he handsome?"

Mr. Ding smiled sheepishly, and Lavender giggled, embarrassed.

"Total dreamboat," I agreed.

"We brought presents," Mr. Ding said, indicating the pink box.

"We felt bad that Yoga Banshee interrupted your cupcakes today," Mrs. Ding said, winking at Lavender. "Mr. Ding worked up a brand-new design."

"My finest masterpiece," the older gentleman intoned dramatically, slowly opening the lid. Mrs. Ding drum-rolled on her thighs. "Death by Karma-mel!"

Lavender and I gasped and applauded at the cupcake reveal—the design was a killer. White frosting generously drizzled with caramel for the base. Nestled on top was a blonde fondant figure tightly wrapped in a yoga mat, like a boa constrictor's final hug.

"This is genius," Lavender declared. "They look amazing!"

"Made the yoga mat out of fruit leather," Mr. Ding said proudly.

"The little "X"s for her eyes are a nice touch," I said with a laugh.

"At first we dyed the caramel red, but that was a bit much," he confessed.

"Keep it tasteful," Mrs. Ding agreed, exchanging a glance with her husband.

"Just some art therapy," Mr. Ding said, glancing down at the unusual confections. "Oh, there's one missing!"

"Probably one of our grandkids, sorry." Mrs. Ding said with a laugh.

"Probably," Mr. Ding said, still looking perplexed. "Anyway—gifts for our new friends."

"We are honored," I said.

"And don't worry, I'm not shocked," my niecling assured them with a grin. "I work with dead people all the time." Mr. and Mrs. Ding blinked in identical confusion. "Thank you. I'll take these upstairs." Lavender scooped the box out of Mr. Ding's hands and wove through the crowd like an expert.

"I'm so glad you're here," I said to the Dings, smoothing over Lavender's casual announcement. I was always impressed by her openness, and a little nervous. I'd spent a lifetime hiding my own woo-woo skills from all but my closest circle, but my niece shared her gifts with admirable confidence. "Let's get you a drink," I said, leading the bakers over to the bar. I worried the seniors might appreciate a lower chair, but the place was full. I realized they were fine when Mrs. Ding scrambled up onto the stool and perched like a cupcake topper.

"My bride and I heard you have Chinese whisky," Mr. Ding said to the bartender. "And we are pumped."

I laughed. I loved this neighborhood and all the colorful characters. I took in the scene with pride—the party was swinging. Time for the entertainment, and I needed to warm up before I let rip with my new repertoire.

"Enjoy!" I gave the Dings a wave and looked around for Xenith. Where was he? I wanted to make sure all was on track before making my way backstage.

A paranormal warning tingled across my skin. Something was wrong. I was always tightly attuned to my family, and Lavender's energy line had suddenly gone from happy kid with cupcakes to deeply worried. I headed in her direction as quickly as the crowd would allow.

"What's wrong?" I asked, meeting her at the bottom of the stairs.

"Ace is really upset," Lavender replied, concern on her sweet face.

"Who's Ace?" I asked, baffled.

"Al's tagalong spirit." Lavender's gaze faded as she listened to a voice I couldn't hear—she looked eerily like my brother. "The spirit's name is Ace. We've been talking. He insists that there's trouble at the yoga studio." She bit her lip. "What if Darien needs help?"

"Let's go," I said, taking her cold little hand in mine as we headed for the front door. Desperately, I looked around for Xenith or Lana, both easy to spot in a crowd due to their height, but they weren't around. The bouncer shot me a puzzled glance as Lavender and I exited the front door.

Moments later, my niece and I stepped into the lobby of Endless Zen and total chaos. Missy Jo crouched in the doorway of the studio, wailing like a fire engine. The foyer was overly warm, and crowded with the yoga class attendees, everyone shouting at once.

"Ladies. Ladies! Please be quiet!" Darien appeared from the studio. He clapped his hands authoritatively and the yogis obeyed. "We need to call 911!"

"Already dialed." Lavender held her phone out and crossed over to the weeping Missy Jo and Darien.

Darien, holding the phone between his ear and shoulder, announced, "Javier is an EMT. He'll take care of Shayla. Someone help Missy Jo."

At his brisk order, two of the yoga students surged forward, ushering Missy Jo to a nearby bench. Darien walked back into the studio, eyes on Javier.

Lavender and I boldly followed, stopping in the doorway and staring into the studio. The tangerine curtains on the enormous window were closed, and the spacious room was ringed in lighted candles, no doubt in preparation for the evening class. The flickering light lent an eerie glow. Shayla lay sprawled in the center of the wooden floor. Javier was kneeling next to her, feeling for a pulse. But even in the candlelight, I could tell it was too late.

Shayla's skin was blue, her sightless eyes focused up at the ceiling. Yoga Banshee would scream no more. A large, irregular-shaped object protruded from her mouth. I grimaced, recognizing the distinctive pink of a Himalayan salt rock. This was definitely Shayla's final corpse pose.

CHAPTER 6 - PINCH OF SALT

The narrow lobby of Endless Zen was mostly quiet, punctuated by Missy Jo's plaintive wails. Lavender and I remained in the doorway between the studio and the lobby, like spirits unable to crossover.

"I need an ambulance at Endless Zen Yoga studio," Darien explained in a shaking voice, giving the address as he moved toward Javier. "There's a, um, body. My boyfriend is an EMT and he's performing CPR." Darien held the phone out so Javier could communicate with the 911 operator as he methodically tried to revive Shayla. Lavender brushed against my side, seeking comfort.

"Is she still here?" I asked in a low voice.

"No," Lavender whispered. "She's crossed."

Well, that was good, Shayla as angry spirit did not sound like fun. The air in the room felt close and far too warm. My shirt was made of ultra-thin fabric, designed to show off my sequined bustier, but I could feel sweat trickling down my spine. Gingerly, I lowered my empathic shields for a peek—fear and confusion permeated quickly, tears sprang to my eyes. A second signature, filled with anger, intruded and I slammed my protection back into place. I'd expected as much; the emotions that led to murder were potent enough to knock me out if I wasn't careful. With a steadying breath, I pushed aside memories long buried and tuned into my regular senses to gather information.

The Himalayan salt rock that had been in Shayla's mouth now lay on the floor by Javier's feet. The lovely pink mineral was thought to purify the air. This specimen was about the size of a duck egg—had she suffocated on a salt rock? Was that possible? I felt unexpected pity for the departed yogi. This death was a sad, messy one.

There was no blood, but I noted what appeared to be vomit spattered throughout the room and puddled around Javier and the body. Lavender tucked her nose inside her shirt, and I followed suit. My brain, sluggish from the shock, suddenly registered that this was not something for a kid to witness. My niece might be a ghost whisperer, but hanging out with the freshly murdered was a very different story.

Just as I was going to usher my niecling away, the quiet night filled with sirens and lights flashing through the glass of the front doors. Tires squealed as the emergency response team and Cedar River's finest arrived at Endless Zen. All of us in the lobby were quickly ordered outdoors by some young, nervous-looking officers. I was grateful for the fresh air and to get Lavender away from the scene.

"Is she okay?" Missy Jo sobbed from the steps of the studio, surrounded by her fellow yogis in a pastel rainbow of workout gear. "Is Shayla g-g-g-going to be okay?"

No, Missy Jo, your sister is not going to be okay.

Crimson streaks, visible between the buildings, painted the horizon. Soon it would be full dark. Lavender and I moved to the lamppost on the corner. The flowers in the basket hanging overhead gave off the barest whiff of fragrance. From our vantage point, we could see The Metal Grind. A handful of folks mingled outside, staring at the police cars. I wrestled my phone out of my back pocket, texting Al and Xenith to break the news about Shayla and that we needed to shut the party down—I wouldn't be making it on stage that night.

"*On it.*" Al replied.

I had a selfish moment of relief that this wasn't our official opening. Would we be able to go ahead with it the next night?

Xenith was still silent. Where was he? I started to text Lana when the obvious answer to Xenith going AWOL hit me between the eyes: the baby! What was wrong with me? Of course, Lana going into labor was
the only thing that could have kept them away tonight and out of communication.

"Goddess be with them," I whispered, and shot off a message to them both saying I had things under control (ha!) and to touch base when they could.

Lavender stood very close to me. Quiet, but steady, absently smoothing her thumb across Stanley's skull.

"I'm so sorry, Lavvybear." I folded her up into a hug. I always thought of her as little, but we were nearly the same size, though my heels gave me an advantage. "This is not the kind of Auntie adventure
I wanted you to have."

"I'm good," she said, muffled into my shoulder. "That was...weird, but I'm all right."

One of the baby cops strutted over to take our information. Lavender put Stanley back in her purse, skull within a skull, like matryoshka dolls.

My nerves jangled in reflex at being questioned, even though the officer was really too youthful to be intimidating. He repeated our names back as if he suspected they were fake—something you get used to when your last name is Cuckoo. And Brionne LeFave actually *is* made-up, but not in a nefarious way. It wasn't until Lavender elbowed me sharply that I realized I'd babbled all of that aloud. Get a grip, Diva!

My emotions were a mess—just like everyone else's—but while everyone else got to manage their own feelings, I got to experience theirs and mine. Always hard to maintain my psychic shields when my own feelings are in turmoil.

Luckily, while I spiraled, Lavender remained steady. She squeezed my hand, answering the officer's questions easily for me while nudging me with her elbow.

"And were you attending the Sunset Zen class?" The officer looked skeptically at our rock-n-roll getups. The streetlight flickered on overhead, like the naked bulb in an interrogation room. I hadn't even
considered how Lavender and I would explain our

presence at Endless Zen. "A ghost gave us a heads-up" was not the right answer.

I stared down at my bloodred boots and started sweating like a horse. I wasn't guilty of anything—why was I acting like it?

"My aunt was giving me a tour of the neighborhood before her show tonight," Lavender said smoothly. "She was nervous about performing and needed a distraction. And our friends were taking the class."

Clearly my best bet was to keep my mouth shut and let the child handle things. I glanced over to The Metal Grind, just as a flurry of guests exited. I wondered what Al had told them. A few curious neighbors

made a point to pass by Endless Zen, getting a look for themselves. Luckily, no one approached Lavender and me.

"Stay here," baby cop said. "Detective Velasco will want to talk to you."

Thank goddess that was over. I considered making a break for it, but I was worried about Darien and Javier. Yes, they were in their twenties and technically adults, but Xenith and Lana were off having a

baby, it was my duty to take care of his nephew and Javier.

Lavender, lost in thought, stared at the glowing orange curtains of Endless Zen. Shadows flickered across behind the cloth. The sill was loaded with statues, crystals, and yoga accoutrement—I wondered at the

irony of a woman who exuded negative energy purporting to guide others to Zen.

I jostled Lavender out of her reverie with a friendly elbow. "What are you thinking about?"

"Who did it," Lavender said immediately. "What else?"

"Well, Nancy Drew..."

"Who's Nancy Drew?" Lavender asked. "Did we meet her today?"

"Never mind about Nancy," I said, making a mental note. "You will find out about her on your next birthday. Who are your suspects?"

"Let's see." Lavender leaned back against the lamppost. "Shayla seemed to have a lot of enemies: you—"

"Me!"

"Obviously," Lavender said. "You've got an okay motive, you'd recently yelled at each other in public, and you just

acted totally shady in front of the police, so I'm sure they've got you on the top of
their list."

"Shady?" I folded my arms across my chest.

"Yeah," she said. "Super shady. *I* started to wonder what you were hiding. Definitely nervous and babbly."

"That is rudely accurate, young lady," I said. "But we know I'm innocent. Who else do you suspect? Please continue, Miss Marple."

"I'm like the opposite of Miss Marple," Lavender said. "I'm a kid."

"You know Miss Marple, but not Nancy Drew?" I shook my head.

Lavender shrugged. "Okay. Suspects: you, Xenith—"

"Well, we know Xenith didn't do it," I said huffily.

"Do we?" Lavender drummed her hands on her purse, not meeting my eye. "He definitely was not around when we left the Grind tonight. And he was acting weird all day. Not to mention literally threatening
to kill Shayla in front of a whole lotta people."

I didn't enjoy hearing my own fretful fears echoed. I gave my niece's shoulder a gentle squeeze. "I know you witnessed him at his worst today, Lavvy, but I can tell you that is a rare thing. Xenith's really
the sweetest guy. You saw how fast he calmed down."

"True," Lavender said. "And you are a supernaturally good judge of character."

"I *am*," I agreed, feeling comforted. My feet were starting to protest my gorgeous boots and the sidewalk. My leather pants would have been so sexy on stage, but at the moment were trying to overwhelm me with constant pressure, like a fashionable tourniquet. I shifted my weight, trying to get blood flowing.

"Mr. and Mrs. Ding made those murder cupcakes," Lavender continued. "Could be suspicious, I guess, but I can't see them actually hurting someone."

"Making the cupcake is almost an alibi," I pointed out. "They're way too smart to be that obvious. And their trouble with Shayla was a while ago. They got the restraining order against her, so why would they
murder her now?"

"Maybe that's why they waited—to avoid suspicion," Lavender mused. "And there's Missy Jo."

"Missy Jo?" We glanced over at the tragic woman on the studio steps. In her signature gray, the poor thing was slumped over as if her spine had been removed. She appeared to be the very definition of harmless and genuinely grieving. "What makes you say that?"

"Did you know there's a hallway that connects The Grind and Endless Zen?"

"Yes." My mind scrambled to keep up with eleven-year-old trajectory.

The backstage door connected to a wide, shared hallway, which ran past Endless Zen's employee entrance to connect to the street. The backway had originally been for the talent, so they didn't have to walk through the public areas before a show—now both businesses used it for overflow storage.

"During your sound check, I was exploring." Lavender leaned towards me. "I heard arguing through the backstage door—so I snuck out into the back hall that connects to Endless Zen and hid behind some boxes to listen."

I felt a momentary qualm as I pictured my unsupervised niece traipsing into a dark, isolated area to eavesdrop on a potentially dangerous situation. Great job, Babe. Maybe her mother was right about me.

"It was Shayla and Missy Jo," Lavender said excitedly. "Missy Jo was accusing Shayla of destroying the sound system."

"Interesting..." I took a step closer, looking around to make sure baby cop was still out of earshot.

"Missy Jo was all 'I can't believe you did that. How could you?'" Lavender continued. "Then Shayla told her to shut-up. I expected Missy Jo to cry or something, but instead she got kind of scary quiet, and she said, 'You know what, Shayla. I'm done. I can't take this anymore.'"

"I wonder what that was all about."

"No idea." Lavender shrugged. "Then Shayla laughs all nasty and says, 'Whatever, Missy Jo.' Then Yoga Banshee slammed back into the studio."

"A fight doesn't equal murder," I said. "Your dad and I used to fight all the time, part being a wonder twin. I only ever *thought* about strangling him—siblings scrap."

"True," Lavender said. "Van and I don't always get along..."

"Exactly," I said. Lavender and her sister were very close.

"Missy Jo cried. I felt kinda bad spying on her." Lavender glanced over at the woman who now stared silently at her hands. "She got herself under control, and then she opened one of the boxes stacked near

their door. She took something out and went back into the yoga studio. I snuck over, opened the box..."

"And???"

"And, inside was...

"The salt rock!?!" I guessed.

"No. Another box!"

I narrowed my baby blues.

"For real," Lavender said with slight smirk. "It was like one of your big moving boxes, and inside that box was a smaller box, like the kind shoes come in."

"That is what grown-up people refer to as a shoebox, darling." Children are fascinating creatures.

Lavender accepted this educational information with a nod. "So then I opened that shoebox," she said, "but there was nothing in it."

"Nothing!?!" I threw my arms in the air, drawing the attention of the nearby yogis. I lowered my energy and whispered proudly, "You're terrible."

"It's the truth." Lavender shrugged. "There was nothing in there. Just some dirt and a pair of plastic gloves."

"That's not nothing, Nancy Marple," I intoned. "That was a clue!"

CHAPTER 7 - NANCY MARPLE

Before we could speculate further on Missy Jo's box of dirt, Darien and Javier emerged from Endless Zen. Their vintage yoga attire was a sharp contrast to their subdued posture; the pair of young heroes looked totally spent.

"Come along, darlings," I said when they reached us. Finally, all my chicks were collected, I spread my wing across Lavender's shoulders and began to walk toward the Metal Grind.

"Aren't we supposed to stay here?" Lavender asked. "For the detective to talk to us?"

"They'll figure it out," I said airily. "Detective, remember?"

Inside The Metal Grind, all semblance of the night's festivities was gone. The work lights were on, music off, café chairs tipped on top of tables—even the scent of coffee and whiskey had faded away. Empty. My stomach twisted. Our fledgling business desperately needed a successful opening—what would all this mean for us? In the face of murder, it seemed a small selfish worry.

Al met us at the door. As Lavender and the boys gravitated to the large corner booth, I filled Al in on what had gone down at Endless Zen. The staff worked quietly in the background, closing-up for the night.

"You'll need coffee," Al said after absorbing the news with a frown. "Go sit."

I obeyed. The other three were slumped in exhausted silence as I slid in next to Lavender. My hideously uncomfortable leather pants squealed against the red leather of the seat, snapping everyone out of their individual thoughts.

"Oh, Lavender, here's your phone," Darien said, handing her the glitter-encrusted black case. "Thanks." He shook his head. "This is so surreal. Everything happened so fast. Javier and I were such a mood, being Yoga Spies and stuff. It was super fun and hilarious, and then..."

Quiet settled over us again as we processed the madness. I took some time to center myself, fortifying my psychic shields as best I could. I glanced at my watch—9:15. The ninety minutes since we'd discovered Shayla's demise felt like a hundred years had passed in a blink.

Al, the coffee angel, appeared tableside. Smelling the healing magic of my Diva's Delight laced with whiskey, I barely refrained from tears.

"Drink." Despite the buzzcut, tattoos, and taciturn style, Al was a total mother hen. I read the name Ace inked on her left forearm as she set hot chocolate in front of Lavender. My niecling and I elbowed each other. The spirit haunting Al and The Metal Grind was someone important enough to warrant a permanent place in her body art. And Ace had done more than play poltergeist games with us; he'd given Lavender the heads up about Shayla's death. Who was this
spirit—an honest trickster?

Al pulled up a chair next to our booth, capturing our full attention. "Talked to Xenith. He lost his phone, called from the hospital. Lana's ok. False contractions. Staying at the hospital just in case.

"What? Oh, no!" Darien gasped.

"Is the baby going to be okay?" Lavender asked.

"Probably Braxton Hicks contractions," Javier explained, putting a comforting hand on Darien's. "Very common, and nothing to be too worried about. They're just being cautious. She's so close to her due date that if the baby came, it would be fine. They may even decide to induce."

"Well, that's one mystery solved," I said, but my relief was still mixed with anxiety. Xenith's absence this evening was explained, but since we didn't know exactly when

Shayla was murdered, he wasn't totally free from suspicion. I reached for my well-earned coffee. "I wasn't sure what the right move was before. But now, I think we should postpone the opening." Just saying it aloud twisted my stomach into macrame. The café was doing well, but the cashflow from evening events was vital to our business plan. Pushing things a week couldn't do that much damage, could it? This was not my area of expertise. "What do you think, Al?"

"Agreed," she said. "It's the best option. I'll take care of it. You tell Zee."

"Agreed." I returned to the comfort of my heavenly Irish Delight.

"I can't believe Shayla's actually dead," Al said, her expression genuinely saddened. "What happened?"

"Missy Jo checked us in," Darien burst out, clearly needing to talk. "Then she went into the studio to see if Shayla was ready for class and came stumbling out again, just screaming and screaming."

"Must've been so scary," Lavender said. "Especially when you realized she was murdered."

"It was horrible," Darien said. "You don't swallow a crystal by accident."

"Himalayan salt rock," I corrected. "I have a lamp made out of one."

"A lamp made of salt?" Lavender's brow scrunched. She seemed more stunned by this concept that having seen Shayla's body. The regular world was still so new to the eleven-year-old, but death was normal.

"I don't think it was the salt rock that killed her," Javier said. "Suffocating someone with a stone would have to be very violent act and there were not visible signs of trauma."

"True," I agreed, mind racing. "And Shayla was really strong, and mean, she wouldn't just let something like that happen to her."

"Exactly." Javier nodded, leaning his arms on the table. "I didn't notice any injury to her mouth or teeth. But there were clear signs of GI distress."

"What's that?" Lavender asked.

"That's fancy future doctor talk for barf," Darien answered, before adding. "I'm pretty sure."

Javier nodded. "My best guess would be an allergic reaction, but considering the salt rock—"

The remaining staff crossed through the café, chatting amongst themselves. "All done, Al!" someone called. "Want me to hit the lights?"

"Yeah," Al replied. A second later, the work lights clicked off. Shadows settled around the café and the soft glow of the booth lamps became the only illumination. I felt myself relax a bit more. "Night." Al raised a hand in farewell to the crew exiting out the front. The heavy door thumped closed behind them.

"Who could have done it?" Lavender wondered.

"Half the neighborhood wanted to shove Shayla's yoga mat down her throat," I pointed out, trying not to dwell on Xenith's behavior that afternoon. "I mean, just tonight the Dings were distributing Death by Karma-mel."

"Death by what?" A dark-haired woman with a badge around her neck stepped up to our table, startling us all. The detective had apparently detected our location. She held up the badge in introduction. "Detective Velasco."

Velasco was neat as a pin, the epitome of the idiom. Hair smoothed into a low bun, without a single escaping whisp — something I've never managed. Her slacks, blouse, and a sweater, all in muted blues, hung perfectly without a wrinkle. She looked more like a bank teller than a homicide detective. She held a small notebook, pen poised expectantly in her hand. There was no escaping now.

"Did you say Death by Karma-mel?" Velasco asked. "Anything to do with this?" She held out her phone, showing a photograph one of the Ding's murder-depicting cupcakes nestled amongst the cluttered windowsill of Endless Zen. One enormous bite, with mini-Shayla's head, was missing.

"Oh no," Lavender whispered.

"From Ding! Cupcakes! across the street, I assume?" the detective said, slipping her phone back into her pants pocket.

"The Dings are a sweet old couple." I sounded defensive, even to my own ears. "They wouldn't hurt a fly. I can't imagine how Shayla got a hold of one."

"I'll find out," Velasco said with a combination of confidence and threat. After glancing at her notes, she raised her eyes to me with cool calculation. "And you are Ms. LaFave?"

I nodded regally, reminding myself that my childhood of crime had nothing to do with this situation and to keep my cool.

"I heard you say half the neighborhood would like Ms. Starr dead," the detective said, plowing ahead. "That does seem to be the prevailing sentiment." She pinned me with her gaze. "I understand your business partner, Xenith Morgan, publicly threatened the victim today. Did you have anything to do with that? Do you know anything about his whereabouts?"

Each question was a sharp poke in my sternum. My hands twisted. "Xenith is at the hospital with his wife," I managed. "She is eight months pregnant and having contractions."

"Which hospital?" The detective asked.

"Overlake," Al supplied.

"And you are?" The detective asked.

"Al Mendoza," she replied. "I'm one of the owners here."

The detective recorded the information and continued. "When was the last time you saw Xenith Morgan?"

"Xenith was with us when we tested the new sound stuff," Lavender piped up.

"Right," I said. "That all sounds true. Right, I mean, right. Lavender is right." Lavender was also slowly pushing a spoon into my leather-wrapped thigh. Her version of a subtle pinch? It helped. My heartbeat slowed. "Around five today."

"Same," Al said thoughtfully.

"And what was his demeanor?" Detective Velasco asked.

"His what?" Lavender's face scrunched.

"How was he acting?" the detective explained.

"Oh! He seemed fine. Right, Auntie Babe?" Lavender nodded at me encouragingly.

"Yes," I said. "A little stressed. We all were, we'd just barely gotten the new sound equipment up and running. Everything was behind."

"And is it true that Mr. Morgan accused Ms. Starr of vandalizing your equipment?" the detective said. "Pouring massage oil in it?"

"We all accused her of that," Al said.

"It was the signature blend from Endless Zen," Darien added. "She wasn't trying to be subtle about it."

"And Mr. Morgan tried to break into Endless Zen to confront Ms. Starr?"

"I wouldn't use the words 'break into'," I said.

"What words would you use?"

"Open a locked door without a key?" I suggested. I swear I heard Lavender roll her eyes.

"He didn't hurt her or the door," Lavender said. "There were tons of witnesses, so you probably already know that."

"Hmph." Detective Velasco eyed us all, expression neutral. "If it was so evident to everyone that Ms. Starr destroyed private property, why didn't anyone contact the police?"

We were silent. The truth was that Xenith had been dead set against it. He said he didn't want anything to get in the way of our opening—was there more to it?

"No time," Al said.

"I see. I guess I'll head over to Overlake and ask Mr. Morgan myself, since he's not answering his phone," the detective said.

"He lost it," Darien said. "Probably left it at home in his hurry to get to the hospital." Javier nodded in support.

"Hmph." The detective wrote something in her notebook and then flipped the lid closed. "That'll do for tonight. I'll have more questions very soon."

With that, our interrogation ended. The detective strode out the door, pausing for just a moment to look up at *Infinite Jest*, as if she'd just noticed the enormous sculpture. With a firm yank on the doors, Detective Velasco made her exit. I knew she was only doing her job, and I appreciated her gentleness with Lavender, but I was glad to see her go. I was also certain we hadn't seen the last of her.

CHAPTER 8 - BURNING SECRETS

As midnight neared, Lavender and I gathered our things from the upstairs dressing room, preparing to leave The Grind. Al had taken the boys home, insisting they were too tired to drive. Lavender and I would be Ubering.

My stuff was strewn all over the furniture and counter tops. Normally I'd be running like a top until 2 am, but this had been a year-long day. Gathering my make-up, my thoughts swirled with the death of Yoga Banshee and worry for Xenith, Lana, and the baby.

"You know what's weird," Lavender said, leaning against the doorway as she watched me.

"Everything about this day?" I replied.

"Yeah." Lavender smiled tiredly. "And Ace. He spent all day following me around. Trying to talk to me. Wanting me to talk to Al for him—they're cousins. I told him I'd do it tonight after the show if he left me alone for a while."

"Did he?" I asked.

She nodded. "Then he popped up again. Totally freaking out, insisting we go to Endless Zen."

"That's right." All packed up, I swung my enormous bag over my shoulder.

"And then when we got back here," Lavender continued, "he totally disappeared."

"Odd, I wonder why." We stepped out onto the catwalk. I closed the door, and darkness enveloped us. "Oops."

When we'd come upstairs, the lights from below had shone through the floor of the metal gridwork catwalk, illuminating our way. I hadn't given any thought to flipping the switch at the top of the circular staircase. Al must have turned off the downstairs lights on her way out with the boys. Luckily, moonlight spilled through the windows. I could make out Lavender's pale face, her eyes lost to the shadows. Balancing on the toes of my boots, I started to pull my phone out of my leather pants—which I could not wait to remove and burn to cinders—when I heard a noise.

"What was that?" Lavender whispered.

"Shhh." I slipped the mace canister off my purse handle. Someone was with us in the dark. Another rustle came from the direction of Xenith's apartment. A muffled oath was followed by the rattle of the door to the stairs leading down to the stage.

"Is that Xenith?" Lavender whispered. She'd turned on her flashlight app, keeping the beam tight against her leg. The up glow did spooky things to her face.

"I think so."

"Let's go see." My niecling nudged me toward the noise and the back stairs. Curiosity overcame my common sense, and I crept forward. I'm sure her mother would not be surprised.

Lavender and I snuck along the catwalk. The door to Xenith and Lana's apartment was closed; no light shone through the frosted windows around the entrance. The door to the back stairs was slightly ajar, opening with a tiny squeak as I pulled it. Perched at the top, we peered down into the darkness. No one was in sight. I clutched the mace, holding it out in front of me, primed. I knew Xenith would never hurt us, but just in case we were mistaken about who we were following, I wanted to be ready. I grabbed Lavender's chilly finger. Closely clumped, we descended the dark stairs. Cool air from the larger backstage space blew upwards, ruffling my hair.

"What is that sound?" Lavender whispered.

I stopped, straining my ears. "I don't hear anything."

"It stopped," she confirmed. We took a few more steps down. "There it is again!" From the step above, Lavender put her mouth my ear. "It's like a creaking, groaning, kind of noise. Like something in pain."

We continued our descent. I heard it too, grimacing as I realized the source. "It's my pants."

Lavender snickered.

"Shut-up, darling," I threatened. "Or I'll make you wear these evil things tomorrow." I could literally feel the brat shaking with laughter as we reached the bottom of the stairs.

A metal clang sounded from the direction of the loading dock. We wove through the backstage with the help of Lavender's cellphone light. In the small shop area, we paused at the exit to the alley. I pressed on the escape bar, trying to quietly ease the heavy metal door open. Through the small crack, I could see a figure at the fence that housed our dumpster. The yellow safety bulbs lit him like a spotlight center stage—Xenith!

"What's he doing?" I whispered.

"I want to see!" Lavender knelt, worming her way in front of me so she could watch from below. Xenith was fully absorbed in his clandestine task. He should have been at the hospital with his wife, not sneaking around in the darkness outside The Metal Grind. Everything about this scene screamed suspicious.

Kneeling next to what Lavender would call "a box that shoes come in," Xenith squeezed lighter fluid onto the contents. He lit a match on the asphalt and dropped it inside. Immediately, flames began to dance over the sides of the box.

I could hear voices approaching. Xenith stiffened. Quickly, he stomped out the flames and tossed the smoldering box into the dumpster.

"Not safe!" Lavender chastised softly.

Xenith closed and locked the fencing, slipping into the shadows on the far side of the dumpster. I held my breath as the group of—happily drunk—people passed by. As their voices faded, Xenith emerged from the shadows rolling his motorcycle with him. The roar of the motor echoed through the alley, and he was gone.

"What is going on?" I wondered.

"Discarding evidence," Lavender said knowledgably.

"Evidence of what?" I asked.

"Well, he's clearly guilty of something," Lavender pointed out.

I couldn't argue with that. By unspoken agreement, we headed toward the dumpster. Lavender scampered ahead, looking briefly dejected when she discovered that Xenith had responsibly locked the gate behind him. She didn't bother to ask if I had the keys—wise child. Divas don't do dumpsters. My eyes stung at the scent wafting from the garbage. No smoke. At least it appeared that Xenith hadn't set the whole thing on fire.

"I think I could climb over if you boost me," Lavender said.

"Yes, or..." I plucked a bobby pin from my hair with a flourish and picked the lock in a matter of seconds.

"Nice job," Lavender said. "Where did you learn that?"

"Yes, interesting skill, Ms. LeFave," a familiar voice said.

I am ashamed to say that I screamed at a pitch very close to the High C I'd used to stop Xenith earlier that day. I clutched at my chest as I whirled around.

"Sorry," Detective Velasco said with absolutely no sincerity. "Didn't mean to startle you while you linger in a back alley at midnight. Is picking locks part of opera training?"

Her unnecessary snark settled me. Repartee, I could handle.

"Just a little something I picked up in my misspent youth," I said, rather coolly. The rush of adrenaline was dizzying. My leather pants conspired to limit my oxygen.

"Passing your skills on to the next generation?" the detective asked.

"Uh. . ." I glanced over my shoulder. Lavender had disappeared into the interior of the dumpster area. "I don't think it's breaking a law if you own the lock you're picking."

"Hi, Detective Velasco!" Lavender popped out of the dumpster gate like a scary doll-in-the-box. "I accidentally threw away the bag with my new lipstick in it, and I was super sad because I bought it with my own money and then Auntie Babe had the idea of looking here and we found it!" She waved the bag from Ink Blot in the air like a flag. "Isn't that awesome!?"

"A dumpster miracle!" I agreed, admiring and fearing the flexibility of Lavender's criminal mind as she casually closed and relocked the gate. Just as I started to think we'd gotten away with it, I realized that something was off with this whole scenario. Finding my best imperious diva tone, I asked. "And what are *you* doing in the alley at midnight, Detective Velasco?"

Velasco shot me a chilly glare. "Looking for Xenith Morgan."

She'd only just missed him.

The pressure started to build. If I was going to protect Xenith, The Metal Grind, and my second career—I need to straighten this mess out. And I'd have to stay one step ahead of Detective Velasco to do it. No more dithering around, this mystery needed solving. Time to stop hiding from my past and use it. I heard my father's voice saying: *Keep it short, klein cuckoo. Stick as close to the truth as you can. Then get out.*

"We told you, he's at the hospital," I said. "With his wife."

"Not when I got there," the detective corrected.

"He probably just stepped out for some air," I said. "I'm sure it's been a stressful night."

The detective didn't answer.

Lavender executed a theatrical yawn worthy of a Tony.

"Well," I said briskly picking up my cue. "We'd better be headed home now. It's been a long stressful day for Lavender, and for me too." My phone buzzed and I was happy to announce. "Our Uber is out front."

"I'll walk you," Velasco said. "This neighborhood isn't as safe as it used to be."

The detective watched until our Uber rolled out of view, as if discovering us dumpster diving at midnight was somehow worthy of suspicion.

Luckily, our ride was short. Five minutes later, we stumbled into my condo and to our separate rooms to get ready for bed. Alone, I was able to concentrate on the one thing that absolutely must happen IMMEDIATELY.

The swearing required to peel off my horrible, horrible leather pants was robust and multilingual (opera teaches a girl many skills.) Finally free, I kicked them into the corner of my bedroom to consider their actions. Then I tried to quiet my restless mind with a steaming hot shower.

Wrapped in my silk nightgown and robe, I made my way to the living room. Lavender and I would need sleep very soon, but we'd agreed to get comfy and touch base first. It had a been a wild night.

Moonlight poured in through the balcony's sliding glass doors. Like any good diva, I suffer from candle addiction. There's no light like candlelight. Lavender had lit everything sitting at eleven-year-old level. Did this count as playing with fire? My nose was picking up an unpleasant chemical note, but nothing inappropriate appeared to be ablaze.

Curled up on my green velvet couch, wrapped in a faux-fur throw, Lavender could have been the subject of an oil painting, except for the giant slice of cold pizza she was sleepily munching on. Her face was placid, her vibes unsettled. Love, worry, sadness, confusion. I felt the tendrils of her emotions brushing against my heart.

"What's wrong, Lavvybear?" I asked, curling up on the cushion next to her.

"Ugh." She flipped on the hood of her skunk onesie and tugged the strings until her face disappeared. "My sister is right. There are no secrets in this family. Especially with you."

When your friends and family react negatively to who you are, it stings—even if it's done with love. It's one thing to struggle with your own innate gifts, another to know that your nearest and dearest do, too. But it was a sting I was used to.

"I'll tell you what I tell your father and your sister whenever they complain. 'That's life with Auntie Empath. Suck it up, buttercup.'" I rubbed the white fur between her skunk ears. How cute was this kid?

"I tried to wait until you were ready," Lavender said emerging from her hood. "But..." She dug under the throw blanket and pulled out a box, streaked with black and smelling strongly of lighter fluid. I winced at the idea of this nasty container on my velvet couch. As she set it on the coffee table, I realized what I was looking at.

The shoebox that Xenith had been trying to destroy.

"Wha? How? Wha?" I moved things forward with my brilliant questioning.

Lavender smiled nervously. "The dumpster lid was open, and it was sitting right on top. The fire must have burned out fast because it didn't even feel hot. So I just put it in the Ink Blot bag!"

"Promise me you will only use your powers for the side of light," I said, only partially joking. "What's in the box, Pandora?" I peered at what seemed to be the burned remains of papers. Letters and photographs. Major damage marred the top layer, but underneath there were singed survivors.

"I'm not sure what it means, but it doesn't look good." I felt her emotions surging, sliding over my skin like the tines of a comb—Lavender was feeling protective of me.

"It's okay, darling," I said, covering my nerves. "I'm tougher than I look. I'm sure Xenith will have a good explanation for anything we find."

Lavender picked up the corner of a Polaroid, lifting it from the mess and handing it to me. A feminine scrawl on the white frame read: Lollapalooza 1993. The photo captured a group of young grunge enthusiasts at the outdoor concert. In the foreground, a young mixed-race couple was locked in a cozy flannel embrace. I smiled, recognizing a young Xenith gazing lovingly at a blonde girl in a hemp choker.

In the background, I spotted Al sipping a Zima—her style hadn't changed a bit. Lavender pointed to the young man next to Al. "That's Ace," she said. "Basically, what his spirit looks like now. He's even wearing that same Soundgarden shirt—maybe he died around the time of the picture?"

The handsome Filipino teen had a grin full of mischief. The Grind's poltergeist looked like trouble—the fun kind. In that moment, he only had eyes for a curly haired girl in a bright yellow babydoll dress. I couldn't see her face, but her body language said she returned the affection. Why would Xenith be burning pictures of a dead boy?

"What made you think I'd be upset by this picture?" I asked.

"You don't see it?" Lavender pointed gestured to the photo. "Xenith, and..."

"And..." I looked closer at Xenith's love interest and gasped—her brows were much thicker and her skin far less orange, but the girl in Xenith's arms was Shayla Starr.

I looked down at the letters in the box. Love letters between Shayla and Xenith. Why was he burning them? Yoga Banshee was clearly an integral part of his past, but he'd never mentioned anything—neither had Al. Xenith's romantic liaisons were vast, and frequently concurrent; could that be the true source of Shayla's animosity? It looked like Xenith had close ties to not one, but two mysterious deaths.

Lavender was right, this did not look good.

CHAPTER 9 - ACE IN THE HALL

My morning brain swirled with clues before I even opened my eyes. A box of dirt, a box of love letters, a disturbingly placed salt rock. Xenith's late-night arson haunted me. Did I leave it alone or confront him? My phone buzzed on the bedside table. I blinked the sleep away recognize that noon was an acceptable time to text—it was from Lana. Worried, I opened the message to see it was Xenith using her phone. He apologized for disappearing; his phone was still missing. He assured me that Lana and the baby were both fine and asked me to meet him at The Grind in about an hour. No rest for the diva. I sent a quick thumbs-up and lay back down on my pillows, mustering my courage. I could hear the shower running, so Lavender was already up and at 'em—show off.

I crawled out of bed and faced the next question: What does one wear to meet their ex-lover, current business partner, and probable murder suspect? It's complicated. I settled for a crimson cashmere sweater paired with flowy houndstooth palazzos. Goddess bless the messy-bun and enormous sunglasses.

After the quick grumbly walk, Lavender entered the front door of The Metal Grind, excited to be trusted to pick up food and Auntie's Delight like the independent modern sophisticate she was. I could see Al and Darien busy behind the bar. My psychic shields were too delicate to navigate the energies of the lunchtime crowd; I opted to avoid the humanity and slink in the back way. I winced at the sight of the concert poster. Brionne LeFave was wearing a banner with the word "postponed" on her chest. I had failed to make it on stage for the first time in my life. What did our cancellation mean for the Grind? Could we bounce back?

Keeping my head low and shields up, I hurried past the dark entrance of Endless Zen to the unmarked door. Stepping in from the street, I pushed my shades onto my head and shut the door behind me. My caffeine headache was starting to pierce its way through my skull like Big Bertha drilling the tunnel beneath the streets of Seattle.

The shared hallway behind Endless Zen was quiet as a crypt. My eyes adjusted to the dim. Cardboard boxes lined the walls, stacked like beige sentinels. At the far end, I could see the fading paint on the backstage door that read: Starrlight Theatre. In a sentimental nod, Xenith and Al had left the old lettering in place.

I felt a little sick at the prospect of this meeting with Xenith. My heart knew he was innocent—if only his behavior matched my heart.

Lost in thought, my steps were slow as I neared the hall entrance to the yoga studio. Pausing at the frosted glass, I wondered how poor Missy Jo was holding up. I knew she and Shayla lived in apartments on the upper floor. Should we stop by with our condolences? Did people do that anymore? Surely Missy Jo had legitimate friends to take care of her.

I started walking again toward the backstage door when I caught motion overhead. One of the cardboard towers swayed dangerously. We hadn't had an earthquake in Seattle in decades. A rat? I swung my bag off my shoulder, ready to smash any incoming rodents with fine leather.

I shrieked as the avalanche of cartons fell, blocking my path. One of the boxes popped open, yoga mats rolling onto at my feet in a log jam. I looked around for any scurrying vermin, but—thankfully—saw no evidence.

"Good goddess!" I exclaimed. "What on earth?"

As if in answer to my question, a sound came from the unmarked door to my right. Some kind of closet, I assumed. The doorknob jiggled. The door itself remained closed, clattering against the frame as if someone were hitting it with their shoulder.

"Hello?" I called. "Is someone there? Do you need help? Are you rat?"

No reply, but the door shook again. I tried to open it—locked. I frowned.

"Hello?" The yoga mats burst into motion, rolling up against the bottom of the rattling door. My coffee-free brain cringed, struggling to process. And then I figured it out—The Metal Grind's poltergeist was sending me a not-so-subtle message.

"Would you like me to open the door, Ace?" I said dryly.

The door stopped its racket.

"I assume that's a yes." I started to reach for a hairpin, but realized this door was more of a credit card situation. I rummaged for my wallet. I'd really been putting my unusual life skills to the test over the past few days. Kicking aside the yoga mats, I slid my much-underused gym membership card into the crack between the frame and the door. "It's all in the wrist," I told the ghost and, seconds later, opened the door.

I flipped on the switch and gasped—I'd discovered Yoga Banshee's shrine.

The small room was thick with Shayla's infamous sandalwood scent. The back wall was a custom bookshelf painted glossy ebony featuring well-lit photographs of Shayla. The wall behind the door was covered with three floor-to-ceiling mirrors, Endless Zen's logo etched diagonally across their surfaces. To the left, two black leather chairs faced a neatly organized Lucite desk. A mandala in signature tangerine covered the far wall.

Not a shrine—her office. Interesting. Helping myself to a tissue from the box on the desk, I smeared any trace of my fingerprints off the door and closed it. Paranoid? Maybe. The giant mirrors showed me a loose curl had escaped. I tucked the renegade back into my bun. Hands behind my back, I peered carefully at the shelves. Some books and crystals, but mostly photographs. Shayla posing with minor celebrities, Shayla winning prizes in fitness competitions, Shayla's headshots spanning the last two decades. So. Much. Shayla.

"Oh my." I took in the details of her most recent headshot displayed front and center, in a—frankly ridiculous—frame worthy of a priceless oil painting. Slanting my brows in silent judgment, I shook my head. As I stared, the mini-spotlight highlighting this monstrosity, popped.

I stepped back quickly as glass tinkled onto the white concrete floor. The smell of electric heat filled my senses as the light went dark on Yoga Banshee's heavily made-up face—probably for the best.

"Art critic?" I laughed shakily, continuing my snoop. An angry spirit with that level of matter manipulation could be incredibly dangerous, far beyond knocking over boxes and stacking toilet paper. Why was he working so hard to get my attention.?

I looked around the room, not seeing anything worthy of ghostly intervention.

"What is it you want me to see, Ace?" I asked.

The wall of mirrors rattled in reply.

"Careful," I cautioned. "I do not need twenty-one years of bad luck. Give me a second."

I peered carefully at the mirrors. A small smudge caught my eye, near the joined edges of two panels, just below the "d" in the logo. Heart beating like a second curtain call, I pressed my tissue-covered fingers to the crack. With a quiet snick, the mirror opened like a medicine cabinet. What was inside? Gold doubloons? Lifetime supply of Botox? Wet bar? Pulling the mirrored panel open, I discovered—another bookshelf.

My initial disappointment quickly changed to curiosity. Why would you need to a hidden bookshelf? Cookin' the books, Shayla?

Unlike the never-been-opened quality of the tomes on the outside shelf, these books were mismatched in height and thickness, some held together with colorful duct tape. The front and backs were decorated with doodles and stickers. Journals? The one uniformity was the years labeled on the spines. I was reaching for the most recent (2014-2015) when 1993-1994 came flying off the shelf at my head. I barely had time to block the book with my forearm —instincts honed from years of living with a twin brother.

"Unnecessary," I snapped, picking the journal up and slipping it into my bag.

Two of the smaller framed photos of Shayla flipped forward, smashing to the ground. "Why are you getting upset?" I asked. "I'm trying to help." Another photo flipped. It was time to get out of there.

Trying to remain calm and not insert any of my own emotions into the mix, I snagged the most recent journal and threw it into my bag. Tissue barrier covering my fingers, I closed the mirror, switched off the lights, and slipped back into the hallway.

The dim lights in the corridor flickered and the remaining box towers swayed. I scrambled over the hill of debris and ran for the back door of the theatre. I kept expecting the boxes to close in behind me in an Indiana Jones scenario. I shot a glance over my shoulder, looking forward just in time to see the stage door gently swing open to receive me. I crossed the threshold, slowing to a walk. The door closed sedately behind me.

"If that was apology, I am *not* accepting," I said through my teeth. What had I done to deserve that? Entirely too much excitement for a woman my age before her coffee.

CHAPTER 10 - GUILTY OF SOMETHING

Still winded from my unruly spirit encounter and flirting with despair due to lack of caffeine, I stomped up the back stairs of the Metal Grind toward Xenith's apartment. Was it only last night that Lavender, my leather pants, and I had followed Xenith down these same steps in the dark?

I opened the door at the top, stepping out unto the second-floor catwalk. Sweet, sweet coffee smells washed over me. So close. Surely by now, Lavender had filled my order and was making her way, very carefully, up the spiral staircase. Like a wanderer in the desert, I stumbled forward.

Xenith stepped out of his apartment scanning the floor like he'd dropped something. He looked up and we locked eyes. The clink of cups and murmur of customers rose from below.

Dressed in an ancient Starrlight Theatre T-shirt and Black Panther pajama bottoms, my old friend appeared rumpled and fragile, dark eyes full of worry. My heart clenched; I'd thought I was ready.

"Still can't find my phone." He shrugged, radiating sadness and guilt. I'd been picking up that vibe since before Shayla's murder—what was he hiding? "Babe, I…"

"How's Lana?" I asked. "The baby? Everything's okay?"

"Yeah." Xenith rubbed a hand over his dreadlocks. "Everything is good. Lana's home, napping now."

"That's good news," I said. "Lana's a strong woman."

"A saint and a warrior," Xenith said vehemently. "I am an incredibly lucky man and I... I don't deserve any of it."

He was sincerely miserable. I tried to keep myself as neutral as possible, safely between my protective layers, but my traitorous emotions hit me with a one-two punch of sympathy and suspicion. Shuddering, I tried to blink my head clear.

"You'll tell me everything and only the truth?" I asked.

"Yes," Xenith agreed. "I promise. That's the only way to go with the women in my life. I don't know why I always convince myself otherwise."

I spotted Lavender at the top of the spiral staircase carrying—a burrito. The child had one job! Before I could throw myself over the balcony and onto the innocent café-goers below. Al and Darien appeared behind her, carrying additional food and my salvation.

"I'm glad you're all here," Xenith said. "I was thinking we could talk in the dressing room." He tapped his fist with his palm. "But, um, it's a pretty adult subject matter."

Lavender heaved an enormous sigh. "Before you try to ditch me, some things to consider." She drew in a breath, ticking items off on her pale fingers. "One: I've already seen a dead body, been interviewed by the police, and had a Coke for breakfast. Two: I promise if I start feeling weird about it, I'll put on my noise-cancelling headphones. They keep the aggressive spirits out. I'm sure it will work on"— she smirked as she added excessive air-quotes— "adult subject matter, and three: I'm your only hope for communicating with The Metal Grind's resident spirit, who knows some stuff and wants to share."

"Ohmygodarewehavingaséance?" Darien bounced in excitement. I eyed my drinks with concern.

"A séance is just theatre," Lavender said, sounding like her mother. "That's for amateurs."

"Oooo, snap!" Darien continued. "Al, it's happening!" He grinned at Lavender. "I made Al watch some episodes of your series to prepare for your arrival—she's totally hooked."

"Cool show," Al agreed.

Lavender blushed and looked at me expectantly. "Don't ruin the best vacation ever by cutting me out now."

"Hard sell!" I slung an arm around my niecling. "It worked. Let's throw the baby in with the bathwater. To the dressing room."

I paused long enough for Darien to hand me my doppio shot. I tossed the espresso back like a Wild West saloon girl. "Bless you, beautiful boy."

I scooped up my Diva's Delight and continued to the dressing room with Lavender in tow.

"You okay, dude?" I heard Al ask Xenith. "How's Lana?"

"Are you sure you're up for this?" I asked in Lavender's ear, hurrying her ahead of the group.

"I am," she said. "I'd figure it all out eventually anyway. Kids always do, you know."

"I know nothing about kids," I reminded her. "You'll have to keep teaching me. Speaking of your superior knowledge," I added as we entered the room, "I just had an Ace encounter in the back hall. He seems unstable."

"He's here now," she said dropping her backpack on the floor and flopping onto the second-hand leather couch. "Looks like he expended a lot of energy. It'll take a while for him to recharge."

I eyed the empty room suspiciously, clutching my Diva's Delight between both hands. If Ace had some mysterious issue with me, I did not want my coffee paying the price.

"He says, he's sorry?" Lavender said. "He wasn't trying to scare you—his emotions get the best of him sometimes. Also, he's smirking, so not sure how sorry he is."

"Hmmmm."

Lavender confirmed my suspicions that Ace enjoyed messing with me. I sat down next to my niecling on the couch. In a show of trust I didn't fully feel, I set my precious drink on the glass-topped coffee table—one of Xenith's designs with a twisted knot of electric guitars as a base.

"What happened?" Lavender asked. "Can't leave you alone for a minute, can I?"

Before I could answer, the rest of our party arrived. Darien hopped up on the make-up counter next to the Dings unfortunately timed cupcakes. We hadn't had the heart to throw them away last night. With one finger he slowly pushed the pink bakery box further down the counter.

Xenith pulled one of the hardback chairs from the counter, turning it around to straddle as he faced us. Al set a hot chocolate in front of Lavender and a plate with my favorite Highway to Hell Hash next to me before taking the side chair on my right.

"Al, you are the wind beneath my wings," I said sincerely. She smirked, but as our eyes met, we acknowledged our mutual worry for Xenith.

I gracefully shoveled breakfast into my mouth, fortifying myself and concentrating on strengthening my psychic shields, which were growing stronger by the moment.

"Before we talk about talking to spirits," Xenith said, "I need to get something off my chest. I've been acting like a tool lately. I know what you all must be thinking, and I want to explain. I threatened Shayla in front of tons of witnesses, disappeared around the time of the murder, and basically look guilty as hell." He rubbed his hands over his face, taking a deep breath. "And that's because, I am."

Darien stopped checking his eyeliner in the mirror staring at his uncle. Al quietly sipped her coffee. Next to me on the couch, Lavender bit her lip. I should have been feeling terrible, but I was strangely relieved. A weight was lifted, almost like *I'd* confessed. The mind-fog I hadn't even realized I was carrying suddenly lifted. And boom— clarity. Being an empath is wild ride, my friends.

Coffee in hand, I leaned back against the dark leather of the couch. Hearing Xenith say he was guilty made me certain he didn't murder Shayla. Woo-woo skills are frustrating like that. Why don't they just work the first time without all the drama in between? There were lots of factors, but when I know, I know. I decided to let the rest of the room in on things—although I thought Al and I were on the same page.

"Don't worry, darlings," I announced. "He's not guilty of murder. He's only guilty of cheating." That habit had also led to the end of our relationship—divas don't share. I didn't introduce that tidbit of dirty laundry into the mix, but couldn't help adding, "And of deeply questionable taste."

Lavender, having been born with our family's innate feel for dramatic timing, punctuated my announcement by dropping the burned shoebox onto the coffee table.

CHAPTER 11 - WHAT'S YOUR POISON?

Xenith stared in shock at the evidence of his dumpster visit on the dressing room table. Lavender sat back on the couch with a flourish. Al raised her brows.

"Cheating! Uncle Zee? Whaa? Who? Who?" Darien demanded, sounding like an owl. Lavender handed him the incriminating Lollapalooza Polaroid. His jaw dropped. "Yoga Banshee?" The poor dear's voice reached coloratura heights.

"Never understood what you saw in her," Al said. "When you were young and dumb—sure. But she was born mean and only got worse."

"It's complicated," Xenith said wearily. "She was my first love—we met when we were teenagers, here at the Starrlight." He leaned away from the chairback, gestured at his shirt. "She and Missy Jo would come from the East Coast and stay with their Uncle Elliot to do summer stock."

"Her uncle! That's why Shayla Starr had two Rs? Like the Starrlight!" Darien said, piecing together something I'd totally failed to notice.

"Her stage name," Xenith confirmed. "She changed it when she moved to LA in '94."

It took every ounce of my diva-level discipline to keep from adding: *to become 'a starrrr.'*

"Long time ago," Al said.

"For real," Xenith said ruefully. "Summer stock is how Al and I got to be friends. We were working on sets and tech for Elliot's shows. Missy Jo did costumes. Shayla was... dazzling. A really good dancer. I couldn't take my eyes off her. She and Al's cousin Ace, were the performers."

Lavender and I glanced at each other—Al was related to The Metal Grind's poltergeist. Or maybe he was the Starrlight's poltergeist.

"Ace was a ham," Al said fondly. "Shayla was a prima donna."

"She was," Xenith agreed. "And back then, I loved it. We'd be hot and heavy in the summer, and then the sisters would go back home for the school year. Even after high school we spent summers together, until 1993."

I touched my bag, thinking of the dates on the journal that Ace had desperately wanted me to find. Al and Xenith exchanged a heavy look. What happened in 1993?

"Elliot died that year; Shayla and I fell out—big time." Xenith rubbed at his stubbled jaw. "I didn't see or hear from her for years, until I came back and started working the Grind."

"I thought you couldn't stand her," Darien said, sounding very young. "How did you end up..."

"Good question." Xenith buried his face in his hands. "Why would I jeopardize what Lana and I had? I don't even *like* Shayla. But one night, drunk, stressed-out, alone—she found me." He glanced uncomfortably at Lavender. "One thing led to another..."

"Dude," Al said, shaking her head.

"I know," Xenith said. "It's not a good excuse, but I was under a lot of pressure—not thinking straight. We'd underestimated—I underestimated—how much work and money it would take to get this building fixed-up. I was the one who convinced Al to invest. Lana and I put every penny we had into the renovation, but financially, we were at rock bottom, credit cards maxed—I thought I'd have to declare bankruptcy and lose it all for everyone."

"And you didn't tell anyone else how bad it was," Al pointed out.

"Right. Big mistake," Xenith agreed. "But I'm done with that. All truth, all the time—from now on. I promise, Al."

She nodded, but her jaw was tight.

Xenith continued. "The next day, I couldn't believe what I'd done. I told Shayla it was a one-time mistake—and I didn't do it gently."

"And she loved that," I said dryly.

"She was pissed," Xenith said. "Threatened daily to tell Lana. Told me she had pictures." He gripped his hands together.

"Yoga Banshee deserves a far worse name than we gave her," Darien said. I agreed, still thinking about the unfairly maligned banshees out there.

Xenith blew out a breath. "After my sound system tantrum, I knew she'd get revenge by telling Lana. I panicked. I snuck up to Shayla's apartment while she was teaching to see if she really had any evidence. Shayla always kept a journal. She was obsessive about it."

"For her memoirs," Al added.

"She always planned on being famous," Xenith said. "Just not like this."

"Did you find her diary?" Darien asked.

"No." Xenith shook his head. "She must keep them hidden somewhere."

I had the answer to that question—literally, in the bag—but I kept my mouth shut for the moment, wanting to hear Xenith's whole story first.

"I found that," Xenith said, pointing to the ruined cardboard box, "sitting out on her bed, like she'd be going through it recently. I was so hyped I dropped the box, stuff spilled everywhere. I had to scramble on my hands and knees to pick it all up. I ended up just taking the whole box back to my apartment. As I was looking through it, all the pictures of me as, well, a stupid kid, made me realize I was reverting to the same place, acting immaturely." He shook his head. "I'm gonna be a dad. I knew I needed to grow-up and tell Lana everything before Shayla did."

"Why come back to burn the box?" I asked.

Xenith sighed. "After I heard Shayla was murdered, I realized I'd be a suspect. If the cops found—"

Lavender stiffened next to me as Darien gasped and scrambled off the counter to his feet. I felt an icy fist in my stomach as I saw Velasco standing in the doorway of the dressing room. My heart slammed up against my teeth. How much had she heard?

"Hi, Detective Velasco!" Lavender said, waving.

"Hello, Lavender," the detective said. "Looks like my invitation to the meeting got lost."

"You're welcome to join us." Xenith said, holding perfectly still.

"You must be the elusive Xenith Morgan," Detective Velasco said as she fully entered the room. She was dressed more casually than the night before, in dark jeans and a navy blazer. I was annoyed by how unfrazzled she appeared, not a wrinkle or hair out of place. She was the anti-Columbo. "I've been looking for you."

"Yes, I heard," Xenith said calmly. "If you check with the station, you'll find out I made an appointment for this afternoon."

I could barely hear their conversation over the warning sirens wailing in my ears. I looked down at the coffee table in horror, only to see Lavender's hoodie casually draped over the top of the tell-tale shoebox. When had she done that?

"Did you find the murderer yet?" Lavender asked brightly.

"Working on it," Velasco said, perching on the arm of the chair between Lavender and Xenith. She seemed to still find Lavender amusing, which I hoped was good sign. "We've got some ideas."

"Do you think the killer will strike again?" Darien asked as he moved to stand behind his uncle. "Should we be scared?"

"I don't think so," Velasco said with enough kindness to make me like her a little. "I'm sure this was all about Ms. Starr and nobody else."

"And her murderer," Lavender pointed out practically.

"Is there anything we should do to protect ourselves?" Darien asked.

"Hide all the salt rocks?" I quipped without thinking.

"You find murder amusing, Ms. LeFave?" Velasco angled toward me.

I fought down the urge to babble like a brook. What was wrong with me? From the look on Lavender's face, she was wondering the same thing.

I waved a hand in semi-apology. "It was a long night."

"Hmph," Velasco replied. "The salt rock isn't what killed her, anyway." She turned her full gaze on Xenith, watching him like a hawk when she added, "We suspect poison."

"Poison?" Al echoed.

"That's right," Velasco said, still staring at Xenith.

My mind went immediately to the cupcake with a single bite out of it on the sill of Endless Zen. The Dings as murderers? I just couldn't wrap my head around it. Were the remaining cupcakes another clue in a box?

"And remind me again," Velasco asked. "Where you were last night, Mr. Morgan?"

"Overlake hospital," Xenith replied.

"Not when I went there," Velasco countered.

Xenith's knuckles tightened on the chairback, biceps bunched with tension.

"And what was your relationship with Shayla Starr?" the cop asked.

"Neighbors," Xenith said carefully. "We weren't cordial."

"Cordial?" Velasco laughed. "I'd say threatening to kill someone is a far cry from cordial. And neighbors, you said? Anything more than that?"

"Not anymore," Xenith said. "Look, I'll be happy to answer all your questions when I come to the station with my brother, this afternoon."

"Your brother?" Velasco asked.

"He's my lawyer," Xenith said, still perfectly polite. I wanted to leap across the table and yank Velasco's bun out of her head.

"Why would you need a lawyer?" Velasco tilted her head inquisitively. "Feeling guilty, Mr. Morgan?"

"No, just cautious. Look, I need to check on my wife." Xenith stood and slid the wooden chair back underneath the counter.

"Does your wife know about you and the deceased?" Velasco stood as well, an aggressive note in her voice.

Xenith said nothing.

"Does your wife know you were in Ms. Starr's apartment recently?"

The muscles of Xenith's jaw twitched. I felt like I was being forced to watch a terrible movie. I wanted to pause, fast forward, make it stop. Al and Lavender were both stiff with tension, eyes on the scene before us. The plates and silverware on the glass coffee table rattled quietly—the last thing we needed was a spirit tantrum thrown into the mix.

"Uncle Zee," Darien said. "I think I should call my dad now." Ear to his phone, he walked out to the catwalk.

"Tell him to meet your uncle down at the station," Detective Velasco said. "That's where we're headed right now."

"Is that necessary?" Xenith asked.

"It is. You see, I've got some good news for you, Mr. Morgan," the detective said with false cheer. "We found your missing cellphone!" Velasco put her hands on her hips, pulling her suit jacket back enough to show her gun and handcuffs. "Under Shayla Starr's bed."

CHAPTER 12 - TO CATCH A MOUSE

Lavender and I walked up the steps of Endless Zen for Shayla's memorial. My tie-dyed maxi dress in sunset shades was not strictly grieving garb but *could* be interpreted as a nod to the colors of Endless Zen. Lavender was rocking her usual Dickensian mourner vibe, so we'd covered our bases.

The previous two days had passed in a head-spinning blur both legal and paranormal, starting with Detective Velasco escorting Xenith out of the Metal Grind in handcuffs. Thanks to Deimos, his lawyer-brother, Xenith was out on bail. He'd been ensconced at home with Lana,

with the exception of one, very important, top-secret, planning conclave involving Al and Darien in my—poltergeist-free—condo.

Shayla's memorial was the perfect place to execute Operation Mouse Trap. After Xenith's arrest, Ace spilled his secrets to Lavender. The poltergeist was quite the voyeur and been holding a whole truckload of information close to his spectral chest. Seeing his Xenith pay the price for his silence was enough to open the floodgates. Ace confessed everything he knew—which was a lot. But one does not simply tell the police a ghost holds the key to the mystery; a little more panache is required. Divas are loaded with panache.

"Ready, Lava Cakes?" I asked as we entered the lobby.

"Lava Cakes?" Lavender looked at me askance. "I don't think so."

"Dark, mysterious, but sweet and gooey in the center?" I pointed out in my own defense.

"Hmmm. We'll discuss later," Lavender said in a disturbing echo of her mother. "Are you ready?"

"Goddess, I hope so."

I marshalled my emotional shields as we paused in the doorway of the studio where we'd last witnessed Shayla's ultimate shavasana. The room was candlelit and redolent with sandalwood. The enormous, framed photograph from Shayla's office was featured on an easel in front of the orange curtains with the dates 1973-2015 under her artificial smile. We were almost the same age, I thought with genuine sadness. Missy Jo had plastered the neighborhood with fliers, but attendance was as low, as one might expect. Shayla's relationships had been about power dynamics instead of affection, and the results spoke for themselves. Most of the attendees were here not to mourn Shayla, but to support her sister or for curiosity.

Cassie from Ink Blot, the Dings, and Javier stood chatting quietly with Missy Jo near a rack of folding chairs. Shayla's sister looked depressed and frail in her black jersey dress. A handful of yoga students clumped together in their corner, conspicuous in their expensive similarity. Shayla's classes catered to the Lulu Lemon set, not the granolas. Under the low murmur, I could hear sitar-forward music playing quietly over the speaker system.

The mark was identified, everyone's roles defined, and Act One of Operation Mouse Trap was ready to open. I saw Al and Darien standing at a folding table, setting out disposable cups and plates for our carefully selected menu. The Metal Grind and Ding! Cupcakes! were providing refreshments for the evening. Darien gave us a wave and a too-enthusiastic thumbs up. The dear was not caper-ready.

Al gave me a subtle nod of greeting. All was in place. There was a layer of sadness over Al's usually contained vibe. Her first reaction to finding out her cousin was the resident trickster spirit had been amusement, as if confirming her own suspicions. But while she'd accepted the fact of Ace's death years ago, enough for a memorial tattoo, hearing the shocking details of his demise had reawakened her grief. I'd felt it settle on her like a layer of dust. Closure comes at a price.

"What's the Ace status, Lavvy?" I whispered.

"He's hee-re," Lavender sang quietly.

"A little on the nose, don't you think?" I asked.

"What's on my nose?" Lavender swiped a sleeve across her face.

"I meant the quote, darling." I did my best not to laugh at the funeral.

"Oh, you know Dad loves *Poltergeist*. He thinks it's hilarious." She shrugged in perfect pre-teen.

"How do you think our trickster spirit will react when we unleash our plan?" I asked.

Lavender made a face that confirmed my suspicions and did not bode well for the breakable items in the room. Ace was protective of those he loved, and for our plan to work —we'd have to put one of them through the wringer.

We moved over to Missy Jo to offer our condolences. I was relieved and alert when Detective Velasco walked into the room. When Xenith lost his cell phone picking up memorabilia in Shayla's room, he'd secured himself as Velasco's prime suspect. I wasn't positive the detective would show up. But she was as meticulous as she appeared. And now, everyone was place. My palms damp, I dried them in the folds of my sundress. Digging up the grifter skills of my past made me uncomfortable on many levels. How slippery was this slope? How rusty was I? Xenith's freedom, the fate of the Metal Grind, and all the money we'd risked hung in the balance.

"Thank you for c-c-c-coming everyone," Missy Jo said quietly. "We're g-g-going to open with a chant and then people can have a chance to share, if they'd like. Find yourself a c-c-c-comfortable position and we'll start."

People gathered, pulling folding chairs into a loose circle in front of Shayla's picture. Someone read a poem and a few yoga ladies spoke of how Shayla had inspired them to better health. Everyone else chose the second half of "if you don't have anything nice to say," which made for a rather short memorial. Eventually, after some uncomfortable silence, Missy Jo thanked everyone for coming. That was my cue: on to Act Two.

"We've brought some refreshments tonight," I said, gesturing to the table. "As you know, Shayla had some strong feelings on the subject of food and drink." This understatement brought on quite a few smiles. "So I want to assure you that these are all natural, sugar-free cupcakes and, instead of coffee, we're serving Shayla's favorite mushroom tea."

People started standing, some folding their chairs and helpfully putting them in the rack. The yoga students left their chairs in place, quickly gave their farewells to Missy Jo, and exited en masse. I heard the words "wine bar" mentioned in hushed, desperate tones. Lavender gravitated to Darien and Javier. Most of those left seemed to, not surprisingly, avoid the refreshment. I served as lonely table hostess, waiting patiently until Velasco approached Missy Jo, who was stationed in a chair near Shayla's portrait.

Perfect. Time for Act Three.

I assessed my psychic shields. Empathy would kill this operation dead in the water. I'd had two days to rebuild— my protection was strong and ready. I nodded to Lavender, who returned the signal and went to look for Mrs. Ding. Javier put an arm around Darien's shoulders and tried to curtail his boyfriend's nervous excitement.

"Excuse me, sorry." I approached Missy Jo and the detective, feeling none of my previous nerves. I'd devised a con and I knew how to execute. Showtime. "Can I bring you something, Missy Jo? Tea?" I clasped my hand in front of my heart. "Oh, I hope you don't mind, we found your open box of mushroom tea in the hallway. We thought it would be fitting to serve Shayla's favorite. I'll be happy to replace what we've used. I know you make it yourself. Just let me know where you order your ingredients."

Missy Jo looked confused. "Tea from the hallway?"

"Yes," I said, nodding. "Lavender noticed you stored Shayla's special tea in the boxes right outside the backdoor. We thought it would be fitting to use your personal recipe for the guests tonight. I hope that's all right."

Missy Jo jumped to her feet, turning in horror towards the refreshments. Detective Velasco took a step backward in surprise at the sudden movement. Lavender and Mrs. Ding stood like salt and pepper shakers right in front of the table in a perfect stage picture. They both held cups of mushroom tea.

"No, no, no," Missy Jo whispered.

Mrs. Ding and Lavender "clinked" their paper cups together and raised them to their lips with the enthusiasm of one about to dose themselves with cough syrup.

"NO!" Missy Jo cried. "STOP! Don't drink that!"

The subdued room became silent. Detective Velasco's surprise turned to pointed interest.

"What's wrong, Missy Jo?" I asked oh-so-innocently. "Why shouldn't they drink?"

"Because, because..." Missy Jo began to look wildly around and laughed brittlely. "It's disgusting, that's why. Truly vile. No one in their right mind would drink it."

"That's okay," Lavender said brightly. "I'm into trying new things. Right, Al?"

Al, standing with Cassie near the door, gave my niecling a thumbs-up.

"I didn't think spicy hot chocolate sounded good," Lavender continued, "but Al suggested it to me, and I really liked it." She raised her glass high. "Might as well try this too! Ready, Mrs. Ding?"

Mrs. Ding peered suspiciously into her cup and nodded. "I'm in if you're in, Lavender, honey."

In exaggerated slow motion, they brought their cups to their lips. Lavender a bit too slow-mo to be believed, in my opinion, but Missy Jo bought it.

"NO!" The normally timid woman shoved her way through the ring of chairs and knocked the tea out of their hands. Then she tipped over the folding table. Beverages and cupcakes fell to the floor in a torrent of splashing and squishing. Everyone stared in shock at the spectacle. Even my jaw dropped. I'd been looking to elicit a reaction— Missy Jo did not disappoint.

"I'm sorry," Missy Jo said, staring helplessly at the mess.

"I'll find a mop," Al said. Lavender appeared by my side. I put my arm around her shoulders.

"I'm sorry," Missy Jo said again. "I'm not really feeling well—you understand." She started to weave her way toward the door, intent on escape. "Please..."

Detective Velasco stepped between the desperate woman and the exit, inserting herself into the drama as if she'd read the script. "What's going on, Missy Jo?"

Missy Jo froze in place, staring at the floor.

Darien and Javier started to gently herd the other attendees out of the room and over to The Metal Grind as planned. The Dings, focused on Missy Jo, stayed behind. I felt a tinge of guilt at involving them in our little plan without their knowledge. But I knew their affection for Missy Jo would help her later. Al returned with a mop and paper towels.

"Anything you'd like to tell me?" Velasco asked Missy Jo, who had yet to move an inch. "We confiscated all the tea found in the studio; why didn't you mention additional storage? If I have this tea tested, what will they find?"

Missy Jo opened and closed her mouth. No sound came out.

Lavender stepped forward and spoke gently to Missy Jo. "The night Shayla died, I heard you two arguing in the back hall. And after she left, you took something out of the boxes. When I looked in the box, I thought it was dirt. But later, Auntie Babe said it was probably mushroom tea."

Velasco turned sharply toward me. I didn't think our theatre was fooling her anymore, but that didn't matter— we had her attention, and she had the scent.

"Are you going to let Xenith take the fall for you, Missy Jo?" I asked quietly. "He told us how you two managed Elliot's hospice together. Xenith said how much he admired you, how strong you were that whole summer. How you helped each other through that awful time. Do you really want him to be punished for Shayla's death, when you know he's innocent?"

Missy Jo looked away, biting her nails. Poor thing. I wanted this over and soon.

"We know you're a good person, Missy Jo," I said. "You didn't let anyone drink the poison tea. You protected them." No need to mention the tea had been basic Lipton.

"I never meant to use it on anyone else," she mumbled miserably. "Shayla wasn't supposed to drink it."

"Of course not," I said, as my heart broke for her.

Missy Jo wiped her eyes miserably. "The tea was for me."

CHaPTer 13 - BEST SERVED HOT

Missy Jo's announcement hit the people in the yoga studio like a slap, even those of us who knew it was coming. Emotions pressed on me from all sides like cabin pressure —but I was ready. Missy Jo put her face in her hands and wept. I felt horrible making her reveal her private pain in such a public way, but I knew ultimately it would help her with the other burden she was carrying—guilt.

In an echo of the earlier memorial, we moved away from the door and back to the center of the room, curving our chairs around the grief-stricken woman. Detective Velasco brought Missy Jo a chair. Mr. and Mrs. Ding flanked her with grandparental comfort.

Lavender and I sat together giving Missy Jo space; now was not the time for us to intrude. Act Four of Operation Mousetrap should unfold naturally from that point—we hoped. My niecling whispered that Ace was standing behind Missy Jo's chair. Detective Velasco sat in front of her, posture open and non-threatening.

"Go ahead, Missy Jo, honey," Mrs. Ding said, "tell us everything. You'll feel better."

"Where do I start?" Missy Jo wondered. Al, finished with cleanup for now, slipped a bottle of water into her hand and came to stand behind Lavender and me.

"Start with the tea," Detective Velasco suggested. "I'm going to record this, okay, Missy Jo?"

"Yes," Missy Jo agreed.

"Where did you get the tea?" Velasco prompted, as she set her phone on the floor to record.

"I made it," Missy Jo said. "Foraging is a passion of mine. Shayla hates the outdoors, so I g-g-g-go alone. To be by myself in nature and really think. When I found the Death C-c-c-caps, I recognized them immediately. I harvested some, almost before I realized what I was doing. I remember thinking: this is my way out."

"Out of what?" Detective Velasco asked.

"Life, myself. I don't know." Missy Jo shrugged. "I've never really been right in the head. Even as a k-k-kid, I c-c-c-couldn't interact normally with other people. I'd panic, stutter like a fool. It was really hard on Shayla to have to deal with me all the time. It's a wonder anyone ever talked to me—I was such a loser."

I could almost hear Shayla's voice transcribed over Missy Jo's, calling her 'not right in the head' and moaning over her own perceived slights. I am sure it was a monologue Yoga Banshee performed ritually. She probably even believed it—Missy Jo did.

"Not true," Al said, leaning the mop against the wall. "The theatre kids, we all liked you."

"You're just shy," Mr. Ding added. "No one thinks you're a loser."

"People don't really notice me when Shayla's around," Missy Jo said. "She was the star. Beautiful, talented, and smart—although people never really respected her, always underestimating her because of her looks."

Al sat down in a chair next to Lavender and me. We shared a look at that statement.

"Shayla k-k-k-kept me in line, made sure I didn't embarrass us—protected me from the world. I know, I know that you all thought she was short with me. But that's just because she was frustrated. Ever since Uncle Elliot died and Ace... disappeared. Ever since that summer, I've been a huge burden. I couldn't g-g-get myself back together. I'd be okay for a while and then—boom—Missy Mess-Up would be back. If there's something that c-c-can g-g-get messed up, I'll mess it." She gave a sad laugh. "And today certainly proves that."

I glanced at Detective Velasco. Her face remained passive, but I thought I saw sympathy in her eyes.

"Shayla was really stressed out lately," Missy Jo said. "Money issues."

"Money issues?" Velasco echoed.

"Bad investments, I think." Missy Jo waved a hand vaguely. "Not a big deal, but Shayla handles all our money; she takes the responsibility seriously."

"It's actually a pretty big deal," Detective Velasco said. "A routine look at Ms. Starr's finances shows a lot of red flags. This building is mortgaged to the hilt, and in arrears."

"No, no, that c-c-can't be." Missy Jo shook her head in denial. "I own the building outright, inherited from my uncle."

"There are multiple mortgages against the property," the detective said. "Held jointly with Shayla."

Missy Jo frowned. "Shayla does all the money stuff because I'm hopeless. I just sign where she tells me. But I own the building, free and c-c-clear."

My heart hurt. Classic gas-lighting set-up. Make the victim feel inept and set yourself up as savior. My father had been an expert. Lavender put her hand on my leg and tapped her fingers. Her eyes tracked movement that no one else could see. I imagined Ace pacing behind the chairs, as the uneasy spirit reached the nefarious the conclusion ahead of Missy Jo.

Detective Velasco leaned forward in her chair. "Is it possible that Shayla could have gotten those mortgages without you realizing?"

Lavender jabbed me in the thigh. Ace was ramping up. I readied myself for the fifth and final Act.

"Why would she do that?" Missy Jo said. "She knows how much this building means to me."

Al started to say what we were all thinking. "Because she was a b—"

The easel holding Shayla's glamour shot suddenly tipped over, hitting the floor with a slap. Mrs. Ding squeaked as everyone jumped in surprise at the noise. The window curtains rippled, as if blown by a breeze in the closed-up studio. We all watched the phenomenon with wonder.

"What is happening?" Mrs. Ding wondered.

Hands clasped, Lavender stood up. This next act rested fully on her eleven-year-old shoulders. Luckily, she was an expert. Through the weave of her fingers I saw the glint of

Stanley-the-Comfort-Skull's shiny head. My heart squeezed in pride as my niecling pushed back her shoulders and spoke. "Um, Missy Jo?"

Missy Jo raised her head, looking at my niece in puzzlement.

"My name is Lavender. We haven't met, exactly, I guess, but I'm a spiritual medium."

I saw Velasco's eyes roll up into her hairline. My Auntie Bear growled an internal warning. Then the detective shrugged and settled back into her chair, arms crossed, ready to observe. Likely she thought she'd be able to pick up a tidbit of information amidst the nonsense. The detective was about to be rewarded for her patience—a twofer dropped straight into her lap.

Lavender bravely took a few steps closer to Missy Jo. "I have a message for you."

"A message?" Missy Jo asked blankly.

"Lavender is the real deal; you can trust her," Al said.

"I have a message from the spirit world," Lavender said.

"Shayla?" Missy Jo suddenly looked scared.

"No, Shayla has crossed over." Lavender pushed her shoulders back, more confident now that the ball was rolling. "I have a message from Ace."

Mrs. Ding gasped. Mr. Ding looked perplexed.

"Ace?" Missy Jo looked as if she were about to faint. "He's here? Is he angry?"

"Ace? Who is Ace?" Velasco asked, keeping her closed-off posture.

"My cousin," Al said, shifting in her chair. "Disappeared in '95. Never been found."

"Ace is on the spiritual plane now," Lavender said. "He's been in these two buildings ever since his murder."

At the word murder, Velasco gave up her pretense of merely tolerating the proceedings. She straightened in her chair. "How do you know that?" she demanded

"Ace is here?" Missy Jo asked, oblivious to the drama playing out around her.

"He's here." Lavender indicated the empty space next to her, looking upward at the taller person the rest of us couldn't see.

Missy Jo got up, took a few steps forward. She reached out a hand in wonder, as if hoping to make physical contact with the spirit. "I'm so sorry. I don't even remember what happened. I don't know how I c-c-c-could have hurt you, Ace, but I would never have done it on purpose. I love you."

Al let out a breath. The Dings looked at each other, communication passing silently between them. Mrs. Ding slid into Missy Jo's empty chair, and her husband put an arm around her. Tears trailed down Missy Jo's face.

"Why did you keep your relationship a secret, Missy Jo? You and Ace?" Al asked. "We would have been happy for you."

"We were planning to tell people," Missy Jo said. "But it was romantic. Our secret. Shayla wouldn't... I loved him so much."

Lavender glanced over her shoulder at me. I nodded my encouragement.

"Ace loves you too," Lavender said. "He was going to ask you to marry him that night." She paused to listen a bit, eyes tracking back and forth as Ace paced the studio. "You'd both been drinking that night, and smoking stuff. Ace wanted to help you relax. Your uncle had just died; you were so stressed out and sad."

"Ace took me up to the roof," Missy Jo said, smiling dreamily. "He'd set up a picnic for us. It was magical. I always remember that part. The before part." She frowned. "But after, it gets blurry."

"What *do* you remember?" Velasco's voice was low.

"I remember Shayla woke me up," Missy Jo said. "It was still dark. I didn't feel well. I never drank or smoked, so I wasn't feeling well. She told me Ace and I had a big fight. She said I pushed him. He was lying at the bottom of the stairs." Missy Jo's voice cracked, breath quickening as she became lost in the horror of the memory. "His... his neck. It was broken. We had to hide him. Or I'd go to jail."

"Where did you hide him?" Velasco asked.

"In the basement," Missy Jo whispered, rubbing her forehead. "In the basement. There's kind of a hidden room under the stairs, dirt floor. We buried him. C-c-cold down there. I was worried he'd be c-c-cold. It was all my fault. I loved him. Why would I push him? Shayla said I'd ruined both of our lives."

The crystals and candles on the windowsill rattled ominously as Ace's emotions surged.

"I'll tell her." Lavender was addressing Ace. "Just calm down and give me a chance, okay? It won't help if you freak everyone out." My niecling neatly put the upset spirit in his place, then turned to Missy Jo. "Ace wants you to know that he remembers everything that happened that night and you are totally innocent. He never left you; he never crossed over, because he wanted to stay with you and protect you."

Missy Jo stared at Lavender with rapt attention. Her face was a heartbreaking combination of hope and sorrow.

"You and Ace fell asleep..." Lavender blushed. "Shayla came up to the roof and Ace woke up when he heard her. She was angry about being left out of your uncle's will and looking for a fight."

"She was so livid," Missy Jo said. "I told her we'd share this building, but it wasn't enough. She'd expected Uncle Elliot to leave her this place and the theatre."

"Ace tried to get her to leave," Lavender said. "He told Shayla he was going to propose. She told him he was trash and she'd never allow you to marry him and steal her inheritance again. *They* got into an argument and *Shayla* pushed him down the stairs. Then she made you think you'd pushed him. Tricked you into helping *her* hide his body."

"It wasn't me?" Missy Jo shook her head in slow motion, trying to process. "It wasn't me. I loved him. I...Shayla..." She put a hand to her throat. "Ace, oh, Ace."

"He doesn't want you to cry," Lavender said. She paused, listening to Ace's next words. "He hated how your sister treated you. Shayla made you think you were guilty and lower than dirt. He's sorry he couldn't help you more." Lavender frowned and I felt her chill of nerves at what she heard next. "He says, not to worry, he evened the score."

"What?" Detective Velasco asked. "What does that mean?"

Lavender took a breath. "Ace knew that Missy Jo was planning to drink the poison. He couldn't let her go through with it. She had the infusers loaded with tea, Shayla's usual blend, and the deadly one for herself. The infusers were next to their cups—Shayla's orange, and

Missy Jo's blue. While she was waiting for the water to boil, a customer came in."

"That's true," Missy Jo said.

"You were still helping the customer when the tea whistle blew," Lavender said. "The noise irritated Shayla. She stormed into the kitchen, made her own tea and went into the studio to get ready for class."

Missy Jo nodded. "She must have taken my infuser by accident."

"It wasn't an accident," Lavender said. "When you stepped out of the kitchen, Ace switched the teas."

"How?" Missy Jo and Detective Velasco asked in unison.

"Ace is a poltergeist," Lavender said. "He can move small objects."

"He does it all the time," Al confirmed. "Plays tricks at The Grind. Just like when he was alive. We've all seen it." She gestured to the fallen portrait. Velasco looked skeptical as the rest of us nodded in agreement.

"Want to demonstrate?" Lavender asked Ace. She followed his movement, turning to face the window. We all shifted, mirroring her gaze. The orange curtains pulled open with violent speed to reveal the evening street. In rapid succession, a pair of finger cymbals, a pile of eye masks, and a tiny Buddha leapt off the windowsill, sliding across the room and landing at Missy Jo's feet. She squealed, stumbling backwards.

It was an impressive display and cleared up another little mystery.

"The salt rock," Velasco muttered to herself. "That part never made sense."

"Ace calls it his artistic signature," Lavender said. "Shayla was always using her words to be cruel, especially to Missy Jo. She needed to be silenced."

Ace was incredibly dangerous, I added silently. We needed to get him crossed over and soon—hopefully our plan would continue to roll without a hitch. So much depended on Missy Jo.

"Oh, Ace," she said. "I...this is so...overwhelming. He's been here all along? With me?"

"He loved you," Mrs. Ding said simply, leaning into her husband's side.

"He couldn't leave you alone with Shayla," Al added, her voice thick with emotion. "We always believed he'd never leave us, and we were right."

Missy Jo sat heavily in the chair next to the Dings, wiping at tears.

Lavender kneaded her fingers together. "He wants you to promise you will never try to hurt yourself again."

"I won't," Missy Jo promised. "It just was a moment of weakness. When it was time to drop the mushrooms in the water—I c-c-c-couldn't do it. I realized I needed a break from Shayla. I thought I would move out for a while. I went back to the breakroom and threw the poison tea in the garbage. Or at least I thought I did—I guess it was already in Shayla's c-c-c-cup."

"What's going to happen?" I asked Detective Velasco. "Xenith is cleared—right? But what will happen to Missy Jo?"

The detective ran a hand over her perfectly smooth hair. "I'm not sure." She picked her phone up off the ground and switched off the recording. "I don't think 'a ghost did it' will work as a defense, but I think we can make a good case that it was an unfortunate accident."

"These will help," I said. Reaching into my leather bag, I unveiled the journals. The arch of my arm and wrist flick weren't strictly necessary, but the spotlight calls. "Say what you will about Shayla, but she was a meticulous journaler. Details her harassment of Xenith and the night of Ace's death."

Detective Velasco raised a rather diva-like brow as she took the books from my hand. "And how did you come to be in possession of Ms. Starr's journals?"

"Ace helped me find them." I said, leaving off the breaking and entering bit.

"Ace is certainly helpful," Velasco said dryly. I braced myself for further interrogation, but I wasn't too worried. She had bigger fish to fry.

"And Xenith?" Al asked, kindly interrupting our exchange.

Velasco nodded. "I'll get him cleared." She stood, tucking the journals under her arm. "But Missy Jo, I'll need you to come with me to the station."

Three glass candles tipped off the sill and shattered onto the wooden floor.

"No, it's okay, Ace," Missy Jo said lovingly. "I'm ready to face it. You don't have to protect me anymore."

"We'll be with you," Mr. Ding said, gallantly helping his wife to her feet.

Lavender and I looked at each other There was one final move essential to close Operation Mousetrap successfully. If the mouse in question did not behave as we hoped, things could get violent quick.

"What about Ace?" Missy Jo asked.

"I'll help him cross over," Lavender said hurriedly. "Now that he knows you're okay, Ace likely won't have the energy to hold on much longer anyway."

Hmmm. That was not true, to my knowledge. Generally, once they find a way to communicate, spirits like to stick around. Lavender was playing Ace.

"This may be your last opportunity to give Missy Jo a message," she said to the spirit.

Brilliant. The best way to make the mark do what you want is to make them think they want the same thing.

"Sounds private," Al said. "Let's give them the room." She'd been able to have her own moment with Ace and Lavender earlier, if not a formal farewell, an opportunity to reconnect that few people were ever gifted. "Goodbye, little cousin," she added. "I love you, dude."

My throat tightened knowing Al would grieve all over again.

Velasco stood reluctantly. I watched her assess the scenario, realizing that Missy Jo would be visible through the window of the studio. "We'll be right out front. Make it quick."

Aw, Detective Velasco was a softy.

I reached into my purse and handed Lavender the canister of salt she'd requested. I hesitated; there was no way I was leaving her alone in the room with a murderous ghost, but I wanted to give Missy Jo and Ace their moment. I settled for standing right next to the door, putting on Lavender's noise-cancelling headphones, and making myself unobtrusive as possible. Not my best skill.

With Evanescence playing in my ears, I watched Lavender pour a ring of salt, about the size of a hula hoop, onto the golden wood floor. Ace was now contained within the circle, and she could safely open the veil to the other side.

The star-crossed lovers said their farewells. Lavender was poised and confident; I was incredibly proud. I read her lips as she performed the ceremony.

"Your work here is done, Ace Mendoza. Here in the presence of the one you love..." She looked at Missy Jo. "It is time to cross over."

CHAPTER 14 - THE LAST DROP

The morning after Operation Mousetraps success, the sun poured aggressively through the many windows of The Metal Grind. My trusty sunglasses offered glamorous protection as I tossed back my opening doppio shot. I leaned back into the red leather of the corner booth and waited for the magic.

"Is it working yet?" Lavender whispered as she slid in next to me, clutching the Montezuma that Al had let her make herself behind the bar.

Something comparable to a growl sounded in my throat.

"Don't get too close, Hot Stuff" Xenith warned Lana. "Babe's coffee hasn't kicked in." Lana hit him on the shoulder, laughing as they pulled two chairs up to the edge of the booth. I admired her exuberant messy-bun and how it emphasized her graceful neck—she looked like an Egyptian hieroglyph. Xenith hovered around his wife like a supplicant, glowing with happiness as if the bun was in his oven. News of his exoneration had spread through the neighborhood and people kept stopping by to offer their congratulations and relief. Why there were so many humans out and about at 11 a.m. was beyond me.

"Diva's Delight!" Darien executed an admirable pirouette before placing my coffee on the table. "I cannot be-LIEVE I missed the séance last night. Tell me everything."

I drank, listening to the quiet talk around me. I thought about young love, potential cut short, and the dangers of long-held bitterness.

"And Ace just agreed to go into the light?" Darien asked. "After all these years?"

"His work was done," Lavender said. "Missy Jo helped convince him. They really loved each other."

"What do you think will happen to him?" Lana asked.

Lavender shrugged. "I don't know. The crossing over is always the same; what happens next is a mystery."

The table settled into thought. Darien went back to work. My drink was partially finished when Mr. and Mrs. Ding approached the table. He cradled two pink bakery boxes in his arms, and she held a drink carrier with three Metal Grind to-go cups. I was able to produce a genuine smile for the charming bakers.

"Good morning," Mrs. Ding said. "Quite a wild night we all had."

"Thank you for taking such good care of Missy Jo," I said.

"Missy Jo is a good girl," Mr. Ding said. "We always worried about her and how Shayla treated her."

"I'm still worried about her," Xenith admitted.

"Your brother was great," Mrs. Ding said. "Handled everything last night at the station."

"We're going to her apartment now to visit, with our care-package," Mr. Ding said, patting the pink lid.

"That is so sweet," Lana said, hands circling her belly. "Above and beyond."

"Deimos is confident she'll be cleared," Xenith said. "Not sure what happens after that though, if Shayla spent all their money. It's a shame for Missy Jo to lose the building. Elliot would be crushed."

"We might have a plan for that too," Mrs. Ding said. "Don't you worry, Zee, honey. We'll take care of Missy Jo. Give Lavender her present now, Mr. Ding."

"We were so impressed by you last night, Lavender." Mr. Ding set one of the boxes on the table. "You inspired my latest creation."

Lavender eagerly opened the lid to reveal six purple cupcakes, each with a mischievous-looking marshmallow ghost popping up from the glittery buttercream.

My niecling gasped in wonder. "They're beautiful."

"We're calling them 'Shades of Lavender'," Mrs. Ding said.

"Thank you," Lavender said, blushing sweetly. "I've never had a cupcake named after me."

"First of many," Xenith said.

We said our good-byes. My caffeine levels were fully balanced. Gingerly, I eased my sunglasses up on top of my head—a move I would regret later when the nosepiece stuck in my curls.

"She emerges!" Lavender declared around a mouthful of purple cupcake.

"You are adorable, aren't you?" I said sincerely. "New shirt?"

Lavender proudly leaned back to show off her long-sleeved black T-shirt emblazoned with The Metal Grind logo. "Al said I should help advertise."

"Speaking of Al," I said, my cylinders fully firing, "I have an idea."

I waved the barista over, getting Xenith and Lana's approval for my plan as Al made her way across the café. I smiled up at her when she stood silent and stoic at our table. Lana wiped a tear from the corner of her eye.

"Al," I said, "We've been talking."

"Yeah?" She glanced at me as she gathered empty cups from the table, wisely leaving my Diva's Delight alone.

"I know we agreed to move the soft-open and concerts to this weekend," I said, "but—"

"We're almost sold-out," Al said.

"What?" I looked at my coffee levels to see if I could possibly be hallucinating.

"Yeah," Al said. "Surprised me too. The neighborhood really rallied for us."

"That's fantastic," Xenith said, his voice laced with relief.

"Huge!" Lana agreed. "And even better for Babe's plan."

Al looked at me expectantly.

"We've got an idea," I said, picking up the thread with a grin. "We'd like to add an additional element to our—nearly sold-out—event."

"Okay." Al nodded.

"It'll be a benefit concert as well as an opening," I said. "A memorial for Ace and a fundraiser for the Ace Mendoza Memorial Scholarship, which will go to a graduating senior from Cedar River High School who wants to study the arts."

Al's jaw clenched and unclenched. Her hazel eyes glimmered with unshed tears. She nodded tersely. "Sounds good," she said, and turned to leave before adding, "Thank you."

"Wish we would have thought of it earlier." Xenith gazed at Infinite Jest, the enormous sculpture he'd created in honor of Elliot. "Maybe in a couple of years we could look into an arts training program here too. Internships, that kind of thing? Elliot would approve."

"So do I," I said. "It's a perfect idea. We've already got mentors in place: tech, sculpture, opera, and pottery—" Lana moaned. "Okay, Lana will have her hands full for a while," I conceded. "We'll put the pottery internship on pause."

"No, I'm in," Lana assured, though her voice sounded a bit strained. She pressed her hands to her belly. "But I think this future young artist has been inspired by all this talk. Call an Uber, Zee. Let's get to the hospital."

Xenith jumped up, frantically searching his pockets for his phone—which was in plain sight on the table. Lavender sighed and set down her cupcake. "I'll call the Uber. Xenith, you get Lana's bag. Auntie Babe, you do your breathing thing with Lana."

We all obeyed her eleven-year-old wisdom. Minutes later, we stood on the steps of The Metal Grind as Xenith and Lana were bundled off into their ride. Patrons of the café were lined up at the windows to wave them on their way.

"So exciting," Darien said, clutching his hands under his chin. "I'm going to be a guncle."

"Get to work, Guncle," Al said brusquely, shooting me a bright grin as they headed back inside.

I looped my arm around Lavender's shoulders, finally enjoying the warmth of the noonday sun. "Well, niecling, I'd say your summer visit started off with a bang. Hopefully, things will be appropriately boring from here on out."

"Nothing's boring with you around," she said dryly. "But maybe one quiet day?"

"Tomorrow," I said confidently, "tomorrow I will be totally boring."

"Then today we should probably get my ears pierced," Lavender said with the nonchalance of a bored countess.

I looked down at her oh-so-innocent face. "What would your father say?" I asked, though I suspected he wouldn't care.

"He'd be cool," Lavender said. "Mom says only trashy people let their children get their ears pierced."

"Reeeeally," I said, with a slow smile. "Let's start with a mani-pedi and see where the day takes us."

"Best vacation ever!" Lavender declared, skipping back into The Metal Grind.

I drew in a breath and glanced at the poster of heavy-metal Brionne LeFave. Who knew what adventures awaited? But first—my second Diva's Delight.

THE END

About the Author

Kate Swenson is a playwright and author living in the Seattle area with her husband and two urban chickens. Her plays for young actors have been produced across the country and are available at www.pinkllamadrama.com and you can find out more about her fiction writing at www.kateswensonwriter.com.

Websites
www.pinkllamadrama.com
www.kateswensonwriter.com

DEJA BREW

by Brenda Beem

CHAPTER ONE

I waited in traffic for the light to change and stared at my reflection in the rearview mirror. My hair was a frizzy mess from the surgical cap I'd worn all day. I combed my fingers through the crazy curls, then gave up trying to regain control.

As my lane began to move, I thought about my evening to-do list. The first thing was to stop by Deja Brew, my favorite coffee shop, have a latte, and see my friends. Then I would begin a search for a good realtor to help me sell my mother's house. I'd been putting it off since her recent funeral.

Memories of Mom sent a wave of grief through me. Without thinking, I reached for the amulet she had given me years ago. My fingers came back empty. The necklace I'd always worn wasn't there. Even the chain was gone.

Panicked, I searched around my collar bone and then in my bra. It had to be there. I drove with one hand on the wheel, checked my purse, and patted my pockets.

"Calm down," I told myself as I replayed my day. I'd had the amulet on when I'd arrived at work. My schedule had called for me to take our first patient for an MRI and then, right into surgery. I can't wear metal around MRI machines, so I'd hung the pendant on a hook in my locker.

That's it. I'd left it in my locker. "Well, at least it's not lost." I sighed with relief.

I'd been foolish to leave the amulet at work, but it would be okay. I'd just go back and get it.

I glanced at the clock on the dashboard. "Darn," I muttered. If I returned to the hospital now, I wouldn't have time to stop for coffee. And I had been looking forward to it all day.

"You'll be okay for one night," I told myself, but my heart pounded a warning in my chest. I could almost hear my mother's voice. "You must wear your amulet at all times. You must wear your amulet..."

This was madness. I had tomorrow off. I could just go to the hospital in the morning and pick up the amulet. I'd be fine. Besides, nothing crazy had happened to me at the hospital all day, and I hadn't worn the amulet since early morning.

I thought about that for a moment.

"That's strange," I said to myself. "Why *didn't* ghosts seek me out today?

* * * * * * * * * *

Seattle has always been my home. I love the constant changes in weather, and yes, even the rain. When the sun does shine, the city sparkles. The hospital I work at sits high on a hill with views of the Seattle's skyline on one side, and Mount Rainier on the other.

Unfortunately, the operating room where I spend most of my days has no windows. But my surgical team had done a good job today. Our patient now had a chance for a long life. And I got to enjoy the views on my drive home.

Without thinking, I again reached for the missing amulet. I felt naked without it. As I headed for my favorite coffee shop, I thought back on the night my mother had given it to me.

Shortly after my eighteenth birthday, I'd begun to see things no one else did. Wispy see-through people I knew were ghosts appeared to me. I was frightened, but soon realized that most of the ghosts I met were simply sad souls. Lost and seeking help. I wasn't sure how I could help them, but I decided to try.

I went online and read that the best way to help spirits was to tell them to go into the light. I began using that line often, and sometimes ghosts left me alone. For a little while at least. But then one day a ghost shoved me from behind and I fell into the street. Another ghost threw garbage at me when I told him to go into the light.

I soon became terrified and isolated. I was afraid to go anywhere.

Even home wasn't ghost free. There were spirits there as well. They materialized at different times and in different ways, but all were confused.

A middle-aged businessman often appeared. He was always searching for the money he had literally lost. He was obsessed and sometimes accused me of taking his money. I gave up telling him to "go into the light." I began to point to different rooms in the house and tell him I'd seen a box of money in that room. His face would light up and poof, he'd be gone. Until the next day.

A young woman in a wedding dress materialized every evening at ten o'clock, no matter where I was in the house. She'd asked me if I'd seen her fiancé. "The wedding is about to start," she'd cry. "Where is he?" When I told her I hadn't see him, she'd usually leave. But not always. Sometimes I'd have to tell her I saw him in the yard. She'd step outside and disappear.

The third ghost was a youngish man who spoke in a strange language. His dark hair was long, and he wore hand-stitched leather and fur clothing. I guessed he was an early settler. Maybe a fur trapper. He grew angry and frustrated when I didn't understand him. It did no good to tell him to go anywhere. He didn't understand me, and I didn't understand him. I just had to wait out his tirades, and sooner or later, he'd leave.

My older sister, Noelle, was in the car with me the first time I met a ghost on the road. I was the driver and a misty apparition appeared up ahead. I tried to point it out to her.

"It's right there!" I yelled, begging my sister to see what I could. "Look!"

She leaned closer to the windshield and shook her head. "I don't see anything!"

She began to worry I was going crazy and needed help. I pleaded with her not to tell Mom, and never mentioned ghosts to her again.

But then one night, the woodsman spirit became over-agitated. He shook my mattress as he babbled at me. Exhausted, I yelled at him to stop.

My bedroom door opened, and Mom came into my room. The woodsman disappeared. Mom sat on the edge of my bed and brushed the sweaty hair off my forehead. "I heard you scream," she said as she bent down and kissed my cheek. "Are you seeing and hearing things that scare you?"

I shook my head in denial. I knew what happened to people who saw things that weren't there. The least I'd face would be counseling and drugs. The worst would be that I'd be locked away.

"Was it the guy who looks like a fur trapper, who gets angry when you don't understand him?" Mom stood and paced the room. "I've tried for years to make him leave."

My eyes must have grown as large as saucers. "You've seen him?"

She sat back down on my bed. "Yes, baby girl. He came with the house. I think maybe he was here before the house was built. He's hard to get rid of because he doesn't understand English, and he's just been dead too long."

Mom looked sad. "The ones who have not gone into the light after a while get stuck. They ask for the same things over and over, but the things they want are long gone."

She reached into the pocket of her fluffy robe and handed me a necklace. It was the same as the one she always wore. Her voice grew low and serious. "I wish you'd come to me sooner. But I'm here now. And I can help."

I shook my head. "What can you do? And don't try to tell me the ghosts aren't real. I've tried to...."

She placed a finger on her lips for me to quiet down. "In every generation, there is at least one family member who is psychic. Our gifts emerge as we become adults. We can see and speak to spirits. Sometimes we know things that are about to happen. This amulet has been handed down for centuries."

She placed the necklace around my neck. "If spirits are seeking you, this will hide you from them. Most spirts are harmless, but not all, as I'm sure you've learned. You should wear this night and day."

"You said 'we' and 'our gift.' You have the gift too?" I asked.

"Yes, sweetheart. And when I die, you will keep my amulet to give to one of your children or your sister's children."

"Why me? Why didn't Noelle get this fun 'gift'?" I asked.

Mom laughed and began to pace my small room. "I don't know. It's only one person per family every generation. Maybe our ancestors could only make so many amulets."

I turned the pendant over in my hand. On the face of the tooled silver amulet was the engraved image of a fairy. Its large wings were spread out wide behind it.

"Do only girls get this gift?" I asked.

"No, boys get the gift as well. That's why the fairy image has no face." Mom sat back on the bed and pulled my covers up. "Now, get some sleep. We can talk in the morning. Just know that when you wear the amulet, no ghosts will bother you."

The next morning, Mom and I sat and talked. "When I received my amulet," she said, "I spent years searching to find another person wearing one. We couldn't be the only family with protection against ghosts, right?'

I nodded.

"Well, I have never seen another amulet like mine, besides the one that grandma wore, of course. The one you are wearing, it was hers." Mom took a sip of coffee.

I reached down and felt the necklace. I vaguely remembered seeing it hanging around Grandma's neck.

"There must be others of course, but I think they have their own designs and maybe different symbols. It's not like I can walk up to someone and say, I like your necklace. Does it keep ghosts away?" Mom laughed.

I chuckled at the thought. "Did Grandma tell you if any of our ancestors had any other superpowers besides seeing and talking to ghosts?"

Mom looked confused for a moment. "Superpowers? Ha! That's funny. Yes. My great grandpa was able to find water.

And one of his nephews was good at gambling, especially cards and dice. He seemed to know what every player was holding. I think he just had a ghostly friend walk around the table and tell him what to play."

"Now that would be cool." I smiled, thinking maybe this ghostly thing wasn't so bad after all.

Mom laughed. Noelle walked into the kitchen. Mom stood and began to make breakfast.

"I heard you two laughing. What's so funny?" she asked.

Mom and I smiled at one another. In that moment, I knew that the amulet was our little secret. I also saw how left out my sister felt.

Over the years I'd take the amulet off, just for kicks. A few times I found newly departed spirits whom I tried to help. But I never could solve their problems. And there was often a cost to me. One time I lost my job. Another time my boyfriend heard me talking to the ghost, thought I was crazy, and broke up with me.

After that, I vowed to always wear the amulet. I graduated college as a surgical nurse, got married, and started to live a normal, ghost-free life.

Working in a hospital posed a bit of a problem, however. Metal can't be worn around MRI machines. I asked my supervisors if I could avoid them. But somedays, taking a patient for an MRI was unavoidable. And every time I'd taken the amulet off, ghosts had flocked to me.

But today I'd been at the hospital all afternoon without my amulet and hadn't seen even one ghost. "Why not?" I wondered.

What if I didn't need the amulet anymore? My childhood allergies had gone away. Perhaps I'd outgrown being a ghost magnet. "Maybe I've outgrown my superpower?" I said to myself.

For a moment, I felt excited. Free.

Maybe I could even start wearing normal necklaces.

CHAPTER TWO

I told my car audio to play the soundtrack to *Hamilton,* one of my favorite musicals. "The Room Where It Happens" began. I turned up the volume and sang along as I drove to Deja Brew.

When I pulled into the parking lot in front of the coffee shop, it was full of cars, which meant the shop would be busy. But not so busy that the owners wouldn't take time to greet me as I came in.

"Nicole! We've missed you." Linda, a petite blond woman and one of the owners, grinned up at me as she wiped down the counter in front of her.

"Missed you too. I just got back into town yesterday," I said with a smile.

The line of customers turned to me. A few scowled. Others checked the time on their watches or cells.

"Thought maybe you were cheating on us. If you were, please don't let it be with Starcafe." Teri, an attractive dark-skinned woman and co-owner, shuddered playfully at me.

"Never," I cried.

"All right then. Your regular?" Teri's face softened as she reached down into the glass case and gathered a lemon scone onto a thin sheet of waxed paper for her next customer.

"Yes please!" I smiled. The aroma of roasting coffee wafted around me, reminding me of my mom and mornings. She loved her coffee too.

"How was Hawaii?" Linda asked as she steamed a beaker of milk for another customer.

I shrugged. "My plans changed. My mom died unexpectedly. We moved our Hawaii reservation to sometime this fall. Kevin flew to Denver for business, and I drove home to be with my family. Not a fun trip, but always good to be with family."

"Sorry for your loss," Linda said.

"Thanks," I replied as tears I thought I was done with swelled in my eyes.

Teri patted her heart.

I tried to smile. When the tears spilled over, I gave up the effort and turned away, as if looking for a place to sit.

I headed for my favorite small table and fought to control my emotions. Two women were already sitting at it. I huffed in quiet frustration and searched the room. A couple of men, one dressed for success, the other in a hoodie with rumpled khakis, were having a heated discussion at a four-person table. I thought about asking for one of the chairs, but when a woman with bright red hair joined them, I changed my mind.

Then I noticed that near the front of the shop sat two stuffed chairs. One was empty. A middle-aged woman with long dark hair occupied the other. She was staring out at the parking lot. Nothing was on the table between the chairs.

Perfect, I thought to myself as I approached the empty seat. A flier, advertising a local florist laid on the cushion. "Is this place taken?" I asked as I held the flier up for her to see.

Slowly the woman turned and faced me, a surprised look on her face. She tilted her head and studied me. Then she went back to studying the parking lot view.

She's a strange one, I thought, but I'd been looking forward to my coffee since lunch and nothing was going to keep me from it. I settled my purse on the floor and my phone on the small round table next to me. The chair was a little too cushy for my taste, but it would do.

Teri arrived and handed me my tall skinny latte and then a small plate. On it sat a blackberry scone. I could feel the warmth of the scone through the plate and the aroma was beyond incredible.

I looked up at Teri in surprise.

Teri smiled. "I know. I know. But you look like you needed more than just a skinny latte today. On us!" Terry hurried to the counter without waiting for a response.

The taste of fresh blackberries, butter, and cinnamon was heavenly. It would ruin my dinner, but it was so worth it. I ate every last crumb, set the plate on the table, and sighed.

My husband Kevin had been right to suggest that I decompress someplace other than home after one of my long shifts. "I don't want to get home from a long day at work and watch you message everyone under the sun," he'd told me soon after we were married. "Stop on your way home from the hospital or wait until after dinner. When you are with me, I want you present."

His advice had seemed harsh at the time, but as usual, he had been right. I'd made two new friends, Linda and Teri, my messages from the day were replied to, and I was relaxed by the time I arrived home.

Phone in hand, I began to check my messages and sipped my latte. After eating the sweet scone, the latte tasted bitter. I reached for a couple of packets of sugar. Just as I began to pour the sugar into my coffee, someone hit the back of my chair, hard. Sugar flew across the table.

A man with large shoulders opened the exit door behind me and left without even an apologetic glance at me.

"Nice," I muttered as I hurried to the counter to get a rag to clean up the mess.

The long line of customers had grown shorter, but I received annoyed looks from those who had been in line behind me earlier. They must have thought I was going to cut in.

I held my hands in the air. "Just need a rag. I spilled."

"We'll be over and clean it for you in a minute," Teri said with a smile and turned to take the next order.

I went back to my chair and realized that the woman who'd been across from me had left. She must have left in a hurry, I mused. I'd only been gone a few minutes. I searched for her through the large plate glass window and scanned the parking lot, but there was no sign of her.

I brushed sugar off the face of my phone onto the already sugar-covered table. I watched to make sure none of the mess fell off the table, then moved in for a closer look. The splatter of sugar that had landed on the dark wood table had been drawn in. I bolted out of my seat and moved around the table as I studied the spilled sugar from all angles.

A word was written in the sugar. I studied the letters.

"What are you doing?" Teri asked from across the room.

"Someone wrote in the spilled sugar." I could just make out a word. "I think it says, 'Help.'"

I glanced up in time to see Linda and Teri silently communicating. Linda shook her head, raced to my side, and quickly wiped off the sugar.

"Ha, ha," she laughed up at me. "You're seeing things. Guess you do need a real vacation."

My hand reached for the amulet that wasn't there. I should have known. It was too good to be true that I might simply have gotten over my "gift." Weird things happened to me when I don't wear it. And now a weird thing had.

I needed to go back to the hospital and get the amulet.

I sighed and poured another packet of sugar in my mug. "The scone was amazing. Thank you. Would you mind getting me a to-go cup?"

"But you just got here. The rush is almost over." Linda looked at the last two people in line.

"We want to hear about your time at home. Sorry about your mom and all," Teri added.

"I left something at the hospital and I need to go back and get it." I followed Linda to the counter. "Wish I could stay longer, but I'll be back Sunday. Maybe we could grab a bite to eat when you close?"

Linda handed me a paper cup. "That sounds good. Are you okay?"

I shrugged. "I'll tell you about it Sunday."

"Sunday it is," she said as she carried my ceramic mug hurried back to the counter.

CHAPTER THREE

Once I was situated in my car, I just sat for a moment, then gazed up through the windshield at the wispy clouds. "You were right, Mom. I should have gone back to the hospital the moment I realized I didn't have my amulet."

"Of course, I'm right," Mom answered.

I yelped, leapt from the car, and continued gawking up at the sky.

"Oh, for heaven's sake, why does everyone think that the dead float around on clouds?" Mom said, clearly annoyed.

"Mom?" I asked, my eyes still searching the heavens.

"I'm right here," she said.

"Here? Where?" I turned this way and that.

"I'm inside your car. If you would quit staring up at the sky, you would see me." I heard her say.

I bent over and peered through my open car door. And there she was. Sitting in the passenger seat. As plain as day. Looking just like she had in her coffin a few days before.

Tears flowed down my face as I climbed in behind the wheel. I turned to her and began to sob. "Mom!" My arms lifted and I moved to hug her but stopped at the last moment. I couldn't bear having my arms go through her.

"None of that now," Mom said, a bit gentler. "There were enough tears to last me a lifetime at the funeral." She got a thoughtful look on her face, then chuckled. "That was kinda funny, don't you think?"

I sniffed and wiped my eyes. I forced myself to smile at her. "You aren't any funnier now than you were before."

"Ha!" Mom laughed at our lifelong banter about who was funnier. "That's my girl." She nodded approvingly. "No sense crying over spilled milk. Now, tell my why you are not wearing your amulet."

My smile this time was genuine. "Oh Mom, I have missed you so much, and here you are, lecturing me just like old times."

"I don't lecture. I just came to check on you before I, well... you know. Pass over. And a good thing I did. Do you know how many ghosts I had to scare away from you at the hospital today, and then at the coffee shop?" She began to silently count on her fingers.

"I screwed up," I confessed. "I left the amulet in my locker at work." Mom always managed to make me feel twelve years old. But then I thought for a moment about what she'd said. "You scared away ghosts? How did you do that?"

Mom shrugged. "I have my ways."

I tipped my head. "What ways?"

She looked at me with her twinkly brown eyes. "I simply told the newly departed to go to the light. Do you know there really is one?"

"A light? Really? I've always told ghosts to do that, but I was never sure."

"Yes! Well, you were right. But the ghosts who have hung around too long can't see it anymore. I had to threaten them. I said I'd send them to, well, you know."

"Is there really one of those places?" I asked.

"Guess I'll find out one way or the other." Her forehead creased.

"Are you worried about where you might go?" I asked, surprised. "I'm sure you will go to the good place."

"No, I'm not worried. At least not much. It's not like I can do anything about it now, anyway." Mom studied her fingernails. "I'm so glad I had a manicure just before..."

"So, you don't know what happens?" I asked.

"I saw some stuff, but I didn't go in. It felt warm and good. I want to be with your dad, and I will go. But I needed to see you and your sister before I'm gone."

"So, when you threatened the ghosts, you really couldn't send them anywhere."

"Of course not. I'm just a spirit, like they are. I'm not in management. At least not yet." She raised her eyebrows.

I was so happy to hear her self-confident self. I loved the image of Mom taking over heaven. Then my tears began to fall again. "Can I hug you?" My voice cracked.

For the first time, Mom looked sad too. "No! Some spirits go through a medium, but I wouldn't like that. I mean, you would be hugging the medium's body, not mine. If we did hug as we are, you wouldn't feel anything but extreme cold, so not worth it."

Then her face brightened. "But *you* can see me and talk to me, at least when you're not wearing the amulet." Then her face fell again. "Your sister couldn't. She's a mess. You really should call her more."

"Yes, Mom," I sighed. "But she will only be angry that I got to see you and she didn't. She hates it when we talk about spirits."

"You'll have you give her an upbeat message from me then. One that could only be from me. I'll work on it." Mom folded her hands in her lap and looked thoughtful.

I turned on the car engine and spied the time. I would arrive at the hospital right in the middle of a shift change. Not the best time, but it couldn't be helped. Even with Mom around to fend the ghosts away, I felt the need to have my amulet back.

I noticed Linda staring out their shop window at me. I must look crazy. Talking to myself for so long. Then I remembered the "Help" message in the sugar. I waved at Linda and backed out of the parking spot.

"The lady in the coffee shop. She was a ghost, right?" I asked as we merged into traffic.

"Yes. And a strong one. Newly departed as well." Mom stared out the side window.

I dreaded to ask. I knew the reason the coffee house ghost would not leave would be unfinished business. And I refused to be dragged into another ghost's tragic life.

"I know you had that one bad experience trying to help a ghost." Mom tried to brush the wrinkles out of her red pantsuit.

"One bad experience? Really? You mean the crazy guy who insisted aliens killed him? He wouldn't leave me alone until I told the FBI. Or the angry drowning victim who insisted his wife killed him for his money. The truth was that he took his boat out during a storm all by himself and fell off his boat." That one had cost me my job. I studied Mom's face.

"Yes, I know. That's why we wear the amulet. Or I did." Mom reached up to hold the amulet that wasn't around her neck anymore either.

"And you were right. I have a good marriage and a great job. When I get sucked into trying to solve ghostly problems, my life falls apart." I pulled into traffic.

"I know. And I don't want that for you. But you were given this gift for a reason." Mom stared out the windshield.

"And you gave me the amulet for a reason." I turned to face her.

"But you hung it up and forgot it today, didn't you?" She smiled at me.

"If I hadn't, I wouldn't have seen you again." I turned back to watch the road.

"That's right. Tell me. How many times have you forgotten your amulet?" Mom asked in her annoyingly smug tone.

I didn't even have to think about it. "I've never, not once, forgotten the amulet since you gave it to me."

"Don't you think that means something?" Mom gestured with her hands.

"You were whispering in my ear is what I think it means," I said softly.

"Maybe." Mom smiled. "But you didn't have to do what I suggested if I was. I think there is a reason I didn't move on, and you forgot your amulet today."

"What is the reason, Mom?" I stopped at a traffic light and faced her.

"We are supposed to help the coffee shop ghost, of course," Mom said.

"I'm not doing this again." I shook my head.

"Even if it is for a good cause?" Mom said softly.

"Ghosts all think their problems are good causes." The light turned and I drove forward.

"Well, this one really is. It affects the life of a living little girl."

CHAPTER FOUR

We sat in silence for a long time. It was rush hour, and traffic was horrendous. I moved us over to the carpool lane, and we sped up a little.

"I don't think ghosts qualify for carpooling." Mom gestured at the carpool sign.

I shook my head and merged back into traffic. "You're right. What was I thinking?"

She nodded. "Do you remember when Daddy died?"

I studied the speedometer and slowed. "I was ten, but of course I do."

"I quit wearing my amulet. I kept waiting for your dad to come back to me. But he never did." Mom pushed on the window open button, then shrugged when nothing happened.

"That's sad. Why not?" I slowed as brake lights flashed ahead.

"I think he'd said everything he needed to say to me, and he'd left us with a large life insurance policy. He had no unfinished business and passed over in peace. I hope he never learned that the insurance company wouldn't pay. They said he must have known he had cancer when he took out the policy. It wasn't true." She stared at me.

"Mom, I didn't know." I glanced back at her.

"You were a little girl. But it was a hard time for me. I missed him so much, I barely functioned. I couldn't afford lawyers to fight the insurance company. I couldn't make enough money to pay for daycare for you and your sister with the skills I had. Our savings account was running dry."

"That's awful," I said and reached over to pat her shoulder, then yanked my hand back.

"I didn't wear my amulet for weeks. I just wanted to talk to your dad. Ask his advice. Instead, tons of ghosts approached me with all their problems. I did my best to ignore them."

"I know how awful that feels," I said.

Mom nodded. "Then one day an old man appeared. His name was Joe. He told me that he'd hidden a metal box full of gold bars down his well. He grew old and forgetful, sold the property to the state for a park, and left the gold."

"Likely story!" I snorted.

"That's what I thought at first too. But I decided, what the heck. What did I have to lose? Do you remember how often we would go walking in the woods after your Daddy died?" Mom grinned.

"We went to the park a lot," I said as we merged onto the freeway.

"We went on lots of picnics. It was something to do and it was a lovely area. Joe usually popped in and out. He got such a kick out of you girls. Looking for the well was a fun adventure and distracted me from my financial problems." Mom pointed to the hospital sign. "There's your exit."

"I remember the picnics." I rolled my eyes at Mom's back seat driving.

"Then one day we found a clearing near a stream. Joe suddenly appeared. 'This is it. See where the stream bends? That is where we had our garden,' He grew excited, then confused. 'But where is my house?' He turned around and around and disappeared again."

"What a surprise," I said sarcastically as I stopped at a red light.

Mom held up a finger for me to wait. "I continued searching the area and found the cement foundation of a house. It was overgrown with blackberries. A house had been there. For the first time, I thought maybe Joe's story was true."

"Really?" I wondered where she was going with this.

Mom ignored my comment. "Later that same day, you and your sister sat down to make daisy necklaces. You found a hole in the ground and stuffed a rock down it. 'Mama, I heard a splash,' you cried."

"You can't begin to imagine how panicked I was. 'Nicole! Noelle! Get away from there.' I screamed as I ran and dragged you to safety."

The car behind us honked. The light had turned green.

"You're supposed to go now," Mom gestured for me to move forward and took a deep breath.

"Do you need to take in air?" I asked.

Mom glared at me. "Let me finish. Anyway, when I scraped the dirt away, there was a deteriorating sheet of plywood under the dirt. Your rock had fallen through a crack in it. Under the plywood was the well opening. If the rotting wood had broken, you two would have fallen in."

"I vaguely remember. I thought you were mad at us," I said as we turned into the employee parking lot.

She laughed. "You were upset because I yelled at you, but I wasn't mad. Just worried. I soon realized the job of getting the box out of the well was too big for me. I contacted a well-digging company and they agreed to help me retrieve the box from the well if I would also pay to have the well filled in."

"I'm surprised there are still well digging companies around." I shrugged.

"Of course there are. People who live in the country have wells. We went to the park the next day and waited for Joe. He finally showed himself to me. When I told him that we'd found the well, he was pleased."

"But it could have been any abandoned well," I said.

"You're right," Mom admitted. "I told Joe that I would be happy to help get the box out, but the well company wanted thousands of dollars. He already knew that your father had died. I hated to ask, but I said, 'If we recover the gold, do you think we could have one of the bars?'"

"What did Joe say?" I began to drive around the lot. It was full.

"He disappeared for a moment, then reappeared. 'The gold is still there.' He smiled at me, but then his face fell. 'I went to see Beth at our facility but couldn't find her. Then I visited the cemetery. She appeared to me there. She'd just died. I told her to go into the light, and I would follow soon. I needed the money for my Beth's care, but she doesn't need it now. We didn't have children. When you recover the gold, it is all yours."

"Mom!" I squealed and almost slammed on the brakes.

"Don't kill us." Mom reached a hand up to hold on, but her hand went through the side of the car.

"You are already dead, remember. Finish the story. What about the gold?" I was growing impatient. I noticed a car backing out of a spot up ahead and sped to wait for it.

Mom grew thoughtful. "The box was recovered, but it was moldy and gross. Joe appeared just as I opened it. I couldn't believe my eyes. It was full of small gold bars, just like he'd promised. Each bar was worth a little more than five hundred dollars. And there were over a hundred of them."

"Oh, my goodness, Mom. What did you do?" I asked.

Mom laughed. "I squealed of course. And tried to throw my arms around Joe, which was weird, because, well, he was a ghost and very cold. You girls joined in the celebration, even though you had no idea why."

"A hundred?" My mouth dropped open. "But that means..."

"A lot of money. Yes." Mom grinned. "When we were through celebrating, Joe said, 'I'm glad I found you and your girls.' He asked me to donate to his two favorite charities in memory of Beth. Then he blew me and you girls a kiss and disappeared."

"What a nice man. And so much money. What did you do with it?" I asked.

"I paid off our mortgage, went back to school, and got my teaching certificate. With my teaching salary, and the interest on the remaining gold, I was able to give you and your sister a good childhood. So, you see. Helping a ghost can be a good thing."

"What a great story, Mom." I beamed.

"It is. And when you and your sister examine my finances, you'll find that there is still gold left. This is the good news you can share with your sister. You can tell her the story." Mom sounded satisfied.

"That's a great idea. I will," I promised.

She reached to take my hand, then remembered she was a ghost. "I've had some bad experiences with ghosts too, don't get me wrong. Most of the time it is best to wear the amulet. I pick and choose, but I also believe in fate. Joe found us."

"Okay! Okay! What does the Deja Brew ghost want?" I sighed.

"She wants us to find her body. She was killed and died with something of the killer's in her hand. She wants us to give the evidence to the police, and make sure the killer doesn't get custody of her eight-year-old daughter."

I snorted again. "Find a killer. You want us to find a killer?"

"It will be a great adventure. And we're a good team. We found the gold, didn't we?" Mom smiled.

CHAPTER FIVE

I was still trying to wrap my head around the idea that my ghostly mom wanted to find a killer when she vanished from the passenger seat of my car.

"Mom, are you still here? Mom?" I searched this way and that.

"Watch out." She suddenly reappeared and pointed.

I slammed on the brakes. A car was backing out of a parking spot beside me.

"Jeez, Mom," I caught my breath. "Don't do that."

"What? Tell you to stop?" She held her hand up to her heart.

"Disappear and then pop right back. You scared me," I breathed heavily.

"Well, you almost gave me a heart attack. We came inches from that red car plowing into us." Mom held the back of her hand over her forehead in dramatic fashion. "Why, if I hadn't warned you..."

"We were not inches away." I leaned forward for a better look as the red car pulled back into its spot and motioned for me to pull in next to it. "And you don't have a beating heart."

I parked the car and turned to her. "This is going to take some getting used to."

"I'm new to this ghostly business too. Actually, I feel strange right now." Mom turned to look out the side window and then at me. "I didn't bother becoming visible with your sister, since she couldn't see me anyway. But I've been visible a long time with you. I feel weak. I guess it takes a lot of energy to stay visible."

"Really. That's interesting. Do ghosts sleep?" I asked.

"No. but I think I need to re-energize. Who knew? I'm going to disappear for a while. I'm not sure where I'll go, but I'm pretty sure it will help."

I glanced over as she vanished again. I was still in shock. My mother was a ghost. She could vanish and reappear at will. "Who knew is right," I whispered and exited the car.

I kept checking the empty space next to me as I walked. Was she still there, just invisible? Could she hear me? Could she talk to me when she was invisible? Only one way to find out, I decided.

A gust of wind blew snow white cherry blossoms across my path. "Did you see that Mom? Cherry blossoms." I pointed at the tiny flowers. "The trees are in full bloom everywhere. And they smell so good."

I waited for a response, then continued.

"The cherry trees at your cemetery were lovely too. They were just starting to open. A pink one is right above your marker. I bet your grave is covered in blossoms now."

Still no reply.

An ambulance was just pulling up to the Emergency entrance.

"Are you here?" I whispered. Mom didn't answer.

I found my nurse ID and made my way to the service elevators. As I'd predicted, I arrived right as the day shifts changed to night.

Out of nowhere, a ghost appeared. A wisp of a woman holding a baby asked for help. Then an old man ghost blocked my way. "I can't find my home," he wailed.

"Go to the light," I told them both and then repeated the line over and over as more ghosts began to follow me. I ran to my locker. Ghosts floated around me as I worked the lock. I had to reach through a young man ghost to grab the amulet off the hook. My hand tingled with the intense cold.

I quickly drew the amulet over my head and around my neck. One by one, the ghosts disappeared.

I took a deep breath and calmed myself. The hall was now crowded with hospital staff, and I wove my way through friendly nods and hellos from those I knew.

When I got to the car, I wondered if I should leave the amulet on. Would just having it in the car or near me keep Mom from being able to show herself? She hadn't helped me in the hospital. Maybe she'd gone off somewhere far away to power up. Just to be on the safe side, I decided to keep the necklace on.

As I buckled my seat belt, I turned to the passenger seat. "Mom, if you're here, I want you to know I'm leaving the amulet on until we get home. Just so other ghosts don't pop in on me. Okay?"

Still no answer. I didn't really expect one at this point, but just in case she was listening, I decided to continue talking to her. It made me feel better. And if she could hear, all the better.

I turned the car toward home. "You sure weren't kidding about the ghosts in the hospital. They just kept coming."

I fingered the necklace.

"Kevin isn't home tonight. He's on a business trip to New York. He'll be back Friday. We have two whole days of girl talk."

I drove on and waited.

"That doesn't mean I want to spend all our time trying to help your coffee shop ghost. I mean, this might be our... our last few days together."

Most of the houses in my neighborhood were dark. It was late. A wave of exhaustion and hunger suddenly washed over me. I was home.

"It's been a long day. I'm going to take a shower. See you in a few minutes. I'll leave the amulet in my bathroom." I hoped she would show up at my house soon.

I stepped into the hot water and closed my eyes. "What a day," I said to myself. I couldn't stop wondering where Mom had gone. "So many questions."

"Questions?" Mom asked. "What do you need to know?"

"Awh!" I screamed. My eyes flew open. My fully clothed ghost mom stood between me and the shower head. Water sprayed right through her onto me.

"What are you doing?" I squealed. "I'm naked."

"Well, I hope so. Most people take showers with their clothes off. I would if I could. Who picked out this outfit by the way?" She ran her fingers down her red suit jacket.

"Get out. Just get out and go downstairs," I cried as I tried to cover myself with my hands.

"Oh, for heaven's sake. I'm your mom. I gave birth to you. I changed your diapers." Mom muttered as she floated out the shower and then vanished with a poof.

•••••••••••

I tossed back a big gulp of red wine, refilled my glass, and carried it into the family room. Mom stood at the window looking outside.

I quietly curled up on the sofa. With one hand I wrapped a furry blanket around myself while balancing the wine in my other.

"Are you under control now?" Mom said as she floated around to face me.

A shiver raced down my spine. "That floaty thing you do creeps me out."

"Well, excuse me. I'm a ghost. That's just how ghosts float."

I sighed. "Can you please just sit down. I want to hear what the Deja Brew ghost had to say."

Mom made her way to the large stuffed chair in the corner. Although her legs made walking motions, she was suspended six inches above the carpet.

Mom tried to sit, hovered a bit above the seat, and then stared at me. "What now?" she asked.

I realized I'd made a face and forced myself to smile. "Nothing," I sipped the wine. "It's taking me a bit to get used to the new you. That's all. So, tell me about this ghost you met."

Mom nodded. "Okay. The ghost's name is Sonja. The morning Sonja was killed, she started a load of laundry. Her laundry room is in the basement of her house. She left to meet a friend for lunch. When she returned from lunch, she entered her house through the garage. She decided to put her wash in the dryer. As she headed down the steep steps, something bashed her from behind. Her arms flailed. She tried to grab the rail, but she thinks maybe she grabbed a piece of the killer's clothes, or a scarf, something to stop her fall. She has that something in her hand, but it didn't stop her fall.

"When she came to, she was wrapped up tight in a thick carpet. She couldn't move, but could feel something in her hand."

"Oh, my goodness," I shuddered. "How awful."

Mom agreed. "A bit later she came to and remembers her head bouncing off the steps as she was dragged up them. She was wrapped so tight, she couldn't breathe. This time when she passed out, she died. Sonja is sure that whatever is in her hand is from the person who killed her."

"I see." I thought for a moment. "Wouldn't the medical examiner have found the object when her body was brought in?"

"That's the thing. Her body hasn't been found. It's hidden somewhere, but she doesn't know where. She can go into her body, but not above it. Her family just reported her missing yesterday. The police think she was kidnapped. No one suspects she's dead."

"Except the killer." I sighed. "And you said she has a daughter?"

"Yes. Cali is her biggest concern. Sonja grew up with money and was the developer of a small startup business. It did well. She divorced her husband a few years ago and got sole custody of her daughter. Her ex, and Cali's dad, has a substance abuse problem. Cali is eight years old."

"So, Sonja suspects her ex-husband?"

"Yes and no. For the last two years, Sonja has been in a stable relationship with a lovely man named Colin." I went to the kitchen and refilled my glass.

"Can I have some too?" Mom called out.

"But how can you..." I stared at the wine bottle.

"I can look at it and maybe smell it. I haven't tested my sense of smell yet. Besides, it's not good for you to drink alone."

"But if you're not drinking, then I'm still...never mind." I poured mom a glass of red wine and set it on the side table next to her.

Mom stood and studied the glass. "You know I prefer white."

"Really. You want me to open a bottle of white?"

"Please!" She grinned up at me.

I carried the glass of red wine I'd poured for her back to the kitchen. I searched our wine fridge and found a bottle of white wine. I poured Mom a large serving of sauvignon blanc and returned to the family room. "Okay! Now, please finish your story."

Mom floated above the wine glass and stuck her nose almost all the way into the glass. "Humm!" she muttered. "Where was I? Oh yes. Sonja's new guy." She stuck her nose into the glass again. "He wants to marry Sonja and has filed to become Cali's legal guardian. Sonja's ex-husband has been fighting it."

"That does sound like a motive." I brought the wine glass up to my nose, breathed in, and wished I hadn't. Mom was staring longingly at me. I looked away and took a big gulp.

"Sonja's sure her boyfriend wouldn't hurt her, but of course I think he's a suspect too. I tried to listen in on their fight, but you kept distracting me."

"What fight?"

"Remember the two guys who were arguing at Deja Brew? Around the same time Sonja wrote 'Help' in the sugar. The guys were fighting over Cali. And then the ex's girlfriend walked in. She was the fake redhead with the long hair extensions."

I vaguely recalled the table for four the two guys sat at. I'd thought about joining them. I wished I'd paid more attention.

Mom continued. "I was trying to have a conversation with Sonja. She was listening to their argument. I kept trying to become visible to you too. I couldn't believe you couldn't see me. You do not die knowing how to do all this stuff, you know."

"I do now," I chuckled.

"Anyway, that's all she told me. She went 'poof,' and then you left. If you have more questions, we should go back to the coffee shop and talk to her."

"I can't believe both Sonja's ex-husband and fiancé were at the coffee house when I was. Together." I sat down my wine glass. "Why didn't you tell me sooner? Maybe all three are in on it."

"Maybe," Mom shrugged.

I thought about having a third glass of wine, but after my busy day, no dinner, and the shock of seeing my mom, the two glasses were going to my head. I put my glass in the kitchen sink and re-corked the wine bottles. "Okay! First thing tomorrow morning, we go to Deja Brew for coffee."

"Can I have a scone too?" Mom licked her lips. "And a latte?"

"You can have anything you want. Just let me get a little sleep." I turned to her. "You will still be here when I wake up, right?"

She nodded and went back to sticking her nose down into her glass of wine.

I turned to her before I entered my bedroom. "I love you, Mom!"

Mom righted herself and grinned sadly up at me. "I love you too, little one." She blew me a kiss, then nosed back down to her glass of wine.

CHAPTER SIX

The ring of my cell woke me early the next morning. The patter of spring rain hitting my bedroom window added to the commotion. With eyes still closed, I searched with my fingers for my phone, cringing as the cool air outside my warm down comforter hit me.

"Hi babe. Did I wake you?" Kevin's voice came over the speaker.

"Yes!" I groaned as I sat up and glanced out my bedroom window. The sky was just beginning to lighten. "What time is it?"

"Eight o'clock. Time to get up, lazy bones," he said.

"That means it's six o'clock Seattle time. It's my day off." I groaned. Mom's ghostly face floated inches away from mine.

I yelped, then gathered control.

Mom's eyebrows cinched as she studied me.

"Nicole! What's wrong!" Kevin yelled.

"Sorry, sorry!" I motioned for Mom to back off. "A big spider was about to attack."

"You shouldn't lie to your husband," Mom scolded and shook her finger at me.

I scooted to the other side of the king bed. "It's okay now. How did your meeting go?"

I muted my phone as Kevin began to tell me about the deal he was working on.

"Mom, please go to the family room. I'll be down in a minute," I begged.

"Aren't you going to tell Kevin I'm here? I want to ask him why he didn't he come to my funeral?" Mom now floated next to the bed with her arms folded.

I shook my head. "Please, Mom. Give me some space."

Her lips turned sad and pouty. She disappeared and I unmuted Kevin.

"So, what do you think?" he asked.

"Are you happy with the deal?" I questioned, not having a clue as to what he'd been talking about.

"Of course," he replied with enthusiasm, and then went on to give me more details.

I continued to half listen while I worried about my mom. Kevin shared insights about the people involved in his new business.

Mom did not come back.

I slowly moved toward the closet, cell in hand. I shouldn't have spoken so harshly to her. These were our last days together.

I told my husband to have a good day and hurried to get ready.

When I finally came down to the family room, I was relieved to see Mom hovering over her glass of wine from the night before.

"You're still here!" I moved to give her a hug, remembered, and stopped. "I'm sorry I pushed you away. Can you smell the wine now?"

Mom thought for a moment. "Not really. But I sense it. I can almost feel the rain, sun, and the movement of tiny creatures in the soil. I understand the joy the bees feel when the grape vines were covered in blossoms. It makes me happy. Every time I get close to the wine, I feel something a bit different. But it all adds up to what is now a glass of wine."

"Mom, that's lovely. I wonder what you'll think of the coffee and scones."

She grinned. "Let's go find out."

• • • • • • • • • • •

Teri and Linda were swamped with customers when we entered the coffee shop. I usually stopped off during my evening commute home, and it was busy, but the morning crowd was twice as hectic. Even with two assistant baristas, the customer line went the full length of the shop.

I slipped my amulet off and stuffed it in my purse. Mom suddenly appeared beside me. I scanned the shop for a free table as we lined up. No one else could see Mom, I reminded myself, and made sure I gave her lots of room. When I was settled in the line, I pulled my cell and ear buds out of my purse and stuck the buds in my ear.

"What are you doing?" Mom asked.

I ignored her question and pretended to answer my phone. "Hi! Yes, I just got here. Did you find a table, Sonja?" I raised my eyebrows at Mom and then scanned the room.

Mom followed my lead. "Right! I get it." She scanned the room. "I don't see her...Wait. She just popped up in the corner."

When I swiveled to where Mom pointed, sure enough, Sonja was standing beside the same chair she'd sat in before. There was a man occupying the chair now, however.

Pretending to adjust the volume of my phone, I said, "I don't see anywhere to sit yet, but by the time you arrive there'll be some. I'll order for you. What would you like?"

Sonja materialized next to Mom. "You should try the lemon and honey scones," she whispered. "I've heard customers say they like them best."

"Okay." I smiled at Sonja and then adjusted my earbuds. "I'll see if they still have lemon scones. What would you like to drink?"

"We can share, you know." Mom suggested.

I snorted a laugh. "Sorry, I didn't hear what you said. Do you want a latte or tea?" I pretended to speak into my phone.

Mom looked at Sonja. "She's talking to you."

"Since I ... died, I haven't had been interested in food or drink." Sonja shrugged.

"Have you tried smelling them?" Mom asked.

Sonja studied Mom, and then looked away.

"Let's go see what pastries they have left," Mom suggested.

I watched the two ghostly moms work their way to the glass case. Sonja was definitely better at navigating. People jerked and rubbed their body parts as Mom passed through their arms and shoulders.

"Brrr! There's a cold spot here," a middle-aged woman wearing jeans and a sweatshirt told Teri. "It's freezing." She rubbed her arms.

"Really," Teri turned to check the thermostat. "It says it's seventy-one."

"Well, it's not where I'm standing," the woman said. "I'll take mine to go."

A method of getting a table suddenly came to me. As soon as the lady ghosts were back, I spoke into my phone. "There seems to be cold air blowing in here. Some of the customers might leave if they get too cold."

"You want us to haunt a table and freeze the people, so they leave?" Mom asked with a devilish grin.

"Works for me!" I smiled at her.

"That's mean." Sonja glared.

"Well, let me know. I won't be able to stand and hold multiple orders very long. And we have lots to talk about, I hear."

Sonja sighed. I watched as she and Mom left to haunt a table. They headed to a table where two young men in collared knit shirts were working. They were concentrating on their computer screens. Mom marched over to the one closest to her, and without skipping a beat, walked straight through him.

"What the...!" The guy cried out as he jumped to his feet. His chair fell with a clang. "Did you feel that?"

"Feel what?" the other guy asked. Then Sonja passed through him. He gasped. "I feel like I was stabbed with an icicle."

"Let's get out of here," the first guy closed his laptop. "Look at my arms. The hairs are standing straight up."

The second guy studied his arms. "I have goose bumps too."

In seconds they were out the door.

I tried not to laugh. Mom was clearly enjoying herself. Sonja, not so much. But then the woman in front of me stepped aside and it was my turn to order.

Linda greeted me. "Nicole! I didn't see you. What brings you in so early?"

"I'm meeting a couple of friends." I glanced around. "I've never seen your place so busy."

"It's mostly commuters. You should see it at seven AM." she told me. "Lots of to-go drinks. What can I get you this morning?"

When I placed my order, she laughed. "You must be hungry."

I grinned. "Well, it's your fault. Everything looks so good."

A few minutes later, Linda handed me my pastries. I started for the table Mom and Sonja had just secured. They were floating above it. Like guard ghosts.

"Please! Sit down!" I whispered as I set a lemon/honey scone, a chocolate pecan muffin, and a sprinkled donut on the table.

Linda brought over a mocha latte, a skinny latte, and a chai latte. "Hope your friends get here soon," she said. "And don't forget, we are getting together Sunday. Let us know what time."

Teri waved at me from behind the counter.

CHAPTER SEVEN

Mom and Sonja passed through the arms of the chairs and onto the seats. Mom hovered a few inches above her cushion, but Sonja looked like she was actually resting on hers.

I placed a drink in front of each of them and picked up the skinny latte for myself. I scanned the area, checking to see if we would been overheard. The customers at the tables near us were engaged in their own conversations, at least for the moment.

The morning haze had begun to clear, and sunshine suddenly streamed between the breaks in the clouds, into the coffee house, and through the pair of ghostly moms.

I checked my cell for actual messages, and then adjusted the wireless ear buds that were about to fall out of my ear. "Hi. I'm Nicole," I said. "I hear you lost *something*." I was still pretending to talk into my phone, although I lowered the phone and stared straight at Sonja.

"I'm Sonja. I didn't lose *something*," she said with disdain. "I was killed, and my body was stolen and hidden a few days ago."

"I understand. My mom told you we would help. What do you want us to do?" I asked.

"I need you to find my body. My family needs to know I'm dead, and I think I have something that belongs to the killer in my hand."

"You know my mom and I are not police or detectives?" I asked.

Sonja sighed. "I know. I wish you were. But you two are the only ones who can see and hear me."

"I love the show Law and Order," Mom said and then made a face. "Or, at least I used to."

Sonja looked at my mom. "I'm sure that will help," she said.

"Okay. I'll put my TV show detective hat on too. What is the last thing you remember?" I took a sip of my latte and felt my muscles relax with the joy of creamy caffeine.

The joy was short-lived when I looked into Sonja's eyes. They were cold and hard. "My house is old, and the laundry is in the basement. I headed down the wooden staircase to move the wash into the dryer. Someone hit me from behind. As I fell, I reached back to stop my fall. I grabbed onto something to stop my fall, fell the rest of the way, and passed out. When I woke up, it was dark. I was swathed tightly in something stiff. I think it's a carpet. I couldn't breathe. I tried to scream, but nothing came out. My head hurt and my vision blurred."

"Why did your head hurt so badly?" I asked.

"When I fell down the stairs, I bumped my head on the wooden steps. My skull was bounced off the steps again as I was dragged back up them. I remember the pain of cracking my skull on the hard wooden slats."

"Did the attacker or attackers say anything? Could you tell if they were a man or a woman?" I asked.

"No! Whoever they were, they didn't speak. I just heard grunts." Sonja spoke softly and then shuddered. "When they were done with the stairs, my upper body was lifted, then shoved into some kind of tight container or space. My legs and feet were hefted up next and jostled in behind me. I must not have fit in all the way, because I was shoved, hard, from the back and sides."

Sonja stared over at Mom, who had been surprisingly quiet.

Mom looked carefully at the people near us before she whispered, "Then what happened?"

I grinned at her. No one could hear her. She had a way to go to accept her ghostliness.

Sonja shook her head at Mom. "I remember hearing the sound of a trunk closing. You know, the automatic ones, who make a hissing noise as they close." Sonja used her hands to demonstrate a trunk lid closing. "I think I passed out again. When I came to, I heard a car engine, and then the sound of tires over pavement. That's the last thing I heard. I couldn't get enough air and died."

"I'm so sorry," I said.

"What a horrible way to die." Mom tried to pat Sonja on the shoulder. Instead, her hand merged with Sonja's shoulder. "Yuck! That doesn't feel so good."

"This just gets weirder and weirder," I said.

Mom began shaking her hand, as if trying to get something off it.

Sonja smiled at mom's antics. "It's just ectoplasm," she said. "Just leave it and you will absorb it."

Mom looked horrified. "We just met. No offence, but I don't want to absorb part of you." She tried to dunk her hand in a glass of water and then wipe it on a paper napkin. When that failed, she brushed her hands on her red pantsuit. "That's better," she said.

"It's all ectoplasm." Sonja shrugged. "Even your pant suit."

"You seem to know a lot about ghosts and such," I said.

"When my parents both died suddenly in a car accident, I got into the occult. I missed them so much. I went to seances at least once a month and read everything I could get my hands on. It gave me comfort then, and now that I'm a ghost, I know a little about what to expect." Sonja said. "But you two must know all about spirits. You can talk to them."

"We mostly wear amulets that keep ghosts from recognizing us," I told her. "Most ghosts aren't as alert as you and my mom are."

"I wish I'd learned more. For instance, I was surprised that I had to wear a polyester red pantsuit for all eternity." Mom looked down at her outfit and scowled.

"Once you move on, it will be different." Sonja smiled, then glanced at her stained capris.

"Different how?" I asked.

"I'm not really sure, but I know that what you are wearing won't be important anymore once you go into the light," Sonja said. "I plan to pass over, but I have to make sure my daughter is cared for before I go. And I want my killer punished."

"Do you have any idea where your body is or what is in your hand?" I asked.

"My body is still wrapped in the tight dark carpet, but it's not in a trunk anymore. It's stretched out and face down. I'm not sure what is in my hand. It feels stringy. Maybe a scarf? I've tried to get a look at where my body is, but I can't get above it enough to look around. I must be somewhere I've never been before."

"Great! That could be almost anywhere."

Sonja nodded.

"I'm worried about my daughter. What if the killer goes after her too? I figured out how to go home. All I have to do it think hard about a place, and I'm instantly there. The day I died, I watched Colin, my fiancé, argue with the police. The police agreed to file the missing person report, but suggested waiting for a day or so before opening an investigation. I hadn't been gone long enough. Colin has stayed home with Cali every day. I spend my nights watching my daughter sleep."

"That must be so hard." I stirred my latte with a straw. "I hate to keep bringing up sad memories."

"Dying is a sad business." Sonja sighed.

"Yes. Yes, it is." I put my coffee down. "Okay then. Going back to the car trunk, did you hear anything else while you were in there?

Sonja closed her eyes. "No. I don't think so."

"Any smells?" Mom asked as she tried to poke at her pastry.

"Nothing I can recall," Sonja said.

Mom smiled. "Tell Nicole about your daughter, Sonja."

Sonja's eyes softened. "My daughter is so sweet. The divorce was hard on her and now she's lost the only stability she's ever had. I want her to be loved as I loved her. Her father cares about her, but drugs blur his judgement and always come first. And his choice of girlfriends goes from bad to worse."

She sniffed, and I wondered if ghosts could cry. "Colin truly cares for her." Sonja's voice broke. "I know he will make a great dad, and I want him to have custody of her."

"I see." I placed my cell, still attached to my ear buds on the table. I went to 'notes' on my phone and began to take some. "What is your ex-husband's legal name?" I asked.

"Marcus James Vorbeck," Sonja said.

When I finished typing his name, I asked. "And where does he live?"

"In a high-rise condo in Seattle." She thought for a moment. "The address and condo number are on my desk at home."

"And where is your home?" I asked.

She gave me the address of a house in Magnolia, an old and exclusive part of Seattle. "It belonged to my parents," she added.

"Does Cali have any relatives who could care for her besides your ex or your fiancé?"

"No. I'm an only child and my parents died ten years ago in a car accident. Marcus's parents are deceased too. He has a brother, but he's an addict as well." She gazed out at the parking lot.

"Can you go inside Marcus' condo?"

Sonja nodded. "Yes. Ghosts can go anyplace they visited when they were living."

Mom moaned. "You mean I can't go to Paris or on a Disney cruise?"

"Not unless you were in Paris or on a Disney Cruise before you died. And if you were, you could only go to the same places in Paris, and on the exact same Disney boat.'

"Darn. What's the fun in that?" Mom scowled.

CHAPTER EIGHT

Footsteps sounded behind me. Both Sonja and Mom glared at whoever it was. I swiveled in my seat. A young man holding a stack of folders stepped up. "Excuse me, but is this seat taken?" He stood behind the one chair I hadn't put food in front of.

He'd startled me, but I was prepared for this. "Can you hold a minute," I said into my phone and then gestured at the food and coffees around me. "Sorry," I said to the guy. "I'm expecting friends soon."

"This spot looks empty." He placed his hand on the back of the fourth chair.

"You can have the chair, but not the use of the table," I said, and pretended to go back to my cell phone call.

He glared at me and repositioned his files. "I promise to leave when your friends arrive," he offered.

"I'm on a call," I tapped my cell. "My friends are almost here."

He dragged the chair away, muttering to himself.

I knew I wasn't showing coffee house etiquette, but I didn't care. I hoped Linda and Teri didn't either.

"Have you tried smelling the place where your body is?" Mom asked as soon as the guy was gone.

"That's gross," Sonja shook her head.

"Maybe not. Mom, why don't you explain what happened last night?"

Mom explained how she'd tried to smell a glass of wine, something she liked to do when she was alive. But she got more than the scent of the wine. She got the essence of the wine. She could feel the components of the wine and they seemed to tell a story of how the wine came to be.

"You could go back to—" I looked around to see who could hear me. The folder guy was still glaring at me. "If you go back to where *you* are, you could try to use your sense of smell. Perhaps you can learn more about what's around you," I told Sonja.

"That is the most ridiculous thing I've ever heard. I've been a ghost for two days now, and I've never smelled anything." Sonja shook her head.

"Have you tried?" Mom asked. "I mean, really tried."

I pushed the lemon and honey scone closer to her. "Mom's right," I said.

Sonja made a motion to push the scone away. Her hand just passed through it.

"Like this." Mom rose and hovered over the chocolate pecan muffin closest to her. She closed her eyes. "Yes, yes!" she murmured.

"Tell us what you smell," I asked after what seemed like forever.

Mom floated back to her chair and closed her eyes. "The wind is blowing through me. I'm a stalk of wheat. The sun warms me. My roots grow deep, taking nutrients from the soil. I grow straight and tall, reaching for the sky."

Mom shook her head as if to clear it, stared longingly at the muffin, then shut her eyes again. "The air is hot and humid. I can hear the calls of large birds. They land on me, their claws grip my branches. Lizards, insects, and monkeys climb and swing around my limbs. Pods of seeds grow in clusters among my leaves. They are often taken before they can fall and grow new cocoa trees."

Mom sat quietly for a while, then reached out as if to pick up the muffin. At the last second, she pulled back her hand. "I couldn't get much of a reading on the pecans. Maybe they were too old?"

Sonja shook her head. "You guys are crazy."

"So says the ghost." I got ready to unplug my phone. "You asked for our help. Let's go outside and make a plan. It's too hard to talk in here."

"You should smell the scone before we go. I'm sure it's incredible." Mom urged.

"Fine!" Sonja said. She floated closer to her lemon scone, sniffed it, and moved back to her chair. "I told you it wouldn't work. I don't smell a thing."

• • • ● •● ● • • •

I hurried to the counter to get a to-go bag and drink carrier. The morning rush had ended and Teri and Linda were cleaning up.

"Looks like your friends stiffed you," Teri said from behind the counter. "I'm sorry."

"I'm annoyed, but all the more for me. By the way, do you know a woman named Sonja who has a little girl, Cali?" I carefully wrapped the pastries and placed them in the pastry bag.

Teri's face brightened. "They come in at least twice a week. We've watched Cali grow from a toddler. Linda always makes a special drink for her."

Linda smiled.

"Did you know Sonja was missing?" I carefully watched their reaction.

"What?!" Teri asked, her eyes wide with shock. "What do you mean, missing?"

Linda grabbed Teri's hand. "I noticed they didn't come in this week."

Worry crossed Linda and Teri's faces as they moved as one to my table. Teri headed to the chair Mom was sitting on. Horror filled me. "Don't sit there. My...I spilled coffee on that chair."

Mom rose high above the chair, rolled upside down, and peered at the seat cushion. "I don't see any spill."

Teri moved to the next chair where Sonja sat. Before I could protest again, Sonja disappeared.

"Behind you," Sonja said.

A biting cold engulfed me. She had passed through me. I turned and glared at her.

"Just thought you should know what it feels like before you ask me or your mom to haunt someone in that way again."

She was right. It did feel awful. I rubbed my arms and then my legs to warm them. I swiveled back to face Teri and Linda. They were sincerely shocked at my news. I looked around to see who might be close enough to overhear me. The place had mostly cleared out, and those who were left were involved in their own animated conversations.

I lowered my voice to a whisper. "Sonja was killed."

"You just said she was missing." Teri's eyebrows knitted in confusion.

I was doing this all wrong. "Remember when the word 'Help' was written in the spilled sugar? That was Sonja. She's a ghost and has been trying to get your attention. She needs our help."

"None of this makes sense," Teri said.

"Sonja's a ghost?" Linda asked. "Why would anyone want to kill Sonja?"

Finally, Teri spoke. "Strange things have been happening around here. The straws are always messed up when we come in. Sometimes the to-go boxes are stacked up like building blocks, and the pictures on the walls are crooked or on the floor."

Linda nodded. "Letters appear in spills. Once a full pastry cone of frosting was used to write 'Help' on the counter."

"That was Sonja's doing," I said.

"But why would anyone want to kill her? And she has a sweet little girl." Tears filled Linda's eyes. Teri wrapped her arm around her.

"Sonja needs to find the killer," I whispered. "She doesn't want her ex-husband to get custody of Cali."

"We met her ex. He's a jerk," Teri said.

"That's what Sonja told me," I said as I watched a party of four walk in. "This is a longer conversation than we have time for. You have customers. Think about how you feel about helping Sonja. I'll come back later and explain."

Linda and Teri looked stunned. They slowly stood and moved to the counter.

I shoved my drinks into a holder and headed out the door.

CHAPTER NINE

The bright sunlight blinded me as I stepped out the door of Deja Brew. I stood for a moment, letting the rays warm me. The cold from Sonja was finally starting to leave my body. I set the bag of pastries and the coffee holder on the hood of my car.

I rubbed my arms. "That felt awful."

"Told you." Sonja appeared. "Those two young guys didn't deserve what we did to them."

Mom materialized next to her. "Oh, come on. Give it a break. It was funny. The guys were young and healthy. If I'd known you'd want to take all the fun out of being a ghost, I wouldn't have asked my daughter to help you."

"Ladies, ladies!" I said, and then realized a couple heading into the coffee shop had heard me.

I reached up to my ear. Thank goodness my ear buds were still in. I retrieved my cell from of my pocket.

"Sonja, why don't you give me your address?" I punched the address into my cell as she told me. "Do you have a hidden key or garage code?" I watched the couple get into their car. "Maybe if we go to the scene of the crime, you will remember something."

"That's a great idea," Mom said. "Detectives always start at the scene of the crime. I can't wait."

"You'll have to wait. In the car, remember. Unless you visited Sonja before you died," I reached for the coffees and placed them in the cup holders.

Mom folded her arms. "Stink on poop, I hate being a ghost."

"Being a ghost stinks in so many ways." Sonja waited while I set the pastries on the back seat. "There's a garage code and a hidden key. My daughter should be in school, and my fiancé will be at work. I'll meet you at the house. I'll check it out before you get there to be sure everyone is gone."

"Aren't you going to ride with us? Give us directions?" Mom asked.

Sonja sighed in frustration. "I can't get into your car, remember? I've never ridden in your car before." She turned and vanished.

Mom popped into the passenger seat as I buckled my seat belt and entered the address into my car's GPS.

"When I was growing up, we didn't have seatbelts," Mom reminisced. "My sister and I would lay in the back of the station wagon and play Barbie dolls as we drove across the country."

I smiled. "That must have been fun. Dangerous, but fun."

Mom smiled. "We didn't know it was dangerous."

I stared at my GPS. "I'm not sure we should have gotten involved with Sonja. She needs real detectives. I'm a nurse and you were a teacher."

"Well, we are the only ones she can talk to. Besides, I'm just getting into this detective vibe. It's going to be fun," Mom said.

"I guess we can hire detectives if we start to mess it up," I said and immediately had second thoughts. How would I explain Sonja to a private investigator? And my husband watched our bank accounts closely. I'd never told him about my gift. How would he feel about my spending money on private investigators? Would he think I was spying on him? He had been traveling a lot.

"Let's give it a few days and see how it goes." I turned to Mom. "Can you still see the light? I want you to stay with me, but I don't want you to miss your chance to be with Daddy."

"I'm good. It's still as bright as ever. And this feels important. I want to meet the little girl," Mom said.

"Okay, but tell me when the light starts to fade." I exited off the freeway and headed into a neighborhood of beautiful historic homes with perfectly manicured lawns.

"Wow! These are lovely." Mom's head swiveled to view one side of the quiet street and then the other. Each mansion was lovelier than the next.

"Your destination is on the right," the sexy female voice of my car told us.

"Which one?" Mom asked.

I confirmed the address and pointed at a beautiful Tudor-style home. Red brick siding dominated the lower part of the house. White shake dormers and steeples jutted out and pointed to the sky on the top half of the house. Black beams trimmed the windows and made starburst designs across the white siding. Chimneys rose on both ends of the house.

When I pulled up to the front, I caught a glimpse of Puget Sound and Mount Rainer between the houses.

"The view off the back of this house must be stunning," I said wistfully.

"I wish I'd found enough money to raise you girls in a house like this." Mom sighed.

"Oh Mom. A beautiful house does not make a happy home. You gave us the perfect home. You were the best mom. And I'm going to miss you so much." Tears again filled my eyes.

"This will be our last adventure. Let's enjoy it. No tears." Mom's smile was shaky.

I nodded and wiped my eyes. "Are there any other ghosts around?"

Mom shut her eyes. "I can feel some, but they seem to belong inside their houses. Maybe we can question the ghosts at Sonja's house."

"She didn't mention ghosts at her house. And she's been back there watching her fiancé and daughter. But you're right. If there are ghosts, they might have seen the killer." I studied the front of the house, searching for Sonja.

"This street is so quiet. Someone might see your car. We need to be stealthier," Mom whispered.

"You know no one can hear you, right?" I said.

"Well, you can. And if I speak loudly, you might answer me loudly. Soft voices and stealthy actions are our motto. Sitting in a car outside the victim's house is definitely not stealthy."

"Is that your new word for the day? Stealthy?" I asked.

Mom grinned. "I rather like it."

"You watch and let me know if you see Sonja. It's harder to see you guys when the sun is shining."

"There she is. On the porch." Mom pointed. "See?"

I had to squint. I could just make out Sonja's wispy form as she hovered on the shade-covered porch.

"Okay. I'll ask her where to park and be right back." I grabbed an empty shopping bag and opened the door.

"I'm coming with you," Mom turned to pass through the door. "Stealthy remem..."

"No, Mom. You can't," I said, but it was too late. Mom disappeared the second her foot left the car.

I shook my head and headed up the path. Sonja came forward to meet me. The sun shone through her, and at times she was barely visible.

"What are you doing?" Sonja asked.

I put my ear buds back in my ears in case anyone was watching me. "I'm putting a bag on your porch. Any looky-loo will think I'm a delivery person."

Sonja studied the Nordstrom bag. "Humm. Maybe."

"Where should I park?" I asked. "And how do I get in?"

"There's a key hidden under a flowerpot on the back deck. There is a garage code, but the door from the garage to the house is locked. Leave your car at the park down the street, walk around the block, and come through the back yard." She turned to check on Mom. "Where's your mom?"

"She got so caught up in being a detective, she forgot she's a ghost," I said.

Sonja chuckled. "I like your mom. I did that a few times in the beginning, too. I always ended up back at my body. I had to concentrate to return to where I'd been. She'll be fine." Sonja turned toward the side of the house. "See you on the back deck in a few minutes."

"That's a big ten four," I said.

"What does that mean?" Sonja's eyebrows knitted in confusion.

"I think it's military talk for 'yes.'" I smiled. "Mom thinks we need to be stealthier."

"You two are having a lot of fun with this. I'm not sure I'm comfortable with that." Sonja frowned.

I thought for a moment. "I can't know what it's like for you. But these are the last few days I have with Mom and you have with your daughter. I'm so sad you are both dead. I'd do anything to change that. But all we can do is make the best of it. That's what my mom wants to do, so that's what I want, too."

"I guess. As long as you find my body and the killer." Sonja shrugged.

"We will do our best. I promise you." I hurried to my car and saw that Mom wasn't back.

I drove around the block, found the park Sonja had mentioned, and parked in the lot. I grabbed my phone and hospital rubber gloves, glanced at the empty passenger seat, and steadily jogged toward Sonja's house.

CHAPTER TEN

I slid the rubber gloves over my hands, found the key, and turned the key in the lock. I could not believe I was breaking and entering. "Are you sure those cameras aren't working?" I asked Sonja as I pointed at the security camera above my head. I'd seen another by the front door.

"I'm sure. My parents put a security system in years ago, but never activated it." Sonja scanned the neighborhood.

I had trouble steadying my hand. "That's too bad. The cameras might have shown the killer. Any chance your boyfriend put in a new system?" My stomach felt queasy. The fear of getting caught was growing by the second.

"I'm sure he didn't. Colin suggested we install new cameras many times, but we never did. These are the same old ones that have been here forever." Sonja disappeared and then reappeared. "Hurry up. One of the neighbors just came home. If they look out their back windows, they might see you."

The lock finally clicked, and the handle turned. I stepped through the door and entered a long narrow hall with a single row of coat hooks on one side. "Where do we go now?" I asked as I gawked at the hooks. "Jeeze, how many coats do you have?"

Sonja glided by me. "They are for friends and family." She floated/walked over to a lone pink parka that hung off a hook. She reached her hand out to it. Instead of brushing the jacket, her fingers went through it. "I bought this for Cali last Christmas," she said softly.

I gave her a few minutes. I could not begin to imagine what pain she was going through. However, even though I felt a bit safer now that we were inside, I was not comfortable. "Where are the basement stairs?" I asked quietly as I spied a number of doors.

She continued to stare at the jacket.

Finally, my nerves got the better of me. "Come on! I want to get out of here before your family gets back. They can see *me*, remember?" I resisted the urge to go ahead and find the staircase myself.

Sonja motioned for me to follow her. I stayed close behind and watched as she passed through a door at the end of the hall.

I yanked opened the door, stepped onto a landing, and right into Sonja. The stinging cold shocked me again. I screamed so loud I was sure visitors at the Space Needle could hear me.

"Shush!" Sonja put her finger to her lips and started down the stairs. "I thought your mantra was 'stealthy.'"

I began shaking with the painful cold from Sonja, as well as fear. "Don't you ever do that again!" I clenched my teeth to keep them from clacking together.

"Me? Look where *you are* going. You walked into me. I was just pausing to pull myself together." Sonja glowered at me then turned around. "I haven't been down there since I died. It's not easy to return to where you were brutally murdered, you know." She snorted and continued her descent.

The door behind me banged closed and darkness surrounded me. I reached out tentatively to find the handrail. "Where's the light switch?" I whispered as I gripped the rail.

"Oh," Sonja said. "Sorry. I forgot you can't see in the dark. The light switch is on the wall, just above your left hand."

Relief flooded me as light flicked on. With my eyes on the wispy form of Sonja, I began my descent, making sure she stayed well in front of me. The stairs were made of simple wooden planks. At one time they had been painted, but only bits of blue paint remained on the edges. Many of the steps were slightly loose. I took a deep breath, pulled up my big girl panties, and inspected each board.

"Here!" I pointed. "That looks like dried blood. Fourth step from the top."

Sonja began to float up to check it out. "Don't touch it," she cried. "Maybe the police will find it."

"I won't disturb it. Besides, I'm wearing gloves. But don't run into me again. Wait until I'm all the way down before you check it out!" I shivered.

She nodded, disappeared for a moment, then re-appeared in the basement.

Soon I joined her. Although the washing machine and dryer were new, nothing else in the basement was. Open beams with wiring going up to the house hung over our heads. One bare lightbulb hung over the center of the room; another lit the staircase. The floor was cement.

"There. That's where the carpet was." Sonja pointed to a bare space on the floor near the base of the staircase.

"I see a partial outline," I moved closer to the bare area where the carpet must have been. Lines of dust and dirt showed where the rug had been. I found my tape measure. "The rug is six feet by nine feet."

I checked around the rug area and then on rest of the basement floor, all the while careful to not disturb or leave footprints in the dust. Under a rustic workbench, I found an earring. I held it up. "Is this yours? I asked.

Sonja turned her head to the side. "Yes. See. I'm wearing the other one."

"So, you lost it when you were captured?" I laid the earring down near a post where it would be spotted.

"Yes. But none of this helps. All the blood does is show possible foul play here at my house. The clues here point to Colin, and I don't want that. The earring is mine. But I could have lost it any time." Sonja sounded frustrated.

"If we need to get professional help, we can tell them about the clues. We'll leave the evidence here. There's blood on a step, a carpet is missing, and an earring is on the floor. When we find your body, the earrings will match. What color is the carpet by the way?" I asked Sonja.

"It is a kind of a reddish/burgundy. It's old and threadbare in places. A fake Chinese style design," she said.

"And you said the fuzzy side is around your body." I searched the floor for more clues.

Sonja began to explore around some garden tools. "Yes. The hemp backing is what will show if we decide to try and find it."

"Don't say *if*. We *are* going to find..."

Before I could finish my thought, an elderly woman spirit appeared. "There you are!" she cried as her ghostly form somewhat solidified. She was wearing an old-fashioned house dress and her hair was done up in a tight bun. In her fading form, it was hard to tell what color her hair or dress had been.

The elderly ghost looked around fearfully. "Why must you do this to me? Your mother already knows you are not in bed. If your father finds out... Back to bed. Both of you."

Sonja appeared next to me. "Oh! I forgot to tell you. We have a ghost."

"Really?" I almost rolled my eyes.

"She must have been haunting the house for years, but I didn't see her until I became a ghost myself. I don't recognize her, but I'm pretty sure she worked as a nanny here at one time. I've tried to tell her that she doesn't have anything to fear. She needs to go into the light. But she won't listen to me." Sonja waved at the elderly ghost.

"None of your nonsense, now. Go to your rooms." The nanny ghost pointed up the stairs.

"She may have seen your killer. Did you ask her about that night?" I was speaking to Sonja, but studying the nanny ghost for some sign that she might be following our conversation.

Before Sonja could answer, the nanny ghost screamed, "He's home!" and vanished.

Sonja stared at me in shock, and then disappeared as well.

Since I wasn't sure why they both vanished, there was nothing I could do but wait. I continued to quietly search the floor for clues. As time passed, I grew nervous. I tried to come up with a good excuse as to why I was in the basement. The best I came up with was to insist that Sonja had hired me to inspect for rodents. But since I didn't wear a uniform or have business cards, I was sure that would not fly.

I was also disappointed I hadn't had time to question the nanny ghost. If there was a clue somewhere in that muddled ghostly brain, would I be able to access it? Clearly, she thought we were the children she was in charge of. Could I work with that in some way?

Sonja popped back. "Colin and Cali are home. They just opened the garage door. Something must be wrong. Cali should still be in school. Oh, I hope she's not sick. Colin hasn't had any experience with caring for her when she was sick. What can I do? I feel so helpless."

"Sonja," I interrupted her tirade. "Focus. They can't find me here."

She wrung her hands. "Of course. Hurry out the back door, the way you came in. I'll go outside and make sure none of our neighbors can see you."

The adjoining backyards were a bit busier than they had been when I snuck in. As I headed out the door, Sonja motioned for me to drop to the ground and hide. I crawled beneath a shrub while the neighbor on the left cut a bouquet of roses from her backyard rose bushes.

When I raced full speed around the right side of the house, I almost ran into a gardener carrying a heavy load of fertilizer. At the last moment, I jumped behind the closest tree. Sonja directed me to keep moving around the wide tree trunk until the gardener passed by. I don't know how he didn't spot me, but apparently, he didn't.

Since my car was parked in the neighborhood Sonja grew up in, she was able to stay alongside me until we reached it.

I peered through the dash window. Mom was not back yet. "Why is it taking her so long to return?" I mused.

"She seems to have a bit more trouble navigating than I do." Sonja shrugged.

I nodded and opened the car door. An idea hit me and I slowly closed the door. "What is your cell number, Sonja?" I asked.

As if looking for her cell, she patted her pockets. "What am I doing?" She sighed and then gave me her number.

I entered the number, waited for her voice mail, and left a message. "Sonja! Where are you? I've been waiting for an hour. Call me back," I said.

"What was that all about?" Sonja asked.

"What do you think about me going to your door and talking to Colin? Does he know you visit Deja Brew?" I asked.

"Of course. The three of us go there often. And I told you, I saw him at Deja Brew yesterday with my ex and his girlfriend. They were fighting over Cali."

"Good. I'm going tell Colin that you and I had plans to meet up today at Deja Brew, but you never showed up. You haven't been officially reported as a missing person yet, so if we actually had made plans, I'd have no way of knowing you wouldn't be there, right?"

Sonja thought for a moment. "That's right."

"I'll say I was worried when you didn't show up and decided to stop by your house and check on you. If Colin searches your phone record, or asks the police to, my message will be there. Just cross your fingers he doesn't realize that the message and my visit were almost at the same time. But it's a pretty safe risk I think." I pushed the lock button on my car door.

Sonja appeared skeptical. "I guess. What are you going to ask him? I already told you he isn't the killer."

"Sonja, he is a suspect. I know how you feel, but I want to get a read on him. You can listen and tell me if he's not being truthful. You can suggest questions for me to ask as well."

Sonja agreed. "I like it. But you might want to get the leaves out of your hair and dirt off your knees first."

CHAPTER ELEVEN

Sonja paced in front of her house as I parked. Her obvious unease made my nervousness soar. What in the world was I doing? I've never been a good liar, and here I was, ready to tell a whopper. I breathed deep and searched for words I could say that would be mostly true.

Sonja quit patrolling back and forth and waited for me to join her on the porch.

I strode quickly toward her. "Ready?" I said softly as my finger hovered over the doorbell.

"No! But just do it," she snarled.

We heard the bell ringing inside the house and waited for what seemed forever. Finally, the door opened. A tall thin man around forty-five stood in the doorway. He held a pretty little girl who looked exactly like her mom in his arms. Her long dark hair was pulled back in a ponytail.

"That's my baby girl." Sonja floated inside and got as close to her daughter as she dared.

"Hi," I said. It was hard not to look or react to Sonja. "I'm Nicole, a friend of Sonja's. Is she home?"

The man I knew was Colin responded curtly. "No! She's not."

I held out my hand. "Sonja and I met at Deja Brew the other day. You must be Colin." He shook my hand but didn't speak.

I smiled at Cali. "And you must be Cali. Sonja told me all about you. Your mom and I had such a good time, we made plans to meet again this morning. But she didn't show up. Since I was passing by, I thought I'd stop and see if she's okay. Guess I should have called. She probably just forgot about our plans."

"You're babbling," Sonja hissed.

"You're a friend of my mom's?" Cali asked. "Do you know where she is?"

"Are you a reporter?" Colin cut in. "The police said that reporters will show up as soon as the report is filed. If you are, you are legally required to tell me."

"What?" Shock must have appeared on my face. "What's going on? No, I'm not a reporter."

Colin kissed Cali on the cheek and lowered her to the floor. "Cali, why don't you go get a snack? I'll join you in a moment."

"Can I turn on the TV?" Cali asked before she left.

"Yes. And have some grapes. I just washed a bunch. They're in the colander in the sink," Colin said, then turned to me. "Her mom limits the hours she can watch TV."

"Sonja sounds like great mom." I smiled at Sonja.

Sonja burst into quiet sobs.

"Can I see some ID?" Colin asked.

"Okay, but what's happened?" I found my wallet and handed Colin my driver's license. "I'm a surgical nurse at Seattle General Hospital." I also showed him my hospital ID badge.

"Sonja is missing." Colin took photos of my identification cards with his cell and seemed to relax. "Can you come in for a moment?" He stepped back and gave me space to enter the house.

"Missing?" I acted as surprised as I could and stepped inside.

"The police will be here soon. I filed a missing person report two days ago. They think she may have been kidnapped. Her purse and wallet are gone, but her cell phone and car are here." He motioned me into the living room. "She would never leave us. She would never leave Cali."

"I don't know what to say. How can I help?" I looked at Sonja.

Colin asked, "When did you last see Sonja?"

Sonja moved beside Colin. It was easier for me to look at her now. "I was at Deja Brew last Wednesday," she told me. "During Cali's playdate with a friend from school."

"Wednesday, last week." I replied to Colin. "We really hit it off, but then Sonja had to leave to pick Cali up from a play date."

"What did you and Sonja talk about?" Colin motioned for me to sit, and for a moment rested his head in his hands. I thought maybe he was crying, but when he raised his face, his eyes were clear. Dark bags hung below his large blue eyes.

"Tell him we both like to read science fiction novels," Sonja said.

I moved to a stuffed accent chair and glanced around the room. Photos of Sonja, Colin, and Cali covered an oval corner table. A goofy one of them in Disneyland made my heart ache.

Sonja hovered over Colin. I turned to face him. "We talked about books. It turns out we both like science fiction novels. I told her I was enjoying audiobooks and offered to share one of my favorites with her."

Colin sighed. Obviously, this didn't help him. "Did she mention going on a trip? Was she upset about anything?"

"She didn't mention any trips. She was excited to marry you. She thought you were wonderful for adopting Cali." I smiled at him.

This time I did see Colin's eyes water.

"Thank you for saying all of that." Sonja sniffed.

I made a note to myself to ask Mom if ghosts have runny noses.

Then Colin sniffed too. "I'm surprised she shared so much with you. She usually keeps personal information to herself."

I kicked myself for not waiting for Sonja to tell me what to say. "Well, I was talking about my mom. She died recently. Guess when I shared, she felt comfortable sharing back."

Colin seemed to accept my explanation. I stared at Sonja, hoping she'd provide a question for me.

"Ask him if the police have any leads?" Sonja told me.

I did.

"Not so far." Colin replied, sounding discouraged. "The police are going to be here to check out the house soon. If there are kidnappers, they haven't made any demands. Sonja inherited a lot of money from her parents and was an investor in a very successful startup company. That's how we met. But I don't have access to any of her money. Maybe a kidnapper wouldn't know that, but since we're not married yet, you'd think they would."

"Why do the police think it's a kidnapping?" I asked.

"Because Sonja is wealthy, and our company has been in the news lately. I made quite a bit of money on the sale too, and would spend it all to get her back, but I don't know. Kidnapping just doesn't make sense to me."

"Everything he's said is true. Ask him how Cali is doing?" Sonja floated over to the photo table.

I asked about Cali.

"She's doing well. Her mom travels a fair bit, so Cali's used to her being gone. For the last three years, I've worked from home and watched Cali while Sonja was away. I've tried to shield her from any negative news. But the police want to question her today. I'm worried about that."

Colin checked his watch and stood. "I want to get lunch made for Cali before the police get here. Would you mind if I shared your info with them? They might have questions for you."

"Please. I would be happy to talk to anyone who is trying to find Sonja. I will do anything I can to help her." I got to my feet. "Would you mind texting me if you have any new information? I know the owners of Deja Brew were close to Sonja and Cali too."

"Sonja and I went there sometimes too. I'll ask the police to question them," Colin said.

We exchanged cell numbers, and Sonja and I left.

When we were out of hearing range, Sonja told me she was going back in. She wanted to be there when the police arrived. She could kick the earring out in front of a policeman if she had to. Or move the dirt that framed where the carpet had been. Anything to get their attention.

"Good idea," I said. I told her I was headed to the coffee shop to talk to Linda and Teri.

"I don't know how to thank you for all you are doing." Sonja tried to smile but it turned into a grimace.

"Thank me when we find your body. I really liked Colin, but we do need to check into him a bit. Con-men can be lovely."

"He's not a..." Sonja started. "Do what you need to do. I'll see you at Deja Brew."

• • • ●• •● • • •

Mom was waiting for me when I got into my car.

"What took you so long?" she asked.

I fastened my seat belt. "What do you mean? I moved the car a few minutes ago and you weren't in it."

Mom glanced back at the house as we drove away. "Isn't Sonja coming with us?"

"No, she's staying. Besides, she can't ride in my car. Remember?" I pulled away from the curb.

"Oh. That's right," Mom said.

"So, where have you been?" I asked.

"Well, I came here, to your car, but you weren't around. So, I decided to go to your house and enjoy the wine a bit more. But it was gone." Mom's lower lip turned into an exaggerated pout.

"You went back to sniff the wine I poured yesterday?" My jaw dropped.

"Well, it not like I can pour it myself, now can I?" Mom snorted.

I grinned. "You know, craving the smell of wine is a little crazy."

"So is having a ghost mom. But here we are. And you cannot imagine how wonderful a glass of wine smells. It is like heaven in a glass."

I smirked and shook my head.

We drove in silence for a while.

"Where are we going?" Mom asked.

"Back to the coffee shop. Sonja is going to meet us there," I said.

"Oh good. Can I have a brownie this time?" Mom rubbed her wispy hands together in anticipation.

I sighed. "I guess so." There had to be a way I could save seats at a table without buying out the café.

We talked for a while about my visit with Sonja's family. I told Mom how much I liked Colin and how Cali looked like a mini-Sonja.

"I wish I could have gone in with you," Mom sighed.

"Maybe Colin will bring Cali to Deja Brew," I said.

"That would be nice." Mom stared out the window. "Too bad they don't serve wine at Deja Brew."

"It's only a little before one," I smiled. "You have lots of time left to sniff wine."

"I don't sniff it, I...you're making fun of me," she accused.

I grinned at her. "Maybe a little. Do you prefer I say you snort wine?"

Mom's lips twitched as she struggled not to smile. "Don't knock it 'till you've tried it."

I laughed. "I'll pour you a new glass when we get home and leave it out until you are done or it smells like vinegar. Deal?

She smiled from ear to ear. "Deal!"

CHAPTER TWELVE

For once, Deja Brew was relatively quiet. Linda was in the front window washing the glass as we drove up. She waved enthusiastically at me.

As I climbed out of the car, Mom disappeared. She was at the pastry counter, her nose halfway through the glass by the time I entered the shop.

A wave of sadness washed over me. Mom enjoyed life. She loved little pleasures. It was such a shame that she died in her sixties, and now, even her time as a ghost was limited. I would miss her so much. I shook my head to clear it. I had to focus and concentrate on Sonja.

"Hi!" Linda said as she picked up her cleaning gear. "I love children, but why do they have to put their sticky fingers all over the windows and glass doors?"

Teri stood up from behind the coffee station and looked around to see if anyone was listening before she said, "Any update on Sonja's situation?"

"That's what I wanted to talk to you about." I searched for a table. No one was in line and the last of the lunch crowd was finishing up. I put my purse on a table in the far corner.

Linda and Teri joined me.

"You told us she was dead and needed help, but you didn't say what kind of help," Teri said.

Linda began to wipe the already clean table. "And you didn't explain how you got involved in the first place."

I sighed. "It's a long story. Basically, I can see and talk to ghosts unless I wear a special amulet. It's a gift that runs in my family. Yesterday, I accidentally left my amulet at work, and came here. I met ghostly Sonja but didn't recognize her as a ghost. She wrote 'Help' in the spilled sugar. My mother, whose funeral I attended last week, materialized in my car after I left Deja Brew. She had been inside Deja Brew and chatted it up with ghostly Sonja while she waited for me. Ghostly Mom heard how ghostly Sonja was killed, and how her killer might end up raising her little girl. Mom insisted we needed to help Sonja find her killer and save the little girl."

Teri wrapped her arms around Linda. Tears gleamed in her eyes. "Poor Sonja," Teri muttered. "How did she die?"

"That's the tricky part. Sonja was reported missing, but only Mom and I know she's dead." I proceeded to describe how Sonja was killed and how her body was taken.

Linda stepped back and scanned the room. "Is she here now?"

"No. But my mom is. She's at the counter looking at the pastries. She told me she wants a chocolate brownie." I sighed.

"What?" Teri asked

"Why does she want a brownie?" Linda made a face and glanced around again, this time looking for my mom. "Ghosts can't eat, can they?"

Mom floated over to me, hands on her hips. "I've changed my mind. They have blueberry tarts. I'd like one of those, please."

I turned to Mom. "You're the one who wanted to help Sonja. Focus on helping, please."

"Is your mom standing right there?" Linda pointed in the direction I'd faced. Her eyes were huge.

"Yes, although she more floats than stands," I said.

"This is all too strange." Teri shook her head.

"What do you want us to do?" Linda asked.

"Can you sit for a moment?" I asked.

They glanced around the café. There were plates and napkins to be picked up at one table, the garbage was full, but still no new customers.

"This is our slow time, but we still have work to do," Teri said as she they joined me at the table.

I turned to Teri. "Didn't you tell me once that you did clerical work for the police department?"

"Yes," Teri said.

"So, you know how to look into people's backgrounds and finances?" I looked at her hopefully.

Teri glanced at Linda. "Well, most of that information was already in the police database or available from the internet. I still have contacts that might be helpful if you need to dig deeper into financial or criminal stuff."

"Time is of the essence. The longer it takes, the worse the chances are of finding Sonja's killer. Sonja's fiancé said the police think she may have been kidnapped. She disappeared without her car, car keys, or cell phone. The only thing that is missing besides her is her wallet and purse."

"Sounds like it might have been a kidnapping gone wrong," Teri said. "Did she have money?"

"Yes, both she and Colin, her fiancé, made big money."

"How much?" Linda asked.

"I didn't ask. I pretended to be a friend of Sonja's from Deja Brew." I thought for a moment and turned to Teri. "Could you check out the financial background of Colin, and Sonja's ex-husband, Marcus James Vorbeck?"

Teri wrote down the information. "Anyone else? No promises, but I'll probably only get one shot at calling in this favor."

"Sonja doesn't like Marcus' girlfriend," Mom said as she floated beside Linda.

"That's right." I recalled Sonja was hostile about the thought of Marcus and his girlfriend raising Cali. "What was the girlfriend's name?" I asked Mom.

Mom shrugged.

"You're not talking to us, right?" Linda moved closer to Teri.

"Sorry. No, I'm talking to my mom. She reminded me that Sonja really dislikes her ex-husband's new live-in girlfriend. We can't remember her name though."

"It's Gloria Polinski," Sonja suddenly materialized beside Mom.

I glanced at Sonja. "Good. You're here. How did it go with the police?"

"Not very well. They didn't stay long. They're still tapping our..." Sonja choked. "I mean, Colin's phone, but of course no kidnapper has called."

I repeated to Teri and Linda what Sonja had said.

"Tell her how sorry we are," Teri said softly.

"She can hear you." I pointed to where Sonja stood.

"We promise to do whatever we can to help." Linda stared at the space I had gestured to, only now Sonja had floated next to Mom.

I didn't bother to tell Linda.

"Did the police find the clues you wanted them to?" Mom asked.

"Yes, but they still think it points to a kidnapping." Sonja huffed in defeat.

I nodded.

"Don't nod. What did she say? We can't hear, remember?" Teri said.

Again, I filled Teri and Linda in on Mom and Sonja's conversation.

A new customer entered the shop and both Teri and Linda stood.

"Teri, how long will it take to get some information back on our suspects?" I asked.

"I should be able to get a preliminary report today, if the precinct isn't too busy," she replied.

"I can handle things here if it would be faster for you go and ask your contact in person," Linda offered.

"It might speed things up," Teri agreed.

"Great." I told Teri and Linda. "Call me when you get the reports." I turned to where Sonja and my mom hovered. "Sonja, would this be a good time to go to your ex's apartment?" I asked.

"As good as any," she replied. "I can enter and scout around. If the coast is clear, I'll try to find a way to sneak you in."

"Sounds like a plan," I stood and turned to Linda. "I'd like a blueberry tart, a breakfast cookie, and a large latte."

"Is this all for your, umm, your mom?" Linda asked.

"No, just the tart." I handed Linda my credit card.

"Just wondering." She leaned in close to me and whispered, "We don't charge ghosts."

I chuckled. "I'll tell her. And thanks."

Mom hovered by the pastry counter. "I heard Linda. Tell her thanks from me."

"Mom says thanks, too." I stood and moved beside Mom.

She shook her head. "You should suggest she sell wine. Deja Brew could be a wine bar at night, and a coffee shop by day."

"You could spend eternity here, then," I teased.

Mom thought for a moment. "If Deja Brew served wine, I probably could."

CHAPTER THIRTEEN

I was entering Sonja's ex-husband's address into my car's GPS when Mom appeared on the passenger seat.

"Where are we going now?" Mom stared hopefully at me. "Your house for some wine?"

I shook my head. "No, we're off to search Marcus and Gloria's condo." I checked the clock in the dash. "It's almost three. Let's hope they're not home."

Mom leaned close to the dash to check the time for herself. "Who's Marcus and Gloria?"

I peered over at her. "You weren't listening at Deja Brew, were you? And why aren't you wearing your glasses."

Mom raised her eyebrows. "My daughters didn't bury me with my glasses on."

"Really? I'm pretty sure we gave your glasses to the funeral home," I said.

Mom shrugged.

I searched my memory. The funeral had been so emotional, I couldn't remember if she'd been wearing glasses or not. "I'm so sorry. Can you see at all?"

Mom shrugged her shoulders. "I can see pretty well, actually. It's just fine print I can't read. But my sense of smell is off the charts. So, it all works." Mom started to put her seat belt on, stopped, and sighed. "I keep forgetting that I don't need a seatbelt."

She sat back and gazed out the windshield for a long while. "Who did you say Gloria and Marcus are?" she asked again.

"I didn't say. Marcus is Sonja's ex-husband. Gloria is his live-in girlfriend."

Mom rubbed her hands together and smiled. "The plot thickens."

"Well, not for you, I'm afraid. You can't go inside again, remember?"

"Why not?" Mom looked forlorn.

"Mom! Come on! You know the spirit rules. You can only go where you've been when you were alive. Sonja picks Cali up from her dad's place sometimes, so she's been there. She's waiting for me now."

"She gets all the fun!" Mom pouted.

"Really? I bet she'd trade places with you in a minute. You're sixty-three years old, your children are raised, you're..."

Mom threw her hands up in defeat. "Stop. I get it. But I don't want to just sit here while you're being all sleuthy. Maybe I'll go check on your sister. Or go back to the coffee shop. I think they are making apricot bars this afternoon."

"That's a great idea. Go back to Deja Brew. If Teri uncovers some information on our suspects, you can report back to me." I knew Teri would text me the info, but it would give Mom something to do.

"Great. I'm on it. I'll be back in a flash with the cash," Mom grinned. And poof, she was gone.

I chuckled to myself. The saying didn't work at all, but at least Mom was smiling. I turned on my music and sang along with, "Who Lives, Who Dies, Who Tells your Story", the final song from Hamilton.

A half an hour later, I pulled up across the street from a mostly glass twenty-story high-rise condominium and checked the address.

"Wow," I mumbled as I peered up at the building. "Sonja's ex must be doing okay."

The condo number was ten-fifty-two. It would be on the tenth floor. The entrance was a double wide glass door that was at least twelve feet high. I crossed my fingers there wouldn't be security at the entrance or in the elevator.

I glanced around. I'd only seen Gloria and Marcus once, but there was no sign of the pair or anyone even closely resembling them. Sonja was nowhere to be seen either.

I texted Teri. "Any news?"

She texted back. "Colin had quite a bit of debt until the sale of his and Sonja's last venture. He had two businesses that failed, and he'd borrowed heavily on them. He paid off most of the debt, but he isn't wealthy by any means. He had a DUI three years ago and lost his driver's license for a year. I'm still waiting for more on him."

That didn't sound good. Darn. I liked Colin. "What about the other two?" I wrote.

"Still waiting." Teri replied. "The divorce between Marcus and Sonja actually made the news. I guess she was some big socialite. She comes from family money, and lots of it. Cali is one rich little girl. I'll let you know when I have more."

"Great," I wrote. "And just so you know, my mom returned to Deja Brew. She wants to bring me news, so text me, but also give her any information you find. Her name is Arlene. Call her name and give her your information. She will hear you."

"Ha-ha!" Teri texted back. "Will do."

"Oh, and if the apricot bars are available, would you mind setting one out for her?"

Teri added a shocked emoji. "Of course. You know, this just gets stranger and stranger."

"Tell me about it!" I slid my phone into my pants pocket and checked the street one last time. Two young men walked by.

Sonja materialized next to my car door and motioned for me to hurry.

"Step back so I can get out," I said as I opened my door.

She moved away and stood with her arms folded. "Where have you been? They could be back any minute now," she snapped at me.

"I had to drive, remember?" I told her. "Did you find anything?"

"I read an open letter on the kitchen counter. Marcus was just fired from his job. Not sure what he was doing, but he got a final paycheck."

"Great," I said. "Anything else?"

"There was a framed photo of Gloria on the wall that I didn't see when I was there before. I think she is an actress. An unopened envelope was on the table. I couldn't read it."

"Okay. I can do that." I stepped to the back of my car and opened the trunk.

"What are you doing?" Sonja whined.

"I'm getting out some nursing gloves. If you want me to pick up stuff and look around the apartment, I want to be wearing gloves."

"That's smart, I guess," Sonja said. "Oh, and I forgot the worst news. There are signs of cocaine and other drug use on the coffee table. I need you to take pictures. Marcus was warned by Child Services that he had to stay away from Cali if he does drugs. I need proof."

I nodded. "But how would I explain taking the pictures? And none of this proves they killed you. Or tells us where your body is hidden. Did you find receipts from a dump or a National Park?"

"I didn't see any laying around, but that doesn't mean there aren't any. I can't open drawers," she said.

"So how do I get in? Is there security?" I asked.

"There are security cameras on the front doors. Residents scan their key cards in the elevator to get to their floor and unlock their doors."

"We don't have a key card, do we?" I asked.

"No, but since it you took so long to get here, I had lots of time to look around. The cleaning supply and maintenance room is on the first floor. The janitor was in the maintenance room when I arrived. The door was ajar, and I peeked in. I didn't see any, but I bet there are master key cards somewhere in that room."

"So, you are just guessing?" I frowned.

"Yes, I couldn't go in and look around. Rules!" She smirked. "And there are security cameras all over the place. Do you have a coat or sweater with a hood?"

I nodded, went back to my trunk, and pulled out my raincoat.

"Good!" Sonja looked up. "It's starting to drizzle again, so your raincoat works. I'll go ahead and make sure the way is clear for you to go to the maintenance room. Just follow me."

"Okay." I flipped the hood up over my head and faced the automatic doors. "Lead on."

As I began to step away from the car, Mom appeared inside my vehicle. She waved frantically at me through the passenger window.

"What's going on?" I asked as I turned back to the car.

"They are there!" Mom squealed with excitement.

"Who are where?" I narrowed my eyes and opened my car door. "Slow down and tell me who you are talking about."

My cell phone dinged. I studied my texts.

Teri messaged, "Marcus and Gloria just walked into Deja Brew."

I wrote back. "Great. Keep them there as long as you can. We are just headed into their condo."

"Will do," Teri responded.

Mom floated in front of me. Her ghostly body hovered, half in and half out of my car. "Did you hear anything I said?" she shouted at me. "Marcus and Gloria. They're at Deja Brew. You gotta get there. Fast."

I started at Mom's appearance. "Don't do that," I sputtered and worked hard to regain composure.

Sonja had materialized near the front of the condo building and gestured frantically for me to hurry. I held my hand up for her to wait.

I pointed to the passenger seat. "Mom. Would you please come all the way inside the car?" I waited until she was settled. "Sonja and I are headed in to check out Marcus' condo. It's great to know we won't run into him or Gloria. Thanks for letting me know. Now, I need you to head back to Deja Brew and help Teri and Linda keep Marcus and Gloria there. Sonja and I will dash to Deja Brew as soon as we can."

"Fine." Mom sighed with disappointment and disappeared.

Sonja stood with her hands on her hips near the front of the building. I threw up my hood and headed for the entrance. An elderly couple carrying groceries approached the double doors. I ran ahead and held one door open for them. "Let me get this for you," I said as the husband shook the rain off their umbrella.

A young man at the front desk hurried over to the couple. He grabbed their grocery bags and began exchanging pleasantries with them.

I hung back to admire the beautiful flower arrangement on the lobby table. As soon as the threesome had their backs to me, I ducked and scurried over to Sonja. She headed down a short hall and stopped in front of a door marked "Maintenance."

"I watched the janitor leave a few minutes ago." She pointed at the door. "I'll let you know if I see him returning."

I turned the doorknob. It surprised me that he'd left the room unlocked. He probably wasn't planning to be gone long. I entered the room alone and closed the door behind me. It was pitch black inside.

I couldn't risk turning on a light that might shine under the door, so I pulled out my cell and brightened the screen. Even the flashlight app would be too bright.

The room was very tidy. Along the wall hung hammers, drills, wrenches, saws, shovels, brooms, shelves of pipes, and replacement pieces.

I went directly to the small desk at the back of the room and began opening drawers. The bottom drawer held a number of files. I pulled a few out. They contained info on repair specialists, plumbers, and electricians.

The drawer above held files for receipts and invoices. I opened the center drawer and rifled through the many pens, markers, rulers, super glues, and tape measurers.

"He's coming back. Hurry!" Sonja shouted from the hallway.

My heart raced. I was about to close the center drawer, when I spied a stack of white key cards in the far corner. They had the name of the condo on the front, and a magnetic strip on one side.

These had to be the master keys. I grabbed two in case one didn't work, closed the drawer, and moved to the door.

"Is it safe to come out?" I whispered, hoping Sonja had her ear to the door.

"Wait," Sonja said. "A resident just called out to the janitor. As soon as his back is toward us, I'll let you know. Move fast," Sonja said loudly.

I started counting to slow my breathing. "One Mississippi-in. Two Mississippi-out. One Mississippi-in. Two..."

"Okay! Now!" Sonja yelled.

I opened the door wide enough to squeeze through, shut it behind me, and hurried after her.

She headed back toward the lobby. My chest ached. I began to shake with nerves as I waited for the janitor or the resident to yell at me to stop and explain why I'd just came out of the maintenance room.

Soon I was ten feet away from the janitor's door. Then I was twenty. No one yelled at me to stop. At forty feet, I spied an exit sign above the door on my left.

Sonja walked straight through it.

I opened the door and hurried after her. We were at the bottom of a utility staircase. We'd made it. I leaned over, inhaled, and willed myself to calm.

When I'd caught my breath, I held the key cards up for Sonja to see. "Let's hope these are the masters."

She smiled. "Good job. Now we need to walk up to the tenth floor. It's not safe to use the elevators. Too many cameras."

"Ten stories?" I groaned. "Where's the 'we' in this? You get to float or materialize wherever you want to go." I glanced up the winding steps. "And what about the rules? When did you ever climb this staircase?"

"I am, or was, a very active person. I always climbed stairs instead of taking an elevator. I took this staircase almost every time I came here to pick Cali up from her dad's."

As we turned to go, I explained that Marcus and Gloria were at Deja Brew.

Sonja froze. "They are?"

"Yes, And Teri, Linda, and my mom are going to try and keep them there until we show up."

Sonja grinned. "That is such good news. If they are there, they won't find us here."

"Yes, but we still should hurry. I'd love to confront that pair and see what happens," I said.

Sonja nodded. "Me too."

CHAPTER FOURTEEN

I glanced at the staircase I was about to tackle. The stairwell had been built in a tight space. I couldn't see beyond the second floor and hoped I wouldn't meet anyone on my journey. What excuse could I use for sneaking up the stairs?

A good lie is always based on a bit of truth, my husband says. So, what truth could I use? I finally decided I'd say I was picking up Cali if I met someone as I climbed to the tenth floor. On the way down, I'd say I'd just dropped Cali off.

I put my foot on the third step and stretched my calves. Although I was on my feet for sometimes twelve hours a day in the operating room, stairs required muscles I didn't use. I was going to feel this exercise in the morning.

A few minutes later, Sonja appeared. "You're only on floor three? Are you crawling up the steps?"

"Go away," I replied. I was doing okay. More the turtle than the hare, but getting closer to the finish line.

When I hit floor five, she showed up again. Startled, I almost fell.

"You're only halfway? Hurry up. It will be dark before you finish," Sonja goaded me.

I huffed. "I'm doing this for you, you know."

I stopped for a moment to rest on floor six and heard the access door above me open. Had someone been ahead of me on the stairs this whole time? Or was someone headed down? I grabbed my cell out of my purse and put an ear bud in my ear. Cautiously I moved forward, replaying my conversations in my head. Had I said anything that might give me away? I was trespassing and fear settled in my gut as I froze and listened for footsteps to approach.

But no one showed up to pass by me. I made it to floor ten without seeing anyone except Sonja. I collapsed near the access door and resisted the urge to crawl through it to the hallway. Instead, I sat on the last step and gasped for air.

Sonja appeared. "About time!"

"Water!" I begged, although I knew she wouldn't be able to carry any.

"In the condo." Sonja pointed.

"You're so mean." I got to my feet and stumbled through the door. Thank goodness there were no other people around.

I quickly slid the master key card into the slot. Nothing happened.

"Turn it over," Sonja suggested.

I turned it over and click. The door opened.

The smell of weed and stale whiskey or bourbon—I never know which is which—overwhelmed me as we entered the condo.

Sonja floated across to the living room and pointed at the remains of cocaine lines on the coffee table. "That's why I can't let Marcus raise Cali." She stared for a moment at the evidence of drug use. "He wasn't like this in the beginning. I guess success went to his head."

"What a waste. I'm so sorry." I stared at the debris.

Sonja sighed. "Yes. Lots to be sorry about. But Cali must be the focus." She moved to a large, framed photo on the dining room wall. In the background were tables of well-dressed guests. I peered closely at it checking to see if I recognized any famous people, but I didn't. Gloria stood, center stage, dressed in a floor length, shiny golden gown. Her long red hair was done up in a simple knot. She had a big smile on her face and held a large trophy in her hand.

I'd seen the golden winged woman holding an open globe statue before. "What is this award?" I asked.

"It's an Emmy. Gloria must have been pretty good on some television program. Will you look and see if there is a date written on the back of the picture?" Sonja asked. "I can't read the engraving on the trophy."

I lifted it off the wall and turned it over, but nothing was there.

"Okay, Thanks." Sonja moved to an entryway table and pointed to a large legal envelope. "This is the letter I'd like you to open for me."

I tightened my gloves and picked up the envelope. It was addressed to Marybelle Winters.

"I thought her name was Gloria?" My eyebrows cinched.

"She's an actress. I think Gloria is her stage name. Can you open it?"

I turned to the letter. The envelope was only sealed in the middle. I put a finger under the side of the flap and carefully lifted it up.

Guilt overcame me and I placed the envelope back on the table. "This feels wrong. Isn't mail tampering against the law?"

"If it bothers you, take the letter out and lay it open on the table for me." Sonja offered.

Before I had too much time to think about it, I slid out the letter, closed my eyes, flattened it on the table, and walked away.

Sonja floated above it.

"Do you have any places you'd like me check out while you're studying the letter?" I asked.

Sonja looked up. "How about the closets? Check pockets. Look at receipts of anything that might lead to where my body was dumped. Search for tissue with dried blood on it. I must have bled all over someone."

"That's a lovely thought," I muttered as I headed to their bedroom.

If the idea of reading someone else's mail felt intrusive, snooping around their bedroom felt twice as bad. I shook my head. I was not cut out to be a spy.

The master bedroom was huge and held two large walk-in-closets with built-in dressers. "This is everywoman's dream closet," I called out to Sonja. Then I turned around and spied row after row of shoes. Each pair was neatly arranged by style and color.

"Boy, she sure loves shoes," I picked up a red heel. "I bet this shoe would cost me a month's wage."

Sonja appeared next to me. "And it wouldn't even be comfortable. Can you check for blood on the bottoms of them?"

I checked the soles of her casual shoes, found nothing, and turned to another wall of shelves. "What's in all these cloth bags?" I asked.

Sonja began reading labels. "I think they're purses. Designer purses. I couldn't open the bags to see when I was here before."

I adjusted my gloves again and brought the closest bag down from the shelf. "Versace!" I slid the purse out of the bag. "You were right. These are designer purses."

"Well, she likes purses and shoes. And already has a ton. Doesn't prove much. What did you read in the letter?" I put the purse back on the shelf.

"It was from her agent. He mentioned that she had done good work on commercials and a daytime drama show." Sonja glanced at the drug table. "What a shame." She sighed. "He went on to reject her request for him to represent her. He was glad that she had gotten herself straightened out, but he had given her a second chance already He suggested she try to find work locally and re-build her resume."

I texted Teri. "We just found out that Gloria also goes by the name of Marybelle Winters. She's an actress."

"Will do. The suspects are still here but are getting ready to go. I don't know how long we can keep them," Teri texted back.

"Okay. We'll leave here in five minutes," I messaged.

I turned to Sonja. "We should go soon if you want to see your ex and Gloria before they leave Deja Brew. Want me to quickly check out Marcus' closet?"

"Just the bottom of his shoes," Sonja said. "He doesn't have many."

"Okay, I'll be fast. Look to see if the way out is clear." I began turning over all of Marcus shoes.

Sonja vanished.

I didn't find any signs of blood on Marcus' shoes and moved to the hall closet. Sonja hadn't come back yet. I stared at the closet door. It would only take a second for me to inspect the coats.

"All clear," Sonja announced, her head sticking through the middle of the exit door.

"Just a minute." I began pulling out bits of papers, tissues, and business cards from the pockets of long coats and jackets. I shoved the scraps of paper into my purse. We could look at them later.

Then I glanced down. On the floor amongst umbrellas and rain boots, sat two identical gym bags. "Looks like they joined Atlas Health Club." I pointed at the name on the bags.

When I opened the first bag, there was nothing in it except a stainless-steel water bottle and a hand towel. The other held the exact same items.

Sonja materialized beside me.

"The bags are brand new," I said.

"Wait a moment. Look at the bottom of the one you just held up," Sonja pointed to the bottom corner of the bag.

I turned over the bag. "What is this? Dirt? Coffee?" I moved closer to sniff at it.

"I think it's blood," Sonja said softly.

I bolted back. "Blood?" I stared at it closely. "Let's take a scraping to Teri and see if she can have it analyzed."

Sonja kept staring at the sports bag. "This might be the murder weapon. The thing that knocked me down the stairs."

"Slow down," I said. "We don't even know if the stain is blood. And we can't tell whose bag this is." I set it down. "Wouldn't the police have found the bag when they were here?"

Sonja huffed. "I'm still just a missing person. The police didn't have a search warrant. They could only ask questions."

"Well, I'm going to get a sample. If it's blood, we'll find a way to tell the police." I ran to the kitchen, grabbed a couple of sandwich bags from a drawer, and a knife.

"I'm going to Deja Brew. Meet you there," Sonja snarled and vanished.

The angry look on Sonja's face terrified me. I had to hurry to Deja Brew. I didn't know what she might do to Marcus and Gloria.

I used the knife to scrape some of the brownish substance from the sports bag into the sandwich bag. I wasn't sure how much I might need but wanted to leave enough on the gym bag for the police to find. I zipped the baggie closed and headed for the door.

Before I left, I checked to be sure I hadn't left anything behind. Then, I scooted out the door, listened for the automatic lock to engage, and raced down the stairs. All my worries about trespassing were over. I needed to get to Deja Brew before Sonja did something awful.

My cell rang as I was halfway down the staircase. "Where are you?" Linda wailed.

"I'm just leaving Marcus' condo." I flew past floor four. "What's going on?"

"It's crazy here. Napkins and straws are flying all over the place. Marcus and Gloria are hiding under a table," Linda screamed into the phone.

"Call the police. You can't let Marcus and Gloria leave. I'll be there as soon as I can." I sped up.

"What do I tell the police?" Linda asked.

"I don't know, but if Marcus and Gloria leave, they will destroy the evidence we found."

"Wait!" The condo security guy called out to me. "Who are you? What are you doing here?"

"I'm a friend of Marcus and Gloria. Sorry. Emergency. Can't stop."

From the corner of my eye, I watched the guy trying to decide to go after me or not. He looked around to see if anyone was watching, then went back to his seat.

I pushed through the entry door and headed to my car.

CHAPTER FIFTEEN

Mom waved frantically at me from the passenger seat as I approached.

I opened the car door, threw my purse onto the back seat, and climbed in. "I know, I know! Sonja is going nuts."

"How do you know?" Mom asked.

"Linda just called." I started the engine and raced toward the freeway. "What happened?"

"Sonja told me that you found some blood on a sports bag in Marcus' condo. She was upset, but under control. She kept insisting we call the police and arrest them both. But nobody could hear her but me."

I shook my head as I sped around a corner.

"But then something else must have happened. I don't know what. Sonja began screaming at Gloria. Of course, no one, including Gloria could hear her. And that made Sonja even more frustrated." Mom's hands flew around as she talked.

"Why is she so sure the killer is Gloria and not Marcus?" I glanced at her.

She shook her head. "I don't know. She is just scary angry."

"I was afraid of that." We stopped at a red light, and I turned to Mom. "Go back and try to calm Sonja down. She needs someone to talk to."

"But..." Mom whined.

"Please, Mom. I'm on my way." I sped off as she reluctantly disappeared.

I asked my GPS for the fastest route. It was the middle of the day and traffic was light. I took a couple of back roads, and ten minutes later, arrived at Deja Brew.

A police car with flashing lights sat in front of the coffee shop. I grabbed my purse with the sandwich bag of what I hoped was blood and hurried inside.

A policewoman blocked the door. "Police business. The shop is closed," she said.

"I'm a friend of the owners. They asked me to come." I stepped aside so I could see what was going on.

The police officer blocked my way. "Identification?" she asked.

I pulled out my driver's license and handed it to her.

"Teri," the police officer called out. "Do you know a Nicole Woods?"

"Yes! Yes! Let her in," Teri replied.

The officer stepped aside. "Okay, you can go in, but stay down. Stuff is flying around."

A few napkins and a couple of straws were slowly floating in a whirlwind fashion around the four-top table that Marcus and Gloria were hiding under.

Teri popped up from behind the counter. I could see just the top of Linda's head beside her. Sonja was floating with her face inches from Gloria's. She was screaming at her.

"Sonja! Stop!" I cried, then immediately glanced around. Who had heard me? The officer who'd let me in stood with her mouth agape as the napkins and straws dropped.

Sonja appeared next to me and pointed. "She has my purse. She was in my house when I came home for lunch. I had that purse with me. She stole it and then she killed me."

"Okay." I said as softly as I could and searched the room for the officer who'd been staring at me."

"Excuse me, Officer...?" I waved.

"Cooper." The policewoman turned to her partner, told him to guard the door, and moved cautiously to me.

I met her halfway. "Officer Cooper. My good friend Sonja is missing. That is Sonja's purse." I pointed to the purse on the floor next to Gloria. "I think Gloria may be responsible for what has happened to Sonja."

The officer was quiet for a moment. "What do you think has happened to Sonja?"

"Something bad. I know that Sonja had that purse with her the day she disappeared."

"Is there a way you can prove that?" the officer asked.

Sonja floated over to me. "Yes," she said. "There is a false bottom in the purse. A copy of my passport, a hundred-dollar bill, and a credit card are hidden under the bottom piece. I used that card when I paid for lunch at Carmines the day I died."

I repeated most of what Sonja had told me to Officer Cooper, except for the dying part.

"Gloria, may we examine your purse?" Officer Cooper asked.

"No," Gloria wailed. "I know my rights. You need a search warrant."

Marcus scooted away from Gloria and stood next to the table. "What did you do, Gloria? Where is Sonja? Give them your purse."

"No," Gloria yelled. "I want my lawyer." Suddenly her voice had a southern accent. She was going for the fragile female.

It was not going to work in this room.

I moved across the cafe. "I need to use the bathroom. I'll only be a moment." I gestured for Mom and Sonja to join me.

"I thought you didn't want me in your bathroom," Mom snarked.

"Not now, Mom," I sighed. "Listen. I want you to smell or whatever it is you do, the stuff in this baggie." I set the sandwich bag with the brown scrapings on the bathroom counter. "See if you can identify it as blood, and anything else you can find out about it."

"But I don't know what blood essence is like," Mom complained and then turned to Sonja. "Sorry, Sonja."

"Give her your blood to sniff," Sonja demanded of me. "She'll have a baseline for what blood is like."

Mom glanced at me and shrugged.

I searched my purse for something to draw blood with. All I could find was a nail clipper. I yanked a paper towel out of the wall dispenser and began clipping the side of my finger until it bled. I blotted the blood on the paper towel and laid it next to the baggie.

I turned to Sonja. "You and my mom need to work together. No more outbursts or flying objects. The police need to find the blood on Gloria's gym bag. I can't give it to them, or they might think I've planted evidence. It wouldn't be admissible."

"But she has my purse," Sonja wailed.

"Identifying the purse is huge, but it won't be enough. If we can know for sure this is your blood, we can push hard to get the police to search their place."

"You sound just like the police on Law and Order. I've never been prouder," Mom said.

"I want to freeze her socks off," Sonja snarled. "She killed me. She stole my life. She stole my purse."

"Freeze her if it makes you feel better," I said softly. "But don't go too far. We don't want her to get off on an insanity charge."

"Okay," Sonja sounded defeated.

"We are going to get to the bottom of this. We will find your killer. I promise, Sonja." I went back out to the shop.

"How soon can you get a warrant?" I asked Office Cooper.

"Captain is already working on it. But I need some background on all of this. Can you fill me in?" She gestured to a table in the corner.

I told Officer Cooper what I knew about the relationship between Sonja, Cali, Gloria, and Marcus. I chose my words carefully.

Sonja periodically poked Gloria. Gloria yelped and pleaded for Marcus to help her. Marcus shook his head, turned his back on her, and leaned on the pastry glass. Tears streaked his face.

Officer Cooper was on her cell. She hung up. "A search warrant is on its way,"

We heard the sirens as more police approached.

Mom floated over to me and announced, "It's blood."

She floated over to Sonja, who was looking worn out. If staying visual was hard, the anger and whirlwind she'd created must be taking a toll on her.

"There is blood in the baggie, but unless you have something with Sonja's blood on it, I can't be sure it's her blood," Mom told me and then turned to Sonja. "And I know you were killed in the early afternoon, so there's a good chance it's not your blood. Not unless you'd been drinking that morning. There were traces of wine in the blood."

Sonja's eyes grew huge. "I had a glass of wine with lunch. Oh, my goodness, the blood is mine." She faced me. "The blood is mine. Will this be enough to charge her?"

I smiled and pointed to the storage room. When Mom and Sonja joined me, I whispered, "We still don't know whose bag it is that has your blood on it, but I bet there will be fingerprints. We can't rule out Marcus just yet."

Mom was clearly pleased with her contribution. "I could sense the wine in the blood. The alcohol, but also the sugar and grapes. I'm pretty sure it was white wine, which as you know, I love best."

"Good job, Mom," I whispered, wishing I could say more, and looked around for a wastebasket. I found one, carried it out to the tables, and began picking up straws and napkins.

Officer Cooper put gloves on and dumped the contents of the purse atop a small café table. A wallet, cell phone, make-up bag, brush, tissues, and a couple of receipts fell over the top. The officer opened the wallet. It had Gloria's driver's license and credit cards in it.

Gloria sniffed. "See! It's my purse."

"Look for a false bottom piece." I stopped picking up and pointed at the purse.

The officer reached in and pulled out a slice of leather the same color and size as the bottom of the purse. She set it aside and hauled out a baggie. She opened the baggie and held up a copy of a passport with Sonja's name on it. The hundred-dollar bill she left in the baggie, but the blue plastic credit card she also showed us. It had Sonja's name on it too.

"I have reason to believe Sonja used that credit card at lunch at Carmines the day she was killed," I said.

The officer turned to me. "And how do you know that?"

"Sonja told me she was going to Carmines for lunch," I said.

"But how do you know that this is the card she used?" Officer Cooper asked.

"Just a feeling I have," I shrugged. "But it wouldn't be hard to check, right?"

Officer Cooper shook her head at me. "We have enough to take that couple in for questioning." She turned and ordered the two newly arrived police officers to cuff them.

I let out a breath I didn't know I'd been holding.

"Look," Mom suddenly yelled and pointed at one of the receipts that had dropped out of the purse. "Look where it's from."

I moved to see what Mom was pointing at, but I couldn't get close enough to read the receipts. Mom and now Sonja were going crazy, jumping around and pointing. I moved back and gestured for them to calm down.

Officer Cooper opened an evidence bag and carefully began loading it with the contents from the purse. "What's this?" She picked up and read the larger receipt. She called to one of her assistants. "Take a look at this. North Seattle Recycling and Disposal. That's the city dump!"

The assistant officer turned with a look of disgust and glared at Gloria.

Officer Cooper picked up her radio. "This is Officer Cooper. I need a search team with search and rescue dogs at the North Seattle Recycling and Disposal. I have reason to believe a homicide victim's body was dropped off there."

She turned to Gloria and Marcus who were being marched out the door. Gloria was now wailing, claiming it was all Marcus' doing. She claimed he'd planned it all.

Marcus lowered his head and let the tears fall.

Officer Cooper told the officers escorting the suspects to stop. She moved closer to them and said, "You are both under arrest for suspicion of complicity in the disappearance of Sonja Woods. You have the right...."

•••••••••••

Officer Cooper was the last to leave Deja Brew. She motioned for me sit with her for a moment. "Lots of strange things happened here this afternoon," she said as she closed her notebook.

"Yes," I agreed, but didn't say more.

Linda offered her a latte. She declined the offer, but said she'd love a coffee to go.

She kept staring at me as if wondering what to say. She cleared her throat and finally said, "I have a bit of research to do this afternoon. I'd appreciate if you'd stop by the precinct tomorrow morning."

Linda brought over the officer's coffee and a box of pastries. "For the precinct," she said. "We will stay closed for the rest of the day. These will just go to waste."

"Thank you. The treats will be appreciated." Officer Cooper stood and glanced at me. "I'll see you around ten?"

"Ten. I'll be there," I replied.

Teri, Linda and I finished cleaning up. It didn't take long.

"Tell them I'm sorry I made such a mess," Sonja sniffed.

I passed on what Sonja told me to Teri and Linda. Mom blew her a kiss.

"Sonja, I wish we could have done more," Teri spoke to the ceiling.

I recalled talking to the clouds when Mom first appeared. "Let's meet up tomorrow. Hopefully the police will have more evidence by then."

"Do you think they'll find my body?" Sonja asked.

I noticed she was fading. I could hardly see or hear her. "I'm sure they will. Go...well, wherever you go to rest. I'll stop by here after my visit with Officer Cooper in the morning."

"I'm going to stay with Cali tonight." Sonja said weakly and vanished.

"How are you doing?" I asked Teri and Linda.

"Kinda shook up. You weren't here when Sonja made all the napkins and straws swirl around the room. It was like a tornado. And Gloria was trapped in the middle of it." Linda shuddered.

"I'm sorry I missed it." I smiled, then realized Linda and Teri weren't.

"Yes, well, many of our long-time customers were scared. I hope they will feel safe enough to return. Some left screaming." Teri reached out to Linda.

Linda held Teri's hand. "I knew the ghost was Sonja, but it was still really scary."

I hadn't thought about how they might feel about being haunted, nor how their business would be affected. "Let's sleep on it. We can come up with a good excuse for the wind in the morning. Maybe you can claim your air conditioner went crazy."

"Maybe," Linda and Teri said at the same time.

"Come on, Mom. Time to go home and have a glass or two of wine."

CHAPTER FIFTEEN

Mom insisted on riding with me to the police precinct the next morning, although I reminded her again that she couldn't go inside. The morning drizzle stopped, and the misty dark clouds began to lift as we headed south on the freeway. Suddenly Mount Rainier appeared on the horizon. The sun glistened off its pure white slopes. It looked like a giant ice-cream cone, floating in the sky.

"I'm going to miss seeing that mountain," Mom said. "I wanted to climb to the top."

"You should have. I would have gone with you," I told her. We spent the rest of the ride admiring the mountain and talking about the different day hikes we'd taken on it.

A short while later, I pulled into Deja Brew's parking lot for a to-go coffee, but the line to get into the shop went halfway around the block. And there was no place to park. A news van with Channel Five News plastered on its side was taking up both of the handicapped parking spots.

I texted Linda and Teri. "What's going on?" But got no answer.

I didn't have time to wait in the line, so I drove on. After a quick stop at a Starcafe drive thru, and a pause to write an explanation text to Linda and Teri, I arrived at the police department at exactly ten o'clock.

Mom grumbled about being left behind in the car, but I ignored her as I draped my amulet around my neck. Who knew how many ghosts might haunt a police department?

"I'll be right back," I said, and hurried toward the entry doors.

"Starcafe?" Officer Cooper gestured at my coffee cup as she escorted me into her office. "Won't Teri and Linda be hurt?"

I sat my cup on her desk. "I tried to stop at Deja Brew, but the line for coffee went around the parking lot."

Officer Cooper nodded. "I'm not surprised. One of their customers from yesterday posted a video on social media. Here!" She brought up a video on her cell and handed it to me.

I gasped as I watched napkins, straws, paper receipts, even a paper cup spin around the table Gloria and Marcus were hiding under. They screamed nonstop while the rest of the customers shrieked and raced for the doors. The video ended with a quick glance at Linda and Teri ducking behind the counter.

"Oh no!" I sighed. "That can't be good for business."

Officer Cooper shrugged. "You never know. People love unexplained and gruesome events and want to see for themselves. Happens all the time at murder locations. It takes extra manpower just to keep everyone out until we finish our investigation."

"I hope you're right." I took a sip of my coffee and made a face at the bitter taste.

Officer Cooper's mouth grew stern as she opened her notebook. "Okay. I need you to tell me how you know so much about Sonja's death."

I studied my strong coffee, then looked her in the eye. "Do you really want to know?"

She closed her eyes for a moment, opened them, and studied me. "I want a statement from you. I can't let you leave without a statement. She picked up her pen. "You knew Sonja went to lunch and used the credit card that was at the bottom of her purse. How do you know that?"

I looked her in the eye. "Sonja told me."

She wrote down my answer. "Where were you when Sonja was killed"

I nodded. This one I could answer. "I'm a surgical nurse at Seattle General Hospital. I was at the hospital working when Sonja was killed." I handed her my hospital badge.

"How did you know..." she began again.

I raised my hand for her to stop. "Officer Cooper, before you ask me any more questions, can I ask you one? I yelled something when I walked into Deja Brew. What did I shout?"

Her face suddenly paled. "You cried, 'Sonja. Stop!' Then the whirling papers fell to the floor."

I nodded. "Sonja told me everything I know. That is my statement."

"I'm a police officer. I need verifiable evidence." She sounded frustrated.

"Did you find Sonja's body?" I tipped my head to the side.

"Yes. They found it last night. It's at the coroner's now," she said.

"I'm glad. I'm very, very, glad." Sonja was going to be relieved. "So, what was in her hand?"

"How did you know something was in her hand?" Officer Cooper jolted out of her seat and almost flew across the table before she stopped herself. She took a deep breath, then slowly lowered herself back down to her chair. "She had a handful of bright red hair in her hand," she almost whispered.

I grinned. Gloria's hair. We had her. I wanted to do a happy dance but decided the police department wasn't the place for it.

Officer Cooper slammed her notebook shut. "Okay. You've told me all you can. but don't leave town. I may have more questions for you."

I stood to leave. "Before I go, is Marcus still a suspect?" I asked.

"Both Marcus and Colin have good alibis for where they were when Sonja was killed. And we found more evidence against Gloria in her closet and her car trunk."

"Okay, I have a favor to ask. Marcus has applied for custody of his and Sonja's daughter, Cali. She's only eight years old. Sonja doesn't want him to raise Cali. If you have evidence of drug abuse by Marcus, would you pass it on to Family Services, I know your input would go a long way to help the courts decide to award Colin custody."

Officer Cooper nodded. "I will do what I can." She stood and pushed in her chair. "Next time we talk, I want it to be someplace where I can get a drink. A drink with lots of alcohol."

I fingered my amulet and smiled. "Anytime!"

• • • ● • ● • • •

I climbed into the car and removed the amulet. Mom was practically screaming, her arms flailed "What did you learn? Did they find Sonja's body?"

"Mom, settle down. It's all good. Yes, they found Sonja's body. But I need a minute." I checked my cell.

Teri had texted that they were going to close around five. They invited me to come to Deja Brew then.

I texted that I would be there with good news.

I showed the message to Mom, and we headed home. On the way, I shared with her what Officer Cooper had told me. When we were through the front door, we finally did a little happy dance. Mom's moves looked more like the 'Chicken Dance," but it was the relief we felt that counted.

"I can't wait to talk to Sonja," Mom said when we sat down. She poked her nose into her wine glass from the night before.

I was excited to see Sonja too. I told Mom to enjoy herself while I did some household chores, baked an enchilada casserole, and watched the clock.

The closed sign was up and the parking lot was practically empty when we got to Deja Brew.

Teri let us in. Linda came out from behind the counter and wiped her hands on a dishtowel.

"What did you learn? We've been dying to find out all day," Linda said.

I looked around. Sonja hadn't arrived yet. "I'd like to wait until Sonja gets here."

She nodded. "That's a good idea. Sit. What can I get you?" Linda asked.

I went to our round table, set my purse and a food basket on top of it, and motioned for Mom to join me. I turned to Linda and Teri. "You probably didn't have a break all day. I brought some dinner and wine."

Mom perked up at the mention of wine.

Teri and Linda joined us. "This is so nice of you. We are exhausted."

"Tell me what happened here today. I couldn't believe the crowd," I said as I filled paper plates with the casserole.

"We were interviewed for the evening news. Did you see the video from yesterday?" Linda asked.

"Officer Cooper showed me," I said.

"Ha!" Teri said. "Bet she didn't know what to think about it, either. We tried to tell our customers that the whirlwind was from our malfunctioning air conditioner, like you suggested, but nobody bought it. Everyone wanted to know what we knew about the ghostly activity. We started saying it was police business and we couldn't comment."

"It was all peaceful. Everyone was curious, but nice too," Linda added. "And we got lots of new customers. If only half of them come back, we will be on easy street."

"I'm so happy for you. I was worried last night." I pulled out a bottle of red wine.

Mom's face fell.

I tried not to laugh at her obvious disappointment and showed her the bottle of white wine I'd brought just for her.

A cold shiver went up my spine.

Sonja appeared across the table. "They found my body!" she clapped her hands soundlessly.

I told Linda and Teri what Sonja had announced.

"Tell us what happened." I pointed to the chair Sonja stood behind.

"Colin identified my body today. I heard him talking to his mom. He was upset. I wanted to hold him and tell him it was okay. That I was relieved. But he had been hoping the police would find me alive." She looked so sad.

I have news too. "Officer Cooper told me that neither Marcus nor Colin were suspects. I asked her to let Family Services know about the drugs they found in Marcus' condo. She said she would."

"Really?" Sonja perked up. "You did that for me?"

I smiled. "No. For Cali. Guess what they found in your hand? Did Colin talk about it?"

Sonja shook her head.

"A clump of long red hair!" I yelled, stood, and raised my hands in the air in celebration.

Sonja leapt off her seat and squealed. "Is it enough to convict her?"

"What just happened?" Linda and Teri asked. I filled them both in before I answered Sonja. "I guess there was even more evidence in her closet and trunk. I'm sure with the stolen purse, the receipt for the dump, and the blood they found on the gym bag, they have a tight case. Gloria is going to prison for a long time."

Sonja collapsed in the chair. "You did it. You put all the pieces together."

"We all did. We were a good team. And the best is that Colin will get custody of Cali." I did a mock 'hi five' all around.

Sonja stared at me, a bright shimmer in her eyes. "I can go now. This has been so awful. Although part of me wants to stay until after the trial, I'm tired. I feel weak. I want to see my mother. It's time for me to go into the light."

Mom said, "Sonja, before you pass over, you have to experience a glass of wine."

Sonja groaned. "Really? She glanced around the table. "Okay. Okay. I guess I owe you."

"Red or white?" I asked.

"White." She winked at me. She must have remembered it was Mom's favorite.

I helped Linda pass out the wine glasses.

I held mine up in the air. "To Cali," I said.

"To Cali," everyone repeated. Mom and Sonja cheered then bent over and stuck their noses into their wine glasses.

After a short while, Sonja muttered, "Oh my! It's incredible." She smiled at Mom.

"Told you." Mom grinned.

I felt content as I sipped my wine, watched Teri and Linda groan with pleasure as they ate, and Mom and Sonja argue about what they were experiencing with the wine.

Mom had been right about helping ghosts. Sonja could go into the light knowing her killer would be punished and her daughter well taken care of.

I swilled the wine in my glass and wondered how long Mom would stay. I promised myself I'd enjoy every second we had left, and for memory's sake, use my gift more often.

Just then, Mom raised her head and asked. "What's our next case?"

I almost choked. Sonja started to laugh. I told Teri and Linda what Mom had said. They looked stricken and shook their heads. Then I saw the gleam in Mom's eyes.

My jaw dropped. She wasn't kidding.

About the Author

Brenda has lived most of her life in the shadows of giant mountains, near lakes and streams, and exploring the beaches that surround the Puget Sound. Her idea of heaven is a book in one hand and a cup of coffee or glass of wine in the other. She now lives on Lake Washington, which borders Seattle, with her husband. She loves to kayak and watch the resident eagles soar. Her sailboat, Whistler, is moored in a marina a short way away. Summers are spent sailing around the inland waters of Washington and Canada.

You can find her books, *Knockdown, Beached, and Anchored*, at various booksellers.

MIDNIGHT SUN MURDER

by Martina Dalton

CHAPTER 1

My knuckles shone white against the black steering wheel.

It was almost noon, and I'd been driving since five o'clock in the morning. And unless I counted a herd of Dall sheep or a family of grizzly bears, I hadn't seen a single soul since the day before.

The landscape lay spread out before me under the deep blue sky. I passed miles and miles of low green and gold shrubs, even sighting an occasional mama moose with her baby in tow. In the far distance on either side of the highway were mountains in shades of brown, blue-gray, and green topped with snow.

"Mags, the camper is almost out of gas," I spoke through my Bluetooth speaker to my best friend in California. "And gas stations on the Alaska Highway are few and far between. Can you do an internet search for a station closest to me?"

"Okay, but before I do that," Mags said through the crackly speaker, "do you have an extra can of gas stored in the camper for emergencies? I mean, here in Los Angeles there's a gas station on every corner and at every freeway off-ramp, but you're not in L.A. anymore."

"No." I gritted my teeth. Why hadn't I thought of stowing a can of gas in the camper?

"Denali, you've got to start thinking like a pioneer woman! Always be prepared—like they told us in Girl Scouts."

"Yeah, yeah. I know. But I never thought I'd be moving to Alaska to run a café in Gold Rush. I'm truly not prepared for any of this." I stared at the narrow highway ahead. Short evergreen trees stood like toothpicks in the tundra on either side of the road.

"You couldn't have prepared for your uncle Roy dying and naming you in his will," she said. "And you're not just running the café in Gold Rush, you own the whole town!"

I didn't even know my uncle existed until a month ago. My parents had never mentioned him. When we'd left Alaska and moved to Los Angeles thirty years ago, I was only a baby.

The red gas gauge flashed rapidly and dropped another notch. "Shoot."

"Someone's shooting?" Mags said, her voice crackling over the weak connection.

"This isn't L.A., Mags. I said shoot because the needle is almost on empty."

"Tell me exactly where you are so I can look up gas stations in the area," she said.

I glanced at the navigation screen on my phone. "I'm fifteen miles from Gold Rush. Almost there. But I don't want to walk that far to get gas. Especially in the middle of nowhere."

There was a pause while Mags did a search. "As luck would have it, there's a gas station just two miles ahead," she said. "Think you can make it that far?"

"I sure hope so." The engine made a chortling noise. "I really, really hope so."

"You're breaking up. I can barely hear you." Mags sounded like she was talking through a tin can. "I'm going to hang up, but call me back when you get there, okay?"

"Will do." The line went dead. It was just me now. The sky was a vast swath of blue. I could almost see the curvature of the earth up here. I was all alone in this God-forsaken land. The last frontier. How could I survive without my best friend? Or shopping malls?

"Stop being so dramatic," I told myself. "How bad can it be?"

The engine sputtered.

"No, no, no!" I shouted. "You've got to get me there, Bessie!"

Bessie? Since when had I named this camper Bessie?

I shrugged. Apparently, Bessie was the only thing I could talk to now that Mags was thousands of miles away.

Checking my rearview mirror, I noticed a vehicle a mile or so behind me. Maybe if I ran out of gas, they would stop and pick me up. I frowned. But what if the person who stopped was a serial killer just waiting for an opportunity to slay his next unsuspecting victim? Again, I reminded myself to lay off the drama.

"Oh, no." The road up ahead inclined at a thirty-degree angle. Could Bessie make it up the hill? My foot automatically gunned the gas. Momentum might be my only hope of getting over the top.

"Here we go." I gritted my teeth and prayed.

The gas gauge dropped a hair lower as my knuckles turned even whiter on the steering wheel. "Go, go, go!" I urged the vehicle.

Bessie complained as I shoved my foot down on the pedal. The gas light on the dash flashed sporadically and made a high-pitched beeping sound.

"I think I can, I think I can, I think I can," I chanted to her. She was a new-to-me camper, but she was getting on in years. I fervently wished she'd come equipped with a fuel-saving tank, but that was before her time.

We neared the top of the hill. I whooped with joy. "We're almost there!"

A snowshoe hare suddenly appeared on the side of the road, staring straight at me. Its white coat was already turning brown in anticipation of summer.

"No," I whispered. "Don't you dare..."

Too late. The animal darted across the road. If I took my foot off the pedal now, I'd never make it. Would I really sacrifice a bunny to make it up this mountain?

Instinctively, I slammed the heel of my hand down on the horn. The rabbit increased its speed just in the nick of time. Bessie had made it to the top and the bunny lived!

Relief surged through me as I spied a tiny gas station about a mile downhill.

Bessie belched. The flashing red gas pump icon beeped one last time and stayed red. The engine cut out.

"No!" I leaned forward, praying that the downhill momentum would carry me to my destination.

I hitched in a breath as the camper slowed and came to a stop at the apex.

Red and blue lights appeared in my rearview mirror. "Really? A cop out in the middle of nowhere?"

The police SUV stopped behind me.

My shoulders slumped. This was not my day.

I watched in the large side mirror as a tall, broad-shouldered guy in a blue uniform and a hat that reminded me of Dudley Do-Right from the old Rocky and Bullwinkle cartoons approached the driver's side. I tried to roll down the window, but it was stuck. My hands shook as I opened the door a crack.

"Sorry, officer. I can't roll down the window, so this will have to do."

"It's trooper, not officer. Step out of the vehicle, ma'am." His deep voice sounded out of place in the quiet of the wilderness.

I opened the door and slid to the ground, wishing I'd worn something a little warmer. I looked down. And a little less revealing.

My shorts were a tiny bit, well... short. And my tank top revealed a little too much cleavage. I bit my lip. Maybe that was a good thing? My friends often got out of speeding tickets in L.A. by being flirty with the officers.

The big man who looked to be about my age—early to mid-thirties—glanced at my attire, then averted his eyes. "May I see your driver's license and registration?"

He was kind of attractive, I mean if tall and muscular was your sort of thing. I felt even more awkward.

"Sure. Hang on." I opened the door wider and climbed back inside, popping the glove compartment open. I dug out my registration, then grabbed my wallet for my driver's license. I hopped back out. "Here."

He took a moment to review and then handed them back to me. "Denali Dahlgren from California, you are a long way from home. Interesting that you're named after our mountain when you aren't from Alaska."

I shrugged. "I was born here, but my family moved to the lower forty-eight when I was little."

"What brings you out here and why did you stop in the middle of the road?" he asked.

I noticed his steady gaze and earnest brown eyes. "I'm headed to Gold Rush. But I ran out of gas." My cheeks warmed. "I thought I could gun it and make it to the top of the hill, but then I almost hit a bunny and—"

He put his hand up. "That explains why you were speeding."

"Oh, yeah. Sorry, Officer—"

"Trooper. Trooper Jones," he said.

I couldn't tell if he was amused or not. His face was irritatingly unreadable. "Trooper Jones. Nice to meet you. Denali Dahlgren." I held out my hand to shake his.

His hand stayed at his side. "I know your name. Tell you what, I won't give you a ticket this time around. And let me do you a favor. Put your vehicle in neutral and I'll give you a nudge with my SUV. Then you can roll to that gas station down there. Grady will take care of you."

I smiled, relieved he was being helpful. "Thank you, Trooper Jones. I really appreciate it."

He gave me a curt nod. "Here to protect and serve."

Okay, that was pretty cheesy, but I wasn't going to complain. I did as he said, and soon, I was rolling downhill and managed to pull right in front of the pumps.

I watched Trooper Jones' taillights as he continued down the remote highway.

"Huh," I said before I turned to put the gas nozzle into Bessie's tank. "That's the first time a cop was there when I needed one."

While the tank filled, I texted Mags. "Made it to a gas station. Thanks for your help. Call you later tonight."

"Thank God," she texted back. "I almost bought a plane ticket so I could rescue you."

I laughed. Good ol' Mags. She was always there when I needed her.

"Rescue not required. But you could move up here—I might need somebody to run one of the shops in Gold Rush."

"Don't tempt me," she texted. "The pay is too good in L.A. right now. Otherwise, I'd be up there in a hot second."

I secretly hoped Mags would do just that. It would be nice to have a friend in this desolate land. "There I go with the drama again," I said out loud.

When the tank was full, I went in to pay, but there was nobody inside the store. There was a basket on the counter with a little sign that read, "Be back in an hour. Pay what you owe here." There was an arrow pointing to the basket and there were a couple of twenty-dollar bills at the bottom.

The honor system? That would never fly where I was from. It would be stolen in a heartbeat.

I went back out to check the pump. I owed over two hundred and forty dollars! Geez. Between the gas guzzling camper and the outrageously expensive fuel prices, I might go broke before the year was over.

Digging into my purse, I counted out a wad of twenties and tens in cash and placed it in the basket. I congratulated myself for being extra prepared to expect that paper money might be needed on the trip.

Hopping into the camper, I started the engine and rolled back onto the deserted highway.

The landscape changed from an open valley to foothills and a rather steep climb into the unknown. Bessie groaned a bit as we rose higher into the mountain range. There were fewer and fewer trees up here. Maybe they didn't survive well in high altitude. The mountain sides were hued in tones of camel and brown with strips of snow descending from the tops in interesting formations. Clouds hung around the mountain peaks, obscuring the formerly blue sky.

"What the heck? I thought I was almost to Gold Rush." But the road continued up and up until I thought I might have taken a wrong turn somewhere back in Canada. I glanced at my navigation app. "Hmmm. It says I have ten miles to go. It will be a slow ten miles with all this altitude gain."

Finally, I reached the summit. Bessie sighed with relief as we began our descent. The grey clouds prevented me from seeing what was ahead. I wondered what Gold Rush looked like. Uncle Roy's lawyer had told me it had been an old gold mining town. My uncle had bought it for a song. Apparently, he'd invested heavily in remodeling and rebuilding the stores and structures that were there. He'd even added a few new ones that hadn't existed during the heyday of the late 1800s.

Suddenly, the clouds thinned, and I caught my first glimpse of the town below. It was situated on a relatively flat area at the bottom of a foothill. One long main street featured wooden boardwalks and folksy shops. Several cross streets were lined with houses, which I assumed were meant for the shopkeepers and others who occupied the town. All in all, I counted at least twenty-two businesses and about that many houses. The color scheme in town seemed to be rustic wood for most of the structures, but some were painted light blue, red, and pale yellow. They were all styled in that old-timey frontier town kind of way. The type you'd see in an old Western movie.

Small towns weren't my cup of tea, but this one was kind of charming, though I wondered if living here would make me yearn for the big city.

I sighed. Maybe I could ride it out for a year or two and then sell the whole thing off.

When I finally rolled into town, I didn't know what to do or where to go. Was one of the houses on the cross streets mine? I drove slowly down the main road, looking at each shop as I went. There was a cafe, a saloon, a mercantile, something called a bunkhouse, a post office, a library, and a jail. "A jail!" I snorted. "There aren't enough people in this town to keep a cop busy." I remembered the trooper who'd helped me earlier. Was this where he worked?

I rolled to a stop along the boardwalk in front of a small, rustic building that said, "Gold Rush City Hall." If anyone would have information for me, this would be the place. I grabbed my purse and hopped out of the camper. I stood and surveyed the boardwalk, eyeing the shops. They seemed to be quite empty. My stomach turned. Where was everybody?

I walked to the front door of city hall, my footsteps sounding hollow on the wood of the boardwalk. I turned the knob and to my surprise, it opened. An older man with white hair and glasses sat behind a desk reading a Guns and Ammo magazine. He looked up as I entered, his black reading glasses slipping down his nose. "Oh, hello there! I wasn't expecting visitors. The town hasn't officially opened for business quite yet."

I gave him a tentative smile. "I'm not a tourist exactly. I'm Denali Dahlgren. Roy Dahlgren's niece."

His bushy eyebrows rose and disappeared into his disheveled hair. He stood up. "Dahlgren? That can't be..."

I frowned. "What do you mean?"

His astonished look still hadn't left his face. "Roy Dahlgren didn't have any relatives."

Just then, a door down a short hallway to the side of the old man's desk flew open. "Jasper, I thought I heard someone come in." The guy froze when he saw me. A slow smile spread across his ruddy face. "Well, well. Hello, little lady. What brings you in to Gold Rush? Are you lost?"

"Not really," I said hesitantly. "I'm just trying to figure out where I'm supposed to be."

The guy looked to be about fifty years old and was dressed in a buckskin jacket and a cream-colored cowboy hat. His dark handlebar moustache twitched and the glint in his eye made me dislike him immediately.

I tried to think of what to say. Should I tell him I owned this town? No. That didn't seem like a good idea. Instead, I settled for, "My Uncle Roy's lawyer sent me here."

Saying the man looked shocked was a clear understatement.

"Your Uncle Roy? Roy didn't have a family." His face had turned red and he looked—angry.

Well, this was awkward. "I didn't know much about Roy either, to be honest. He was my dad's older brother. They didn't communicate much."

He narrowed his eyes at me. "I'm having a hard time believing you're not just another gold digger, here to claim something that isn't yours."

I glared back at him. "I don't know what you're getting at, but I came up here because Uncle Roy left me this town and everything else he owned. Are you saying I'm not his niece?"

"Damn right, that's what I'm saying. This town is mine. See, Roy Dahlgren and I were business partners. We owned this town together--fifty-fifty."

I frowned. "That's not what his will said."

"Then that will is wrong. Or you forged it!" he blustered.

The older man behind the desk stood. "Now, Soapy, let's hear the lady out. Maybe check her ID."

"Here." I pulled a copy of Uncle Roy's will out of my purse and showed it to Jasper and then offered it to the angry man who seemed way too agitated for the circumstances.

Soapy batted the document away and stepped forward, his face just inches from mine. "I'm going to go see *my* lawyer. How's about that? We'll see who owns this town and who doesn't." He turned and stormed out the same door he'd entered through.

"Wow," I said. "Who is that guy?"

The older man smiled apologetically. "That's Soapy Smith. Don't mind him. He has a mean temper. Just let him cool down before you talk to him again."

"I plan on it." I shook my head. "But I don't think I want to talk to him again."

He nodded sympathetically. "Not many people do want to talk to Soapy. He can be very brash. But I think it's all bluster. You don't need to be afraid of him."

I shrugged uncertainly. "I hope that's true."

"Let's see," Jasper said, "if you're Roy's niece, you'll want to stay at his place behind the Midnight Sun Café. His house is the red one on the cross street next to the café. Come on, I'll show you."

"Thank you, Mr... I don't believe I caught your last name." I followed him through the front door.

"It's Osgood. Jasper Osgood," he said. "My wife and I run The Bunkhouse, but we take turns filling in here behind the desk to greet visitors in case we have any."

"Nice to meet you, Jasper." At least he was a nice man. If everyone in town was as nasty as Soapy Smith, I might've just turned around and driven straight back to California.

Jasper looked both ways, though there were no cars in sight, and crossed the cobble road to stand in front of a cute coffeehouse. The sign above the door said "Midnight Sun Café." "This is the establishment your uncle was planning to run, God bless his soul. The building is original, but completely refurbished on the inside. Such a shame he died before the ribbon cutting ceremony. It's coming up next week."

I hesitated. "How exactly did my uncle die? My lawyer didn't say."

He looked surprised. "Oh, we think he had a heart attack. He was behind the counter fiddling with one of the espresso machines and he collapsed. A terrible thing, that was." He shook his head. "But at least he went quick."

I bit my lip. "Wait. You said you *think* he had a heart attack? Didn't the medical examiner confirm that?"

Jasper shrugged. "This town doesn't have a medical examiner, Miss Dahlgren."

"There's no medical examiner? What about a doctor?" I asked.

He shook his head. "No doctor quite yet. Roy was looking into getting one for the summer months here, but so far, he hasn't been able to find one willing to move here."

Astonished, I rocked back on my heels. "But what if someone gets sick? Especially in the winter months?"

Jasper took a moment to consider the question. "We just built the town up. But most of us have lived in bush towns or remote places before. We have to take a bush plane to Anchorage if we need medical care."

"Anchorage?" I asked incredulously. "But that's so far! What if there's an emergency?"

"Those are the chances we take by living here, I suppose. We have to take the good with the bad."

"My God," I said. "It's even more primitive here than I thought it was."

Jasper let out a loud guffaw. "Primitive! I like that. Welcome to the Last Frontier, Miss Dahlgren." He pulled a ring of keys out of his pocket and handed them to me. "Here. These are the keys to the town."

I ran my fingers over the keys, which were of various shapes and sizes. I assumed that was to help differentiate between them.

"The literal keys to the town?" I stared at them in my palm.

"Yep. As you can see," he pointed to them, "they are all engraved with the name of the buildings. Some names are abbreviated, like this one, because the name was too long to engrave into the metal."

I looked closely at the key he'd pointed to. "8StarsGold. What kind of business is this?"

"Eight Stars of Gold Hardware," he said.

Noticing my blank stare, he added, "Eight stars of gold is the image on the Alaskan flag." He pointed to the flagpole next to city hall. A flag fluttered in the light breeze. It had eight gold stars in the shape of the Big Dipper constellation emblazoned on a background of deep blue.

"That's pretty," I said. And it was. I'd never seen a state flag quite like it.

"Indeed. We are very proud of it. The flag was designed by a thirteen-year-old Native boy named Benny Benson. He did a real fine job with the design, don't you think?"

"Wow," I said, watching the flag blow in the breeze. "I love it."

"Let's go inside." Jasper motioned toward the café door. "Just find the key that says Midnight Sun Café."

I sorted through until I found the right one. Putting the key in the lock, I turned the knob and walked inside.

CHAPTER 2

It was a relatively cozy space with room for maybe twenty to thirty customers. But it was nowhere close to being done. There were no tables or chairs and no decorations on the walls. There were, however, two expensive looking espresso machines all in place behind the counter. The countertops consisted of giant slabs of wood stained a dark, rich brown. There was a sink, a microwave, and a small fridge for milk and cream. A low shelf on one of the back counters held at least a dozen different flavored syrup bottles. A long glass case on one end of the counter was ready for fresh baked goods to be loaded inside.

"Are all the shops unfinished like this?" I asked, feeling a little overwhelmed. "It's already the middle of June. Isn't this supposed to be tourist season?"

Jasper frowned. "Yes, we were planning on opening on June 21st. But then Roy died. Nothing much has been done since he passed away. The other shops are mostly built, though. Because Roy was planning on running this café here, he saved it for last, so the other shop people could go ahead and start up."

"That was nice of him—to give others a chance to open before him. Was that the sort of thing that he normally did? To look after people?"

Jasper smiled. "Yes, Roy was a decent fellow. Though, he did enjoy making money. That's why he didn't allow any of the townspeople to buy their own businesses. He wanted the rent money."

My face fell. "Oh." I had hoped that maybe my uncle was a good guy. But I knew there had been something going on between my dad and him. Otherwise, why wouldn't they have spoken in over thirty years?

Jasper patted me on the shoulder. "We all have our faults, my dear. Greed is a human emotion that just about everyone is guilty of. He had many other good qualities, that's for sure."

I brightened a bit. "I'd love to hear more later when there's time." I turned to look at the bare café. "I don't know where to start."

"Come back into the kitchen." He nudged me through the swinging door that led to the back. "There's an entire shipment of stuff all boxed up. There should be tables, chairs, and all kinds of other supplies in here. This was delivered the day after your uncle passed away. You can start here."

I stopped and stared. There were at least thirty large boxes taking up most of the floor space in the commercial kitchen. "Wow."

Jasper pointed at the good-sized ovens and baking racks. "Roy ordered state of the art commercial ovens, mixers, and racks—everything you need to bake up some loaves of sourdough bread, donuts, and anything else you plan to serve."

I closed my eyes. I was a decent pie maker and even made some pretty good cookies. But I'd never made sourdough bread or donuts. It seemed complicated.

As if he'd read my mind, Jasper opened the refrigerator door and said, "Now, about that sourdough. Your uncle has three jars of sourdough starter in here. You have to feed it regularly with new flour to keep it going. I've been feeding it every day since he passed away. But this is your family sourdough starter—and it's been kept going for over a hundred years."

I put my hand over my mouth. "A hundred years?"

"Yes, indeed. In fact, it's probably longer since it was started during the gold rush days."

"Is that safe to eat? I mean, anything fermenting for a hundred years seems like it would be pretty nasty."

Jasper let out a loud guffaw. "It's perfectly safe! In fact, the older it is, the better the bread tastes. Do you know how to bake bread?"

I shrugged. "I've made a few loaves in my lifetime. But I don't consider myself to be an expert by any means."

"Have you made *sourdough* bread?" Jasper asked.

"No. Not yet. But I suppose I will be doing just that if I want to keep up the family tradition." I wondered why my mom and dad had never talked about this. Or why they'd barely mentioned growing up in Alaska at all.

"I'll send Jade over to show you how to make bread after you've settled in."

"Jade?" I asked.

"That's my wife. She's an amazing baker."

"Jasper and Jade?" I gave him a quizzical look. "Aren't those two kinds of stone?"

He laughed. "Go figure I'd find a girl who complements me perfectly—even our names go together."

I smiled. I liked Jasper. It was a relief to talk to someone friendly after that Soapy Smith character came across so brash and mean.

"Now that you've seen your café, I'll take you out back to your house. Your uncle had just moved in, so it's furnished and equipped. I think you'll find it quite comfortable and cozy."

I followed him out the back door of the café.

The summer breeze had blown in the scent of flowers, earth, and a hint of ocean. I noticed bright pink flowers growing on the hillside behind the row of houses. "What are those?" I pointed toward them.

"Oh, that's fireweed," Jasper said. "Makes great honey. There's a local beekeeper who lives in the hills. He's going to sell his honey to a couple of shops here once we get things up and running."

"That sounds great." I followed Jasper to a two-story red house with white trim. The red paint matched the color of the café. It had a cute front porch and flower boxes in the windows.

"This is your house now." Jasper took the key ring from me and pointed to the key that had "Homestead" engraved on it. He stuck the key in the lock, twisted the knob, and handed the key ring back to me. "After you."

I stepped through the door and into a bright kitchen. Strange that the kitchen would be the entry. But I was immediately taken with the cheery room. There was a bench on the left side where you could sit and take off your muddy shoes. Coat hooks were nailed to the little stub wall to the side of the bench.

"The bench opens up," Jasper said. He opened the hinged lid. "You can put dirty boots or gloves and hats in here when the weather turns."

"Clever." I stepped further into the kitchen. The walls were painted a light yellow and the countertops were white marble. "Nice," I said, running my finger along the white farm-style sink.

"Roy spared no expense on the homes here. He wanted everyone to feel like the houses were homes—not just a place to live during the summer. He was hoping that folks would stay and live here, even during the off-season."

So far, what Jasper had said about my uncle made me think he was a decent man. I felt a twinge of disappointment that he'd died before I'd gotten to know him.

"Well, I plan on staying." I surprised myself with this unexpected declaration. Was I really planning to stay?

"Good!" Jasper grinned. He walked over to a little rectangular table against the wall in the kitchen. A thick binder was on the table, and he picked it up and handed it to me. "These are Roy's plans for the town. You'll notice it's very detailed and well thought out."

I flipped it open to the first page and read, "Gold Rush, Alaska. A historical gold mining town originally established in 1898."

"That's right," Jasper said. "Toward the end of the Klondike gold rush in Canada when the gold discoveries dwindled, adventurous souls desperate to strike it rich came into this part of Alaska to find their fortune. Of course, there were other gold strikes across the state, including Nome and Kodiak, but this one here was lesser known."

"Did they find much gold here?" I asked, flipping to the next page.

"Yes, they did." Jasper pulled out one of the chairs at the table and sat. "Have a seat. I need to take a load off. I'm no spring chicken."

I smiled and followed suit. Despite his white hair and blue eyes, his skin was nearly wrinkle free. Perhaps living in Alaska was kinder to the skin than living in hot climates. Most people his age in California either had skin that looked like tanned leather, or they were injected so full of Botox, they couldn't smile or frown.

Jasper continued. "At first, there was a big gold strike and the town boomed, just like Dawson City in Canada. But then it all seemed to dry up. Only a few people hit it big."

"And they all left the town after that?" I asked.

Jasper nodded. "Not all at once. Some held on for a little while, but when there was no way of making a living, they left."

"Interesting." I flipped open the binder to a page. It was a list of the businesses in town. There was a checkmark next to about half of them. "What do the checkmarks mean?" I pointed to the list.

Jasper peered at the page. "Oh. Those are businesses that already have people running them. Roy was in the process of getting more entrepreneurs to sign on."

My heart sank. "Does that mean that I will have to find people to run those businesses now?"

Jasper gave me a sympathetic smile. "Yes, my dear. But don't worry, if you flip to the next page, you'll see that your uncle already had drafted a list of contacts that he'd been wooing to do just that."

A tiny ray of hope parted my gloom. 'Oh, good. Because I don't know anyone in Alaska. I don't have a single contact here."

Jasper grinned. "You have me!"

I laughed. "I do. Thank you for being my first Alaskan friend."

Jasper pushed back from the table and stood. "My pleasure. Why don't you pull your camper up into the driveway? Roy was planning on buying one of those himself. You'll notice that your side yard has a nice big parking pad." He pointed out the window. "You might consider getting an SUV too. More manageable for getting around, especially in the winter."

I frowned. "You're right. I hadn't thought of that. But where can you buy a vehicle around here?"

"Talk to Denny Harris over at the Miners' Mercantile. He can order a vehicle in Anchorage for you. They'll deliver."

"Won't that cost a lot of money?" I asked. I still had some money left over from Uncle Roy's estate, but I was hoping to save that in case of an emergency.

He nodded. "Yep. There aren't many other options unless you want to drive your camper down there yourself. Guess you could trade it in for an SUV, but I can't guarantee they'll give you a good price for it."

I thought for a moment. "No, you're right. I just bought the camper. I think I'll hold onto it for a while." Internally, I wrestled with the idea of staying in Alaska. If I decided to leave, I might need the camper to get back to California.

"Well, I better head back to city hall. I'll send my wife over later to show you how to make sourdough bread." He stepped onto the porch.

"Wait," I called after him. "How am I going to meet the other people living here?"

He looked over his shoulder as he made his way across the road. "Oh, they're more curious than a brown bear in springtime. They'll find you and pester you with all kinds of questions and chatter."

I laughed. "Okay. Thanks, Jasper." I watched him cross the alley, then slip between the café and the building next to it. He stopped on the sidewalk and then strode across the main road to city hall. "Nice guy," I said to myself.

Before I parked the camper, I wanted to tour my new place. Shaking my head, I still couldn't believe that I owned a house. And a town! Despite the fact that my dad didn't get along with his older brother, I couldn't help but feel grateful to Uncle Roy. He'd left me an incredible opportunity to start life fresh. I had a roof over my head and a tourist town to run. I would be using my master's degree in business after all.

I couldn't wait to see what other exciting things awaited me.

CHAPTER 3

I walked from the kitchen of my new home through to the living room. It was a cozy space, with wood floors and a stone fireplace on the back wall. A plush sectional couch was pushed up against the left wall. The right wall was adorned with a flat screen television with a bookcase below it.

"Nice," I said, fingering the books. Most of them were about Alaska, the gold mining industry, ghost towns, and Alaskan cookbooks. I slid one of the larger books off the shelf. It was a book of poetry by Robert Service. Flipping it open, I noticed the poems were all about Alaska. I didn't love poetry, but maybe his poems would give me a sense of what this state was about.

I wandered out of the living room and into a large master bedroom. It too had a fireplace, though this one was a freestanding pellet stove. I wondered if Roy had been worried about losing power and heat in the winter.

The bedroom was hued in earth tones—a little too masculine for me. The bed was king-sized. I'd never had a bed this large! My apartment in Los Angeles was on the smaller side. I'd had a full-sized bed there, and it seemed like a luxury at the time.

There was a master bathroom with a large claw-footed tub and even a shower stall in the corner. That was good. I figured quick showers were perfect for the summer months, but nice hot baths in the winter sounded comforting. The best of both worlds.

Next to the master bedroom was a guest room furnished with a queen-sized bed but nothing else. The walls were bare, and I could tell my uncle hadn't put much thought into furnishing it.

I left the bedroom to discover a small cleaning closet and then a large pantry near the kitchen, not yet stocked with food. There was only a box of stale cereal and a hodgepodge of canned goods. It didn't seem like there was much to eat. Had Roy eaten elsewhere or had someone else helped themselves to his pantry after he'd passed away?

"No. That's unlikely," I said out loud. Regardless, I'd have to go shopping for food soon. Was the Mercantile the place to buy food? Or did I have to drive to a larger town nearby for that?

I went up a narrow staircase and discovered a loft upstairs. The room was equipped with a desk, a file cabinet, and a cushy office chair. There was also a bookshelf and two comfortable armchairs situated by a large window that faced the back yard. "This will be a nice place to work in the evenings."

Again, the décor was too masculine for me in only muted earth tones, but I could easily change that.

I looked out the back window and was dismayed to see only a dirt yard with a fence around it. There was no patio or deck, no grass or flowers. Just dirt. "Uncle Roy must not have had time to do anything with the yard before he died." I gazed out beyond the yard at the brownish foothills. A few trees poked up from the low brush. The mountains beyond were shrouded in clouds.

Thinking of Uncle Roy's death made me sad again. How unfortunate that he hadn't lived to see the town grow. I guess it was left to me to make that happen.

Now that I'd seen the house, I went outside and stood on the front porch. I watched the back door of one business open, and a man appeared. He hauled a bag of garbage to a heavy dumpster and tossed it in, making sure the lid was snug before he went back in. Was that Soapy Smith? He hadn't been wearing his buckskin jacket or his cowboy hat, but I could easily see that dark handlebar mustache and ruddy skin.

Just before the door closed behind him, his gaze caught mine, and he glared hard at me.

Did he really think this town belonged to him? I made a mental note to call Uncle Roy's lawyer to find out more.

I walked around the corner and crossed the main road to Bessie. I climbed in and drove through the rest of town. Again, I drove slowly and noticed a hardware store, hair salon, theatre, pharmacy, and bookstore. I'd missed identifying a few others as I turned Bessie around and navigated to the cross street called Skookum Jim Road that my home was on. I parked her on the large concrete slab Roy had installed alongside the house.

"There. Home sweet home." It was then I realized that I'd been talking to myself an awful lot lately. The solitude was getting a bit much for this city girl. I was used to being around people all the time. There hadn't been any time or space to really be by myself in L.A.

A faint chill tickled the back of my neck as I stood on the porch and unlocked the door. Perhaps it never truly warmed up in the summers here.

I went inside the house, sat down at the table, and texted Mags. "I made it to Gold Rush. I have my own house! It's cute. Come visit."

"Thank God!" Mags texted back. "I'm in the middle of something at work. I'll call you tonight. Send me pics!"

I touched the thumbs up emoji and put the phone down on the table. I looked around the kitchen. "Now what?"

My stomach growled. "I wonder if there's a good place to eat in this town?" I grabbed Roy's binder on the table and flipped to the page that listed the existing businesses. My index finger followed down the list until it stopped on Eureka. It served hearty frontier food, whatever that was. "I hope they're open."

Each business had a number in parenthesis which corresponded to a map. Eureka was number fifteen. It was next to city hall. I must've just missed it.

I grabbed my purse and made my way back to the main street. I opened the door of Eureka and stepped inside. The restaurant was cozy with dark, rustic barn wood floors. The six tables I counted were also rustic to match. The one in the back was a large table with seating for twelve, while the other tables were set for four people.

No one was in the restaurant from what I could tell. My stomach churned, thinking about how hard it would be to draw business here—especially when I knew nothing about this state or its inhabitants. Would I be able to make this town thrive, or would it end up being a very expensive ghost town?

The doors to the kitchen swung open and a woman wearing Levi's, a western-style shirt, and hiking boots stepped into the dining area. Her eyebrows rose in surprise. "Oh! I didn't hear you come in. Sorry about that." She smiled. Her long brown hair hung in a side braid over one shoulder. She looked to be younger than me—maybe in her early twenties.

"Go ahead and sit wherever you want. It's not like there's a crowd here. I'm Missy, by the way." She stuck her hand out.

"Denali." I shook it and smiled at her. I sat at the table closest to the window so I could look to see if there was anything happening outside. Anything at all. Things seemed a little dead in this town. "How long have you been open?"

She took out a pad of paper and a pencil from the apron at her waist. "This is our first day, actually. We were supposed to have a grand opening, but then the man who built up the town suddenly died."

I nodded thoughtfully. "Yes, that was my uncle."

She gasped. "Roy Dahlgren was your uncle? I thought he didn't have a family."

"That's what everyone tells me." I chewed my lip. "I was his only living family member. But I didn't even know about him until his lawyer contacted me after he died."

"Oh my God! That's crazy. What are you going to do? Are you going to run the town with Soapy?"

"The cranky guy in the buckskin jacket?" I fidgeted in my chair. "I hope not. He doesn't seem to want me here."

"Missy! Who are you talkin' to out there?" A man's voice called from the kitchen. "Do we have a customer?"

She jumped up. "Yeah! I'm taking her order!" Her cheeks turned a rosy red. "Sorry. I got caught up in your story." She handed me a menu.

"No problem." The menu was a one-pager with appetizers and entrees on the front page and sides, desserts, and beverages on the back page. My eyes widened as I read some of the more interesting fare. "Braised moose with Yukon gold mashed potatoes and gravy?"

Missy licked her lips. "Yeah, that's delicious."

I made a face. "Seriously?"

She gave me a blank look. "You don't like moose?"

"Um, I've never tried it. I'll have the salmon with roasted potatoes and broccoli."

Missy shrugged. "That's yummy too. What would you like to drink?"

"Do you have Mojitos?"

She wrinkled her nose. "Mosquitoes?"

I returned her confused stare. "Yeah, you know, it's got white rum, crushed fresh mint leaves, and lime juice?"

"That sounds refreshing. But we don't serve that here."

Geez. Between the entrees and the drinks, I was getting tired of conversation in which I didn't understand what she said, and she didn't understand what I said. I looked back down at the menu. "I'll have a glass of white wine, I guess."

She nodded, jotting something down in her binder. "Riesling, Chardonnay, or Pinot Grigio?"

"Pinot Grigio, please."

"Coming right up!" She dashed into the kitchen.

I sighed. I was feeling like a fish out of water here. For a hot second, I thought Missy could be my second first friend in Gold Rush. But I didn't seem to "get" her. Maybe that would all change in time. Friendship wasn't one of those things you could rush.

While I waited, I thought about running this resurrected town. The summer tourist season was just starting. The realization that I could go into ruin if I couldn't bring in enough money to make this place financially viable was terrifying. How could I live on nothing? I really needed to dig into Uncle Roy's books. Where did he get the money to rebuild this town anyway? He must've had a huge amount of cash to do it. Unless he got loans? The many questions spinning in my head nearly made me lose my appetite.

But when Missy came out carrying a hot plate with grilled salmon, potatoes, and vegetables, my stomach convinced me that I was still famished.

She set a glass of cold white wine in front of me. "Here you go. Do you need anything else?"

"Water would be nice, thank you."

"Got it." She hurried off.

I sipped the wine. It wasn't bad. Nice and crisp, just like I liked it. But the first bite of salmon sent me straight to heaven. It was so light and buttery, it nearly melted in my mouth. It was nothing like the salmon I'd ordered from bougie restaurants at home. It was a million times better. The potatoes, too, were beyond delicious. I felt myself plunging into a bath of sensory and olfactory bliss. Even the broccoli was divine.

Missy appeared with a glass of ice water. "How's everything tasting?"

"To die for," I said through a mouthful of food.

Missy smiled. "I'll be sure to tell the chef. Need anything else?"

"Nope. I'm good, thanks."

She sauntered back into the kitchen, and I dug into my meal.

The door opened and a guy walked in. He was wearing jeans and a red flannel shirt. He was tan and his cheeks were rosy from the fresh air. His wavy, wheat-colored hair gave him that tousled "I just came in from the outdoors" look.

Missy came out of the kitchen wiping her hands on her apron. "Paxson! What brings you back here? I thought you were flying a customer to Anchorage today."

"Oh, hey, Missy," he said casually. "The guy canceled at the last minute. He had a doctor's appointment, but then the doc got sick. He's rescheduled for next week."

"That's too bad." She sidled up to him. "Want your food for here or to go?"

I noticed her demeanor had changed. She was totally flirting with him. Heck, I didn't blame her. He was hot. Though, she was way too young for him. He was more my age.

"For here," he said. Paxson suddenly noticed me sitting by the window. He smiled. "I haven't met you before, have I?"

I shook my head. "Nope."

"You here for a visit or are you running one of the new businesses?" He walked over to my table. "Mind if I join you?"

"Not at all. Please do." I could feel my cheeks warming. It wasn't every day that a handsome stranger came and sat at my table. I stuck my hand out and shook his. "I'm Denali Dahlgren. I'll be running the Midnight Sun Café."

He stared at me. "Dahlgren? As in Roy Dahlgren?"

"That's right. I'm his niece."

"Holy cow," he said. "Does Soapy know you're here?"

I winced. "Yes. I had the misfortune of meeting him at city hall earlier. He didn't think Roy had any family and he seemed to be pretty angry at me."

Paxson leaned back in his chair. "I'll bet. He thought this town was all his to run. Now it looks like he's getting a partner he hadn't bargained for."

This Soapy Smith thing was really starting to irritate me. "See—that's just the thing. When I talked to my uncle's lawyer, he didn't say anything about Soapy Smith. The will says the town and everything in it was left to me."

Paxson raised an eyebrow. "You've got to be kidding. I thought Roy and Soapy had joint ownership—though, now that you mention it, I don't think Soapy has put a dime of his own money into developing this town. Figures he would want to reap the rewards of your uncle's hard work and grab it all for himself."

This was getting more interesting by the minute. "So, Soapy thought he was going to just take over and get everything Roy left behind?"

Paxson shrugged. "Yep. And he made sure that everyone knew it."

Missy came back. "I see you two have met." She gave me a nervous smile.

Was she afraid that she'd lose Paxson's affection to the new girl in town?

"What can I get you, Paxson?"

He glanced at the remaining food on my plate. "I'll have what she's having. But instead of wine, I'd like a beer. Thanks, Missy." He smiled at her, and she blushed.

"You want the Alaskan Amber?" Missy asked him.

"That would be great."

She turned to me. "Are you all finished with your meal?" Missy eyed my mostly cleaned plate. "Care for some dessert?"

I was pleasantly full, but I still had room for something sweet. "What do you have?"

"We've got mud pie, Alaskan wild berry cobbler with vanilla ice cream, and cheesecake with blueberries."

I tried not to drool. "The Alaskan wild berry cobbler sounds divine."

"You'll love it," Missy said. "Good choice." She took my plate and looked over her shoulder as she headed toward the kitchen. "Care for some more wine or maybe some coffee to go with your dessert?"

"Decaf would be great," I said.

Paxson smiled at me. "Where are you from, Denali? You don't seem to be from these parts."

I self-consciously ran my fingers through the ends of my blonde ponytail, still highlighted from the sun. "Los Angeles."

"Nice place. A little too busy and populated for me, but I've enjoyed my visits there."

"Oh? What part have you visited?" I asked.

"Disneyland—when I was a kid. My mom and dad took me there for my tenth birthday. Then I traveled down a few years ago to pick up a new bush plane."

"You flew it all the way up to Alaska from California?"

"Sure," he said. "Of course, I stopped in a couple cities on the way to rest and get fuel."

"How long have you been a pilot?"

"About eight years, give or take. It's a great job, and I get to be my own boss."

Missy arrived with the cobbler and a cup of steaming hot coffee. "Here you go, hon."

The cobbler was baked to a light golden color. Juicy berries peeked out here and there, creating shades of pink and purple where the juices seeped into the dough. A small scoop of vanilla ice cream sat on top and melted into a pool of yumminess around the edges.

"That looks delicious, thank you!" Though I wanted to devour it, I held back. It would be rude to eat in front of Paxson. He hadn't yet gotten his meal.

"I'll be right back with your salmon, Paxson." Missy went back to the kitchen.

He leaned forward. "So, what are your plans for the town? Are you going to sell it and head back to California or stay here and run it?"

I sighed. "To be honest, I'm not sure." I took a sip of wine. "Before I got here, I thought I'd want to bide my time for a year or two and then sell it off. But I don't have a lot to go back to in California, except my best friend, Mags."

"No husband or boyfriend?" He glanced at my ring finger.

I felt a little flutter in my stomach. "Nope."

Did I imagine it, or did he seem pleased?

"Well, I think it would be nice if you stuck around, California girl."

That seemed like a line, but he said it with such sincerity, I kind of believed him.

"We'll see." I smiled.

The door pushed open. A tall, dark-haired woman stepped inside with such force, I thought she was going to pull a gun. The sneer on her face looked a little familiar.

"Well, well, well," the woman said. "What do we have here?"

An older, mousy woman came through the door next, and stood by the younger woman's side. Her face was expressionless, and I wondered who she was.

The younger woman's ruddy skin bloomed with anger. She would've been pretty had she not had the expression of loathing distorting her features.

Paxson sighed. "Hello, Tiffany. Hello, Adina."

Tiffany barely gave him a second glance. Instead, her laser focus cut into me like a hot knife. "So, you're the faker who says she's Roy Dahlgren's niece? Ha!" She pointed at me with a long finger. "You think you can just waltz in here and run this town when my father put his blood, sweat, and tears into this place?"

"Tiffany, dear. Let's not be so accusatory," the mousy woman, Adina, said.

"Wait." Shocked, I stared at the younger woman. "Your father?"

"Cool it, Tiffany." Paxson stood. "Denali—this is Tiffany Smith—Soapy's daughter. And her mother, Adina."

The realization hit me, and I frowned. "Look, I'm not here to cause trouble. I'm here because Uncle Roy named me in his will."

Tiffany's brown eyes had turned black with anger. "That's BS and you know it! Roy didn't have a family. You're just a gold digger."

Adina remained quiet.

I could see that no matter what I said, Tiffany wasn't going to listen to reason. "I'm sorry you feel that way. You'll have to talk to my lawyer if you want to learn the truth."

"You little—" Tiffany reached out to slap me, but Paxson put himself between us. "Stop it, Tiffany. If Denali says she's Roy's niece, then she's Roy's niece. Now back off and leave her alone."

I could practically see the steam rising from her head. To my relief, she spun around and shoved her way through the door. As it was closing behind her, she shrieked, "We'll just see who owns this town, you poser!"

Her mother, still quiet, opened the door and followed after her daughter.

I put my hand over my heart. "Wow. Is Tiffany always like that?"

Paxson sat and blew out a breath. "Only when she doesn't get her way."

"Is that often?" I asked.

"Not often enough, if you ask me." He leaned back in his chair. "Forget about her. She's all bark and no bite. Most of the time, anyway."

I laughed. "Geez. I'll try to stay out of her way, though that might be hard, given that this town is so small."

We finished our meal and left the restaurant together. Standing on the boardwalk, I was suddenly at a loss for words. It felt like the end of a first date where neither person knew what to do. Hug? Shake hands?

Paxson cleared his throat. "See you around?"

"For sure. Um, thanks for having dinner with me. I'm really glad we had a chance to talk." I stepped off the boardwalk and headed across the street. I turned and said, "Have a nice evening!"

"Likewise!" he called as he headed down the boardwalk.

I watched him walk away and wondered if he lived in Gold Rush or if he only came here to deliver clients and other goods in his airplane.

I needed to get back to the house so I could text Mags. I had to fill her in on everything that had just happened.

CHAPTER 4

"Whoa," Mags said. "Your new town sounds almost as dramatic as some of the soap operas they film here."

The sight of Mags on my laptop screen nearly made my eyes mist over. I desperately wanted to see her friendly face in person and to give her a hug. Her long black hair was perfectly styled in loose waves, framing her heart-shaped face. And, as always, she looked glamorous wearing a gorgeous red silk blouse and gold hoop earrings.

I sighed. "I really wasn't expecting to be verbally and almost physically attacked by some crazy lady on my first day here. Geez."

"I'll buy you a ticket home if you want to escape," Mags teased. Her dark eyes twinkled with amusement. "But I'd rather fly up there to kick that Tiffany chick's behind."

Laughing, I brushed a loose strand of hair off my cheek. In comparison, I looked disheveled from my long trip in the camper. My blond hair had partially escaped the messy ponytail it was in, and I was still wearing my driving uniform—a tank top and a pair of old shorts.

"I wish you would fly up here," I said. "You can live with me or in any of the unoccupied houses—your pick."

Mags paused, considering my offer. "I've always wanted to live in a house instead of a condo. And I do miss having my best friend around."

A spark of hope leaped in my heart. "You're really considering it?"

She bit her lip. "I don't know. Things are going well at work right now. But I did hear a rumor that a merger might be coming. That's never good for job stability."

I tried to act upset by the news, despite the fact I secretly hoped for the merger to go through.

"Well, it's something to think about." she smiled. "If I get laid off, I could at least come up for the summer and help in your café."

"I'll pay you a decent salary." I grinned, feeling more hopeful than I had in weeks.

She giggled. "I don't think you could match the salary I get at Modical."

Mags was a project manager for a company who'd developed state-of-the-art software for the fashion industry. It was the latest tech, allowing customers to upload full-body photos of themselves. When the customer picked out clothing, they could see what it would look like on them before pressing the buy button. It was pure genius.

"I don't think Modical would let you go. Or would they?"

She shrugged. "You just never know. No job is forever."

I leaned back. "You have such a great attitude about things. Does anything ever get you down?"

"Just my best friend leaving me." She grinned. "Now, tell me more about this town. When do you think you can get the café up and running?"

I thought about all the tables and chairs I'd have to assemble—not to mention figuring out how to use the espresso machines and make baked goods. "I have no idea. I really need to look into hiring people to help me get started."

"You said your uncle has a binder with tons of info in it. Did he have a list of possible employees?"

"I haven't had a chance to go through it yet. I'll definitely take a look."

She smiled. "Good. Hey, I have to go. Got a hot date tonight."

My mouth fell open. "With whom? You haven't mentioned anyone to me!"

"His name is Rad."

I stared at her.

"I know, I know," she laughed. "He's a stunt man. And he actually lives up to his name! He's taking me to the premiere of his new action flick. Exciting, right?"

"So jealous!" I put my hand over my heart. "But I hope you have a great time. Call me tomorrow and let me know how it went. I need to tell you more about this guy I met today, too. He's a pilot."

"Sexy," she said. "Pilots are hot."

"He is very handsome. I hope he doesn't have a girlfriend." Thinking about Paxson made my stomach flutter a little. Or was that just the excess food I'd consumed?

She waved her hand. "Even if he does, he'll dump her for you. You're a catch!"

"You're good for my ego, Mags. Have a good time on your date."

We ended the video chat, and I closed my laptop. It was time for me to study Uncle Roy's binder.

• • • • • • • • • •

I sat in the recliner near the fireplace with the binder in my lap. I'd read through countless pages already. So far, I'd memorized each and every existing business name and learned of my uncle's ideas to fill the vacant shops.

The most helpful section was on the Midnight Sun Café, which I would be opening soon. There was a list of equipment and furniture he'd ordered, plus a menu he'd planned with all the recipes. Suddenly, I felt a little better knowing that I'd have some guidance to get me started. I was pleased to see my uncle's instructions for keeping the sourdough starter alive as well.

Tomorrow, I'd have to practice using the espresso machines.

As I flipped through a few more pages, a note fluttered out and fell to the floor. I bent to pick it up.

It said:

"Roy, please sign the contract and return it via certified mail by June 15th. Mark."

I frowned. "What contract?" I paged through the binder and found the section on signed leases and equipment invoices. But there was nothing that indicated which contract needed to be signed. It was only the beginning of June. I hoped I'd find whatever Mark, whoever that was, wanted signed. Wait. Mark. Wasn't that the name of Uncle Roy's lawyer? I made a mental note to call him in the morning. I needed to talk to him anyway.

A knock on the door startled me. "Who could that be?" I made my way to the door and cautiously opened it a crack. An older woman with her graying hair pulled into a ponytail stood on the porch holding a basket. She was wearing a periwinkle shirt, a purple fleece vest, and a pair of old jeans.

I opened the door wider. "Hi. Can I help you?"

The lady smiled, her blue eyes twinkling. "Hello! You must be Denali, Roy's niece. I've brought you a basket of goodies to welcome you to Gold Rush." She held the basket out, and I took it out of her arms.

"Well, thank you so much!" I was so surprised, I almost forgot to invite her in. Then I remembered my manners. "Won't you come in?"

She stepped past me into the kitchen. "Thank you."

Once I closed the door behind us, she said, "I'm Jade, Jasper's wife. He said you might need a little help in the kitchen. I'm happy to help you get set up. Do you know how to make pastries and the like?"

I swallowed hard. "No. I'm a little worried about that, to be honest."

Jade laughed. "Nothing to worry about. You seem like a smart girl. I'm sure you're a quick study. She pointed at the basket. "In fact, I helped Roy flesh out the menu for your café and came up with the recipes as well. You'll find a good selection of pastries that match some of the recipes in there. Plus, I included a loaf of sourdough bread, a jar of honey from our local beekeeper, and some salmonberry jam."

I blinked. "Wow. Thank you. You don't know how relieved I am to have some help."

She waved my comment off. "No need to thank me. Since Jasper is busy at city hall, I need something to keep me occupied before we open The Bunkhouse."

A sudden inspiration struck me. "Jade, would you like a job at the café? I could sure use some help in the kitchen—

especially from someone who knows what they're doing."

Jade cocked her head to one side and looked up at the ceiling as she thought things through. "Jasper might kill me if I leave him to run The Bunkhouse all alone. But I'd be happy to work here in the early mornings to help with the baking and the first wave of customers."

I grinned and shook her hand. "It's a deal then. I'll draft a hiring contract, and I'll look into employment benefits as well."

Jade seemed surprised. "You know how to do all that?"

"Sure," I said. "I was about to start a new business down in California...but then my partner took off with my money and left town."

"Oh, dear." Jade frowned. "That's awful. Sorry to hear that."

I shrugged. "I'm considering it a life lesson. Don't go into business with someone until you know for sure they are honest."

"Indeed." Jade turned to walk out the door. She glanced over her shoulder. "I'll come by the café tomorrow. What time would you like me to come by?"

"How about eight o'clock?"

"I'll be there!" Jade waved and closed the door behind her.

Relief rushed through me. I had my first employee!

CHAPTER 5

Instead of going upstairs to the office, I sat at the dining table in the kitchen, and worked late into the evening. It was a pleasant place to work and close to the delicious food that Jade had brought over earlier.

I worked on getting an employment contract written up and researching benefit plans for full-time or part-time workers.

Uncle Roy's binder lay on the table next to my laptop, open to the page of possible employees. I was happy to see Jade's name on the list. He must not have approached her about a job before he died, since she hadn't mentioned it.

I yawned and rubbed my eyes. A cup of tea sounded soothing, so I went out to the camper to raid the cupboard.

Outside, the sun was still shining, though it was well past eleven o'clock. How did people sleep around here with the daylight reaching into the night?

The air smelled of alder trees, honey, and something else. Was that the fireweed that smelled so sweet?

I unlocked the camper door and found my tin of chamomile tea. I wasn't planning on staying up too late since I'd had a long day of driving, and I was tired from staring at my laptop screen.

The outside breeze had come in with me, and I shivered as I shut the door. I would have to get used to the cool evenings here.

Back inside the kitchen, I accidentally bumped the table, and Uncle Roy's binder fell to the floor with a thump.

It laid open to a section I hadn't yet explored. I bent to lift it and caught a glimpse of the title on the handwritten pages. "Journal."

Uncle Roy kept a journal in his binder?

I glanced around the room furtively, as if someone would catch me reading his private thoughts. Should I read it?

"Hmm," I said. "If he'd wanted this to be truly private, he would've kept a separate journal and stashed it away."

A draft from somewhere in the house fluttered the pages, and they flipped open to the last page. I sat down at the table and began reading the final entry.

May 20th

Tiffany is coming around the café a lot more. What is she up to? This morning, she brought me a delicious scone. I told her I was on a diet, but when she left, I couldn't resist eating it. Delicious! But why is she suddenly being nice to me?

What a strange entry! Uncle Roy seemed to think that Tiffany had been up to something. She was a spoiled brat from what I could tell. But I supposed she couldn't help it with a father who was equally temperamental and rude.

I read the entry from the previous day.

May 21st

Soapy came over while I was taking inventory of the boxes that just arrived. He keeps bugging me to sign the contract, which just makes me want to call the whole thing off. I hate the idea of going into business with him. He hasn't put any effort into building up this town. He just wants to run it.

So, that was the contract Uncle Roy's lawyer was talking about! Had Uncle Roy signed it, or had he decided not to?

I got up to fill the kettle with water and placed it on the stove. While it was heating, I put an alarm on my phone for the next morning to call the lawyer. Maybe he could tell me more.

When the tea was ready, I carried it up to the bedroom along with the notebook. Maybe I could stay awake long enough to read a few more journal entries.

Once I'd climbed into bed, I opened the binder and flipped through the pages. There was so much information to absorb, but I would start with my uncle's personal opinions about the town and its people.

After fifteen minutes, I rubbed my eyes. I'd read through a dozen of Uncle Roy's journal entries so far. He seemed like a very driven person. Most of the entries I'd read were about the various people who had signed on to live here and work in the shops.

He'd written plenty about how Soapy annoyed him. Why were they business partners in the first place? Uncle Roy had put his money into the town, and as far as I could tell, Soapy Smith hadn't put a penny into it. But he sure seemed like a control freak. Tiffany, his daughter, seemed to fit the whole "apple doesn't fall far from the tree" adage.

Yawning, I set the binder on the nightstand. I clicked off the light and fell asleep.

• • • ◆ • ◆ • ◆ • • •

My alarm woke me at seven o'clock. I hurried to shower and get dressed. I had a quick meal of the delicious sourdough bread and honey from Jade before walking to the Midnight Sun Café. There was so much work to do, and my heart thudded with anticipation, nerves, and excitement.

I unlocked the door of the café and went inside. The atmosphere was still—like the place was holding its breath in expectance. Was it waiting for me to breathe life into it? I turned slowly in a circle, staring at the emptiness. I closed my eyes and pictured people sitting at tables, meeting for coffee and treats, laughing and enjoying each other's company. I could almost smell the scent of sourdough bread and other baked goods—and the aroma of freshly brewed coffee.

I smiled. Yes. This place was a possibility just waiting to happen. And I would make it so. Humming to myself, I went into the kitchen to get started.

Surveying the many boxes piled high on the kitchen floor, I decided those needed to be dealt with first. Luckily,

Uncle Roy had left a toolbox on one of the countertops. I opened it and took out a box cutter and a screwdriver.

I'd taken my uncle's binder along, and now I opened it to the seating chart he'd drawn up for the layout of the tables. I remembered seeing it the day before and was again thankful for his thorough planning and foresight.

"I'll start with the corner table by the window," I said out loud. That was a table for four. I hoped I could handle putting it together myself.

"Need some help?" a woman's voice said from behind me.

I whirled around, my hand over my heart. "Oh! Jade. I didn't hear you come in."

She winked. "You left the front door open. I thought you might be here early and could use a hand." This morning, she was wearing a blue T-shirt that matched her eyes and the same pair of faded jeans she'd worn the day before. She'd come ready to work and to get dirty, I assumed.

"Thanks! I sure could. Maybe you could help me assemble these tables."

"Absolutely."

We located a box that held one of the four-person tables, opened it, and began to attach the legs to the tabletop.

"Hello?" a man's deep voice called from the front of the café.

I got up and brushed the dust off my hands. "I'll be right back," I said. I left the kitchen and walked to the main room.

The state trooper who'd helped push Bessie to the gas station tipped his hat to me. "Good morning, Miss Dahlgren."

"Oh, hello. Trooper Jones." I smiled. "What brings you here? We aren't actually open for business yet."

"I know. I'm here regarding your uncle."

I raised my eyebrows. "My uncle?"

"Roy Dahlgren." His tone was cool and even.

"What about him?" I asked.

"After his death, which we assumed was a heart attack, I had Roy's body taken to Anchorage for an autopsy. It struck me as odd that Roy hadn't had any medical problems before. He was an active man."

"Oh, I..." I was at a loss for words. Uncle Roy's lawyer hadn't mentioned anything about an autopsy. But perhaps he didn't know, given that the police had taken it upon themselves to do this.

"I can tell what you're thinking," Trooper Jones said, his brown eyes boring into mine. "You're wondering what took the autopsy so long."

"Actually, I was thinking that no one told me about the autopsy," I said, crossing my arms.

"At the time, Miss Dahlgren, I didn't know that Roy had any family. Otherwise, you would've been told, of course." The trooper took his hat off and held it at his side.

I couldn't help but notice that he had nice hair—a little smooshed from his silly looking trooper hat, but nice. It was dark brown, short on the sides, and a little longer on top. He was definitely a striking man, with his broad shoulders and straight posture.

"Anyway," he said, "things move slowly up here. I just received this today and thought I should come in person to talk with you."

I uncrossed my arms. "Is that the autopsy report?" I pointed to the folder he held in his hand.

He nodded. "It is. You should know that..." He hesitated a moment before he continued. "Your uncle did not die of a heart attack. Well, he did, but the cause of his heart attack was not natural. What caused it was...poison."

My mouth fell open. "Someone poisoned him?"

Trooper Jones nodded. "Yes. And it's likely that the killer lives right here in Gold Rush."

CHAPTER 6

If there'd been chairs set up in the dining area, I would've plunked right down in one. "Why would someone kill Uncle Roy?"

Trooper Jones took a step toward me, almost as if he meant to steady me on my shaky legs. "I don't know, Miss Dahlgren. But he was a man of power and wealth. That sometimes makes people a target." He paused a moment to reflect. "Though I'm guessing he sunk most of that wealth into having this ghost town rebuilt. I doubt there was much money left."

Wealth. How *did* Uncle Roy get the money to build this town? It must've taken hundreds of thousands—if not millions—to renovate the old buildings and bring electricity and a cell tower up here.

"Trooper Jones, do you happen to know where Uncle Roy got all his money?"

"Oh, yes. He inherited it from his mother and father. They passed away well over thirty years ago, from what my dad told me. But I'm sure you know that."

I frowned. "I didn't know my grandparents had money."

He gave me a curious look. "You didn't? It's common knowledge your grandpa's dad was one of the few who got rich from the gold rush. Didn't your parents tell you that? I'm assuming they themselves are wealthy."

Now I really needed to sit down. Growing up, we didn't have much money. Especially when I was little. We lived in a two-bedroom rental house in South Los Angeles. Later, both Mom and Dad got decent jobs, and we moved to a better neighborhood with better schools.

"My parents weren't wealthy at all," I said. "When they died in a car accident, there was just enough money for me to finish college and go to grad school. There wasn't anything more than that."

Trooper Jones seemed surprised. "Really? That's odd."

"Yes." I paused for a moment. "Yes, it is. I was planning on calling Uncle Roy's lawyer this morning. I'll ask him what he knows about that." I'd said this part out loud, though it was more of an internal musing. The revelation that my uncle had inherited a lot of money when my grandparents died, but my parents had nothing was startling.

Trooper Jones glanced around the empty restaurant. "Looks like you've got a lot of work to do. I'll leave you to it."

"Will you let me know if you find out any more information on who poisoned my uncle?" I asked as he turned to leave.

"Sure. Just—" he turned to make eye contact, "be careful. We don't know who did this. It could've been anybody. Don't trust anyone for now."

I blinked. "Okay."

He left and closed the front door behind him. I quickly crossed the room and locked both the knob and the deadbolt above it. I would have to be more aware and careful until the killer was arrested. *If* he was ever arrested.

On shaky legs, I made my way back to the kitchen and surprised Jade, who seemed to be eavesdropping behind the swinging doors.

"Oh!" She put a hand to her heart. "You startled me!"

I eyed her. "How much did you hear?"

Her cheeks bloomed red. "Just the last part. I'm sorry for listening in. What was Trooper Jones saying about your uncle? Someone poisoned him?"

Remembering what he'd said about trusting no one, I hesitated, not sure how much I should say. I settled for, "That's right. Except, I don't know who would do such a thing."

Jade patted my arm and gave me a sad look. "Me neither. Your uncle was a decent man."

Was he? Now I was unsure. Why did Uncle Roy inherit my grandparents' money and my dad didn't? What had happened to cause such a rift in their relationship?

"How about we finish that table we started putting together?" Jade picked up the screwdriver and held it out to me.

"Good idea." It was better to do something productive rather than dwell on my uncle and dad's relationship. I would find out more later.

Jade and I put together the table in no time and carried it to its spot against the window in the dining area. In the next hour, we assembled six more tables and had placed them in their respective spots.

"Need a break?" I asked Jade. "I could use some caffeine to keep me going. I can run over to the house to make some and bring it back."

"Nonsense!" Jade said. "This is a café! We can make coffee right here."

I glanced at the fancy espresso machines on the countertop. "But I don't know how to use these yet."

"No better time to learn than now. I'll show you." She marched over to the machines and began to wipe down the nozzles.

I stood next to her and watched. "How did you learn to do this?"

"I worked in a coffeehouse in Palmer. In fact, I was the one who recommended which machines to buy for this place. Roy had never run a café before. He didn't know where to start. There's a bit of a learning curve with this equipment, but once you get started, you'll find it's really quite easy. Kind of like riding a bike—you learn it and you just go!"

She reached under the cabinet and pulled out a vacuum-sealed bag of coffee beans. "Now, let's get rolling."

• • • • • • • • • •

A half hour later, I'd made my very first decent latte. "Not bad." I licked the foam off my upper lip. For the first time, I felt that this was an actual café. The rich smell of coffee filled me with possibilities of what this place could be.

"You did great." Jade sipped her coffee and smiled. "Now that you've got the latte down, we'll tackle the Americano."

"Sounds good. But first, I have a call to make. Are you okay to start assembling the next table? I'll be back in a few minutes."

"Sure, sure." Jade waved me away. "Take your time. I've got this."

"Thanks!" I headed out the door and walked back to my cozy house. Once inside, I called Uncle Roy's lawyer. I had so many questions.

"Olmstead, Johnson, and Stern," a woman's voice on the other end said.

"Hello. My name is Denali Dahlgren. Is Mr. Olmstead in?" I asked.

"He just stepped into the office. May I ask what this is regarding?"

"My Uncle, Roy Dahlgren, was a client of Mr. Olmstead. I have questions about my uncle's will. May I speak with him?"

"I'll put you through," the woman said.

The phone rang a few times before he answered. "Mark Olmstead," he said curtly.

"Hi, Mr. Olmstead. This is Denali Dahlgren. Your client, Roy Dahlgren, was my uncle. I'm calling because I have some questions regarding his will."

"Oh, yes, Denali!" His voice took on a much friendlier tone. "I'm so sorry about your uncle. He was a great man and a good friend."

"Thank you. I have some questions, though. I found a letter from your office that said Roy was supposed to send a signed contract to you. But I think he passed away before he signed it. Can you tell me what it was all about?"

Mr. Olmstead cleared his throat. "Ah, yes. That's true. The contract was between Roy and his colleague Soapy Smith. It outlined the business relationship between the two men as partners. Roy would be sixty percent owner of the town and Soapy the other forty."

"Soapy was going to be part owner of the town?" I sat in one of the dining chairs.

"Yes, he was. But because Roy hadn't signed the contract before he passed away, it remained under his ownership alone. And therefore, it now belongs to you."

"Why did Uncle Roy want to sign over forty percent of his property to Soapy? From what I understand, Soapy hadn't contributed any money to rebuilding Gold Rush." I rubbed my eyes.

"Roy and I had long discussions about this topic," Mr. Olmstead said. "Soapy and Roy met when Roy began looking into the prospect of bringing the ghost town back to life. See, Soapy is what I could call a serial entrepreneur. He is in the habit of starting new businesses and then selling them after he gets the attention of investors."

"Does he make enough money to earn a living that way?" I asked.

Mr. Olmstead laughed. "Well, not really. Mostly because Soapy never follows through with anything. If he'd really been driven to be successful, he would get the businesses to the point of thriving before he sold them. He's too lazy for that and he has the attention span of a gnat."

"So why would Uncle Roy want to become business partners with him?"

"I suspect it was just a matter of Soapy wearing him down. That man is like a pit bull when he sees something he wants. Roy mentioned to me several times that he was wary of the deal, but Soapy would threaten him if he didn't agree to a partnership."

"What?" My interest was piqued. "He threatened Uncle Roy? How?" At this point, I was sure Mr. Olmstead didn't know that Uncle Roy hadn't passed away from a heart attack. He didn't know the actual cause of his death was murder.

"Roy didn't say much about it, to be honest. I personally believe Soapy knew something about your uncle that he thought he could use as leverage."

"Like blackmail?" I asked.

"Could be." The lawyer was silent for a moment.

"Mr. Olmstead," I said. "I just learned some disturbing news from a state trooper who drops into town once in a while. He told me that he'd arranged for an autopsy and Uncle Roy was poisoned, and that's what killed him."

"What?" The shock in his voice reverberated in my ear. "It wasn't a heart attack?"

"From what the trooper has told me, the poison stopped his heart. Roy was otherwise healthy with no history of heart problems. It was the poison that caused the heart attack."

"Oh, lord," the man whispered.

"Mr. Olmstead, did Soapy Smith know that Uncle Roy hadn't signed the contract?"

He groaned. "No. I think Soapy thought it was signed and that he was part owner. The contract also stated that if anything happened to either partner, the remaining partner would inherit the whole thing."

"Well, then," I said. "I think we know who killed my uncle."

CHAPTER 7

I took the card Trooper Jones had given me out of my pocket. I entered his number in my contacts list and tapped on the call button.

"Trooper Jones," he said.

"It's Denali Dahlgren. I have some information you might need in the investigation of my uncle's murder."

"All right." He paused. "What is it?"

"Apparently, Soapy Smith pressured Uncle Roy to become business partners. There was a contract that my uncle was supposed to sign, leaving him with sixty percent ownership of the town, and Soapy Smith with forty percent."

"Hmm," Trooper Jones said. "I find that hard to believe. Everyone knows Soapy Smith hasn't put any of his own money into developing Gold Rush."

"But listen, my uncle was supposed to sign this contract —but according to his attorney, he didn't. Soapy, however, believed the contract had been signed and mailed to the lawyer, Mark Olmstead. Here's the interesting part. The contract stated that if either partner died, the other partner would inherit the entire town."

Trooper Jones sucked in a breath. "Well, that is interesting. Looks like I'll be headed into town to question Soapy. Miss Dahlgren, don't speak a word of this to anyone else in Gold Rush. I don't want Soapy to catch wind of it. Rumors and gossip burn like wildfire in small towns."

"Got it. One other thing you should know. Jade overheard our conversation in the café. She knows about the poisoning."

"That's unfortunate. Tell her not to let that secret out," he said.

"I have. And I'll remind her again when I go back to the café."

"Good. Have you found that unsigned contract anywhere in your uncle's belongings?"

"No, not yet. But if I do, you'll be the first to know,"' I said.

"Great. Talk to you later." He hung up.

I stared out the kitchen window. What information did Soapy have about my uncle that would allow him to take forty percent of the town? Whatever it was, it had to be powerful enough to intimidate Uncle Roy into giving up almost half of what he'd worked hard for.

· · · ● · ● · ● · ·

Jade brushed her hands together as we finished assembling the last table. "That's that!"

"I can't believe we got this done in such a short time." I looked around the room in wonder. "It's actually starting to look like a real café."

"Now all you need is a mural on that wall." Jade pointed to the long wall without windows to the right.

"Hmm. A mural. That's a good idea. Do you know any artists who could paint one?"

"Well, there's Brenna Randall. She works in the library. Maybe she'd be willing to come over and paint the mural after the library closes at six o'clock." Jade grabbed a rag and washed down the counter.

"Has she done mural work before?" I asked.

"Oh, sure. She's real good. She's even painted a few in Anchorage."

I glanced at the time. "I might just head over to the library now. Feel free to take a break while I'm gone."

Jade nodded. "Will do. I'm going to whip up some sandwiches for Jasper and me. I'll be back at one-thirty."

I waited for Jade to leave before locking the door to the café. Now, which way was the library? I looked in both directions, then remembered it was a block or two past City Hall but on the same side of the street as my café.

I walked past an empty shop and then stopped in front of a store whose window had been decorated in hunting and camping gear. Soapy Smith's face suddenly appeared as he pushed a backpack into the display. He caught sight of me and stared daggers in my direction.

Not wanting to have another encounter with the jerk, I increased my pace and nearly ran the remaining two blocks. As I rounded the corner and turned into the entry of the library, I crashed headlong into someone, sending us both sprawling to the ground.

"Oh, my gosh! I'm so sorry!" I scrambled to my feet and reached out my hand to help the man up. "Are you okay?"

When he was standing, I realized who he was. "Paxson?" My cheeks bloomed red. Geez. Of all people I had to knock on their butt, did it have to be Paxson?

He brushed the dirt off his pants and his bright blue eyes twinkled in amusement. "Denali. Nice to see you again. Where are you off to in such a hurry?"

"I'm sorry. I wanted to talk to Brenna Randall about painting a mural in my café. Then when I passed Soapy's, store, he glared at me, and I—"

"Wanted to get as far away from him as fast as you could?" He chuckled. "I get it. Soapy can be very intimidating when he wants to be."

"That's an understatement." I sighed. "I don't know what I can do to make him like me."

Paxson shook his head. "Don't take it personally. Soapy doesn't like anybody. Except maybe his daughter Tiffany and his wife, Adina."

"I feel sorry for his wife," I said. I couldn't imagine being married to that brute.

"Don't feel sorry for her. She's not as passive as she seems."

"I guess they deserve each other, then." I glanced at the library, taking in the red siding and fresh white trim. "What a cute library! Is it one of the buildings that was here originally?"

He turned to follow my gaze. "Yes. But it was in a sad state before Roy started renovating the town. He hired an expert carpenter to restore it. Turned out great, didn't it?"

I nodded. Once again, I was reminded how much money Uncle Roy had put into this place.

"Well, I'll let you get back to what you were doing." He glanced at his phone. "I've got to fly Chuck Morrow out to his cabin in a half hour. I better get a move on."

"Oh, okay. I don't want to keep you." I hurried toward the library entrance.

"Hey, Denali!" Paxson called to me. "Are you free for dinner tonight? I should be back around six o'clock."

Surprised, I stammered, "Six o'clock. Yes. All right."

"I'll drop by your place to pick you up." He grinned and his dimples made my heart beat a little faster.

"Sounds good. I'll be ready." I turned to go but had a sudden thought. "Wait! Where are we going? What should I wear?"

"Just down to Sasquatch Saloon. This is Alaska. Just wear something comfortable—and preferably with long sleeves. The mosquitoes come out in the evening."

I shuddered at the thought of mosquitoes, but felt giddy at the prospect of having a date. "Got it. See you tonight."

Turning back to the library, I opened the door and peeked my head inside. The librarian's desk sat in the center of the room, but the chair was empty. Rows and rows of bookshelves hailed categories like "Alaskan History", "Romance", "Science Fiction", and many more. Inhaling the scent of books, I stepped inside and let my shoulders relax. Books were magical, and I couldn't wait to sign up for a library card.

Humming from behind a shelf made me turn to the right. The librarian was in here somewhere. The tune she hummed sounded familiar. Was that *Creep* by Radiohead? I followed the sound, humming along with her.

The humming stopped abruptly, and a petite young woman with a brown bob stepped out from a row of books. "Oh, hello! Were you just humming along with me?"

Smiling, I nodded. "I like Radiohead. They're on my playlist."

She returned my grin and pushed her tortoise-shell glasses up the bridge of her nose. "I'm Brenna Randall. And you are?"

"Denali Dahlgren." I hoped she didn't say what everyone else had said when I'd mentioned my last name. The old "Roy didn't have a family thing" was getting old.

Brenna stuck her hand out. "Nice to meet you, Denali. Are you in town visiting?"

"No." I glanced at the far wall, where a beautiful mural of mountain goats perched on the rocky side of a mountain brightened the room. "I'm getting ready to open the Midnight Sun Café. Jade told me you paint murals. Is that one yours?" I pointed at the goats.

She nodded. "Oh, cool. I'm glad we've got more people moving to town. It's a bit dead right now." Brenna turned to the goat mural. "I just painted this one last week. What kind of mural are you thinking about for the café?"

"Something midnight sun related?" I laughed. "I'm not sure. Or perhaps the northern lights?"

Brenna nodded. "I'll think of something cool. What's the vibe of the café?"

I bit my lip. "I haven't given it much thought yet. I guess I want something eclectic that reflects the people of Alaska —but I want it to feel current and kind of hip, too."

She raised her eyebrows. "I'm impressed. I like it!"

"Good. When can you start working on it?"

"Give me a couple of days to sketch up some ideas. Can I come by and show them to you when I've got something ready?"

"Sure. That's perfect. Just let me know how much I owe you."

"Great!" She smiled and motioned toward the bookshelves. "Feel free to browse and check out some books."

"I've got to get back to the café, but I'll be sure to drop by on a regular basis." I opened the door. "See you soon, Brenna. It was nice meeting you!"

I left with a feeling of hope. Brenna might become a good friend, and at least she was around my age. As I walked back to the café, I scurried past Soapy's store, hoping to avoid his piercing anger.

Instead of heading straight back to work, I swung by my house and made a sandwich for lunch. After I filled a glass of water from the sink, I opened the lower freezer drawer to see if Uncle Roy had an ice tray. He did. I reached to scoop out some ice and spotted something white underneath the metal scoop.

"What is this?" I lifted out a piece of paper. I carefully unfolded it and gasped. It was the missing contract.

CHAPTER 8

I stared at the contract and quickly read through it. It said just what his lawyer had told me—the town's ownership would be shared by Uncle Roy and Soapy Smith —a sixty/forty split. Again, I wondered why.

When I reached the signature line, I noticed Soapy's name confidently scrawled in black ink. Uncle Roy had *started* to sign. His first name was there, and the first letter of Dahlgren, but it abruptly stopped halfway through the letter A. Had he changed his mind? And why had he stuffed the contract into the freezer?

"Uncle Roy, I wish you were still alive so you could tell me what this means." A cold draft fluttered the edges of the paper. The little hairs on the back of my neck stood up. I stared as a shimmering form began to take shape before me.

Was that a—?

Footsteps on the front porch startled me even more than the apparition in the kitchen. I put my hand over my heart and took a deep breath.

The white shape that had begun to assemble disappeared in a poof.

Coming back to my senses, I yanked open the freezer drawer and shoved the paper back into the ice cube tray, shutting the drawer just as someone pounded on the door.

My hands shook as I turned the knob.

Soapy Smith stood on the front porch, his dark eyes boring holes into my skull. "Where is it?" he asked.

"Where is what?" I frowned. What was it with this guy? His bluster made my fear disappear, and now a red-hot anger bubbled in my veins.

"You know exactly what I'm talking about." He pushed his way into my kitchen. "What did you do with the contract? Roy said he signed it and sent it to his lawyer, but I just called the guy. He told me Roy never sent it."

I glared at him. He had some nerve. I'd had just about enough of his accusations and rude behavior. "Look, I don't know why Uncle Roy didn't send the contract. Maybe he changed his mind. Did you ever consider that?"

He stepped closer to me. I could smell his tobacco-laced breath, and my stomach churned.

"Listen here, missy. I'll bet you somehow convinced Roy to destroy that contract. You knew you'd inherit everything if your uncle kicked the bucket, didn't you?"

Anger welled up inside me. I took a step toward him and poked him in the chest with an index finger. "For your information, I didn't even know my uncle. In fact, the only reason I knew he existed is because his lawyer called me and told me he'd died. I have no idea why Uncle Roy would sign something that would give you forty percent of this town when everyone I've met so far has told me you've put *no money or work* into it yourself. How dare you come in here and accuse me of being greedy. I think we all know who the greedy person is, don't we?"

Soapy turned tomato-red. I could almost see the steam rising from his ears.

"Why you... you... I could throttle you!" He reached his hands out toward my throat.

I took a step back.

"Not so fast, Soapy." Jade boomed from behind him.

Soapy dropped his hands and whirled around.

Jade stood on the porch, her hands on her hips. "Just what do you think you're doing, threatening Denali?"

The air seemed to leak out of Soapy. "I wasn't threatening her."

"Oh, yeah?" Jade said. "What would you call it then? Harassment?"

Soapy narrowed his eyes at her. "Mind your own business, you old bat."

Jade shook her head. "Leave, Soapy. Or I'll call Trooper Jones."

His eyes shot daggers at the two of us. "Fine. But this isn't over. This town is rightfully mine, and I'll find a way to prove it."

I had no words. There was too much anger inside me to respond.

"I said, leave." Jade pulled out her phone. "Trooper Jones will be very interested to hear about your threats. He'll finally have reason to arrest you. You've been harassing folks without consequences for too long. It's about time the law puts a halt to it."

Soapy pushed Jade out of the way and stormed off.

"Thanks, Jade. I think he was about to hurt me." I watched him disappear into the back of his store.

"He's a bully, but I don't think he'd physically harm you. He's all bravado."

Jade hadn't seen the look of malice in his dark eyes. I was certain he would've hurt me if Jade hadn't interfered. Was he the person behind my uncle's death?

"Come on," Jade said. "Lock up and let's go to the café. Don't let that idiot get in the way of your work."

I nodded. "Go ahead without me. There's something I need to do. See you in a few minutes."

"All right," Jade said as she headed back to work.

After my call to the trooper to tell him I'd found the contract, thoughts of the partially-signed document niggled at me as I strode to the Midnight Sun Café. What had happened to cause Uncle Roy to change his mind about his partnership with Soapy?

• • • ● • ● • • • ·

Jade and I set up all the tables in the café and she'd even started teaching me how to make sourdough bread. Uncle Roy had left me the family recipe. With Jade's help, I baked my first loaf. It was the best thing I'd ever tasted.

"Let's call it a day," I told her. It was five o'clock, and I needed to get ready for my date.

Hurrying home, I glanced around nervously, expecting that weird white shape to reappear. When nothing happened, I rushed to my bedroom and unpacked a box of clothes. I laid the outfits on my bed, feeling defeated.

Paxson had said I could wear whatever I wanted to The Sasquatch Saloon. The problem was my date clothes for L.A. were all short dresses and heels. This didn't seem like the place for those outfits. Instead, I rummaged in another box and found a pair of distressed jeans, a white tank top, and a military jacket. I dressed quickly, then headed for the bathroom to do something with my hair and makeup.

Twenty minutes later, my blond hair was styled in beachy waves. Then, I applied a light application of makeup to accentuate my tan. "There." I left the bathroom and grabbed my credit card and ID for the bar.

Just as I entered the kitchen, a knock on the door made my heart leap. Geez. Ever since my encounter with Soapy earlier, I was as jumpy as a tick on a jackrabbit. I opened the door and there stood Paxson. He wore a pair of khaki-colored jeans and a denim shirt. His wavy hair was styled in that carefree way that indicated he'd been out in the sun and nature.

"You look great!" we both said, and then laughed.

I stepped out onto the porch and locked the door behind me. "Lead the way." I pointed to the road and smiled.

"It's a short walk. I didn't bother driving. Hope that's all right," he said.

"It's a nice evening. The walk will be good." I gave him an awkward smile. When I'd met him in the restaurant the night before, I hadn't been nervous at all. But now I could feel my heart rate accelerate, and I was worried about saying something stupid or weird.

"So, what do you think of the town so far?" he asked.

"I'm not sure. It's been two days since I arrived here, and I've only visited a few places." I counted on my fingers. "My café, city hall, the restaurant where I met you, and the library."

He turned his twinkling blue eyes to me. "Well, then, I'll just have to give you a proper tour of the town after dinner."

I returned his smile. "I'd like that." Hanging out with Paxson almost made me forget about Uncle Roy and the mysterious circumstances surrounding his death.

CHAPTER 9

The Sasquatch Saloon was hopping.

I glanced around, admiring the log cabin interior and the old photos of adventure seekers during the heyday of the gold rush. On the wall behind the bar hung a weathered wood sign depicting a sasquatch drinking a beer.

Paxson grabbed my hand and pulled me to an open table near the bar. "Have a seat. What kind of drink can I get you?"

My eyes roamed the tables, where it seemed as though everyone was drinking beer. "When in Rome," I said. "I'll have a beer."

He grinned. "Coming right up."

A minute later, he set a tall frosty glass in front of me. "Alaskan Amber."

"Thanks." I took a sip. "This is really good!"

"Only the best. They brew it in Juneau. It's an Alaskan staple." He took a sip.

A waitress came by and smiled. "Hey, Paxson." She turned to me. "I don't think I've met you before. I'm Trixie."

"Nice to meet you. I'm Denali." I shook her hand.

"I see you already have your beverages." She handed us menus. "Do you need a few minutes to decide?"

I nodded. "That would be great."

She went to the next table while we perused the menu. When she returned, I asked for fish and chips and Paxon ordered a burger.

When the food arrived, we tucked into our meals as we chatted about the town.

"Roy was so strategic when he built this place. I know it took him years and years of planning before he dipped a shovel in the dirt."

"I could tell by the level of detail in his binder." I reached for a French fry.

"The cool thing was, he recruited people to run some of the stores and gave them new housing—and he's not charging them rent for this entire first summer. It's a great way to attract people to live and work here."

"Wow. He really thought things through. I wish I had known him. I have a master's degree in business, but I think I would've learned much more from him than I did in school."

He nodded. "That's probably true."

My thoughts turned darker—toward what Trooper Jones had told me about the cause of Uncle Roy's death. "Is there anyone in town who didn't like my uncle?"

Paxson sipped his beer thoughtfully. "Well, to be honest, Soapy Smith tried to bully Roy into doing things his way a lot. They had this weird relationship—one moment Soapy was nice, almost kissing Roy's butt. The next moment, he was demanding that Roy consider trashing the plans he'd drawn up and exchange them for Soapy's vision for the town. It must've driven Roy nuts."

"Why do you suppose Roy let him get away with that?" I wanted to get to the bottom of this.

Paxson shrugged. "I have no idea." He paused. "I have a sneaking suspicion that Soapy was blackmailing Roy."

I raised my eyebrows. "I was thinking the same thing. But what did he have on Roy? It had to be something big."

The door opened and Soapy, Tiffany, and Adina strolled in.

"Speak of the devil." Paxson tipped his chin toward the threesome.

"Oh, no."

"Did you save room for dessert?" Trixie suddenly stood before us. "We've got blueberry pie or chocolate mousse with whipped cream.

Paxson caught me eyeing Soapy and his entourage nervously. "Want to get dessert to go?"

Grateful, I nodded. "I'd love the blueberry pie."

"Make that two," Paxson said. "Can we get the check?"

"Sure." Trixie headed to the kitchen. "I'll be right back with the check and the pies."

"Mind if I stop at the restroom before we go?" I stood.

"No problem. They're to the right." Paxson pointed.

I made my way to the short hall and entered the bathroom with two stalls. As I was coming out of the far stall, Adina entered.

Not knowing if I should acknowledge her presence or not, I gave her a nervous smile and turned on the faucet to wash my hands.

She cleared her throat. "It's Denali, isn't it?"

I looked in the mirror at her reflection. "Yes, that's right."

"Listen." She fidgeted with the buttons of her jacket. "I want to apologize for the behavior of my husband and daughter, Tiffany. It's not your fault you inherited your uncle's town."

"Oh!" Surprised that she was much nicer than her family, I smiled. "Thank you. I hope they will come around. I don't mean anybody harm. And I certainly don't want any bad feelings between us."

Adina gave me a little nod, patted her mousy brown hair, and left the restroom.

Well, that was odd. But I was glad that at least one person in their family seemed decent.

I joined Paxson by the front door. He grinned and held up a paper bag and two plastic forks. "Ready to go?"

"Yep." I followed him out the door. "Where are we going to eat our dessert?"

"I thought I'd walk you to the end of town. My cabin is right on the lake, and I have a nice picnic table facing the water. Is that okay with you?"

"Sure, sounds nice."

As we walked, I told him about my encounter with Adina.

"Really?" His eyebrows rose. "She was nice to you?"

I tilted my head, curious at his reaction. "Yeah, why do you ask?"

"Because Adina isn't really like that. She's usually kind of —prickly."

"Maybe she thought Soapy and Tiffany were being over-the-top mean. I don't know. Anyhow, I think it's nice of her to apologize for them. I know they aren't likely to apologize themselves."

"Hell would freeze over first," he said.

The road turned from cobbled to dirt, and Paxson led me down a side road. We stopped in front of a small log cabin. Just as he described, it sat near the shore of a large blue-green lake shimmering in the evening sun.

"Nice place!" I admired the rustic cabin, complete with a willow rocking chair on the porch. I turned to see a dock past the picnic area. There was a ramp at the edge of the dock, a float plane tethered on top.

"Thanks." He pointed to the picnic table. "Have a seat."

We sat on the same bench facing the water while we ate our pie.

"Delicious," I said, taking the last bite and licking the fork clean.

"So, what are your plans for the town?" Squinting into the sun, he watched an eagle soar overhead.

Before I could answer, I spied Trooper Jones' vehicle driving slowly past. The officer glanced out the window and caught sight of Paxson and me. He backed up and drove down the side road toward us.

Paxson waved at the officer as he climbed out of the police SUV. "Good evening, Trooper Jones!"

The trooper nodded. "Hello, Paxson. Denali, I have some news I thought I'd share." He sat across from us at the table. "The report came back from the lab on your uncle's cause of death. The poison I talked about came from foxglove—also known as digitalis."

I frowned. "You mean the tall plant with the pretty bell-shaped flowers?"

"That's the one," Trooper Jones said. "The contents of his stomach—sorry to be graphic—contained some sort of pastry. It's likely that whoever killed him, baked it into a treat which he ingested. The toxins in the plant are actually used to make potent cardiac medicine. But if not given under medical supervision, can be lethal."

"Oh, my God." My hand flew to my mouth. "That's awful."

Paxson shook his head. "Wow. I had no idea."

Trooper Jones took off his hat and laid it on the table. "The toxin can wreak havoc on the heart—causing an irregular heartbeat and making it either too fast or too slow. In Roy's case, that proved to be fatal. I'm sorry, Miss Dahlgren."

Words failed me. Someone baked treats and had given them to Uncle Roy with the intent to kill him. What a heartless and cruel crime.

Trooper Jones gave me a sympathetic look. "It's a lot to take in. I'm going to do everything I can to get to the bottom of this."

I swallowed hard. "Thank you."

"Please remember, that whoever killed your uncle is still out there. Be careful, and if you see or hear anything unusual, call me right away."

"I will." I sat, numb, as I watched him return to his vehicle and drive away.

"Wow." Paxson reached over and covered my hand with his. The warmth of his touch was reassuring. "Sorry, Denali."

Glancing at our hands, and then back at his kind face, I said, "Do you have any idea who would do such a thing?"

Paxson shook his head. "Honestly, no. I mean, even though there were people who didn't exactly like your uncle, I don't think any one of them could commit murder."

But he was wrong. Someone in this town was a killer. But who?

CHAPTER 10

There was an awkward pause as Paxson and I stood on my front porch. Our date had left me intrigued, and I thought about inviting him in. My stomach fluttered. Would he kiss me?

Paxson's gaze lowered to my lips.

My phone buzzed. I recognized Mags' ring tone. She had terrible timing.

Paxson smiled. "You better get that."

I tried to hide my disappointment with a cheerful grin. "I had a great time! Thank you for the lovely evening."

The phone in my pocket continued to ring.

"I'll call or text you tomorrow." Paxson gave me a quick hug, then bounded down the stairs to the sidewalk.

Sighing, I answered the call and switched to video.

"Denali! You look great. Alaska agrees with you."

Mags was one to talk. She looked radiant in her sunny yellow top—like a ray of sunshine on a cloudy day.

"I was on a date with Paxson. In fact, it just ended. How about you? You look amazing as usual. Are you still dating that guy, Rad?"

She shook her head. "Nope. He turned out to be a jerk. I went out with a couple of friends from work, instead. We had cocktails at a new bar. It was totally upscale, and the drinks cost twenty bucks a piece! I only had one."

I laughed as I unlocked the front door and let myself in. "You were paying for the ambience—not the drink."

"You got that right. So, tell me about your date."

"I think he was about to kiss me when you called." I gave her a stern look.

"Oops. Sorry."

I filled the tea kettle and set it on the stove. "Hopefully, there will be another chance to get that kiss. I like him. Paxson is a really nice man. Handsome and caring."

"I'm so glad you met him!" she said. "Where did you go on your date?"

"A place called Sasquatch Saloon. It was fun until Soapy and his family arrived," I said.

"Uh oh. What happened?" Mags leaned forward. "Did you get into a bar brawl?"

I laughed. "No, of course not. But Soapy and his daughter have both been awful to me, so Paxson and I took our desserts to go. Before we left, I visited the bathroom and Soapy's wife followed me in."

"Oh my God! Is she awful, too?"

"No. She actually apologized for her husband and daughter. She said she was ashamed of the way they acted toward me earlier."

"Good. Maybe she has a conscience." Mags sat back in her chair.

"There's something else you should know." I let the words hang uncomfortably in the air, wondering how I should tell her.

Her eyes widened. "Is Paxson married?"

"No! He's not married. "It's about Uncle Roy. Trooper Jones told me that Uncle Roy didn't die of natural causes."

"Huh?" She frowned.

I told her about the poisoned pastry and the unsigned contract.

"What in the world? Denali—I don't think it's safe for you to be there. If Soapy killed your uncle thinking he'd get the town, what's stopping him from killing you?"

I shook my head. "But he has nothing to gain if he kills me. Uncle Roy didn't sign the contract. Soapy has no legal claim on the town or anything in it. If Soapy kills me, he still won't get what he wants."

"Well, who would inherit it, then?" she asked.

"Whomever I named in my will. But I don't even have one of those. And I don't have any next of kin."

"Soapy might think he can worm his way around it. Maybe he'll draft up some fake document that says you're a relative or something." Mags pointed a finger at me. "You'd better come back to Los Angeles where it's safe. Please, Denali—I'm really worried."

I rolled my eyes. "Did you just hear what came out of your mouth? I think a small town in Alaska is a heck of a lot safer than Los Angeles."

"Ha!" She narrowed her eyes at me. "We may have our fair share of road rage and random murders, but at least we don't have grizzly bears, freezing temperatures, and weird people named Soapy who might kill you."

I snorted. "You've got me there. But Mags, I'm starting to get excited about running a tourist town and making it successful. This is a once in a lifetime opportunity!"

Mags remained quiet as she looked away from the screen. "You're right. It is." She turned her attention back to me. "Promise me you'll be careful."

I smiled. "You're a good friend. I promise to be extra cautious. Listen, we've only been talking about me. What's going on in your life? And when can you come up for a visit?"

"Sadly, I can't come up for a while. My grandma just passed away unexpectedly and my mom and her sisters are fighting over the stuff in Grandma's house. I mean, some of her stuff has sentimental value, but they aren't fighting over that. They're fighting over money, the house, and other valuable stuff." She shook her head. "It's a hot mess."

"Oh, Mags, I'm so sorry to hear that. I know how much you loved your grandma." I watched a few tears roll down her cheeks.

She fanned her face and grabbed a tissue. "I didn't mean to cry. It's just sad, you know? All that stuff in Gran's house means nothing. It's just stuff. Why do people fight over material things when what's important is family?"

"I agree. Family is everything." My mood plummeted. I was the only person in my family still alive. Everyone else was gone. The tea kettle whistled, and I poured the water into a mug and dropped a tea bag into it.

"Did your dad and your uncle ever fight over your grandparents' stuff?" she asked.

I stopped wallowing in self-pity and considered her words. "They must've fought over the money, but I'm not sure about the other material things. Dad never talked about his parents or Roy, so I'm guessing there must have been lots of tension there. I wish he was still around to ask."

Mags sniffled, then laughed. "Listen to us! We are a couple of Debbie downers. Let's talk about something else."

"You got it. Tell me what happened with Rad."

• • • ● • ● • • •

After chatting for another half hour, I washed my teacup and stared out the kitchen window. It was after ten o'clock at night, yet the sun still shone like it was the middle of the day. Thoughts of Dad and Uncle Roy tumbled through my mind. Did they fight over my grandparents' estate? Was that what divided them and why we left Alaska for California?

Curious, I opened my laptop and did a search for my family's names.

After getting distracted reading about Uncle Roy buying the town of Gold Rush, I scanned through some other articles with little to no luck. That is, until I stumbled upon the obituaries for my grandparents, Ollie and Elsa Dahlgren.

Ollie had died in a small plane crash. Elsa had died a few months later of pneumonia. The obituaries mentioned that my family's forefathers had struck it rich during the gold rush in the 1800s. My grandparents had grown their wealth by making investments in land, property, and by buying up other Alaskan businesses. So, why were my parents poor when they left Alaska for California? Wouldn't my grandparents' fortune have been divided evenly between Uncle Roy and Dad? I set a reminder on my phone to call Uncle Roy's lawyer in the morning. He had to know something about the family money.

I read more articles about Uncle Roy. He'd started several businesses of his own after his parents' death and had done very well.

My eyes burned after staring at the screen as I tried to dig up more information. I yawned. It was well after midnight, and I'd planned to meet Jade at the café at eight o'clock. I stood and stretched, trying to relieve the tension in my shoulders.

As I made my way to my bedroom, I thought about broken relationships, family drama, and lost opportunities. Having at least one family member alive to talk with about the past would've been incredible. But as it was, I had no one to fill in the details of my family history and no one to guide me while I figured out how to plan my future. I was a boat without paddles, afloat in the middle of a vast ocean.

CHAPTER 11

The morning sun streamed through the kitchen windows, nearly blinding me with its radiance. Bleary-eyed, I stirred honey into my tea, hoping it would at least jumpstart my energy.

I sat down at the cozy little table, tea in hand, as I called Uncle Roy's lawyer. After his secretary put me through to him, I said, "Mr. Olmstead? Do you have time to answer a few questions about my uncle?"

"Please—call me Mark. What would you like to know?"

Wasting no time, I blurted out, "What was the relationship like between my dad and my uncle? Why did Roy inherit so much money, but my father didn't? Why didn't I know Uncle Roy existed until after he died? And why did he leave me his money and the town when he didn't even know me?"

There was a long pause before I heard him sigh.

"Denali, I understand this must be very confusing for you. I'll do my best to explain," he said.

I took a sip of my tea. "Please do."

"Your uncle was the oldest of your grandparents' two children. Therefore, they entrusted him with the responsibility of managing their money in the event of their death. He was the executor of their estate."

"And?" I asked. "He took it all for himself?"

"Let me back up. Roy had always been good with money. He knew how to take a little money and grow it into a large sum. I guess you could say he had a head for business. Your dad, on the other hand, was more interested in holding down a steady job—but he often spent the money he earned on more frivolous things. For example, when Roy had money, he invested it in a business. But when your dad had money, he would buy a car or something else that would depreciate the moment he bought it. Naturally, your grandparents knew that Roy would take the family fortune, invest it, and make it grow. And they counted on him to share the money with your dad."

Thinking back to my childhood, all I remembered was living in poor, rundown neighborhoods. We had a car, but it was old and rusty. It was a constant concern for my parents, as they tried to keep up with the cost of repairing it.

"Frivolous? But Dad never bought fancy cars," I argued. "We had one beat-up sedan that my parents shared. I don't think you can call that frivolous spending."

"The point is," Mark continued, "your grandparents put Roy in charge because he would manage it better."

A ribbon of anger uncoiled inside me. "Why didn't he give at least some of it to his brother? Did Roy understand that sometimes my mom had to dig through the couch cushions searching for coins so I could have lunch money for school?"

Mark sighed. "I don't think he knew that. Your dad refused to talk to Roy."

"Probably because Roy cheated him out of his inheritance!" I tapped my spoon on the tabletop. I knew that part of my anger had to do with not getting enough sleep. But a lot of it came from the mystery of not knowing anything about my family. I took in a breath and let it out slowly. "Look, I'm sorry. None of this is your fault. I guess I'm just upset."

"Totally understandable," Mark said. "Roy and your dad got into a big fight. Roy told him that he was going to invest the money. After the money grew, he'd planned on giving Peter his share plus the profit from the investments."

"Go on," I said.

"You had just been born and your parents needed the money right then. They asked for cash to buy a house and for a college fund for you."

I waited while Mark paused again.

"Roy declined the request because the business he'd just purchased was going through some changes, and he didn't want to risk pulling any funds from it. He was worried it would destabilize the company and cause it to go bankrupt."

"I see." Out of the corner of my eye, a white mist began to gather. Alarmed, I sat up straight and watched it intently. Was this a ghost? More importantly, was this Uncle Roy's ghost? My heart banged in my chest as my gaze fixed on the gathering mist.

"Anyway," Mark continued, "out of anger, your dad packed up his little family and left the state for California. Roy tried to contact him to explain, but every attempt failed. Soon, Roy was too busy to keep trying, and your dad never reached out to hear Roy's side."

The misty shape came closer and hovered next to my chair. The hairs on the back of my neck stood on end, and I shivered.

"Roy told me it was his biggest regret. He'd unintentionally severed the only family relationship he had left. And that's why he changed his will, leaving everything to your dad—and subsequently, to you. I think his guilt ate him up over the years. He knew he had to do the right thing."

"So, originally, he was going to leave everything to Soapy?" I asked, confused as to why he would want that awful man to get what my family had worked hard for.

"Just the town," Mark said. "He was going to leave whatever money was left to your dad. But he didn't know that your parents had passed away."

My eyes narrowed at the misty form hovering to my right. Not knowing whether to be terrified or angry at the ghostly presence, I said, "When he found out Mom and Dad were gone, he thought of me."

"Yes." Mark hesitated. "He felt terrible about what he'd done."

I angrily fanned my hand at the white mist. "Go away!"

"What?" the lawyer asked.

"Not you. Just a pesky fly." I glared at the dissipating mist.

"Denali, your uncle carried a lot of guilt about what happened between him and your dad. He began to reflect on the situation. He knew you were grown and probably needed the money. He even had me snoop a little to find out what you had accomplished in your life."

"So, he wanted to know if I was worthy enough to get the money he owed my dad?" I stood and then paced through the small kitchen.

"No, not at all. Roy was curious, that's all. He was pleased to find out you also had an entrepreneurial spirit—just like him. Roy told me he wanted everything to go to you when he died. Even Gold Rush."

"But why was he planning to leave the town to Soapy originally? Why would he enter into a partnership with him?"

"Because Soapy found out that Roy had taken all your grandparents' money. He threatened to tell everyone— media included—that Roy had cheated your dad out of his fair share of the family fortune. It would've ruined Roy's reputation and killed any opportunity to partner with other businesses."

"I see. So, when he decided to leave Gold Rush to me, he was taking a big risk, wasn't he?"

"Yes," Mark answered. "Roy knew that when Soapy found out of the change in plans, he would be livid. And he knew Soapy would ruin him."

I stared at a few tea leaves left at the bottom of my cup. "Thank you for sharing that with me, Mr. Olmstead."

"You're welcome. But it's Mark."

"Thank you, Mark." I ended the call and stood. The white mist had gone, and the chill had gone with it.

At least one piece of the puzzle had snapped into place.

But who had killed Uncle Roy? Soapy?

CHAPTER 12

After a restless night, I arrived at the café an hour earlier than I'd planned. Thoughts of my parents, grandparents, and Uncle Roy still swirled unhappily in my head. Uncle Roy had cheated my father out of what was rightfully his. No wonder Dad wouldn't have anything to do with him. It made me extra mad because I *wanted* to like my uncle. Now I was left with a sour taste in my mouth whenever I thought of him.

Shaking off my anger, I practiced making a latte with an espresso machine. The caffeine would help me clear my head and think. The first two tasted burnt, so I dumped them down the drain.

My third try yielded a decent latte. Pleased with my efforts, I sipped my coffee and flipped through Uncle Roy's binder to find the menu he and Jade had created. Even though I was livid at what my uncle had done, I still needed the information he'd gathered to make this town succeed.

I thumbed through the pages until I got to the menu section. The titles of the items were quite bland. Apple fritters, scones, chocolate chip cookies, and the like. It would be more unique to name each pastry and baked good something related to Alaska. "Stampeders Salmonberry Scone" sounded way more fun than a plain old scone—at least, it did to me.

So, I set about creating a spreadsheet on my laptop, listing the plain-named items in one column and a new

Alaskan or gold rush themed name in the next column. I researched the flora, fauna, and history of Alaska as I came up with even more names.

I'd just typed in Motherlode Cinnamon Rolls when Jade entered through the back.

"Oh! You're here early." She set down a plate of fresh oatmeal cookies. "Would you like one?"

"Thanks." I took one, but then remembered what Trooper Jones had said about poison in the pastry my uncle had eaten. Uneasily, I set the cookie down next to the binder.

Jade had brought me treats earlier. I'd eaten them and hadn't died. Now that I was accustomed to eating her scrumptious baked goods, it would be easier to lure me into eating one of her delicious cookies. And then, I'd be dead.

"Not hungry?" Jade asked as she reached for a cookie and took a big bite.

"I'm just a little preoccupied with naming items on the menu. The cookies look delicious." Well, she had eaten one herself, but what if she'd turned the plate to make sure I took the poisoned one?

But why would Jade want to murder my uncle? What motive would she have? Had he been mean to her? Threatened her? It didn't make any sense.

Just then, someone knocked on the entry door.

"Who could that be?" Jade asked. She walked through the café to the front and unlocked the door.

Adina Smith stood with a basket in her arms. "Good morning. I brought a gift for Denali. Is she here?"

Jade gave her a curious look and pointed to me. "She's sitting at the table."

"Hello?" Brenna Randall, the librarian, peeked out from behind Adina. "I brought some sketches for the mural and my famous chocolate muffins for Denali. Is she here?"

I frowned. Was everyone in this town a baker? I stood. "Come on in."

Adina eyed Brenna's basket of muffins and scowled. "Those look... interesting."

Brenna rolled her eyes. "Unlike your perfect poppy seed scones, Adina, my chocolate muffins are absolutely delicious."

Uh oh. Were these women going to fight over who offered up the best baked goods? Had one of these three women poisoned my uncle and were now aiming to kill me?

"Thank you both." I forced a smile. "Can I get you a coffee? I just learned how to make a latte." I lifted my cup.

"I'd love one," they both said at the same time, then glared at each other.

Jade looked from me to Brenna to Adina with a curious expression. "I'll make the coffee. What would you like?"

"A vanilla latte, please." Brenna set her basket on the counter.

"Just a plain, black coffee, for me." Adina glared at Brenna. "I don't go for those frou-frou fancy drinks. So indulgent and unnecessary."

Unfazed, Brenna sat next to me. "Want to see my ideas for the mural?"

I nodded, grateful to concentrate on anything other than the tension in the room.

Adina placed a scone on a plate and brought it to the table, setting it down next to me. "This will go perfect with your coffee."

Ignoring her, Brenna flipped open her sketchbook. "Here's the first option."

Jade fired up the espresso machine and the scent of coffee filled the café. My stomach rumbled, but I resisted the urge to devour the scone. Instead, I gulped my latte and peered at Brenna's colored pencil sketch.

A large bull moose stood majestically on the vibrant tundra with the backdrop of a pink and orange sky.

"Oh," I breathed out the words, "it's magnificent." The details and colors were so rich—it was as if I were standing in the scene with the moose.

Jade finished making the vanilla latte and brought it to Brenna. "Here you go. Adina, I'll get your drip coffee to you in just a few minutes."

Adina gave her a curt nod and then nudged the scone toward me.

Brenna flipped to the next page.

I gasped. This mural was just as magnificent, if not more so, than the last one. A brilliant, white polar bear stood on an ice float, with its nose in the air—probably sniffing for seal. Behind it, the last vestiges of sunset tinted the sky pink at the horizon. Above the sunset, the northern lights lit the star-filled heavens with streaks of green and purple.

"Oh my gosh." I looked up at Brenna with tears threatening to spill onto my cheeks. "These are both so beautiful. I don't know which one to choose."

Jade brought Adina's drip coffee and a plate of Brenna's chocolate muffins, Adina's scones, and her own oatmeal cookies before joining us at the table.

"Let me see," Jade slid the sketchbook over and looked at both images. "Wow, Brenna. You've outdone yourself!"

Adina cleared her throat. "Yes, yes, the pictures are lovely. Denali, please eat something. These lemon poppy seed scones are my specialty. Your uncle loved them."

My uncle loved them? A feeling of unease crept into my chest. "Thanks, but I had a big breakfast," I said, just as my stomach growled loudly.

A ghostly mist began forming behind Adina. It gathered quickly into the shape of a man. As the features began to arrange themselves, I realized it looked just like the photo of Uncle Roy hanging on the living room wall of my house. In the photo, he was standing with my grandparents in front of their home in Anchorage. The beating of my heart accelerated as I watched the apparition.

"Hello?" Trooper Jones entered through the open front door. He stepped further inside and took in the scene. I hoped he wasn't bringing me a baked good too.

Jade jumped up. "Good morning! Can I get you a cup of coffee?"

"No, thank you, Jade. Did I miss the ribbon cutting? I didn't realize you were open for business already." His brown eyes sought me out and then slid to Brenna, Adina, and then Jade.

Adina cleared her throat. "We were just looking at Brenna's ideas for Denali's mural."

"Hello?" Tiffany, Adina and Soapy's disagreeable daughter, poked her head through the open door. In her arms, she held a plate of apple fritters. She spied her mother sitting at our table and her expression darkened. "Mom? What are you doing here?"

"Just being neighborly," Adina said.

Tiffany frowned. "Since when are you 'neighborly'?"

"The better question is, what are you doing here? And why did you bring fritters? I thought you didn't like Denali." Adina's lips flattened. Somehow, the look on her face scared me more than the fully formed ghost, now standing between Adina and me.

"I saw you come in here with a basket of scones," Tiffany put the fritters on the counter next to the other baked goods. "I only brought the fritters because I want to persuade Denali to sell them when the café opens. A girl's gotta make a living, you know." She fixed her gaze on her mother. "Why are you here engaging with the enemy?"

Adina chuckled. "Don't be silly, Tiff. Denali is a friend. I just wanted to welcome her to Gold Rush."

"Hello?" Jade's husband, Jasper, stepped inside. "Are you open for business already?"

"No, dear," Jade answered. "But it seems like the welcome wagon is here for Denali."

"Oh, good," he said holding out a plate. "I just whipped up some moose nugget fudge. If Denali likes it, I'd be happy to make a fresh batch every day for her to sell at the café." He came in and set the fudge on the counter.

"Moose nugget fudge?" I started to laugh at the thought of the name. How would I market that? When I saw his hurt feelings, I stopped. "Sorry, but everyone has been so nice to bring me goodies, I can't wait to try them all. But I'm not hungry right now." As if on cue, my traitorous stomach growled again.

Covering my mid-section with my hand, I glanced from one dessert to another. Why was everyone trying to feed me? Suspicion seeped into my thoughts. Had one of these desserts killed my uncle?

I noticed Trooper Jones had made his way to the counter and was carefully scrutinizing each dessert.

Adina nudged the scone closer to me. "You should really try this first, Denali. You'll love it as much as Roy did."

Uncle Roy's ghost suddenly materialized fully. He wasn't even white anymore—he looked like a solid person. At over six feet tall, his imposing figure loomed over Adina.

Swallowing hard, I looked from person to person. "Do... do you see that?" I pointed to Uncle Roy.

"See what?" Brenna asked.

"I should really be going." Adina shivered and tried to stand. But Uncle Roy laid his ghostly hands on her shoulders, and she slammed back into her chair.

Startled, I stared at my uncle's ghost.

He eyed the scone and shook his head.

Picking up the scone, I held it up for him to see, wondering what he would do if he thought I would take a bite.

"Don't eat that!" Trooper Jones shouted as he rushed toward me.

Uncle Roy beat him to it. He slapped the scone out of my hand. It fell into my lap in a crumbling heap.

Quick as an arctic fox, Trooper Jones scooped the pieces of pastry into a plastic bag. Then, he turned to Adina. "Adina, did you make the scones with the poppy seeds?"

She hesitated. "Yes. Why do you ask?" She gave him a frosty look. "You should try one."

Trooper Jones fingered the handcuffs on his belt and reached for Adina's arm. "You're coming with me for questioning."

The defiant look on Adina's face could've melted a glacier. "For what?"

Soapy appeared in the open doorway and spied Trooper Jones with his hand around his wife's wrist. "What's going on?" he boomed.

"I'm taking Adina in for questioning on suspicion of murder," Trooper Jones said in a calm but firm voice.

Soapy's eyebrows furrowed, and his expression darkened. "Murder? What murder?"

"Roy Dahlgren's," Trooper Jones answered.

Soapy barked out a laugh. "What are you talking about? Roy had a heart attack."

Roy floated over to Soapy and glared at him.

Soapy shuddered and zipped up his jacket.

"Roy Dahlgren was poisoned—that's what caused his heart attack." Trooper Jones' held up the scone he'd placed in a plastic bag. "The coroner's report stated there were poppy seeds in the pastry he was poisoned with."

Tiffany stared, open-mouthed, at her mother. "Mom?"

Soapy stormed over to the trooper. "That's ridiculous. What makes you think my wife poisoned Roy? She had no reason to. Besides, poppy seeds can't hurt anyone."

"True," Trooper Jones said. "But it will be interesting to see if the lab in Anchorage finds digitalis in these particular poppy seed scones."

"Digitalis?" Tiffany asked.

"Otherwise known as foxglove," the trooper answered.

Tiffany's eyes grew large. "Like the flowers we have growing in our side garden?"

Adina's face turned a deep red. "Enough, Tiffany. I don't even know what those flowers are."

Jade frowned. "I thought everyone knew that foxglove is poisonous."

Trooper Jones cuffed Adina and led her to the door. He turned back only to say, "Don't anyone touch those scones. In fact, Denali, put the rest of them in a plastic bag. I'll pick them up later."

Soapy's face drained of color. "Don't worry, Adina. I'll call our lawyer."

"Better call a divorce lawyer while you're at it, you idiot. This is all your fault!" she screeched.

"What?" Soapy looked stricken. "What are you talking about?"

"You said that Roy had already signed the contract and it was a done deal." Her eyes narrowed, and her voice pitched higher. "I can't believe you didn't follow up with Roy's attorney. The town was supposed to be half yours. The contract stipulated if one partner dies, the other gets ownership of the entire town. I was *helping* you, don't you see?"

Soapy shook his head. "I can't believe you would—kill Roy."

"I did it for you. For us!" Her eyes flicked to Tiffany. "This town would've been our legacy. And we could've passed it down to our daughter. But you had to go and mess it up, just like you mess up everything. All those businesses you started and bailed on before they were mature enough to make a return on investment."

"I—I was ready to move onto new things. I sold them before I got bored." Soapy tugged at the collar of his shirt.

"You have the attention span of a flea," she grumbled. "I had to take matters into my own hands. And if it hadn't been for the missing contract, we would be sitting pretty right now."

"Come on." Trooper Jones tugged her out the door. "You have the right to remain silent—"

His words faded off as he and Adina walked further away from the café.

The rest of us stared at one another. Then Soapy snapped out of it and grabbed his daughter's arm. "Come on, Tiffany. We need to get your mother a good lawyer."

CHAPTER 13

A small crowd surrounded me outside Midnight Sun Cafe, talking excitedly about the grand opening of Gold Rush. Jasper, Jade, and Brenna stood close beside me and gave me encouraging smiles. Soapy and Tiffany stood across the road, glowering at me.

A giddy feeling of pride overcame me and I took in a breath of fresh Alaskan air and let it out slowly. The town was reopening to the public for the first time in over a hundred years—and only a week behind Uncle Roy's initial schedule. Summer had arrived.

I hadn't filled all the stores, and there was still so much left to do, but it was a real town. This place would become a fantastic tourist destination and a great place for the town's inhabitants to live.

"Denali," Paxson said, "what are you waiting for? Cut the ribbon." He grinned and motioned toward the red ribbon. Jade held one end and Jasper held the other.

My phone buzzed. It was Mags.

"Hey, Mags!" I held my phone to my ear in one hand and clutched the giant pair of scissors in the other. "I'm just about to cut the ribbon for the town opening. Can I call you back?"

"No, you can't," Mags said.

"Huh?" Was she mad at me?

"Turn around." Mags giggled.

I turned slowly and saw a petite woman with long dark hair approaching me. "Mags?"

She laughed and ran toward me, arms outstretched.

"What are you doing here?" I said into her hair as she crushed me in a hug.

Mags stepped back, grinning wildly. "Do you honestly think I would've missed this?"

I gave her a sheepish grin. "I thought you were too busy to come."

"See, that's the thing," Mags said. "That merger came through—I'm out of a job."

"Oh, Mags." I patted her shoulder. "I'm really sorry."

"Don't be," she said. "I got a great severance package, so I'm keeping my summer open. I thought I'd hang out here and see if I can help you get this place up and running."

I dropped the giant scissors and hugged her again. "Oh, my gosh! I can't believe it. This is the best day ever. How did you get out here so fast?"

"I flew into Anchorage and then Paxson picked me up in his bush plane."

My mouth hung open. "How did you get his number?"

She linked her elbow through mine. "There's this little thing called the internet—you should really check it out."

I rolled my eyes.

"How many pilots named Paxson do you think live in Alaska? It was a piece of cake to find him." She gave me a smug look.

I turned to Paxson. "Why didn't you tell me?"

"Mags said she'd kill me if I did. She sounded pretty serious, so I did what she said." He winked at me.

"Is the ribbon cutting going to happen soon?" Missy, the waitress from the restaurant across the street, said. "I've got to get back to work."

"Oh, right." I picked up the giant scissors.

"Wait!" Mags took out her phone and stepped back. "I'm going to take photos so we can include them in the press release and post them to our social media sites."

"Well, then," I said, "I'd better set up those sites right after this."

"Don't tell me you haven't done that yet," Mags said in mock horror.

"I was a little busy with all the murder stuff."

Mags raised an eyebrow. "We have a lot to catch up on. But for now, say cheese!"

I raised the giant scissors, smiled at the camera, and snipped. "Gold Rush, Alaska is officially open for business."

• • • • • • • • • •

Epilogue

It was evening and the sky was tinged in a warm, pink glow. With the grand opening behind me, I was glad to get a few moments of quiet inside the Midnight Sun Café. I sat facing the beautiful mural of the polar bear and hoped that Brenna could paint the moose on the opposite wall at a later time.

I'd sent Mags to my house for the evening. Tomorrow, we'd look at the newly built homes in town, and I'd let her pick the one she wanted to live in for the summer.

Paxson had asked me out on another date. I couldn't believe how much my life had changed for the better in just a couple of weeks.

Looking down at Roy's binder on the table, I paged through it, not really knowing what I was searching for. A cool breeze ruffled my hair. Wait—a breeze? The doors and windows were closed. I peered over my shoulder, afraid to see what was causing the icy current of air.

When I felt the cold intensifying, I turned my gaze to the chair across the table from me. White mist swirled and solidified until finally, it gathered into the ghost of Uncle Roy. He looked so solid and alive, I could hardly believe he was dead.

"Uncle Roy?"

He nodded and waved his hand at the binder. The pages flipped one after the other, until it stopped on a page with a pocket. A handwritten letter was tucked inside.

I stared at the paper and then looked at my uncle. "You want me to read this?"

Again, he nodded.

"Dear Denali," I read out loud, "If you're reading this, it means I'm dead. First of all, I'm sorry for what I did to your dad—and to your family. I was foolish to think I could take our parents' money and double it before giving

Peter his share. While I did eventually succeed, it was too late to repair my relationship with him. What I did was inexcusable, and I am so very sorry.

It took me a long time to realize my mistake. To make it right, I didn't sign the contract specifying Soapy would get half ownership of the town. I was ready for the truth to come out, and that freed me from his threats and blackmail. You'll find the unsigned document in the freezer at my house. I stashed it there when Adina paid me a surprise visit asking if I'd sent the contract to my lawyer. I lied and said I had. She is just as awful as her husband. Those two deserve each other.

I hope you can find it in your heart to forgive me. Take care of Gold Rush. Do good things. I have faith in you.

Love,

Uncle Roy."

I looked up from the letter. Uncle Roy gave me a tentative smile. His eyes brimmed with sorrow.

Emotions rose up inside me—feelings I'd stuffed deep down when I buried my parents. So much loss. I felt sad that Dad and Uncle Roy hadn't been able to mend their relationship before they died.

"I forgive you, Uncle Roy. Thank you for the letter. Thank you for giving me the opportunity to run your town. I promise to take good care of it."

His face relaxed and he smiled. I could almost feel his relief.

With one more burst of ghostly energy, he opened his mouth and whispered, "Thank you for your forgiveness. I am free to go now."

"Wait—" I said, holding out my hand. "Say hello to my mom and dad when you see them. Tell them I love them."

He nodded before disappearing in a swoosh of light, until there was nothing left to reassure me he'd been real.

My phone buzzed. It was Mags.

"You coming?" she texted. "I opened a bottle of champagne. We're celebrating."

"Be right there," I texted back.

I stood and took one more look around my beautiful café before closing the door behind me.

This was going to be one heck of an adventure.

About the Author

Martina Dalton writes mysteries and lives in the Pacific Northwest with her family. Born and raised in Alaska, she can nimbly catch a fish, dress for rain, and knows what to do when encountering a grizzly bear. Now living in the Seattle area, she uses those same skills to navigate through rush-hour traffic. Visit www.martinadalton.com to learn more about her books.

Click here to download a FREE book in Martina Dalton's humorous mystery series.

See her other books on Amazon: Martina Dalton's Books

THE CLOCK STRIKES ONE

by Maren Higbee

CHAPTER 1

An awful scream cut through the air, growing louder with every second. No, this wasn't the sound of a brawl or a murder. It was coming from the little old lady ghost tottering into my store, Mystique Antiques. When I had accepted the vintage clock, a family heirloom deeded to the eldest girl of each generation, I had forgotten all about Mrs. Thomas, the ghost attached to it. Now that Aunt Birdie was moving into an old folks' home, she'd begrudgingly decided it would finally go to me.

I shoved the overdue bills into the counter drawer and rushed to the delivery man, who was jockeying the large mahogany clock around the tight corner into the shop.

"Where do you want it, ma'am?" he asked.

"Please, put it over there, next to the grandfather clocks."

Mrs. Thomas turned to me, an annoyed expression on her wrinkle-creased face. "Remember, this is a hall clock, my dear," she said, shaking her head before rushing away after her clock. "Mind the finish, boys!"

A crash echoed through the store.

"You twits!"

I was grateful the men could not hear the non-stop complaints of our new resident.

For generations, the women in my family had run this little antiques store in Seattle. The ghosts attached to some of the vintage items were often a source of enjoyment for the owners, though sometimes they caused frustration. The spirits who became attached to a piece usually had attitude.

"I hope she doesn't stay long," another ghost named Abner said, appearing from behind the heavy crystal ashtray to which he was attached. Abner took a puff of the long cigar that constantly hung from his lip. Cherry tobacco temporarily overpowered the musty aroma of my shop.

"Shhhh, Abner," I pleaded. "Other ghosts can hear you, remember?" Abner rearranged his burgundy ascot and took another puff. The woman's shrieks only grew louder.

"Who the hell is this, waking me from my nap?" Tiffany said as she stormed into the middle of the shop. Tiffany was the most temperamental ghost in my store, a sixteen-year-old blond ghost attached to a 1980s digital alarm clock. Usually, ghosts were attached to items they loved. Why a teenager would love an alarm clock was beyond me. Like a typical teenager, she refused to tell me.

Mrs. Thomas now sat on a chair next to her clock. She looked over her round glasses at Tiffany. "Hush-hush, dear. The terrible beeping of that ugly clock is enough to alert the cops." Then, turning her scowl into a broad, taunting grin, Mrs. Thomas leaned back and laughed heartily, shaking the big round belly covered by her floral dress.

"Like you're one to talk. You haven't shut up since you got here." Tiffany rushed past me to her clock. I stepped back in an attempt to avoid the terrible smell of her teenage Exclamation perfume. I got a nose full of it and sneezed.

"You trying to wake the dead, Sanne?" Harvey, my best friend, laughed as he swaggered into my store. Two years ago, when his mother had passed away, Harvey had inherited the Coffee Café next door. We had grown up forced to work at our family stores while other kids went to the beach. Now that we were the ones in charge, we worked alongside each other and commiserated about the challenges of running a business, sometimes over cigarettes in the back alley.

Soon after he had taken possession of the Coffee Café, Harvey had changed its name to Someday Café. It was a joke between the two of us that *someday* we would both get to do what we wanted and not have to run the family business. I had grown to love my shop, but Harvey still held onto that resentment from our teenage years. He wanted to own a gym and hire someone else to run the café.

To give Harvey peace of mind that someone would be watching over the café even after he left, and to keep my antiques store alive, we had a doorway cut between the shops to connect the businesses. That way, our customers could easily move back and forth. It had increased both businesses' profits.

"Harvey, you are not that funny."

"No, I'm not funny. I'm hilarious." He threw his arms in the air and ran toward me like a monster. "I know, I know. You see dead people. Are you allergic to them too?"

I rolled my eyes. "It's not a joke. That's why it's so loud over here. We have a—"

"A new ghost with this big beauty?" Harvey walked over to the new clock and watched the delivery man finish adding the weights and the pendulum to the case.

"Wanna get it started?" the delivery guy asked.

I pushed my way past Harvey. "I do. It's my family heirloom."

Harvey shimmied his way beside me and winked. "Let's do it together."

We both put our hands on the pendulum, mine up higher than his, and started the beautiful old clock. I grinned as I heard that tick. In the decade since my mom died, Aunt Birdie had never wound it, never let that gorgeous chime ring out. She just left it sitting in her hallway, a lifeless piece of furniture, and now, with the worsening of her dementia, she couldn't remember to wind it even if she wanted to. That was sad to think about, but did I ever love the sound of the clock.

Harvey noted my satisfied grin. "If it's that special, why are you going to sell it?" he chided. Since we were children, Harvey had had a way of pushing my buttons. We weren't family, but it sure felt like it most of the time.

"I think that's everything," the delivery guy said, holding out a clipboard for me to sign.

"You want the truth, Harvey?" I asked, signing and passing the clipboard back to the man and smiling. He nodded and left. I turned back to Harvey.

"If it's going to be about ghosts, you can spare me," Harvey said.

"Nope. I'm even more behind on the bills than I've told you. It's really bad. I'm not sure if I'm going to make it." Tears welled up in my eyes. I looked away.

Harvey wrapped his arms around me. "I'm sorry. I wish I had more liquid cash. If I did, I'd help you in a heartbeat."

"I know." I leaned into his broad chest.

"I may hate myself for saying this, but maybe it's time to let it go? Get a tech job like all the other good little Seattleites?"

"I don't want a tech job. As much as I hated this place as a kid, I love it now. More than just a single clock, the shop is my heritage. If I can sell the Seth Thomas, I could pay rent for three months." As I finished that sentence, the bell on the front door of my shop rang. The face in the doorway was far more imposing than any of the ghosts.

CHAPTER 2

"Sell it?" a stern voice echoed. "You can't be talking about the Seth Thomas clock your mother left to you." I turned to see Aunt Birdie standing behind me, salt-and-pepper curls peeking out from under her lavender hat. "That has been in our family for over one hundred years."

"I...I..."

"She was talking about the big clock next to it," Harvey exclaimed, pointing randomly toward the back.

Aunt Birdie ignored him and glared in my direction. "You're forcing me into an old folks' home, taking our heirloom, and getting rid of it? Disgraceful!"

Harvey shook his head and strolled back to his shop.

"I don't want to sell, Aunt Birdie, but it could save the shop, which, mind you, has been right here in Ballard for over one hundred years as well. Doesn't that mean more?"

"Dear, I'm sorry to say that poor management on your part does not justify the sale of an heirloom. Your grandfather treasured that clock more than just about anything. He said it was the luck that would save our family when we most needed it. It must stay around. Shall I take it back and give it to Calvin?" she asked.

"No," I said, staring at the floor. "I'll find a way to keep it here."

"Thank goodness," Mrs. Thomas said, shuffling over to us. "I rather like this family and find most others genuinely appalling."

Just as she finished speaking, the three clocks in the back struck five in unison.

"Looks like it's closing time, Aunt Birdie," I said, pushing past her to turn the sign on my glass door to closed. "Did you take the bus?"

"No, dear. I had Calvin drive me. He's trying to find parking. I thought we could have a nice family dinner tonight," she said, pulling her thin white gloves off one finger at a time. "Maybe we can reconsider this move to that strange nursing home? Are you available?"

"I'd love to, but I have plans with Harvey," I said. As if on cue, my cousin Calvin began banging on the door. I unlocked it to let him in. He gave me a quick hug and whispered into my ear. "It's been non-stop complaints while I've been cleaning out my mom's house."

"I can only imagine," I whispered, then stepped out of the hug.

Aunt Birdie and her son Calvin were the only family I had now. He and I had grown up together but fought a lot. While I rode bikes with the neighborhood kids, Calvin sat on the ground playing with bugs and talking to himself. I understood why the other kids picked on him. When I was around, I would stand up for him, but his awkwardness never ceased.

Calvin heard a chime and beelined to the Seth Thomas clock. "The sound of this clock is pure magic. It's even more beautiful than its description in Grandpa's letters." He turned to his mother. "Why didn't you ever run it?" She shrugged and stared off into space. Dementia had started to affect her ability to function safely, and Calvin couldn't handle it anymore on his own.

I turned my attention back to Aunt Birdie. "I'm sorry I can't join you tonight, but soon I promise I'll take you both to a fantastic little spot called Joli, where the pharmacy was when you were a kid." I smiled. "It's fairly new, but the food is amazing."

Aunt Birdie raised an eyebrow. "Calvin, it appears Sanne is too busy for us tonight. Let's go." Calvin pressed his ear to the clock one last time and grinned, then ran after his mother. "I'll see you soon, Sanne!" he called out.

"What is wrong with your family?" Harvey said, leaning against the doorway between the shops. "You have ghosts and love affairs with inanimate objects?"

"He means well. He's just always been a little off, you know that. Plus, we should give him a break because that boy has a long night ahead of him. Aunt Birdie's furious right now. Truthfully, she's not that bad all the time, but dementia has made her grumpy. You know, if I hadn't been twenty when Mom died, I'd have gone to live with her."

"Then you'd be weirder than you are now." He grabbed me for another tight hug.

CHAPTER 3

When Harvey left, a wave of calmness flowed through the shop. Harvey knew I liked to be the last one here to clean up and say goodnight. I put a white lab jacket on and pulled my curly red hair to the top of my head before grabbing a duster. The ghosts began to appear from behind or around their antiques.

When my grandmother Jessie was training me to eventually take over the shop, she taught me about keeping the books, buying antiques, and the usual business practices. But she spent the most time in our lessons insisting that I honor the ghosts that made their homes with us in our small antiques shop.

I began my evening routine. A clean scent wafted past my nose. It smelled a lot like White Shoulders lotion, the floral smell that was distinctly my grandma. The scent had been extreme whenever she bent over and put a little apron on my five-year-old body, her long silver hair tickling my face. I would scrunch my freckled nose and turn away, which always made her laugh. Once I settled, she'd hand me a bright purple feather duster. Then she would kiss my cheek and whisper, "Respect your elders. Bid them goodnight and peaceful rest, and assure them you will be back in the morning. Can you do that, Bits?"

I'd follow directions and dust each item, causing many ghosts to laugh, some to grumble, but most to thank me.

Many would comment to Grandma Jessie how sweet her little redhead could be.

Tonight, I began with Mrs. Thomas's clock. She was new to the store, so I felt she needed a greeting.

"How are you settling in, Mrs. Thomas?" I asked as she plunked her broad backside into the chair near her clock.

"Now that I've recovered from my journey, it is quite lovely here to see so many folks from my time. But that young man, Calvin, I had hoped that when I moved here, he would be gone. Is he here often?" she asked.

"Not often, but he was pretty mad your lovely clock came to me," I said. "And just wait until Aunt Birdie tells him I might have to sell it."

"Dear, I'd prefer to stay with your family, but as long as I get away from that young man, I will be fine. Since they started clearing out the house, he has suddenly become handsy with me. He makes my finish crackle."

"Give him a chance. He's an odd guy, but he appreciates the fine quality of the clock. He only comes in and helps occasionally. You'll be safe."

"Thank you, dear." She smiled.

"I know moving is hard, Mrs. Thomas, but today you were a little over the top, don't you think?"

"It's hard on my old bones to move. And these whippersnappers are just not careful."

"But will you try?"

"Yes, dear. If you keep me here as long as possible."

"I'll try, Mrs. Thomas. I'll try."

I continued on my usual journey around the store, listening to the ghosts' commentary about the day or their items. Mr. Welbey, as usual, commented on his weak ticker. Each night I promised him I'd wind his clock in the morning. Elva and Vera wanted to be sure all the spots were off of their Depression glass. Once I cleaned them up, the sisters dropped to their knees and prayed for a family to bring them home. They missed the sound of little ones filling up a household.

In the back corner of the store, I checked on the toy section. The kids back there had played well together until Crissy and her Cabbage Patch Doll arrived. She liked to fight with the other toys' ghosts, especially with the classic Barbies, who would band together and lock themselves up in the dream house for days on end. It looked as if Crissy was sound asleep, thankfully.

I finished my rounds by grabbing Abner's ashtray and bringing it upstairs with me. With the financial stress and Aunt Birdie's failing health, I had reverted into a smoker, and taking Abner up with me made me feel less alone.

CHAPTER 4

Later that night, Harvey unwrapped an incredible spread of Mexican treats while I set the round wooden table just outside my small open kitchen.

"Those tacos look amazing!" I said, putting out a cigarette in the ashtray. Abner sat in a blue velvet wingback chair off to the side, puffing on his cigar, watching us eat.

"Wait until you try Vicente's pork verde. It's so good you will swear it was born in the sauce. The only person who made these better was my mom," he said, holding up a taco before taking a huge bite.

"I remember how sweet she was."

"Yeah, sweet, and a pain in my butt."

We filled our plates with pork, rice, refried beans, roasted jalapenos, and fresh corn tortillas. This was my favorite kind of Friday night. Harvey and I were gorging ourselves on Mexican food and margaritas, blowing off the stress of the week. I was incredibly grateful for his company tonight.

"Your aunt seemed extra uptight today, even for her," Harvey stated through a mouth full of food.

"Her dementia is getting worse, and truthfully, she has a point," I said, gulping my second margarita. "The Seth Thomas clock that arrived today was created specifically for my family after a depression in the late 1800s. My uncle Olaf was friends with Seth Thomas himself. It's one-of-a-kind. It has been passed down for generations, and here I am about to sell it."

Harvey took another big bite of a tortilla stuffed with meat. As he chewed, he stared at me and grinned. "I have an idea. My uncle, who is a big-time New York City antiques guy, is coming to town tomorrow. I'd bet he would buy a lot if I can get him in here. Maybe the clock or, even better, enough of the other items to keep you afloat while you figure out a new plan."

"Really?" I brightened. "You've never mentioned him before. Why?"

"I haven't talked to him in years. He called me last week and said he is passing through town and he'd like to take me to dinner. He's my only surviving relative, so I feel like I need to see him. Honestly, I'm hoping he's nicer than I recall him being when I was a kid."

"Do you think he'd make time to check out Mystique? I don't want to use the guy, but maybe this way I can keep the Seth Thomas."

"Why not ask? Join us for dinner tomorrow night at Joli, and we'll see what he says." Harvey smiled. "Cheers, my friend, to keeping your shop open."

I raised my glass, feeling hope for the first time in months. "To saving the Mystique!"

CHAPTER 5

My head throbbed as I flipped the sign on Mystique Antiques to open the following day.

"Lovie, you sure we were on a toot last night," Abner stated, leaning back in the Eames chair near the register. I ignored him and went about searching through my paperwork. "You realize we all need you to survive, but selling Mrs. Thomas?"

"I may not have to, Abner," I snapped.

"Don't get short with me, young lady. I'm trying to help." He took a puff of his cigar and exhaled. "Can't you get a loan and not rely on some mysterious chap from New York to take some of us away from you?"

"Last time we were running low, I took out a loan. I'm tapped out on credit, Abner. Just let me figure it out, okay? Maybe Harvey's uncle will help." I walked away and into the back storage area. Out of reach of the ghosts, unless I carried their objects with me, this windowless back room was my hiding spot when things got to be too much. Selling that clock would be challenging, but losing the shop was even worse. I paced until I heard the front door jingle.

I headed back out front starting to say, "May I help you with—" but stopped mid-sentence. There was the lady who always came into my store and touched everything but never purchased anything. During the first few years of her visits, I'd check the shop to see if she had stolen anything, and she never had. She always wore a big hat, a hood, or something hiding her face, as well as a big shawl wrapped around her, making it look as if she wore a blanket to stroll around the neighborhood. All of this garb made her stand out in any crowd.

"Hey, you want a Butterfinger?" Harvey said, using our nickname for this particular customer as he came around the corner. I burst into laughter. Harvey brought me a paper cup filled with coffee.

"You look like hell, but this will help." He winked. "Jimmy made it." He liked to put a shot or two of Jim Beam into our coffees after a night of drinking.

I took a sip and shook my head. "Wow, Jimmy put extra effort into this one. It's strong."

Butterfingers continued her trip around the store. I watched her hands caress the vintage hats and purses on the south wall. She then moved to a shelf filled with crystal. She picked a few items up as if to weigh them. I watched, glad for something to do since the shop had been dead quiet for the last three hours. Butterfingers headed back to the clocks and paused directly in front of Mrs. Thomas's clock.

"It's a nice grandfather clock, isn't it?" I said. Her head snapped up toward the face of the clock. I stared, curious if she would answer me this time. She nodded.

"Shame on you." Mrs. Thomas stormed into my line of sight.

"It's a hallway clock, not a grandfather clock. And you call yourself an antiques dealer. Shame on you." She shook her head and plopped her wide bottom into the chair next to the clocks.

A moment later, I heard Mrs. Thomas wail, "Get your hands off me!" This made Butterfingers jump as if she'd heard her. I tried not to laugh as I rushed over to find Butterfingers opening the clock to touch the pendulum.

"I'm sorry, ma'am, but please do not touch the running clocks." Butterfingers avoided eye contact as she strode away into Harvey's café.

"I best get back to it," Harvey said, following her. I watched them walk away and wondered why Butterfingers seemed to hear Mrs. Thomas.

"Did she see you?" I asked Mrs. Thomas.

"My, my, Sanne, your breath smells like whiskey," Mrs. Thomas said, walking right up to my face. "It smells delightful. And to answer your question, yes, I do believe she did."

CHAPTER 6

"I'm off to the gym!" Harvey yelled to me around four o'clock. "I locked my door and put up the sign to enter through your shop."

"Thanks! See you soon," I called back.

Knowing that, if all went well over dinner, Harvey's uncle would be coming to look at all my antiques made me nervous. I began moving all the vases, coffee cups, statues, and silver to dust under them. I checked all twenty-two of my mantelpiece clocks and my three tall clocks. I wound them and made sure each one was running on time. Then I went to the glass cases holding all my vintage jewelry. I moved them around just slightly to alleviate my frayed nerves.

"My dear, those jewels look lovely. You must relax and have a spot of tea," Mrs. Thomas said. "Adding a dash of whiskey helps, too."

"I quite agree," Abner said. "A spot of tea sounds lovely. Rest yourself, woman. You redheads get huffy about everything."

"You gingers are weird," Tiffany said. "Why not have a Coke or something good? Tea is so gross."

Many of the ghosts appeared, each giving their two cents about tea.

"Stop," I shouted. "No one is having tea. Go back to your items and leave me alone."

"Well, that's just rude," one ghost complained, drifting back into her sizeable mid-century star brooch.

• • • ● • ● • • • •

I actualized the books for the day, happy that I'd sold about five hundred dollars worth of items. Thankfully, a tour bus had stopped nearby, and the tourists seemed to like the old Seattle World's Fair memorabilia. It was a good day, but not enough to save the shop.

At five o'clock sharp, I closed up shop as all the clocks chimed right on time. I grinned at the sound of my prize clocks all running well. This was something Uncle Julio ought to appreciate.

I went upstairs, hoping to get a shower in before Harvey arrived with his uncle. But just as I stepped into the shower, I heard a loud crash. Luckily, my robe was within reach. I grabbed it and let the wet droplets soak in as I rushed back down to the shop.

"Hello?" I called out. "Is anyone there?" No one answered. I walked the aisles. Nothing was on the floor, nor was anything out of place. The clocks that struck on the half-hour bonged, a sign I was running out of time. I took one last look around the shop before returning to my shower.

CHAPTER 7

The smell of fresh baking bread, roasting meat, and spices wafting outside Joli was terrific. Inside, the small cozy restaurant bustled with people. Luckily, Harvey had made reservations. I could see one booth open, saved for us.

Hopefully, the next two days would save my antiques store. At least for a little while.

Just a few minutes after I arrived, Harvey entered with a man in a trench coat, who looked like an older version of him with silver-gray streaks in his slick black hair, an uncanny resemblance.

"This is my uncle," Harvey said when they reached our table. "Uncle Julio, this is the friend I told you all about, Sanne."

"Hello!" I said, bouncing to my feet and holding out my hand. "Shall I call you Mr. Sanchez or—"

Harvey interrupted me. "You can just call him Julio." His uncle nodded.

Uncle Julio slid into the booth across from Harvey and me, and no one said another word until we each ordered our drinks and a meal.

"Are you two dating?" Julio said with a mouthful of buttered bread, finally breaking the silence. "Or are you still intent on shocking people by dating men, Harvey?" I turned to my friend, appalled, grabbing his leg.

"Nope, still gay, Tio. Your only relative is a gay man."

"That is very unfortunate," Julio said as our drinks arrived. Julio took a sip. "So tell me, what kind of antiques do you have?"

"Mystique Antiques features some of the best antiques in the Northwest, in my opinion," I said. "My family has owned it since 1910. We sold memorabilia from the old country, then expanded into antiques from around the world. Our clock collection is most popular. We have a gorgeous Welbey and three calendar clocks, from Ithaca, Sessions, and Ansonia, respectively. We also have costume jewelry from Boucher, Dior, Carnegie, Sarah Coventry, and Trifari."

"Got it." Julio slammed his drink down, looking for a server. When he didn't see one, he turned to Harvey. "How do I get a server back over here, twinkle toes?"

Harvey shook his head, patted my leg, and whispered, "Some things never change, I guess." I could hear his voice catch.

Julio turned his attention back to me. "Do your clocks run, or are they just for parts?"

"Every one of them is running perfectly. As I left tonight, they all chimed at the same time. It was glorious."

"Wow, I haven't heard that in a while. You wound them all?" Harvey said with a grin.

Julio's drink arrived, and he took a big swig. The air seemed to get cold all of a sudden.

"Well, what do we have here? No time for family, but plenty for... I'm sorry. Exactly who are you?" Aunt Birdie tapped the edge of our table, interrupting our meal with her disapproving scowl. She moved her gaze to Julio.

"This is Julio, Aunt Birdie. He's an antiques buyer." Julio continued to drink and stuff bread into his mouth while looking past Aunt Birdie at the old movies that Joli had projected onto a back wall.

Aunt Birdie leaned into me. "Well, hopefully, he's not here for the Seth Thomas clock."

"No, Aunt Birdie. He's coming to the shop later. What are you doing here?"

"I just wanted to see it. Ethel is over there—"

"I can't see," Julio interrupted, finally looking at Aunt Birdie.

"Sorry." She straightened up. "I should get back to my friend."

"Good riddance," Julio muttered under his breath.

Aunt Birdie's head snapped to the side. "I'll go. I needn't be where I'm not wanted." She spun on her heel and left us.

I vowed that I would call her later to check in. For now, I had to focus on saving my store.

"Harvey tells me you have traveled the world for antiques. What's your best story?" I asked Julio.

He shrugged. "My trip to Israel was quite amazing. I was able to purchase a large trunk filled with treasures. It made me a mint." With this, he kept talking about himself, allowing us a break from the stress and a chance to eat.

An hour later, Julio finally stopped talking. We finished our meal, and the bill came. Uncle Julio immediately stood and left the restaurant, standing outside smoking a cigarette and talking on his phone.

"I guess I'm paying?" I said to Harvey, picking up the bill. It was over four hundred dollars.

"Don't you worry, I've got this one." Harvey put down his credit card, and I hugged him.

"You are the best, thank you."

• • • ● • ● • ● • ● • •

When I got home, I kicked my shoes off and poured two fingers of whiskey over a big ice cube. I needed one more drink to recover from the evening. I was beginning to think this was a waste of time. I could only imagine how Harvey was feeling. My phone rang.

"He's all snug as a bug at the Four Seasons," Harvey said. "He'll take a cab to us tomorrow around closing time to check out your shop."

"Thank you, Harvey." I paused for a moment.

"Sanne, what is it?"

"It's just. Well... I don't want to do business with a homophobic jerk. It's not worth it. He was awful to you, and ..."

"I know. But let me handle my relationship with him. I'm disappointed, sure. But now I can put any questions about whether I should have a relationship with Julio to rest. I don't need a person like that in my life. Family is not just blood. It's who you choose. And you, Sanne, you are family."

"I feel the same... but I feel guilty that you have to play nice with him because of me. He was terrible to you."

"You didn't know he'd behave like that. For that matter, neither did I. But let's get something out of this guy. Whatever you do, stand your ground tomorrow, and don't let him negotiate you down. He has the money. I hope he can help you by doing something good with it. Make that jerk pay!"

CHAPTER 8

At four fifty-five the next day, I nervously wandered my store straightening every piece that was slightly out of place. As much as I didn't like Uncle Julio, he could be the answer to my problems, at least for a while. I wanted my shop to look its best when he arrived.

Butterfingers visited the shop and headed directly back to Mrs. Thomas again. Watching her stare into the glass distracted me until I heard the bell next door at Someday Café and then a familiar voice, loud enough for the last few customers to hear. "You support yourself on this? I guess you take 'one cup at a time' seriously, Harvey."

"Knock it off, Tio Julio. I do just fine. You know, you don't have to be such an asshole. Go over to see Sanne's shop."

Pulling out my sales records for the day, I began to actualize my day's work. I heard Julio walk in and tried to act casual. His long, dark trench coat brushed past me on his way to the clocks.

I went back to my work, trying to ignore my nervous stomach. The next thing I heard was someone say "get out of my way" followed by a big crash. Butterfingers lay on the floor, and Julio was stepping over her. Was he so rude he pushed her to the ground, then just continued on with his shopping?

Harvey came through the doorway to see what was happening. I rushed over to Butterfingers to help her up. I had just reached out my hand when my cousin Calvin appeared at my side. Butterfingers ignored my hand. Her long, dark hair slowly fell out from a rubber band that had been holding her loose bun under a green floppy hat. She dropped a bright yellow scarf that she had picked up on the other side of the store.

"Are you okay? Did you slip?" Calvin and I said in unison. She looked up, hand shaking as she pointed to Julio, who was now at the front of the store inspecting the Chihuly sculptures, Depression glass, and a miniature Horiuchi painting I had in the window.

Butterfingers finally grabbed my hand, and I helped her to her feet. A stern expression on her face, she whispered, "Do not allow this man to take any of your treasures. He will destroy their souls. It will be the beginning of the end." With that, she put the scarf on the counter and strode out the door and into the cold night. I stared after her as she went. I had never heard her voice before. Calvin and I looked at one another for a moment.

"So, who is this guy?" Calvin asked.

"That's Julio, Harvey's uncle. He's an antiques dealer. If he buys enough, I could stay in business and keep the Seth Thomas clock," I said quietly enough that I hoped Julio wouldn't hear.

"Oh, I see. My mom is upset you may get rid of it."

"I'm not getting rid of it if I can help it."

"Well, good. Did I tell you about finding Grandpa's letters? They're like a journal. Grandpa loved that clock. He wrote about it a lot. Please keep it."

"I'm trying." I patted his shoulder and walked toward Julio.

Harvey stopped me. "Did she actually speak to you?"

"Yep, apparently she can see the ghosts too."

"You and Butterfingers, one and the same!" He laughed. Calvin joined in, as if he was in on the joke. Calvin always had to do something weird after a moment of normalcy.

The smile left Harvey's face when he glanced over at his uncle. "I'm going to close up my shop and head to the gym. Could you make Julio an espresso or something when he's done? I'll get him at my café later, much later."

Harvey had obviously reached the limit of his patience with Julio. I mouthed the word *Sorry*. He nodded. "Does that plan work for you, Julio?" I asked.

"Fine," he said, refusing to take his eyes off the hallway clock.

"That one is not for sale," Calvin stated.

Julio turned around and stared at my cousin.

"Good," Calvin said, crossing his thin arms as if he were a bouncer at a nightclub.

Julio shook his head. "We can finish our business once you clear out of the shop."

Calvin came to stand at my side. "You cannot sell that clock. Especially not to that guy. If you don't want it, give it to me."

Mrs. Thomas appeared and chimed in. "That man is up to no good, little miss. He will not honor that exceptional clock."

"Listen, Sanne," Julio said. "I want to buy things, but I am running out of time and patience." He waved his hands in the air with irritation.

"I need you to go. I'll talk to you later," I said, pushing Calvin to the door.

· · · ● · ● ● · · ·

Half an hour later, I had a list of the items Julio wished to purchase. My stomach lurched when he told me he wanted the Seth Thomas hallway clock. My mind jumped to the generations of family members who have enjoyed the gorgeous chime of the clock over Christmas holidays, mornings to rush out to school. I could almost hear my mother sing along with it as she did while she cooked her famous beef stroganoff. My heart hurt.

Julio followed me to the counter as I wrote up the order, my hand shaking and eyes filling with tears. I brushed a stray tear off my face, hoping that Julio didn't see.

"The hallway clock is eighteen thousand dollars before shipping," I said. "The grandfather clock next to it is on sale and worth a lot more. Maybe you prefer that one instead? I'll make you a deal."

"I'm no idiot, kid. Just write it up, and let's be done." He leaned against the counter, seeming quite pleased with himself.

His whole order, including most of my Depression glass, ten of my mantel clocks, and the hallway clock, added up to almost thirty thousand dollars. This one sale would keep me afloat for another six months at least.

Julio pulled out a few wads of cash, counted out the right number of bills, then rolled up the rest and shoved them back into his pocket.

"Doesn't that seem fishy?" Mrs. Thomas interjected.

"Cash? I'm okay to take cards or checks, if that works better."

"This is easier on the taxes."

I didn't want to argue and risk losing the sale. "Thank you, Julio. Let's get you that espresso."

As I finished the transaction, an angry mob of ghosts surrounded me, begging to stay here in Ballard. When I ignored their pleas, many of them disappeared, sobbing. But Mrs. Thomas and Abner were relentless.

"This is disgraceful, Sanne, just disgraceful," Mrs. Thomas slurred.

"I concur. Can't you see this man is no good?" Abner said.

"I'm so sorry, guys, but I need this," I said with tears in my eyes.

Next door, at the Someday Café, I delivered a small white ceramic cup to the round table where Julio sat reading his phone. "I'm going to run upstairs to my apartment. I'll be back in five minutes." I didn't wait for a response. Back in my shop, I grabbed the massive lump of cash. It was the most cash I had ever seen in person.

"You're going to regret this, my dear," Mrs. Thomas insisted. Abner was pacing, puffing on his cigar. He dragged his feet on the ground, making a loud swishing sound he knew drove me crazy.

"Oh, Abner," I said, shaking my head as I grabbed Abner's ashtray and left.

Upstairs, I sat down on my couch and smoked a cigarette, tears streaming down my face. The wad of cash sitting on my coffee table was the solution I had been looking for. So why did I feel so terrible? My phone rang, breaking the silence and scaring me. It was my aunt. I didn't answer, but the persistent ringing felt like Aunt Birdie was lecturing me as I took the cash to the safe in my closet. With a pang, I placed the large sum of money inside next to my father's coin collection and my mother's wedding ring. What would she have thought of our heirloom leaving the family? I shut the door and spun the lock. It was done now. I finished my cigarette and dropped it into Abner's tray before heading back downstairs to throw it away.

When I got back into the store, everything was quiet. All the ghosts seemed to have gone back to their items. Julio's phone and coffee were on the table in the café, but there was no sign of him. Figuring he must be in the bathroom, I began cleaning up the store. As I got to the front display, I noticed whiskey in one of the crystal glasses I had for sale. Who would leave whiskey over here? Maybe Harvey had needed the relief of a shot after his uncle's dismissive comments and left the glass there when he'd rushed into the shop during the commotion earlier. I put the glass on the counter near my register to clean later.

Mrs. Thomas appeared next to me, sniffing. "Smells delicious."

I smiled, glad she seemed to have calmed down about the sale of her clock. "Agreed. I'll be getting one of those drinks when I finish up here. Did Julio find the bathroom in the back?"

"Who cares where that imbecile is. And you, you are not forgiven, my dear." She spun around and disappeared.

"Julio?" I called out. "Would you like another espresso?" There was no answer. The bathroom door was wide open. My mind raced. Had Julio just left? Had Harvey arrived and they were outside? I wasn't quite sure what to do next.

Walking back toward the window to peer outside, I slipped on the wet floor. My arms flailed, trying in vain to catch my balance. What came next was a series of impressions, each worse than the last. Hard cement. Dark liquid. Uncle Julio beside me, his face bloody and his eyes vacant. I screamed.

CHAPTER 9

When Harvey arrived at the café, I was still sitting on the floor. I could hear him dialing 9-1-1, his voice shaking as he described the scene of finding his best friend crying on the floor next to his uncle's corpse. Harvey hung up and helped gather me up to my feet. Everything felt so surreal. So blurry as nausea set in. I had never seen a dead body, but how was Harvey helping me and not breaking down on his own? He held me tight and helped me into the bathroom to clean up a little and put some distance between Julio and us.

Soon, the cops pulled us out of the bathroom and separated us to opposite sides of the café. Harvey was near the front door at one table, and I was near the back, closer to the body. Thankfully, they had covered Uncle Julio.

"I'm Detective Trak. And you are?"

I stared up into the face of an older woman with short silver hair. "Sanne Sorensen. I own the antiques store next door."

"So tell me what happened."

I explained what little I knew. "After I ran our transaction, I went upstairs to put the cash in my safe, and by the time I got back down here..." My voice faltered, and I broke down crying. Detective Trak's expression didn't change at all. She continued taking notes, glancing up at me only occasionally.

"Cash, you said? How much cash?"

"A lot. Almost thirty thousand," I said, wiping my nose with the sleeve of my blue shirt.

"Who carries that kind of cash on them?"

"I don't know. It seemed odd to me, and he had a roll of bills left over, but he said something about avoiding taxes."

"Hey, Benny," she called out, "did you find another wad of cash in his coat or pants pockets?"

"Nah," he answered. "But he's got a few twenties in his wallet."

She nodded, continuing to write. "Do you know anyone who would want him dead?"

"No. Julio wasn't the nicest guy, but he didn't deserve this." My voice trembled, and tears sprung to my eyes.

• • • • • • • • • •

Detective Benny took me to the station after that and collected my clothing and fingerprints. I got back to the store at nine that evening, but it seemed later. There was yellow crime scene tape blocking off the entrance and the whole sidewalk—not good advertising for Harvey or me. I paused. How could I be thinking about my advertising? A man had just died right here in this building. And that man was Harvey's only relative. I needed to call him.

"Ma'am, you need to move along now."

I turned to find a cop sporting a stereotypical brown mustache. I reached toward the door.

"Sorry, ma'am, you can't go in there."

"I own the shop and live upstairs. How am I supposed to get home?" Not that I relished the idea of going to sleep above the scene of a murder.

"You'll need to use another entrance or stay with a friend," he said, mustache blowing with each word. I nodded.

When I turned the corner, I saw a person in a black jacket with a yellow scarf near the door that led to my apartment. I squinted, trying to see a face, but the shadows blocked a clear view. I could only gauge that the person was a bit taller than me. They abruptly turned and ran. Before I could think about it, I followed. I paused, looking from side to side, but had already lost them by the time I got to the corner. What had I thought I would do? What if they were armed? What a terrible idea to randomly chase a potential murderer. I walked back toward my door and kicked something that clinked along the pavement. I picked it up and examined it as I climbed the stairs to my apartment. It was like a safety pin, but much larger and thicker. What could it be?

Once inside, I heard a sound downstairs. I paused. Was it safe to check it out? I listened carefully, leaving my key in the lock so as not to draw any attention to myself.

After listening intently, I realized that sound was Abner, swishing his feet across the floor. I entered the back of the shop. It was a ransacked mess. Why had the cops left it this way? Taking a deep breath, I covered my face with my hands and fell into one of the café chairs. My life felt out of control, moreso than it was before Julio had arrived.

A handful of ghosts appeared in front of me, each asking a flurry of questions. I couldn't hear a single thing as the voices rang through the air.

"What happened?" "How did that guy die?" "Are you a suspect?" "That guy deserved it. He was a douche bag." The last comment was from Tiffany, standing near her clock, tightening the neon-pink scrunchy in her side ponytail.

I got up and walked around, a handful of ghosts behind me. The cash register was open, still full of cash. My jewelry and brooches were askew. Even the clocks were all out of sync. The voices and questions were getting on my nerves."Enough. I don't know. They asked me a lot of questions about the shop, who was here yesterday, and what I knew about Julio's last hours."

"Did you tell them about us, lovie?" Abner asked, a hint of cherry tobacco hitting the air.

"Of course not. Do you think I'm crazy? Did any of you see anything?" I saw a lot of heads shaking no. Once they realized I didn't know anything, the majority of them returned to their objects.

"Abner, you are usually around. You must have seen something."

"I did not see anything because we were upstairs at your safe. But if I do say so myself, I'm glad none of us have to leave with him. Were I you, I'd be grateful for the killer. Now we can stay together, and you have the money."

"That's a terrible thing to say, Abner."

Abner shrugged.

"Also, the money is gone. The police took it. Every single dime. The cash is now evidence."

"Pity," he said with a final puff before disappearing.

I looked around the shop, trying to decide what to do. Fingerprinting dust covered the tables, and the thought of the blood on the floor in the café made my stomach hurt. They'd insisted I stay out of the café until they cleared the scene. That was fine with me. The mustache outside watched me through the window. I waved and grabbed Abner's ashtray so I could go upstairs and smoke. The cop nodded and turned his back to me. With him there, I felt a little bit safer.

Once inside my apartment, I locked two deadbolts, secured the chain, and then tested the door to be sure. It didn't budge. I sat down in my big wingback chair and settled in for a cigarette. Abner appeared.

"Everything will be okay now, Sanne. You'll see."

CHAPTER 10

At nine in the morning, I stumbled to the door to stop the loud banging. "I"m coming, I'm coming. Settle down." I assumed it would be Harvey wanting to debrief, but it was Detective Trak. I pushed my auburn curls behind my shoulders and tied my bathrobe tighter.

"Miss Sorensen, I'll need you to come downstairs immediately," she said, lips pursed into a tight line.

"Let me get dressed, and I'll be there in a minute."

"No, now." She pulled me toward the stairs.

"I'm coming." I pulled my arm from her grip. She walked in front of me, stopping every few steps to be sure I was following.

My shop looked as it had last night, completely ransacked. I was tired, uncaffeinated, and annoyed at this woman's audacity. "You know, this kind of shutdown is hard on us, but to make it look like this is just rude. Why did you leave such a mess?" I exclaimed.

"This," she said waiving her hand in the air in a circle "was not us. In fact, I was going to ask you the same thing. Were you down here last night?"

"Well, yes, I was," I admitted, "just a few minutes. But it was this terrible when I came home. Just ask the mustache you had out front. Then I went to bed. If you didn't do it, who did?"

Detective Trak rolled her eyes and said. "Last night, you gave us all the money Julio paid you for the antiques he planned to buy?"

"Of course I did."

"So does this look familiar?" She held up a plastic bag of rolled-up bills.

"Yeah. That's how Julio kept his money."

"Any reason this would be under your counter?"

"What? No. I put all my cash in the safe upstairs every night."

"I'm going to need you to take a seat right over there." She pointed to a chair occupied by Mrs. Thomas.

"You're going to have to move," I said to Mrs. Thomas, under my breath. She just kept knitting. "Please, I don't want to sit on you."

"Dear, I don't feel well. Find another chair." A faint scent of whiskey lingered in the air.

"I can't. Do you see what's going on here?"

Mrs. Thomas looked up. Surprise washed over her face.

"You really didn't notice."

"No, dear, I was up late last night."

"Move!" I demanded.

"What?" Detective Trak asked.

"Nothing," I muttered, sitting down in the chair. Detective Trak left my shop and went into the Someday Café. I could hear Harvey's voice, but I couldn't see him. I wondered if they were giving him just as hard a time.

For almost an hour, I sat there watching the cops dig through all of my drawers, handling all of my antiques. They even pulled out all my jewelry and laid it on the counter, checking to see if anything was hiding in the matting that held the pieces. They were making my already disastrous store look even worse. I wanted to jump up and shout, *Stop!* I wished I could rewind the hands of time, but I couldn't. I was stuck here in this chair like a child in time-out.

An officer approached me. "Would you please join Detective Trak in the café?"

Inside I found the detective at one of the rectangular tables with Harvey. Harvey jumped to his feet, and I ran to him, giving him a big hug.

"Please sit. We need to talk." She tapped her pen loudly on her notepad. "Harvey here says he did not put the cash under your register."

"Right. I said there was no reason for it to be there." The idea of this wad of cash made my stomach hurt. How did it get under my register? Had someone tried to frame me? Could Harvey be setting me up for some reason? No. He would never do that, right?

"But it was there, in your space. You are also struggling with your payments." She pulled out my overdue bills. "Is it possible you saw how much money he had in his pockets, and you decided to murder him while your friend was out?"

"What? No! I never touched any of his money other than the bills he gave me, which I put in my safe." My clocks began to chime ten times, drowning out any sound from Detective Trak.

"Can you please go back to the other room while I speak with Harvey?" Detective Trak asked. I got to my feet. Harvey gave me a reassuring nod, and I left the room.

About ten minutes later, Mrs. Thomas's hall clock began to chime. They had all been in unison yesterday. Why was the Seth Thomas clock running behind? It was about seven minutes slow. I approached it and opened the door.

"Ma'am, this is a crime scene. Don't touch anything." An officer grabbed my shoulder, pulling me away, then yelled, "My God! Detective! I need you." Confused, I looked back. There was blood on the pendulum.

CHAPTER 11

The interview room smelled of sweat, burgers, and mold. It made me nauseous. I took a sip from the water bottle they had given me and noticed my hand shaking. I put the bottle down and paced the room. Up in the corner, I spotted the camera. Like the detective TV shows depicted, one wall was a huge sheet of one-way glass. This room had been my holding place now for three hours. My stomach felt like a hard knot. Sweat beaded up on my forehead, even though the room was a bit cold.

The door opened. Detective Trak sauntered in. "Do you want to come clean now, or do we have to continue to play this game?"

"I didn't do it."

"Everyone in that chair says they're innocent. But the facts are simple. You are the last person to be seen with the victim. Your business is failing, which is understandably upsetting. You saw the thousands more he had in his pockets. People have killed for a lot less than that. And oh, yeah, we found the likely murder weapon in your clock. Now, doesn't that seem clear to you?" Detective Trak leaned forward, gritting her teeth like a hungry grizzly bear.

I leaned back, away from her stale coffee breath, gripping my stomach with both hands. "I did not do this."

"Then who did, Sanne? Who killed Julio?"

"I don't know. He was a jerk to everyone, it seemed. He knocked one of my usual customers down to the ground. She was so upset she said something about him being a bad person. Maybe her? She's an odd character." I continued to cry. Then it occurred to me. "Wait, did I tell you someone was by my apartment door in the alley the night of the murder? After you dropped me off? Maybe that person did it."

"Interesting that this is the first we have heard of this." She did not seem impressed. I sat quietly and stared at her. The room stayed eerily silent.

"Could you describe the person for us?"

"Not really. They had a long black jacket on and a bright yellow scarf. That's all I could see in the dark as they ran away from me."

"That's all you have?" she asked. "Sounds to me like you are grasping at straws. Any chance you staged a robbery and that is why your shop is turned over?"

"What? I would never..." Then it dawned on me. Someone was setting me up.

"But?"

"I thought I heard there were no signs of a break in. Wouldn't a person trying to stage a break-in make gouges around the door as they tried to pry it open?"

"And wouldn't a guilty someone point that out?" She sneered at me.

"Are we done. I want to go home." I wiped my eyes. "Unless I need to call a lawyer?"

"You can go, for now, but don't leave the area. We'll be back once we get the test results for the blood found on the pendulum. I can't imagine that is going to bode well for your shop." Her gaze was terrifying. I looked away.

"Someone is here to take you home," she said finally.

At the front of the station, Aunt Birdie and Calvin were waiting. "Harvey was taken in for questioning, so he asked that we come get you." Aunt Birdie shook her head slowly. "My word, what kind of trouble have you gotten yourself into?"

CHAPTER 12

By the time we got back to the shop, the police tape and guard were gone. I had managed to tell Aunt Birdie and Calvin the whole story.

"Let us come in and help you, honey," Aunt Birdie offered. "It would be our pleasure." It was nice to see a glimmer of my kind Aunt Birdie. Dementia had taken a real toll on her. Beyond the forgetfulness, she was starting to get an uncharacteristic mean streak.

"Thanks." I sighed, knowing there was a lot of work to do between Someday Café and Mystique Antiques. I picked up the overdue notices scattered around my cash register.

Aunt Birdie nodded. "They asked me quite a bit about your financial situation and mine." She pulled her white gloves off one finger at a time. "I find it quite classless to ask about money, but I guess they must." She finished with her gloves, taking her fitted blue coat and matching hat off and hanging it on a coat tree near the door.

Calvin walked to the clock and examined the case. "Why isn't it running?" he asked.

"They found blood on the pendulum, so the cops took it into evidence."

"Oh no, that's terrible." He turned to the clock and ran his hand down the side and knocked a few times.

"Enough!" Mrs. Thomas came storming out of the clock. She yelled into his face, "Stop knocking all over the place.

It makes my head hurt!" Aunt Birdie and I both laughed while Calvin, oblivious, continued.

"Do you know why the men in our family don't see them?" I asked Aunt Birdie.

"Maybe they could if they would open their eyes?" She began to survey the mess. "Hop to it, Calvin. Let's help your cousin get this place in order so she can get back into business tomorrow and maybe save that lovely clock."

Calvin stood motionless, as if unsure where to start.

I tapped his shoulder. "If you want to help me, please straighten this up." I squatted down and looked at the silver section of my jewelry. The police had taken each pin out of its cushion. Cleaning up this mess was going to take hours. My mind wandered to the pin I found out in the alley, but Calvin interrupted my train of thought by kneeling down beside me.

"What did the police interview you about?" I asked.

"They asked me where I went Sunday night after leaving the shop. I have a bagpipes class. They also wanted to know more about our relationship. I painted it as if we were great friends. Remember when we used to be?" he said. "I played the Scotsman and you the Viking on the ship. Those games were a blast! We were so close, and we always helped one another."

"Yup, that funny Viking hat was great. How many tartan scarves of your mom's did you ruin? I always wondered why you didn't want to be a Viking like your dad and my mom. Instead, you went for your mom's Scottish side."

"I guess I just liked plaid," he said. "We still had fun with it, didn't we? It was better than hanging out with the kids on the dirt bikes, just being loud." He stood up and moved over to the glass counter and peered down at me as I worked at sorting out the brooches in the case. The corner glass distorted his face into some grotesque shape, obscuring his mousy brown hair and green eyes, which were just like my Uncle Jack's.

"We did, Calvin, yes."

"I have to go to the bathroom," he said abruptly, leaving the room.

I stood up to give my back a rest and looked over at Aunt Birdie and her perfectly tight French twist, working away.

"You know, Sanne, I hope this turns out okay."

Tears sprung to my eyes. "I am in an impossible situation." I knelt down and went back to work, hoping to hide my tears. "I feel like it's the antiques shop or the clock."

"You're a smart girl. You will figure it out."

I went over to Someday Café. There was still dried blood on the floor where Julio had died. I sat down next to it, gazing at the stain, wondering who had murdered him.

A little while later, I felt a hand rest on my shoulder. "Your mom will be home soon. Pick up your toys now and put them away." I looked up and saw the aunt of my youth. I smiled.

"Okay, Aunt Birdie." I walked her over to Calvin.

"It might be time to go. It seems that I need to clean up my toys." Calvin nodded. "Come on, Mom. Let's let Sanne finish this up."

"Okay, honey, as long as you promise me you will not leave this mess for your mother." Aunt Birdie stared me down.

"I promise."

"If you want to give me a key, I can come back later and clean some more," Calvin offered.

"I think I've got it, Calvin, but thanks." He nodded and took his mother's arm.

I watched Calvin walk with his mom, helping her gently into the car.

CHAPTER 13

Behind the counter at Someday Café was an absolute mess. The to-go cups and boxes scattered about the floor. The cops must have looked behind the containers for the murder weapon before finding the blood on the pendulum of my family's antique clock.

I was removing dirty cups and putting the clean ones back when Harvey came through the door. "Oh my God. Are you okay?" I said, running into his arms. "What happened?"

"It turns out I'm the sole heir to Uncle Julio's estate. The police are suspicious because I have access to the antiques shop," he said. "They let me go, but told me they'd be watching." Harvey walked over to the bloody spot on the floor and stared. "Even in death, Julio is a jerk. He ruined my childhood by showing up drunk to my birthday parties and insulting my friends, or by promising to help me with college and backing out at the last minute. He was a jerk. And now he's ruining my adult life. It's always a mess around Uncle Julio. Serves him right to be murdered."

"Wait, what? Harvey, you don't mean that."

"I wanted him to come here because I hoped he had changed. That maybe the heartbreak he caused my mom would be worth it. That maybe I'd have some semblance of a family again. Since Damon broke up with me, I've been missing family. But I should've known better. I'm glad he's gone."

My stomach lurched, hearing him speak so poorly of his uncle. Julio may have been a jerk, but no one deserved to be stabbed to death.

Harvey let out a big sigh. "That Detective Trak is a real piece of work. They are treating Julio like he was some kind of saint when he was alive or something."

I tried to push past my nausea to support my friend.

"They do have to solve the case. Like him or not, don't you want to know how someone got murdered in our space? And about family, think of it this way, at least we have each other," I offered weakly. "Friends are the family you choose."

"Yup, I wouldn't give you up for nothin'." Harvey smiled and wrapped me in his arms. "Will you help me get this place back in order so we can open tomorrow?"

"You bet. Why don't you let me clean up what's left of the blood."

"Thanks, I'll take you up on that."

I grabbed the mop and the bucket and filled it with bleach and water. Mopping the area and seeing it become clean was rewarding.

"Will you help me figure out who did it?" Harvey asked as he replenished the cups and tops that I had been working on when he arrived.

"Of course."

"Thanks," he said, a tear streaming down his face. He brushed it away and went back to work.

CHAPTER 14

An hour later, Harvey and I sat in Someday Café at the table where Julio had spent the last few moments of his life. Now that the café was clean, we thought it would give us the energy to find the murderer and take them down.

"What are your clues?" Harvey asked.

I told him about the person with the yellow scarf and held up the large, shiny safety pin I had found right after they fled the scene.

"Did you tell the cops about this?" he asked.

"I tried, but they were too preoccupied with the clock pendulum," I said.

"Wait a second. If you can talk to ghosts, why can't they tell you who killed my uncle? Isn't that a no-brainer?"

"I asked, but they said they didn't see anything. Truthfully, the only one I'd trust is Abner, the older gentleman attached to the ashtray, but since I started smoking again, I take that upstairs with me at night. So he was with me when the murder happened."

"What about the lady with the clock? Can you try again?" He stared me down.

"Are you seriously asking me to go talk to the ghosts you don't believe in? Maybe something good did come out of this—now you believe me!" We laughed for a moment.

"I am serious." He smiled. "Pretty please?"

"Sure." I got up and walked over to my shop. Harvey followed, keeping a good amount of distance between us.

"Mrs. Thomas?" I opened the door of the clock and looked inside where the pendulum used to be. "Are you here?"

"Yes, my dear?" she said, appearing from behind her clock.

"Do you remember the night of the murder?" I could hear Harvey behind me snickering. "Hey man, I'm doing this for you. You stop."

"Well, no. I do not recall many evenings since I arrived here." I smelled the cherry tobacco and turned around.

"Abner, hello." I smiled.

"That woman is a drunk. Every morning I come down to find her hungover or still in the throes of intoxication." He exhaled a large puff of smoke. "I find it most distasteful."

"Calling the kettle black, sir?" she slurred. "Smoking is no longer considered charming. I don't enjoy the smoke any more than you enjoy my whiskey."

"Wait, you can get drunk?" I asked. "How does that work?" I had a faint memory of my grandmother laughing with my grandfather as a child, telling him not to leave his whiskey out or it could get nipped.

"Are you asking ghosts about getting drunk?" Harvey laughed. "This is getting ridiculous. Let's forget this and get back to work," he said, walking to the café.

"Gimme a minute. This is important!" I shouted back.

I turned back to Abner and Mrs. Thomas. She hiccupped and then disappeared.

Abner shook his head and tightened up his ascot. "A ghost can over-imbibe from the fumes coming off an open glass of whiskey," he said. "So, stop leaving them around the shop, and she will sober up."

"I haven't left whiskey out around the shop. But I did see one glass up by the purses and another behind my desk. Wait a second." I ran over to the café. "Harvey, have you been doing shots of whiskey after hours and maybe forgetting your glass over here?"

"No. Why? Are your ghosts partying too hard? This is too much, but I do appreciate the laugh." "I'm not kidding. I've been finding shots of whiskey around the shop. I'm going to see if there are any others."

"Whatever you need to do," he said, continuing to chuckle. Back in my shop, I took a closer look at the hallway clock. To the side was another shot glass of whiskey. I grabbed it.

"Dear, give me that," Mrs. Thomas begged, appearing next to me. I shook my head no and took it to the café. I wanted to help her sober up. She could only follow if I took the clock into the café.

"What about this?" I said, holding the glass up for Harvey to see. His mouth fell open. "Isn't that one of the shot glasses we keep in the back for special occasions?"

"Mmm hmm," I said. "it also smells like the Maker's we keep right next to it." I walked to the hallway that connected our two shops. The shelving still held our Maker's Mark bottle, but there was only one shot glass where four usually rested. "Only one is still back there. Two more of our glasses are gone. This is so weird. Do you think the killer did it? And if so, does that mean this person has been here repeatedly? Now that is creepy. Dang it, I shouldn't have touched it. Oh no!"

"Don't get worked up. That makes no sense. But this pin, this is an odd thing," Harvey said, holding it up in the air. As he examined the pin, I walked to the shop's front and peered out the window into the night.

"I wonder if the murderer came in through the back or the front that night? I mean, there were no signs of forced entry. Was the lock picked? Was it someone that had a key?"

"Only you and I have keys that I know of," Harvey stated.

"I think that's it. I even took Aunt Birdie's key a while back. I didn't want her coming here if she was having an episode and leaving the place open. I just wish I knew. That night, I was in my apartment. The killer could have come in either way."

"Are you sure you locked the door?"

"Pretty sure. But no, not one-hundred-percent sure."

Harvey nodded and went back to work.

"Look, there is Butterfingers again." She was walking up the sidewalk on our side of the street. When she got to the café, our eyes locked, then she ran down the street. "Now that's weird. I remember having a scarf like that in the store. A yellow scarf that disappeared the day Julio died. Maybe she did it."

"Why would Butterfingers want to kill a stranger?" Harvey asked.

"Maybe Butterfingers cracked. You're not going to believe this, but I suspect she too can see the ghosts. If that is the case she could have heard the litany of complaints about leaving the store and she decided to take the matter into her own hands. Maybe she's mentally ill. It just kinda makes sense, don't you think?

Before he could answer, the café doors swung open, and three cops appeared, along with Detective Trak. "Harvey Hernandez, you are under arrest for the murder of Julio Hernandez." They swarmed him and locked his wrists in handcuffs.

"Arrest?"

"Your fingerprints were discovered on the murder weapon."

My jaw dropped. "Call my lawyer, Sanne," he called out as they dragged him away. I had never been so relieved that both the café and my shop were empty.

CHAPTER 15

After calling Harvey's attorney, I sat down on my couch. The lawyer had advised me to stay home and let him handle the cops. I took a big swig of white wine and stared across the coffee table at Abner's ashtray, which was sitting next to a Cabbage Patch doll I had brought up in order to remove a stain from her hand. I took another drag of my cigarette and wondered out loud, "What if Harvey had done it? What if his fury with his uncle became too much to take?"

"I don't like it here. There's no one to play with," the little girl attached to the Cabbage Patch doll cried out, breaking my concentration.

"Great, I'm not in the mood," I said, finishing my glass of wine and pouring another.

The little ghost stomped her feet, dark pigtails bobbing up and down on each side of her head. I couldn't help but laugh a little.

"Lovie, please get that little one to be silent. I was trying to nap," Abner complained.

"I wanna go home! I want to go home now! I want my toys! I want my mom!"

I begged her to quiet down, but the little voice became more shrill with each scream.

"If we go play with the other toys for a while, will you please stop it so I can get some rest?" I asked. With a snotty little grin, she nodded.

Once we were in the store, the little ghost ran to the toy section and began to play. I decided to take the time to clean up around the shop and catch my breath. Just then, a cold burst of air hit my shoulders, sending a shudder down my spine.

I put my wine down and strode to the back of the shop. The loading dock door was slightly ajar. I looked outside. The alley seemed normal. I stepped into the brisk wind rushing up the alleyway and only saw a few people out on the main sidewalk.

As I tried to shut the door, something made a scraping sound under my shoe. It was another big safety pin. I shoved it into my jeans pocket and shut the door, shaking the handle to make sure the lock clicked into place.

"Hello?" I called out into my shop, fearful that the murderer was back.

There was no answer, but I heard a rumbling back in the store. I rushed into the central part of the store and didn't see anything other than the little girl playing with a few other ghosts. A crash followed a loud rustling sound. I ran back by the clock and found the Seth Thomas hallway clock door open. Next to it was Mrs. Thomas.

"Did you see anything?" I asked her.

"Something moved back toward the door I think. I wasn't really looking. But, my dear, can you be a gem and pour me some more whiskey?" she asked, pointing to a shot glass on the floor. I stared in disbelief—another shot glass. I rushed to the back door to make sure it was still closed. It was. I checked the shelf with the Maker's Mark on it, which was also still in place but short quite a bit. But this shot glass—it hadn't been here earlier. "Darlin', please," Mrs. Thomas begged.

I glared at her. "Are you drunk again, Mrs. Thomas?" "My heavens, child. Just get me a spot of whiskey."

As I leaned over to grab the glass and Mrs. Thomas let out a sigh of relief, I noticed several pieces wood on the floor. "Why are parts of your clock on the floor?"

"I'm not sure, dear. It's been quite a night." She let out a belly laugh. "Why don't we discuss it over some more spirits?"

I went into the back and poured her another shot. I looked around again and saw no one. Hopefully, the cops had left the door open earlier. But hadn't they come in the front?

Mrs. Thomas took a big sniff of the glass I gave her. "Thank you, dear. Now, what are you fussing over?"

"Was someone here? Did you see someone come in the back? And why are there pieces of the clock on the floor?"

"Slow down, you are rattling on like a train. One question at a time." She took another sniff.

"Did you see anyone in the shop after I left?"

"Nothing bad happened if that is what you are worried about."

"What? Does that mean someone was here?"

"Well, yes, dear, someone lovely, but they left. That's where my whiskey..." She passed out in the chair before she could finish. I reached out to shake her, but my hands rushed through her shoulder and hit the chair. Mrs. Thomas disappeared.

"Dang it!" I cried out, slipping to my knees on the floor. With my face in my hands, I sobbed until I heard a little voice next to me. "Are you okay?" the little girl with the pigtails asked.

"I"m sorry. What was your name?"

"Jennifer. Why are you crying?"

"I'm just frustrated and a bit scared. Have you seen anyone in the shop since we got down here, Jennifer?"

"Just my friends," she said. "That lady was acting weird."

"Yeah, I know. She does that sometimes." I smiled, not wanting to try to explain drunkenness to a child.

"That wood shouldn't be on the floor," Jennifer said, pointing to the pieces. "You should fix it. Can I play longer?"

"Of course," I said. I had forgotten about the chunks of wood lying around the base of the clock.

This clock had been carefully pieced together upon delivery. There were no extra pieces. Surely I had swept here earlier before Harvey was dragged out in cuffs. I opened the clock door and looked inside. The piece from the floor seemed to be from a secret compartment I hadn't known about. On the right wall of the clock inside, a board slid up into a small square slot. This piece was perfectly fitted, making the seams barely visible. The next piece on the floor was similar but from the left side of the clock. A prickly feeling ran up the back of my neck. Maybe this clock's secret compartments had held something valuable, something worth killing over.

CHAPTER 16

"Mystique Antiques, Sanne speaking. How may I help you?"

"Sanne, I'm in deep trouble here. They seem like they want to press charges. You've gotta help me."

"You didn't do this, right?"

"Seriously, are you going to doubt me at a time like this?"

"Sorry, no. I just... Well, you said some things that threw me off." "Sanne, knock it off. No, I did not kill my uncle."

"Right, right, right. Okay, so this is going to sound weird, but the loading dock door was open last night when I came downstairs after closing."

"That's creepy."

"And someone has been pulling the Seth Thomas clock apart and getting into some secret compartments."

"That has to be the killer."

"And even weirder? Butterfingers was outside creeping around. Humor me for a second. Remember we were looking at the whiskey glasses the other day? Maybe the person who did this knows about the ghosts. They realized that they need to get them drunk to carry through on a murder. So they left the glasses around, and voila, no one remembers anything."

"That seems like a lot of knowledge and planning. It's not like we knew that Julio would be here," he stated.

"But what if it's not about Julio? What if it's about one of the antiques that Julio bought? Remember my theory about Butterfingers? Maybe she sees and hears the ghosts too. I think she does."

"I suppose that could be true, but which ghost would be bugging her? The clock?" he asked. "It seems more likely that Julio pissed someone off. He was a real gem, remember. He also pushed Butterfingers over, and she was really upset. It could be her?"

"That's what I'm thinking. I'll bet someone was digging around in the clock searching for something when your uncle found them. The person and Julio likely got into a fight, and when Julio thought they were gone, they came back in and murdered him. I'll find the killer and get you out. I promise. I'm sorry I doubted you."

CHAPTER 17

It was a busy Saturday since I was covering both my shop and Harvey's. All this work gave me little time to figure out why someone was digging around inside Mrs. Thomas's clock. I had just finished making room for a new grandfather clock that would be delivered soon and was starting to fill several coffee orders when a tourist bus stopped in front of the shop. For help, I called the only other person who knew how to run the store.

Ten minutes later, Calvin arrived, still clad in his kilt and long socks from bagpipes class. I don't think I'd ever been so happy to see him. The store rumbled with the sound of shoppers and caffeine addicts, all looking for their next treat.

"I can see that you rushed here. Thank you so much for coming so quickly. I was dying over here!"

Calvin grimaced. "Too soon."

"Right. So, can you help the delivery guy and watch the register on the antiques side?" I asked.

"Okay," Calvin said, stalking away.

"I appreciate the help. Truly."

Making coffee drinks wasn't my favorite thing to do, but I was good at it, from what I heard. Five caramel macchiatos, two soy lattes, more flat whites than I could count, and two teas, and finally, the line disappeared. I washed my hands a final time.

The sound of items moving around came from the back; my clock had arrived. I could hear Calvin greeting the driver, so I straightened up in the toy section so I could keep an eye on any customers coming in.

The delivery man and the clock appeared around the corner, followed by Calvin, who showed the man the perfectly cleared square intended for this new clock. Calvin turned to me. "Where's Harvey?" he asked.

"He's in prison. Can you believe it?"

"Wow. Do you think Harvey murdered his uncle? That's crazy." He looked away.

"No."

"I mean, I know you're close, but he could have. When did Harvey go to jail?" Calvin asked as he helped the delivery guy shimmy the clock back closer to the wall.

"Last night. It seems like they're going to charge him."

"What? That's horrible. But if he did it, I hope they lock him up."

"He did not do it." I walked away, leaving Calvin to finish up with the delivery guy. I couldn't bear to hear someone else suspect Harvey, even if I'd had my own doubts until recently.

Two more tour buses stopped on Main Street before the end of the day. When the final customer left, I locked the door.

"I couldn't have made it through today without you. Thank you so much. Would you like a coffee or glass of wine?" I asked Calvin.

"Sure," he said, sitting down at his favorite table near the window.

"What's your poison?" I asked before glancing at the corner where Uncle Julio had died. I cringed.

"Red wine. You have any?"

"Sure. I talked to Aunt Birdie yesterday. She said you're all absorbed in some family stuff you found in the basement. Anything that may work for the shop?"

"Nah, it's just a bunch of old letters and journals that Grandpa wrote. He seemed to keep track of Grandma's delusions about ghosts."

I put down a glass of red wine in front of him and held up my glass of white.

"To family, history, and all the help today. Cheers."

• • • ◐ • ◑ • ◑ • • •

After Calvin left, I began to dust and sweep the antiques shop, listening to the ghosts complain about the departure of Bella Bing Bong, one of the most popular clocks for all her wistful bells and melodies. Then I moved over to the café. As I picked the glasses up, I stepped on another large safety pin just like those I found in the alley and back behind the chair. Had the killer been in the café today or had it been here all along, escaping the cops' notice and mine? I left my chores unfinished to double-check the locks and caught a glimpse of Butterfingers out the window, staring at me. She was still wearing the yellow scarf and black jacket. A chill trickled down my spine, making my hands quiver enough to drop the pin on the floor. I bent to pick it up, and when I stood again, she was gone.

I had to know once and for all.

CHAPTER 18

Pushing through my side cramp and my screaming legs, I raced after Butterfingers, who had a big head start but was still barely in view. Until now, I had thought there were only two things I would run for, my life and the bus. But apparently, I also ran after suspected murderers.

I tracked her to a large Victorian house, painted pink with purple details around the peaks and surrounded by a picket fence. I stopped on the sidewalk and gazed at it. Through a window, I could see the warm light in a living room where a few older people played cards at tables. Butterfingers appeared without her jacket on. Her mouth was moving quickly until a younger woman came in and put a hand on her shoulder. Butterfingers turned and pointed at me. I looked behind me, forgetting that, in this situation, I was the voyeur. My instinct was to panic, and I started to walk away.

After two steps, I stopped. If I wanted to know what was going on, I should stay and see if either woman would come outside and talk to me. The younger woman helped Butterfingers into a chair. Then she waved at me to come inside.

I hadn't knocked yet when the door opened, revealing the young Black woman with a warm smile.

"May I ask why you followed Mrs. Boone tonight?" she said. "She was quite frightened."

"She comes to my antiques store every day and touches everything. But a few days ago, my shop got broken into. I saw a person in a black jacket with a yellow scarf flee the area. I wondered if it was her. I just meant to ask, but she ran."

"Mrs. Boone?" The woman laughed, making me feel silly. "This is a long-term recovery home. Mrs. Boone has been with us for many years. She is a charming, shy woman. That yellow scarf is interesting, though. She came home one night with a huge grin on her face. She had seen this lovely yellow scarf in your store and it reminded her of one her mother had. I remembered we had a box of hers in storage. And wouldn't you know it, there was that yellow scarf of her mother's in that box. She hasn't stopped wearing it since."

The woman walked through the wide archway to the other room. There, she crouched next to Butterfingers. They chatted for a moment. I heard the woman ask her if she wanted to speak to me, and she frantically shook her head no.

The caregiver walked back to me. "I'm sorry, she can be quite shy."

I looked over at the woman now sitting peacefully. "Do you have any idea why she is always watching my shop?"

"Ah, she often talks about your antiques shop. She comes from an abusive background and is keeping an eye on you. She worries about such a pretty young lady working on her own at night. Ever since the murder, she has been obsessed with keeping you safe."

Butterfingers smiled at me. I grinned and nodded before turning to the nurse. "I feel like such a jerk. Sorry for any anxiety I caused her."

The woman smiled. "Your antiques shop brings her joy and reminds her of her mother. She will be fine, don't worry." She shook my hand, and I left the house.

CHAPTER 19

"Oh my gosh, I'm so glad to hear your voice, Harvey," I gasped out as I answered the phone. "Are you okay?" I wandered over to the counter and began manically arranging and rearranging the brooches and necklaces under the glass. "Yeah, but it looks like they have more evidence against me. The police apparently have a tip from an anonymous source that I was arguing with Julio in the alley the night of the murder."

"But it's not true!"

"I know, but we need to find the real killer." I heard a loud voice in the background yelling about something unintelligible. "Please, Sanne, get me out of here. These other guys are terrifying."

"Have you been hurt?"

"Last night, some guy wanted my dinner roll. Before I even knew it, he socked me in the eye and took it." He laughed weakly. "Little does he know I'm on a low-carb diet."

"Not funny. Did they get you medical treatment?"

"I'm okay for now, Sanne, but you have to help me. Any new tips or leads?"

I told him about my pursuit of Mrs. Boone and how the mystery of the scarf had clarified. It was not likely a good lead. But I'd found another of the pins.

"What do you think the pins are for?" he asked.

"I'm guessing to pick the lock?"

"You be safe, Sanne. I can't lose you too." I heard a voice yell in the background. "Time's almost up, Sanne. Please be careful, but also get me the hell out of here!"

There was a crash in another part of the shop. "What the hell just happened? Harvey, hold on."

Mrs. Thomas was lying on the floor with Abner and Tiffany standing over her shaking their heads.

I couldn't see what had made the noise.

"Looks like that shot glass over there fell."

"That's not all, Abner," I said. "Out with it. What is she doing?"

"Trying to get totally blasted. That's what," Tiffany said, popping her gum and tossing her crimped blond hair over her shoulder. I stared at her and had an idea.

"Can you guys help get Mrs. Thomas settled?" Tiffany and Abner nodded. I went into the café to finish my call.

"Bear with me, Harvey. I think that maybe one of the ghosts did this."

"You think a ghost murdered my uncle? You have got to be kidding me. Seriously?"

"Tiffany hated your uncle, and she has a terrible temper. If Mrs. Thomas can get drunk, maybe Tiffany found a way to wield a pendulum."

"Okay. I'll bite. Test your theory about Tiffany."

"Done."

CHAPTER 20

I pulled the plug on Tiffany's clock as I dusted the items and said hello to the ghosts.

"Be a gentle young lady. Please," Abner begged.

"Sorry, Abner," I said, moving on to the plates and teacups, whose ghosts—the ladies of tea time—always whispered their rumors and asked for tea and cakes to enjoy with their gossip. I don't believe they were aware they were dead. Once I got to the Viking hat, the store lit up with old Norse cursing and hollering. I knew this would bring Tiffany out of her clock.

"Why are those annoying dudes always yelling? I was trying to sleep in. And who unplugged my clock? I feel out of it without the electricity. I need it to help me think. Duh." She stormed over to me, her jelly bracelets sliding up and down her arms.

"Fix it yourself. I'm busy," I said, knowing this would set her off.

"You are so lame."

"I'm busy."

"Um, hello McFly, I can't do it."

"Right. Whatever, Tiffany. I don't believe you." "Fine." Tiffany went over to the cord and tried to grab it. The cord didn't move. Tiffany tried kicking it, to no avail.

"Lovie. You know better." A cherry-scented puff escaped his mouth. "She cannot manipulate the cord herself unless, of course, she feels a strong emotion. Irritation isn't enough. Please help the young lass, so we don't have to listen to her moan and complain all day long." She flailed around, trying every which way to move the plug. It looked like some kind of terrible dance. After a few minutes, she plunked to the ground. "Like, really? Now fix it!" she demanded.

"What kind of strong emotion do you mean, Abner? Could one of you have hurt Julio because he was going to take you away?"

"Lovie, no. Love, fear, deep hatred, maybe, but not annoyance about a new locale."

"What about Mrs. Thomas? She really objected to going."

"Hah!" Abner laughed. "Drinking makes it nearly impossible for her to focus or care enough. If she could move anything, it would likely be a bottle of whiskey, not her beloved pendulum. She also wouldn't be able to make it all the way to the café. That's quite a distance."

"I'm right here, guys. Shut up and plug my frickin' clock in!"

I plugged the clock back in. So much for the theory that one of the ghosts killed Julio.

I headed toward the café to get the cigarettes stashed behind the counter, but halfway there I sat down and cried. I missed Harvey. I wanted my life back to normal. Abner stood over me, puffing on his cigar.

My foot kicked something on the floor, another large safety pin. I picked it up. "Abner, do you know what this is?"

"I do believe that is a kilt pin."

"A what?" I screamed. "A kilt pin... Oh my god!"

"Dear, please be careful. My head is sensitive to all this ruckus," Mrs. Thomas said. "My clock has been off ever since they stole my pendulum. These weights are not quite right anyway, but running a little slow is nothing compared to not running at all. But I will feel much better when I get my pendulum back. When might that be, my dear?"

"Shhhh." I scratched my head.

"I do believe she has a plan." Abner let a ring of smoke escape his mouth as he grinned at Mrs. Thomas.

"I think I'm going to need some help at the store tomorrow." I smiled. "I'd better call and see if my family

will help."

CHAPTER 21

I climbed up on the counter and installed a camera that pointed directly at the Seth Thomas clock. It was a fancy camera with night vision, so I knew the camera would catch any action that happened in the store around that clock. I checked my phone app to make sure I could see the clock. Then I made the call.

"Hey, Calvin, how are you?"

"I'm good. Sorry I couldn't pick up when you called. But I did talk to Mom. She says you need me again tomorrow? I'm busy trying to get her ready to move into the home at the end of the month. Can I let you know later?" he asked.

"Sure, I'll be out tonight visiting Harvey, so just text me when you figure it out. I can also help you later with Aunt Birdie if you do me a solid."

"Oh? You're out tonight?" he asked. "Where is he being held?"

"They moved him to a holding area downtown somewhere. I'm going to have to find out."

"I hope he's doing okay. I gotta run. I'll text you when I know if I can help tomorrow."

"Thanks!" I said with a big grin on my face.

• • • • • • • • • •

A few hours later, I sat on my couch, watching my phone to see if anything was happening in the shop. I heard a banging on my apartment door—Calvin checking to make sure I wasn't home, presumably. I'd moved my car out of sight, about ten blocks away. The knocks became louder. I ignored them, and after three more tries, the eerie silence returned.

Next, I heard a slow squeak of the back door's hinges. I sat perfectly still. Nothing was in view yet.

Slowly, a person dressed in all black crept into the frame and disappeared for a few minutes. I heard the clink of a glass, and fluid being poured. I watched the person set down what appeared to be a shot of whiskey. Next, he began digging around the clock with a glinting object—the kilt pin—to open the compartments and pull out the wood from the base. Then he knocked on wood up the sides. After pulling what looked like a journal out of his pocket, he paused and held it up to catch the streetlight coming in the window.

The figure moved the clock's weights from side to side and continued knocking on the back. Mrs. Thomas must have been ignoring the sounds because of the whiskey. Was he trying to find a secret panel? But what did he think was hidden there?

Now what? I hadn't thought this through. I dialed 9-1-1 on my phone. There was a big bang downstairs before I got an answer. I ran toward the noise. Disoriented by the darkness, I collided with the figure by the clock. I found myself eye to eye with my cousin Calvin.

"You lied," he said, his eyes vacant and cold.

"What the hell, Calvin? Why are you here?"

"You had to ruin it. You don't get to have everything, you jerk. Everyone always favored you. Well, this, this fortune is mine."

"Fortune? There is no fortune. It's just an old clock."

"Screw the clock. Grandpa stored gold in here. You can't have it. You can't have that an the antiques shop." He pulled a knife out of his pocket and swung it toward my head.

I stumbled backward into a table of trinkets that crashed to the floor.

"My mom sure is going to miss you." Calvin was serious.

"Why, Calvin? You can have it. You can have the damned clock. Stop it. Stop now!" I ran over to the side of the store, where I had heavy cast-iron pans hanging from the wall. I grabbed the biggest one I could swing and held it up. Calvin laughed.

"A pan? Get real. I'm stronger and smarter and I have this plan. I learned a lot from Julio. Now I carry a knife all the time." He ran at me, swinging his blade. I dodged him again.

Abner appeared. "Oh dear, this is not good. Sanne, run!"

"Sanne, you were going to sell the clock to that idiot from New York. I *had* to stop it." He grimaced and crept closer to me, holding his knife in front of him. "That clock is magical and worth a lot more than your measly eighteen thousand. Our family stored their gold in there during the depression in the late 1800s. It's all in the letters and journals Grandpa kept. I knew there was a secret with the clock. I didn't know what."

He lunged forward. I stumbled backward and fell hard on the cement floor, pain running down my leg.

"Stop, Calvin. We're family. You don't want to do this," I begged as he stood over me with the knife.

"This is going to hurt me more than it hurts you."

I closed my eyes and screamed.

There was another big thud. I opened my eyes just in time to see Calvin fall to the floor. Behind him was Abner. He dropped his ashtray to the ground.

"Sanne, are you okay?" he asked, kneeling next to me.

"I think so."

Calvin came to and started to get up.

"Freeze right there!" Detective Trak came barreling into the room, pointing a gun at Calvin. "Are you okay, Sanne? We heard the whole thing. You have the 9-1-1 line open on your phone." She put her foot on Calvin's back, pressing him into the floor.

"Stop," Detective Trak said, and she dropped to her knees, rolled Calvin over, and put cuffs on him. "You're under arrest. Anything you say can and will..."

As she talked, tears welled up in my eyes. How could this have happened? Julio was gone because of a clock. Detective Trak and another officer took Calvin out of the room.

Abner stood next to me, clapping and blowing smoke rings.

Detective Trak came back in. "What happened here? How did you get him to the ground?"

"I'm not really sure. It's a bit of a blur."

"I see," she said.

A flurry of ghosts popped out from their antiques and began to chatter. I ignored them. "Can I please come to get Harvey now? It's clear he did not hurt Julio."

"Follow us."

· · · ● · ● · ● · · ·

Aunt Birdie and I stood in shock at the door of the police station. Harvey rushed out and gave me a big hug.

"I'm so sorry. I just... I just didn't know," Aunt Birdie said. Harvey hugged her tightly as she began to cry. "Calvin had been so engrossed in those letters from Grandpa that I just thought he was taking an interest in the family business. My son, how could he?"

"It's not your fault, Aunt Birdie. Did you know there was treasure somewhere in that clock?" I asked. She shook her head.

"Hey, ladies, I think we should get going?" Harvey asked.

"Of course." I hugged Aunt Birdie one more time before we left.

· · · ● · ● · ● · · ·

The next day, the sun was shining brightly over the mountains. It was as if Mother Nature herself was celebrating that we knew who'd killed Julio and that he would get what he deserved.

Harvey and I came in early to enjoy some time together in the café and decompress.

"So, did you find the gold he was looking for in the clock?"

"No, but I did get the pendulum back. Wanna help me get it started again?" I asked. We walked over to the clock with coffees in hand. "I wound it this morning. But this clock always runs slow."

Mrs. Thomas appeared. "Dear, it runs slowly because the gold in the weights is lighter than the usual lead."

"Wait, what? Gold?" I said, pulling out the weights that hung from the clock face, next to the pendulum. "These weights?"

"Yes, dear. Each of the weights is encased in a layer of lead to appear normal, but if you hold the chain on the top and pull, the gold will come out of the center."

I followed her directions to reveal bright shining blocks of gold. I turned to Harvey. "Wow, this is it! My shop is saved! And I'll have money to help Aunt Birdie stay in her own home with the care she needs."

Harvey grinned and hugged me. "How is she?"

"She's a bit sad, but she keeps forgetting it happened. That may be a small blessing."

"Now," Mrs. Thomas interrupted, "can you please put the wooden slats back in place? Those other hidden panels were emptied of their riches years ago during the Great Depression."

I did as she asked. A kilt pin still rested on the floor next to the clock—the tool Calvin used to pry these panels open and pick the door lock.

"Dear, now that I have given you all this information, may I please have a whiskey?"

I laughed. "Let's all have one." I got the Maker's out, poured a shot into Harvey's coffee and mine, and set one on the table where Mrs. Thomas could sniff it.

"Ah, this reminds me of the good old days." She grinned. Abner appeared over her shoulder and took a sniff, then coughed.

"I still do not like the stuff." He puffed his cigar and blew a series of rings. "Does this mean we get to stay here with you?"

"Yes, Abner, it does. You saved me. I wouldn't let you go for anything!"

I hugged Harvey one more time. "I'm so glad you're home."

"Me too!" He smiled, then his expression shifted to curiosity. Butterfingers was outside, staring into the store, but this time she had a grin on her face. She nodded at us and then walked away down the street, her yellow scarf a flutter of color in her trail.

About the Author

Maren Higbee writes fictional comedies and is now taking on mysteries for a change of pace. As the pandemic took hold in 2020, she and her husband Brandon opened an online antique store, inspiring this latest story. Although Maren was born in Seattle, she has lived in London, New York, and Los Angeles to work in film and TV. She returned home to Seattle in 2008 where she met her husband, Brandon. They love sharing the Pacific Northwest lifestyle with their two German Shepherds, Orson and Tippi. Visit her website at www.marenhigbee.com.
You can find Maren's other books on Amazon.

FIRST AND FOREMOST AT THE HIGH GROUND CAFÉ

by Robin Russell
CHAPTER 1

High Ground Café
Dr. Emma Jean Parker, reluctant proprietress
104 Main Street
Gadson Township, Georgia
Wednesday, May 12, 1999

Delia Parker née Mobley, in a whirl of gardenias and purpose, rushed in, causing the bell on the door to thwap more than ring, as if it too were as startled as the handful of patrons turning to face the leopard-print clad woman, who, in 1951, had been the first to be crowned both Miss Gadson and Miss Southern Charm in the same year. She paused, soaking in (as well as making sure she had) the attention of the room, before releasing her breath in a pleased dismissal and flitting (on fuchsia kitten heels) over to her daughter, gushing, "Emma, sweetie, I am so sorry."

With a sigh of accustomed patience, Emma untied her apron and set it on the counter. "Don't worry about it, Mama. Grant's saving me a seat. It'll be fine."

"Well, I don't know how it's going to be 'fine,' which, Lord knows has to be just about the most useless word in the English language and you as an English teacher."

"*Former* English teacher," Emma corrected, grabbing her keys from a drawer and stepping out from behind the counter.

"*Erstwhile,* sweetie, erst—good Lord, Emma Jean, are those dungarees?"

"First of all, Mama," Emma began in a strained tone, "dungarees? Are we Gold Rush prospectors, Mama? It is a *denim* skirt. It's not like I'm wearing overalls. Second, we've talked about making comments on what I wear."

"But people will be there, sweetie."

"Yes, Mama. I know. Half the town will be there, and *third*, this skirt was made for me by Mia Anderson and of all the skirts that have come out of Aaliyah Jones' Home Economics class, it's the most," she scanned her expansive vocabulary in search of a word that would appease her mother, but gave up and settled on, "appropriate."

Delia dabbed the corner of her eye with a carnation-pink handkerchief. "Oh, sweetie. If that isn't the most darling thing I have ever heard."

Emma leaned in to give her mother a quick kiss on the cheek, noticed the dry eyes and unmarred blue eye shadow, and threw her mother an exasperated look. "I need to go, Mama."

"No one's stopping you, Emma Jean. Although why you want to go, knowing it's going to just about break your heart to be there, is beyond me."

This time there *was* a tear and Emma reached out to give her mother a consoling hug. The older woman, bird-like in her youth and even frailer now as she neared her seventh decade, let herself be pulled in to the embrace of her only child, a woman nearing fifty who couldn't be more unlike her in every respect. Nearly six-feet tall, Dr. Emma Jean Parker had inherited her father's hardened features and white hair. Looking like she'd just stepped out of a Dorothea Lange photograph, she held an uncanny resemblance to the iconic Migrant Mother of the Great Depression, even though she'd borne no children and had led a reasonably charmed life—at least until recently.

"Mama, listen," Emma said softly against the Clairol 249 tresses that had been teased to near-mythical proportions. "It's not that I *want* to go. It's that I told 213 kids and their families that I *would* go."

Delia released a sniffled harumph, brought her hands up to cradle the cheeks of a daughter who she was relatively sure had come from her womb and not from a last-minute mix-up at St. Joseph's all those years ago. Delia gave her two sharp pinches on either cheekbone.

"Mama!" Emma glared as she rubbed her cheeks.

"Well, if you're not even going to put on some lipstick, what else can I do?"

"Lord help me, Mama. If I'm not arrested for killing The Roach, I'm going to come back here and murder you!"

With a smile and a best-you-get-going wave, Delia donned the apron, stepped behind the counter of the High Ground Café—the only establishment in Gadson, Georgia where one never needed to wait in line—and muttered, "Good luck with that. I'd kill The Roach myself if I knew a way to do it. Emma Jean, do you know that man has had *three* heart attacks? Even God couldn't kill him."

Dr. Emma Jean Parker, renowned and retired English teacher from Gadson High School, left the café she had half-heartedly bought, and which she had whole-heartedly named in a snub to The Roach, her nemesis and former colleague, who had ruined her life a year earlier when he'd threatened to out her, causing her to relinquish the profession she loved rather than be yet another pawn in his megalomaniacal machinations.

Watching her go, Delia frowned in worry—a frown she quickly remedied as she turned to assist the round man whose curly blonde hair tufted out from underneath a bright green bill cap marked with the gold logo of Culverhouse Trucking. "Skinny Shadrick! Why, it's been a dog's age since I've seen you. Where on earth have you been?"

"New trucking route, Miss Delia. I've been running the 280 into Birmingham most days."

"Well, you have to go where the money is, Skinny."

Skinny nodded his sage agreement. "True enough."

Delia placed her elbows on the counter. "And how's Amelia? And little Maisie?"

The man's face got even rounder. "Not so little now, Miss Delia. She'll be starting school this fall."

"Saints preserve us. Seems like it was just yesterday when she was no bigger than a bean and I could just about put her in my pocket."

Chortling, Skinny said, "It's something alright. Everyone's getting older but you, Miss Delia."

Now it was Delia's turn to smile. "Skinny Shadrick, you precious little devil." She batted her eyelashes with a sincerity that belied their synthetic composition. "Now, what can I get you? You want a slice of cake? We've got—" She stepped back to examine the contents of the glass case at the end of the counter. "Butter Beware Cake, Raisin d'Être Cake, Crunch Cake, Mississippi Mud Cake—good Lord, no one will want that. I might as well take it home. Ooh! Skinny, we've got some Hummingbird Cake here. How does a big slice of that sound?"

Skinny grinned. "Sounds awful good, Miss Delia."

Delia took out a waxed to-go container and dropped in a partially mangled slice of cake. "It's the taste that counts, Skinny," she announced before picking up a chunk that had fallen on the countertop and popping it into her mouth. "Now, what can I get you to drink?"

"Well, it'll be an all-nighter, so let's go with a grande Americano with an extra shot."

Delia, who still made her own morning coffee in a plug-in percolator, eyed the espresso contraption dubiously. "Coffee it is!" She turned around, selected the mid-size cup and poured in the remaining of what had been brewing in the pot, which was enough to fill the cup about halfway. Donning her pageant smile, she set the cup on the counter. "I left some room for cream."

Skinny held out a credit card and Delia recoiled from it, something she thought she'd never do, considering how joyfully she had used her own over the years. She glanced at the small black box of modern technology lurking next to the cash register—a device she wouldn't know how to use except as a paperweight—and she shuddered. Then, delighting in her own ingenuity—and munificence—she announced, "It's on the house, Skinny."

• • • ● • ● • • • ·

Gadson High School
Sheila Simmons, Principal
301 Jenkins Lane

Gadson Township, Georgia
Wednesday, May 12, 1999

In a rare day for Gadson, the humidity was just balmy enough to remind everyone they were still in Georgia without being so high as to endanger the ten gallons of hairspray that had been used to secure the bobs and bouffants, not only of the young ladies of Gadson High School's graduating class, but of all their female relatives in attendance, as well.

Emma scanned the crowd to find Grant Michael, who had defied instructions to sit with the other teachers on the stage in order to keep her company. Theirs was an unlikely friendship, but the dearth of commonalities between them was offset by a shared irreverence for the bureaucratically mundane and absurd. Until The Roach had forced her into early retirement, she and Grant had made weekly staff meetings more bearable by exchanging clandestine challenges. One of her favorites had been her dare for him to insert as many pirate-related expressions in a discussion as possible. No curriculum meeting had ever been more entertaining.

"Nice skirt," he said as she joined him.

"Nice..." Emma gave his sartorial selections a quick scan, but he was as dashing and debonair as always, "manners," she finished weakly. "What did I miss?"

"Not the opening prayer." Grant nodded toward the stage where Reverend Jimmy Ward II, known colloquially as "Reverend Jimmy Junior," embarked on a prayer of epic proportions, sparking about the same number of "amens" from the congregants of First Baptist as scarcely audible grumblings from the congregants of Missionary Baptist, who wondered, as they did annually, why Pastor Josiah was always relegated to giving the closing prayer, when he was, by far and without question, the superior preacher.

Reaching a fevered pitch, Reverend Jimmy Junior finished with, "and Jesus will return in power and glory to judge the world and rule as King of Kings." He took a moment to wipe the sweat from his brow, before mumbling into the microphone. "And may God bless all the graduates and keep them away from drugs and unnatural persons."

Grant leaned in to whisper, "He means you, Dr. Parker."

"Tell me something I *don't* know," Emma muttered.

Next, Carter Bacon, the mayor of Gadson as well as the owner of both Zip-N and the neighboring Tire-N-Lube, stepped up to the podium and stumped for a while. Emma couldn't think of a reason why, considering the man hadn't been opposed in years. Being the mayor of a small town was a thankless job with more complaints than a city, but with significantly fewer resources, but he seemed to revel in the appellation, if not the actual responsibilities, and most folks felt he was welcome to it.

Following Mayor Bacon, were speeches by four-fifths of the school board, beginning with Jackson Jackson of Jackson's Allgoods, Kingston Ledbetter of Ledbetter Dairy and Nevaeh Brown of Guns-Guns-Guns, who each used this opportunity—as they had at the other two town-wide events, the Juneteenth Jubilee and Christmas Wonderland—to garner support, hock wares and pander shamelessly. Of course, to appease Principal Sheila Simmons, who had allotted each of them two precious minutes of the ceremony, all of the members added a perfunctory piece of canned advice to the graduates.

When it was time for Wyatt Culverhouse, the fourth member of the board, to give his speech, no one missed the look of repugnance he directed toward The Roach. However, since it was merely one of a dozen the man had received since the event began, everyone easily relegated it as unworthy of comment, unlike the current weather, the future weather and the scandalous height of Principal Simmons' heels. Even if most citizens of Gadson didn't know them as "stilettos," everyone recognized a fancy pair of "hooker-heels" when they saw them, and the fact that Sheila Simmons had paired the shoes with a conservative gray dress, didn't make a lick of difference. Despite the principal's emphatically tapping on her wristwatch, the speech Wyatt gave was double the length of the others and focused on all *he* had accomplished during his illustrious high school years. Emma had been a freshman when Wyatt was a senior, and one year with him had been more than enough for her to join in the schoolwide sigh of relief when he graduated. Even now, over thirty years later, the man exuded the bombast and delusions that only come from being a lifelong narcissist and bully.

The fifth and final member of the school board, Cyrus Morris, who was a recluse half the town thought was a myth and the other half thought was dead, made no appearance, as usual. Some might have thought having an even number of board members would render decision-making nigh impossible, but The Roach was currently strong-arming or blackmailing all but Nevaeh, so the Gadson School Board was rarely plagued by stalemates.

Next, came the graduates, and Grant handed Emma a small packet of tissues. One by one, the students she had taught a year earlier crossed the makeshift stage, shook hands with Principal Simmons and received their diplomas from Jackson Jackson, president of the board. After posing to have their picture taken by Cooper McBride, town clerk and photographer for the weekly Gadson Gazette, they returned to their alphabetical spot in the bleachers.

At last, Principal Simmons reclaimed the podium to announce this year's recipient of Gadson High School Teacher of the Year, an award that came with a slew of pecuniary benefits, everything from a free oil change at Tire-N-Lube to free lunches at Jill's Grill. The package even included a membership from Might-As-Well Fitness, however, in Emma's opinion, Tiana Brown might as well include colonoscopies for all any teacher ever took advantage of the offer.

As the principal droned on, lauding the accomplishments and attributes of the soon-to-be-crowned Teacher of the Year, Grant undid another button on his shirt and fanned himself with his wilted program. "I feel like I'm sitting in a lukewarm bathtub."

"Welcome to Georgia, Yankee. I'm sure the ladies of Connecticut are ready to welcome you back at any time."

The murmurs of the crowd diminished as Principal Simmons' speech drew to a close.

Grant glared at the stage. "And here it comes. I wonder what he has on her. Former stripper?"

Emma grimaced at the thought. "Don't let the heels fool you. I'm thinking embezzlement. Those shoes don't come cheap."

Principal Simmons took a deep breath, knowing she was about to receive both the revulsion and the sympathy of the crowd, and declared, "With great honor, it is my privilege to announce that our Teacher of the Year is," she paused as if to swallow either actual or emotional bile—perhaps both—before finishing with a half-hearted, "Everett Roach."

Casting around, it was clear to Emma that she and Grant were not the only ones disgusted by the display. However, their collective abhorrence was quickly replaced by dread as The Roach sauntered up to the podium for his annual reign of terror, a lengthy speech filled entirely with veiled threats and innuendos in this yearly reminder of how precarious life could be.

Truth be told, it was primarily the White half of the audience that sat in terror, the Black community having circled its wagons early on, making sure to keep *their* scandals and secrets in house. Instead, they listened in a combination of bemusement and curiosity, grateful that The Roach had yet to infect the lives of Gadson's Black citizens. Occasionally, he'd try, but then Nevaeh Brown of Guns-Guns-Guns, would remind him she knew how to use every item in her inventory.

The Roach took to the stage, smiling broadly. "Thank you, Principal Simmons, for your little speech."

Not unlike reciting a sadistic laundry list, The Roach proceeded through his recycled speech, different every year only in that it got longer as he wielded even more power in a town that universally loathed him. She had no doubt that the comment added last year and repeated just a moment earlier about "unwholesome and unnatural influences on our children" was aimed directly at her.

"Jesus, I'd like to wring his neck." Grant hadn't bothered to lower his voice and Emma thought she detected a few nods of agreement.

"Get in line," she muttered.

The speech ended with a meager smattering of obligatory applause. If there was any gratitude at all, it was probably from those who felt reprieved from public humiliation. It mixed now with the miasma of antipathy pouring forth from the audience.

Fortunately for many of them and extremely fortunately for a few, the reprieve was soon to be permanent. Everett Roach, the scourge and terror of Gadson, would be dead by the end of the week.

CHAPTER 2

Magnolia Senior Center
Scarlet Frazier, Activity Director
1442 Magnolia Avenue
Gadson Township, Georgia
Friday, May 14, 1999

It took forty-eight hours and nearly as many of her mother's "special sarsaparillas," before Emma resumed her equilibrium. By that time, the last vestiges of resentment toward The Roach had returned to the back burner of her brain, and she was able to focus on more pressing matters, like how she was going to pay the café's electric bill and whether or not her mother was overbidding her hand. Emma figured she could worry about the former tomorrow, and her mother, the epitome of a cock-eyed optimist, would *always* overbid her hand.

"Pass," Emma told the other three bridge players, and, in a conscious effort to avoid her mother's predictable eye-rolling, Emma scanned the other quartets spread across the spacious multi-purpose room of the Magnolia Senior Center. She wasn't sure which couple she and her mother would be playing next, but Emma figured she could tolerate the company of all but Reverend Ward and his bothersome wife, Blakely.

Miss Glenda, Delia's best friend of fifty years, rebid her spades and her partner, Mother Coburn, knowing that the reasonable septuagenarian was consistently a pragmatic bidder, settled them into a contract of "four spades."

"Goodness, that thing is as big as she is, poor dear."

Emma turned to see what had distracted her mother from the admonishment she surely had been just about to dole out, and saw the diminutive Paisley Culverhouse, as small as her husband was large and clad in the bright green uniform of Culverhouse Cleaning. She was lugging a vacuum up the stairs, and Emma had a quick flashback to twenty years earlier when Paisley had reached the state finals as the star competitor on Gadson's gymnastics team. Judging by the way she wielded the machine, she looked to be as strong as ever.

Miss Glenda deftly acquired all but three tricks, fulfilling the bid, and Emma wrote down the score, making sure to add the extra points above the line for high honors. Then, for the last hand in the set, she acquiesced to her mother's insistence on "five diamonds," a contract she surely wouldn't make, even if she had the best cards. Rather than watch the bloodbath that was about to ensue, Emma, after completing her role as dummy by laying down her cards, let her mind wander. She found herself returning to thoughts of Paisley. Having at least twenty trucks and nearly as many drivers, Culverhouse Trucking was a lucrative business, and Emma was not the first in Gadson to wonder why Paisley was scrubbing toilets rather than filing invoices or focusing on raising their two sons. Emma suspected that, just as in high school, Wyatt sought out ways to demean and demoralize his girlfriend. And yet, it wasn't a shock to anyone when she married him.

As expected, Delia barely made two diamonds, the second of which being the result of a quick peek at Mother Coburn's hand when she leaned over to take a sip of tea. Also as expected, considering Emma's luck these days, Scarlet Frazier, Activity Director and former recipient of Grant's romantic attention, had paired them with the sanctimonious Wards, although Emma imagined the assignment had less to do with luck and more to do with her being unwilling to serve as an intermediary in Scarlet's matrimonial aspirations.

After the socially required niceties were out of the way, the cards were dealt and Emma savored the silence as they each sorted and assessed their hands. Reverend and Mrs. Ward, delighting in their repeated luck with the cards, were distracted from making their usual comments about why Emma and her mother didn't attend church. Ever since Emma's father had died, some twenty years earlier, Delia had joined Miss Glenda at the Black church, Missionary Baptist. Emma, who had more brains than courage, knew herself well enough to avoid both churches, each of which had a preponderance for casting fire and brimstone at "the homosexual agenda" on a weekly basis. Emma felt a nervous laugh brewing inside her as she considered her own "homosexual agenda" for today consisting of a morning jog, bridge with a bunch of senior citizens and trying to keep her floundering business afloat.

"Oh, there you are, Mrs. Ward," Carla Nesmith called before bustling over to the card table, carrying a pink pastry box. It was stamped on all sides with the title of her out-of-the-house business, Merciful Savior Cakes & Cookies.

Having worked with Gary Nesmith—Carla's husband and Gadson's band teacher—for years, Emma appreciated both his dedication to students and his penchant for dramatic musical performances. His concerts, entertaining from beginning to end, always included some surprising element, delighting his audiences and privately causing Grant to refer to his fellow teacher as "Gary Poppins." Other than at college, Emma had never experienced being a part of a gay community, but she certainly recognized a fellow member when she saw one. She couldn't help but wonder if Carla didn't know her husband was gay or if they had some kind of arrangement. Considering the weekly delivery of free donuts to The Roach, Emma was certain that *he* knew the answer and hadn't hesitated to add the Nesmith's to his blackmailing list.

Blakely Ward took the proffered box in exchange for a cloying smile. "Dear, it's no trouble at all. It's right on my walk. I'll bring it over this afternoon."

"I appreciate it, no end, Mrs. Ward. You're so kind to offer. Miss Delia, Dr. Parker, you're looking well. Reverend Jimmy, your son did a beautiful job on Wednesday." Carla's voice was replete with obsequiousness, and it was only

Delia's warning glare that prevented Emma from rolling her eyes.

"He's just the messenger, young lady," came the pastor's automatic response. "It's the Lord's word."

"Amen," Carla replied with hearty enthusiasm. "And your blood pressure? I hope that's doing better."

Reverend Ward shook his head in puzzlement. "It's the darndest thing. Dr. Dixon tested it and it's gotten even worse. He had Junior William give me more of those pills, but I don't know if they're doing much good."

Carla's features showed genuine concern. "Well, I'll keep you in my prayers, Reverend."

"Oh, don't worry about me. The good Lord has need of me yet."

Emma couldn't help but cough as she thought of all the people—especially teenagers—the man had terrified throughout the years with his threats of hell and damnation.

"Dr. Parker?"

Emma's reverie was broken by Carla's voice, who had been asking her something.

"Sorry, say again?"

"I asked if the High Ground was going to be on the Art Walk tomorrow night."

"Well, of course it is," Delia declared. "And you all must come. Bernard Sinclair will be displaying his work, and you might recognize one of his models."

This time, Emma did roll her eyes.

Blakley gasped. "Bernard Sinclair? The Californian?"

Emma would always marvel that, unless one's parents were born in Gadson, one was either relegated as "tourist" or deemed a "foreigner." If the former, folks wouldn't bother learning your name, and if the latter, you would be appointed with an appellation that vaguely referenced your origins. Bernard Sinclair was a permanent "artist in residence" at the hoity-toity Roundtree Ranch, a mysterious retreat at the edge of town that catered to the rich and famous who needed to either dry out from substance or wait out from scandal. It was owned and operated—as it had been for over thirty years—by Hollywood Briggs.

"Doesn't he paint scantily clad women?" Blakely's accusatory tone sounded like she had a pitchfork at the ready.

"Every chance he gets," retorted Delia.

Reverend Ward cleared his throat and began dealing the last hand.

Carla excused herself with, "I'd best be going. Thank you again, Mrs. Ward."

The last hand was played in silence, but the reproving glares from Blakely to Delia spoke plenty.

When the game was finished, Emma made note of the score and handed the paper to her mother, before nodding to the Wards. "Reverend, Mrs. Ward, always a pleasure to see you both."

"Well, you know, Miss Parker," Blakely said. "You'd see more of us if you came to church."

"Yes, ma'am."

"Remember, you're never too bad to come in, but never too good to stay out."

"I'll keep that in mind, Mrs. Ward."

Blakely huffed. "You do that."

Emma grabbed her bag and walked to the other side of the table. "Mama, I'll see you at home. Be sure to go see Meemaw. And don't say she was sleeping, because she never sleeps."

"Emma Jean," Delia whined. "I am too old to get yelled at by an old woman."

Emma kissed her mother on the cheek. "I know just how you feel, Mama."

· · · · ● · ● · · ·

Magnolia Manor
Meemaw Mobley, disinclined resident
1440 Magnolia Avenue
Gadson Township, Georgia
Friday, May 14, 1999

Emma's daily check on her maternal grandmother always included the same conversation.

"I don't know why your fool mother ever stuck me in this place with all these highfalutin bastards."

"You are welcome to stay with us, Meemaw."

"I am not going to step foot in Geraldine Parker's house! That woman didn't want me there when she was alive and she sure as hell won't want me there now that she's dead."

"Meemaw, that was fifty years ago."

"Don't patronize me, Emma Jean. I know how to count. Why don't you just drive me over to my house?"

"Because your house doesn't have running water."

"It has a well and a pump. If it was good enough for my mama, it's good enough for me. You think I care about using an outhouse? My ass ain't picky, Emma Jean. It's your traitorous mother what was picky."

Emma opened up a bag of butterscotch candies and added them to the empty bowl next to the recliner, which faced the window overlooking Magnolia Avenue rather than facing the small television.

"That's my good girl. It was your money that bought them, you say?"

"Of course, Meemaw," Emma lied.

Meemaw settled into the recliner and reached for a candy. "Because I'll be damned if I'm taking any charity from the Parkers."

"I know." Emma reached behind the recliner to retrieve the crazy-quilt that had seen generations of Mobleys through hard times and harder times. She tucked it around her grandmother and gave her a quick kiss on the cheek.

"No need for that nonsense, Emma Jean."

Emma scanned the room to make sure everything was in its place. She noticed a book and a few candy wrappers underneath the bed.

"I don't know how that got there," Meemaw replied to her granddaughter's skeptical look at seeing the half-naked couple on the cover.

Emma tucked the book underneath the pillow on the off chance that her mother did stop by for a visit. "I love you, Meemaw. I'll see you tomorrow."

"You're a good girl, Emma Jean. Mobley blood runs strong in you."

As Emma reached the end of the hall, she whispered a quick prayer that the three Godbee sisters would still be at lunch. Her visits were always timed to avoid them, but Emma had arrived late today, and as she neared the grand foyer, she saw to her dismay that the three women had returned to their stations. Emma, who had been a classics major, had mentally dubbed them "The Fates" even before her life felt like a Greek tragedy. She wasn't sure which of the women she would consider to be Clotho, Lachesis or Atropos, since she had always just thought of them as Creepy, Creepier and Creepiest.

"You can run from it, Emma Jean Parker," Creepy Godbee called after Emma's brisk retreat from the manor. "But you can't hide."

CHAPTER 3

High Ground Café
Dr. Emma Jean Parker, maladroit proprietress
104 Main Street
Gadson Township, Georgia
Saturday, May 15, 1999

The half-orc growled over the counter. "One mead, barkeep. Here's my coin."

Emma ran the debit card through the machine and proceeded to make a venti macchiato, two of a hundred small things she had learned to do this year. As she deposited the dollop of foamed milk onto the espresso, the chime from the front door of the café jingled, announcing a halfling, a gnome and two elves.

Emma nodded to them as she handed the cup to her patron. "Your fellow champions have arrived."

"Indeed," snarled the barbarian, Grishk, dropping a quarter in the tip jar. "That's for your trouble, wench."

"Kayden, we've discussed this."

"Right," cowered the half-Orc, taking out his inhaler. "Sorry, Doctor Parker," he mumbled, slinking off toward his friends, pausing only to reinstate his bravado before bellowing, "Well met, well met."

Emma smiled after him, cherishing the fact that Reverend Ward's grandson played his weekly game of

Dungeons and Dragons—one of Satan's pastimes—at her establishment.

The halfling druid was the next customer. "Hi, Dr. Parker!" she chirped. "How are you?"

"Just fine, Londyn. I didn't know you all played on Fridays."

"Oh, we don't, Dr. Parker. We're just strategizing." She put her hands on her hips. "Can you believe Malik just dumped us in a valley full of giants and we have to get into Minderhall to kill Urathash and save the world all by ourselves?"

"That's a tall order," Emma agreed.

Londyn released a heavy sigh. "I'll say. Still, Effie says since we're the heroes, there has to be a way to figure it out."

"Well, you'll need your strength. What can I get you?"

"A mocha please, and a slice of that Tennessee Mountain Stack Cake. My sister says no one makes it better than Mrs. Nesmith. She is so talented."

Emma began to prepare the order.

"Also, my mama says she can cover the café tonight for the Art Walk if you want."

"That's awfully kind of her."

"She says it's the least she can do, considering all you've done for our family over the years. She says Hudson wouldn't have gotten into Duke without your help and my dad says that he'll always recognize a preposition because you taught him it's all the places you could hide a dead body."

Out of the context of the classroom, the pedagogical strategy jarred Emma, and she wondered, not for the first time, if telling students they could put the dead body *under* a table or *aboard* the train or throw it *over* a cliff was the best idea. After all, Cooper Wells was now a manager at the peach factory, where he probably put the fruit *in* the can more often than he diagramed sentences *on* his break. Still, it was too late now.

"And no need to worry about our game tomorrow," Londyn added.

"Oh?"

"Mr. Singleton says he was going to be at school grading tests all afternoon anyway, so we can play in his room."

"That's nice of him."

Londyn stared off into the distance. "It is. Miss Roberts says he is such a treasure, that Mr. Singleton, and I agree."

Emma didn't know about that. She'd taught Asher Singleton and she couldn't think of him without thinking of the paper he had submitted as his own work, but which was really the same assignment his sister had submitted two years earlier. He had tried to weasel out of it, explaining that it wasn't plagiarism, since he had his sister's permission, which had also been a lie.

Londyn continued to laud the man. "Did you know that he received the Chickering Scholarship for Academic Excellence? My mama says you can only get that if you have perfect grades."

Emma did know that, but kept her thoughts surrounding his worthiness to herself. "Is that so?"

"Sure thing. And it's the same one Tucker Culverhouse received this year." Londyn lowered her voice and leaned in. "But my sister says that Jace Ellison says that Tucker didn't get into Duke, and he didn't apply anywhere else! Can you believe that, Dr. Parker? Who applies to only one school? That's just asking for trouble if you want to know what I think. My sister applied to fourteen schools, and my mama says it was a good thing, too. I suppose Tucker thought because he earned that scholarship and his brother, Beau, goes there, he didn't need a safety school. I mean, not everyone can be like Mr. Singleton."

For a moment, something tugged at the back of Emma's mind, some story Grant had told her about Beau, but it was shoved out of the way when the front door opened and a life-size painting of her naked mother was brought in. It was soon followed by another, and another.

Emma sighed, thinking of how long the evening would be if she was forced to make small talk about what a wonderful teacher she had been while trying not to see the artwork.

"Actually, Londyn," Emma said, making a gut decision in an attempt at self-preservation. "You can tell your mama she doesn't need to come in tonight. I'll be just fine staying behind the counter for the foreseeable future."

• • • ● ● ● ● ● ● • •

High Ground Café
Dr. Emma Jean Parker, former mortified Art Walk hostess
104 Main Street
Gadson Township, Georgia
Sunday, May 16, 1999

Delia perched on one of the stools at the counter and pouted. "Well, I don't see what all the fuss is about."

Emma sighed her exasperation. "Mama, I may not be the best businesswoman, or even a very good one, but even I know that it's more prurient than prudent to have a café filled to the brim with naked pictures of an old lady."

"Puns are beneath you, sweetie," Delia reprimanded. "And I wasn't naked. I was *nude*. It was *art*, Emma Jean."

Emma was saved from issuing a bitter rejoinder that would have caused even more theatrics by the roaring of a motorcycle engine that halted right outside. In a gust of sweltering heat, the front door flew open and Grant stood in the doorway. "He's dead!" he bellowed to a café empty of customers. It was Sunday morning, so anyone who was not in church was either a heathen or suffering from an illness—whether real or fictional. Normally, Delia would be at Missionary Baptist with Glenda, but they both agreed it was best to abstain this Sunday so as to let the dust settle from the Art Walk.

"Who's dead?" Emma and her mother chorused.

Grant bellied up to the counter. "The most hated man in Gadson, the scourge of our community, our very own Wicked Witch of the South."

"The Roach," came the barely audible and barely believed response from both women.

"None other," Grant announced. "Better yet, he was murdered and his body was shoved in a supplies closet."

"Well, I'll be," murmured Delia. "Someone finally managed it."

"Who killed him?" Emma asked.

"All I know is that Maverick Hall was arrested for it."

"The janitor?" Emma could hardly imagine it.

"How?" asked Delia.

Grant shrugged. "No idea. I was with Jaclyn Hunter, and after a lovely night of—"

"Minding your own business?" Emma interrupted.

Grant gave Emma a conciliatory smile. "Indeed, and she got a call. Apparently, there is actually a new sheriff in town —a lady sheriff—and she started yesterday. Jaclyn said they don't even know the cause of death, but for sure he's dead."

"It could be anyone," mused Delia. "Hell, I'd suspect myself if I didn't have an alibi. We should celebrate! Emma, where do you keep the champagne?"

"Mama, a man is dead."

Delia grinned, her eyes sparkling with delight. "And what a man. The whole town will breathe more easily."

"I'd buy you some champagne, Miss Delia, but there are those pesky blue laws." Grant turned to Emma. "We're still on for this evening, right? Do you want me to pick you up?"

"No. I found you a bunch of boxes, so I'll drive over."

"Sounds good. Well, ladies. I'll leave you to your non-alcoholic celebration. I'm headed to an indoor picnic."

Delia gave him a mischievous look. "Indoor or in bed?"

He winked at her. "First, in the door. Then, in the bed. That is, if we make it that far."

Delia's normal titter was replaced by a giant cackle of delight. "Grant Michael, you little devil."

"Takes one to know one, Miss Delia."

CHAPTER 4

Gadson High School
Grant Michael, chemistry teacher
301 Jenkins Lane
Gadson Township, Georgia
Sunday, May 16, 1999

Gadson High School, a four-story building with brick veneer walls, had been built in 1927 in anticipation of a population boom that never panned out. Designed in the medieval-eclectic style, it contained 30 classrooms, an administrative suite, a cafeteria and science laboratories. It also included a library that, ever since Luna Godbee—Creepiest of the Fates—had retired, students were no longer afraid to enter. She had been replaced by Serenity Smith, a striking beauty with a warm disposition, and daily book circulation was now in the hundreds. Some of those books were even read.

Retrieving the stack of folded cardboard boxes from the back seat of her car, Emma eschewed going through the elaborate main entrance with its five arches in two tiers, opting for the eastside doors closest to Grant's classroom. Entering any school at night feels ghostly, almost as if the atmosphere needs to compensate for the overwhelming vivacity of the day, and Emma shuddered at the prickling idea that the specter of The Roach might be hovering around as well. The dulcet tones of Shania Twain singing

You're Still the One flowed down the hallway, and Emma hollered her presence in a dual effort of not frightening her friend and *definitely* frightening any lingering spirits. Grant echoed her holler and Emma proceeded.

"Country music?" she asked, reaching his doorway.

Grant swathed a microscope in bubble-wrap and said, "When in Rome, pardner."

Emma scanned the room and set down the cardboard. "Where do you want me to start?"

"Those are good to go." Grant tilted his chin to indicate a stack of boxes.

Each one had a series of numbers written and crossed out in permanent marker, serving as a record of the principal's annual direction for Grant to change rooms. Whether out of base pettiness or Machiavellian design, Sheila Simmons had penalized Grant for his refusal to teach Creationism by decreeing that he move from 102, the smallest classroom in the science department, to 105, the noisiest, and then back to 102. This past year, he'd been in 109, which was the worst, being right above where the trucks idled when they were dropping off supplies. And with a room full of hormonal teenagers, it was nearly impossible to focus without the window open. Fortunately, Asher Singleton, with his rarely used degree in physics, had helped Grant develop a contraption that syphoned both teen-stench and carbon monoxide from the classroom.

One by one, Emma carried the boxes back down the hall to room 102, unpacked them and put the items in their designated locations. And with each trip, she passed the supplies closet—now covered in police tape—where the murdered body of The Roach had been found. Also with each trip, when she exited Grant's new classroom, she avoided looking at the door across the hall. Like most high schools, classrooms were grouped by department, but even though The Roach taught history—or his version of it—he'd secured room 101, the large corner classroom in full view of the parking lot, where he could keep an eye on anyone coming or going.

"You never told me how the date went," Grant prompted when Emma returned to the classroom for another haul.

Emma scoffed. "That's because it was less of a date and more of a lecture on investing for retirement."

Grant set down a centrifuge and paused to consider this. "I warned you this was a problem in dating women your own age. You should consider widening the pool."

"It's too weird." Emma sighed before muttering, "I started teaching when I was twenty-two." At Grant's nonplussed expression, she explained, "So if I dated any woman who wasn't at *least* in her late-forties, it would feel like—"

"Like you're dating a student? Jesus, Emma. That's ridiculous."

"I can't help it," she snapped truculently.

Grant gave her a look of combined disgust and disappointment, and with a dramatic sigh, Emma hefted up another box and left the room. Since it was filled with textbooks, the task of unpacking it took all of five minutes, including the walk down the hall. Not ready for another rebuke about her romantic life, she delayed her return by perusing the student work and sundry announcements on the walls. This time, as she reached the supplies closet, she was distracted by a thought. The Roach's body, with its looming height, considerable girth and heart of stone, would have been incredibly cumbersome to move. The man rarely left his classroom, preferring to summon people to him instead, but if he'd been killed in room 101, there would have been no reason to move the body. Pondering the notion of an unwieldy corpse ending up here in the supplies closet, Emma looked at the door directly across the hall, where the nameplate read "Mr. Singleton" above a school picture of a boy—she couldn't help but think of him as anything else—sporting a bowtie, a weak mustache and a stern expression.

Emma retraced her steps until she found herself facing the door of room 101, the den of destruction, the pit of pain, the domain of the demon. As more alliterative appellations occurred to her, she turned the doorknob and entered the room.

Immediately, two things vied for her attention. The first was a spray of white shards illuminated by the fluorescent lighting in the parking lot. The pieces started at The Roach's podium and reached almost as far as the chairs and desks, which had been stacked against the far wall in preparation for summer buffing and burnishing. The second was the pungent scent of strawberries. Under normal circumstances, the first would have been more alarming, but everyone knew of The Roach's deadly allergy to the fruit. Emma followed the scent, maneuvering around the detritus until she reached the desk and saw the coffee cup with a faded "Best Teacher" emblem. Emma's olfactory sense was stronger than most, but she marveled that The Roach hadn't noticed it, until she remembered it was grass pollen season. *Had he been poisoned?* She contemplated this. *If so, why not just leave him here?*

An unmistakable clicking of heels echoed down the hallway that ran perpendicular to the science corridor. Scanning for somewhere to hide, Emma scrambled to the first place she could find. Just as she pulled The Roach's chair back in place, she heard the sound of the door opening. Footsteps repeated the tortuous path Emma had followed just minutes earlier. Just as quickly, they retreated and Emma proceeded to calm her racing heart by mentally reciting *Do Not Go Gentle into That Good Night* once, and then again for good measure. Tipping her head back, she sighed, then noticed a manila folder taped to the underside of the desk. Fueled by curiosity and interest in the potential for posthumous retribution, she took the folder, pushed back the chair and stood. It was instantly clear that the cup was gone. It also subsequently became clear that her movements had caused something in one of the drawers to slither.

· · · ● · ● · ● · · ·

Gadson High School
Grayson Gordon, Animal Control Specialist
301 Jenkins Lane
Gadson Township, Georgia
Sunday, May 16, 1999

Within the hour, Grayson Gordon, a young man who, to Emma's recollection, had never turned in a paper on time, had taken her call, driven out to the school, retrieved an irritated cottonmouth from The Roach's desk and was now regaling her and Grant with tales from his illustrious career at Bacon County Animal Control.

"And today's May 16, Dr. Parker," Grayson announced. "If this here snake," he said, motioning to the contraption that held the hissing reptile, "was put in yesterday, it would have been on the 'Ides of May.'"

Emma tried not to show surprise at his literary reference.

Grayson continued, "Which was not as scary as the 'Ides of March,' when I had to remove a black bear from outside Mr. Roach's house. Strangest thing. It had fallen into a massive hole that had been dug right underneath his back door." Grayson gesticulated his exasperation with his free hand. "The man could have been buried alive if he'd used that door!"

"You don't say," Grant deadpanned.

"Sure enough. And Dr. Parker, here. She taught us all about how to 'beware the Ides of March.'"

Grant nodded sagely. "Useful advice."

"Indeed. Actually, now that I think on it. Dr. Parker, *you* taught us all that poetry. It was *Mr. Wiggins* who had us read Julius Caesar." Grayson sighed. "That Mr. Wiggins, he really made all that Shakespeare come alive. Is he still teaching?"

Emma thought of Floyd Wiggins, a moderately successful actor with the Royal Shakespeare Company who'd left England under the rush of something scandalous and who managed to find a small semblance of joy by introducing the bard to a slew of provincial teenagers, until he left teaching after some mysterious confrontation with The Roach. For a moment Emma considered the snake, the bear and the idea of being buried alive, wondering what a creative, Shakespearean fanatic might have done if he was consumed by vengeance and had plenty of time on his hands. "No," she answered. "He retired."

"Well, that's a shame. And now, with you leaving to start your...uh...darn fine café, well Gadson High is just losing one good teacher after another." Grayson patted Grant on the shoulder. "But we're sure lucky to still have fine teachers like you, sir."

Grant gave him a bemused smile, then glanced at his watch. "Look at the time. We're about done here, Grayson. I just need to drop off some paperwork. Then, we can walk you out and you can tell us more about your bizarre encounters at Animal Control."

Emma picked up the envelope containing the paperwork. "I'll drop this off and catch up to you." She left the room before Grant could offer an alternative suggestion that would involve *her* learning more from the loquacious Grayson.

Not needing much light—partially because of the parking lot illumination, but mostly because she'd taught in the building for nearly thirty years—Emma made her way briskly down the dark hall and turned right, toward the front of the school. The administrative suite was locked, so she slid the paperwork under the door, and as she did so, she heard a faint repeating click. Instantly recognizing the sound, she made her way farther down the hall to the teachers' lounge and work room. A wave of nostalgia hit Emma as she stepped into the room, with its partially functioning microwave, occasionally cold fridge and four broken desks that had been duct-taped together to form a communal table. The clicking was louder in here, and having dealt with it on a daily basis for the twenty-year life of the dishwasher, she opened the door and adjusted the lock so it would work. As she did so, she noticed that the dishwasher was empty except for one item. With an impulse born out of every whodunnit she'd ever read, Emma retrieved a plastic bag, secured the mug and dropped it in her messenger bag.

Not heeding her own warnings to hundreds of teenagers, she ran down the hallway and out the side entrance.

Grant waved after Grayson's retreating van, then turned to her. "He got another call. What's wrong?"

Emma, who still adhered to the daily routine of an early-morning run her father had started when she'd been fourteen, realized she was breathless, not from the physical exertion but rather from some kind of morbid excitement that unsettled her. Tucking the feeling away for scrutiny tomorrow, or never, she asked, "How likely is it that two people tried to kill The Roach on the same day?"

"I'm pretty sure there were *more* than two people who tried to kill him on *every* day. The fact that someone succeeded? *That's* what is so unlikely."

CHAPTER 5

High Ground Café
Dr. Emma Jean Parker, temporary holder of evidence
104 Main Street
Gadson Township, Georgia
Monday, May 17, 1999

Emma was in the middle of explaining the difference between "lie" and "lay" to Chloé Williams (and not for the first time) when the door to the café opened and Emma felt a barometric shift in the room. She looked over to see a statuesque woman with luminous brown skin, sculptured features and a commanding presence. Emma's first instinct was to bow. At the same time, her skin tingled, her face flushed and a flutter hopped between her heart and her stomach. This was the new sheriff in town.

"Dr. Parker, are you okay?"

Chloé's question snapped Emma back from her reverie and her face reddened even more, fearing that her attraction might have been as obvious externally as it had felt internally.

"Grass pollen," Emma coughed.

Chloé nodded knowingly. "Oh, I believe it. It's the worst. Mama says half her appointments are with patients needing subcutaneous immunotherapy. She has pamphlets at her office. I'll bring one over to you. Also, be sure to wear sunglasses and a hat to minimize the pollen getting in your eyes or on your face. Do the Wilsons mow your lawn? Does ragweed bother you too?"

For the first time in her career, Emma was grateful for a chatty student. After giving cursory responses to Chloé's questions, Emma redirected the girl back to her work of correcting sentences, while Emma focused on *her* work of eavesdropping and keeping her heart in her chest. In her peripheral vision, she saw the sheriff approach the counter where she received a hearty welcome from Corliss Stewart, a great-grandmother who wore her fifty-five years split between her hips and her smile. The woman had staffed the café for a few hours each Monday, her day off from the canning factory, so that her granddaughter, Willadeene, the third generation of Stewart teen-mothers, could work with Emma to prepare for the GED.

Willadeene's four children were also there, the two-year-old twins being entertained with endless rounds of peek-a-boo with Harper Coburn and Journee Smalls, friends and fellow cheerleaders of Chloé's. Emma had determined that, despite the fact that formal sex education had never made its way to Gadson—Grant had been able to sneak in some basic precautions under the nose of Principal Simmons in the guise of sophomore biology—no curriculum would ever be as effective in averting teen pregnancy as keeping up with the energy of two well-rested and well-fed toddlers.

However, even with all of this, Emma had no trouble overhearing the conversation. After the requisite southern pleasantries, the sheriff's rich caramel voice, sounding more like a late-night DJ interested in breaking the law rather than a public servant intent on upholding it, asked after Emma.

Delia, as was her wont of late, perched at the counter, surveying all. "She'll be right with you, Sheriff," she crooned, in a flirtatious tone that Emma found disconcerting and could only attribute to a lifetime of ingrained responses to anyone in uniform. "In the meantime, how about some coffee?" In a lowered purr, she added, "Do you take your coffee like you take your men, Sheriff?"

Emma had never listened so carefully in her life.

"I do indeed, ma'am." Presumably, to Corliss, she said, "I'll have some tea. Oolong, if you have it."

"Excuse me, Chloé and Willadeene," said Emma.

She approached the sheriff, noticing that they were of a similar height (hard to tell exactly with the hat) and now that she was closer, she also noticed that the sheriff, while carrying herself with the authority of sixty years, couldn't have experienced many more than thirty. Like cold water, the thought instantly stifled any and all of Emma's romantic rumblings. Thoughts of heaving bosoms and matching Subaru Outbacks were immediately thrown in a safe, which was promptly dumped in wet cement. This psychological task completed, Emma brought herself back to her senses, a place where she was infinitely more comfortable.

She extended her hand to the sheriff, and in a neutral tone, said, "I'm Emma Parker."

Sheriff Walker took her hand and time seemed to stand still for a moment, which gave Emma the opportunity to mentally send the block of cement to Antarctica. "*Dr.* Parker, correct?"

As they released each other's hand, Emma thought she detected a brief glance of pleased appraisal beneath the other woman's professional regard. Beginning to blush in response, she visualized shoving the block of cement onto a piece of floating ice. "Yes, but it's a doctorate in literature, so I generally don't use it."

Delia piped in. "But she should, Sheriff. Lord knows, it'll be the only doctor we ever have in the family. And she worked hard for it. Hours studying, traveling into Savannah, all while teaching these children. Why, she's a credit to our family and we couldn't be prouder."

"Mama," Emma muttered the warning, and the older woman threw her an indignant look.

Corliss, who had been nodding in vigorous agreement, set a steaming cup of tea down on the counter. "Honey?" she asked.

Still looking at Emma, the sheriff answered, "Yes?"

Emma snorted and was promptly drowned in mortification.

Both Delia and Corliss looked nonplussed, but Sheriff Walker smiled conspiratorially at Emma, before amending, "No, ma'am. I reckon I'm sweet enough as it is." Turning to Emma, she shifted back to the business at hand. "Is there a good place for us to talk?"

"Of course," Emma said, motioning to a small table in a far corner.

As they sat down, Delia bustled over and set a glass of water in front of Emma. "You looked thirsty, sweetie."

A jingle of the door preceded the maelstrom that was Janine Ledbetter, who entered heaving a cardboard box. She was followed by her daughter, struggling to carry another box and Grant, balancing a third with one arm. In his other hand he held the coffee mug Emma had given him for Christmas that read, "I make horrible science puns, but only periodically."

"Dr. Parker, where do you want these?" Janine called out.

Emma, grateful for a distraction, even while she was plagued with disinterest, waved vaguely toward an empty wall. "I suppose over there for the time being."

Janine nodded and deposited them. "Kennedy, you get another box and I'll be right with you." Her tone shifted from maternal authority to audacious flirt. "Mr. Michael, you're so sweet to help us. If there's anything I can ever do to repay you..." she left the suggestion out in the open to see how many flies it might collect.

Grant gave an officious and well-worn response. "I'll be sure to let you know, Mrs. Ledbetter."

Emma suspected that it wasn't Janine Ledbetter's married state that precluded Grant's attentions. Emma had it on good authority (her mother) that Grant has been "generous with his affection" with a number of married women over his five-year tenure in Gadson. Emma wasn't entirely sure about that, but she was absolutely confident that Grant would steer clear of anyone he might encounter at a parent-teacher conference.

Grant made his way over to Emma's table, gave a shrewd look at the sheriff, a knowing grin to Emma and a kiss on the cheek to Delia. "Miss Delia, you're looking well."

Delia gave him a once-over and hummed. "Sheriff Walker, it was a pleasure meeting you. I hope my Emma Jean isn't in too much hot water."

Grant motioned to the large cloth bag Delia was carrying with "Not today, Satan" printed in glittering pink letters. A fuchsia yoga mat peeked out of the top. "Headed over to Might-As-Well?"

Delia grinned. "I sure am. Tiana is starting a class today called 'Hot Yoga,' and I'm determined to keep my girlish figure even at my advanced age."

Emma sighed. "It's more like social hour, Mama, and you know it. You're just going over there to spread news to all and sundry."

"Not at all, sweetie." Delia was speaking to Emma, but only had eyes for Grant. "I'm also going to spread my legs." She threw Grant a coquettish wink and sashayed toward the door.

This time it was Sheriff Walker's turn to snort, almost spitting out her tea.

"Mama!"

"Don't start what you can't finish, Miss Delia," Grant called after her.

Emma covered her ears. "Please don't encourage her."

Grant grinned. "So, Sheriff," he began, pulling over a chair to join them. "I presume you're new in town?"

Emma could hear his matchmaking tone loudly and clearly, and she gave him a sharp glare.

"Relatively new," the lawwoman answered, something in her tone seeming to question his, glancing back at Emma in time to see the tail end of her facial expression. Sheriff Walker stifled a grin. "I was deputy over in Watson County, but when my father retired last month, I was moved over on a temporary basis."

"Well, I hope you find a reason to stay in Gadson," Grant said, with a head tilt toward Emma. "We certainly could use another—"

"Jaxon Walker is your father?" Emma interrupted, adding a quick under the table kick. "So, Anya Walker is your niece? She was one of my students. Is she still at Duke?"

Sheriff Walker nodded. "Yes, she is. Pre-med and when I told her I'd be in Gadson, you were one of the first people she mentioned. Said you were her favorite teacher, in fact. It's a noble profession." The sheriff gave the café a pointed perusal.

"Long story," Grant answered her unasked question, rubbed his shin and shifted the topic. "You do know there's no way that the janitor killed The Roach, right?"

Sheriff Walker gave him a skeptical glance. "And why's that?"

As Grant explained his theory, Emma gazed at Sheriff Walker, at first to ascertain any features she shared with her father—something in the jawline, perhaps—and then for the simple joy of it.

"Emma?" Grant's voice cut through the mist of longing and Emma made herself envision tipping the cement block into the ocean.

"What's that?" she asked.

Grant repeated, "That the killer could have been just about anyone?"

Emma considered this for a moment. "Just about," she agreed. "He was a thoroughly hated individual who was blackmailing a lot of people."

Sheriff Walker took a longer look around the café and returned her critical gaze to Emma. In that look, three things were clear. First, that Sheriff Walker had inherited her father's keen skills of observation, and second, that she knew Emma was gay and third, that The Roach had also known, which was the obvious impetus for Emma's recent change in professions.

"We received a call from Animal Control," the sheriff said. "Tell me about the snake."

Emma released the breath she'd been holding in fear that the sheriff was about to reference the secret that only Grant knew.

Grant, recognizing Emma's panicked expression, jumped in. "Grayson said it was a cottonmouth. We figured, it must have been put in there in the hopes that The Roach—Mr. Roach," he corrected after a raised eyebrow, "would open the drawer, get bit and die. The venom of a cottonmouth, left untreated could kill and there wouldn't have been anyone near enough to help."

"And Mr. Roach would have been there when other teachers weren't," the sheriff more stated than asked.

Grant laughed. "Certainly. He was a horrible teacher and I doubt he did much work, but I imagine he did most of his bedevilment from that desk. He was usually the first to arrive and the last to leave. Frankly, I wouldn't be surprised if it was some kind of psychological intimidation. The first thing people saw upon arriving was his Lincoln Continental, and it was the last thing they saw when leaving. He was a horrible person, but he wasn't dumb and knew how to get to people."

Sheriff Walker seemed to consider this as she took a sip of tea. "I appreciate the information. We'll take it from here."

The clear message not to meddle in police business suddenly reminded Emma of the mug. "Actually," she added in a contrite tone. "There is one more thing." She retrieved the plastic bag from behind the counter and handed it to the sheriff. "I forgot that I also found this yesterday. The—Mr. Roach had a deathly allergy to strawberries, and I believe you'll find that something strawberry-related has been smeared on the rim of his cup."

Sheriff's Walker's demeanor, which until now had been serene, showed a flit of irritation. She took a deep breath. "Please explain."

In a nervous rush, Emma relayed how she had entered a room she probably shouldn't have, hid under a desk and listened to high-heeled footsteps that likely belonged to Principal Simmons.

"You're sure?"

Emma indicated her own Dansko clogs and shrugged. "Teachers and nurses."

She had experienced a momentary hesitation ratting out Sheila Simmons, but her mind was quickly inundated with a flurry of memories of the woman using her power to terrify and demean children. Emma added a final confirmation. "I'm sure."

Sheriff Walker scrutinized her, as if noticing another facet to Emma's personality and cataloging it in her steel-trap brain. "Is there *anything* else related to this murder investigation that you'd like to share?"

Emma didn't share about the proximity of the supplies closet to Singleton's room, because the sheriff would know that, just as she would know about the ceramic shards on The Roach's floor. Emma *did* consider sharing about the manila folder she'd found taped underneath the desk, which had contained official school stationery and blank report cards, but since she'd left it on the desk and since sharing about it would extend their time together and since she could feel the cement cracking and the safe with all her reckless yearnings somehow rising to the surface, she found herself giving the answer that would minimize future interactions with this woman whose presence was making it increasingly difficult for Emma to keep her head and heart from spinning. "That's it," she said.

At that moment, there was a squealing of tires followed by a stampede of footsteps before the door of the café was thrown open. The Furies—the secret name Emma had given her mother's lifelong frenemies, Adelaide Cook and the Beauregard sisters—all three clad in tights and Flashdance leotards with matching headbands—hurtled in.

"Emma Jean! It's your mother! She hurt herself," shrieked Chantilly Beauregard.

"It was the *Utthita Padangusthasana!*" added her sister, June.

"I told her not to try it," finished Adelaide Cook.

"I have a stretcher. We'll take my truck." Sheriff Walker took the mug and rushed out the door.

Emma grabbed her bag from behind the counter, then stopped, feeling like she should issue some instructions, but then figured everyone in the café—save the toddlers— probably knew more about how to run the place than she did, so she just ran out after the sheriff.

"We have this, Dr. Parker," Corliss hollered after her.

Sheriff Walker had just started her truck and set the flashing lights, when Emma hopped in the passenger seat. "Head north, then take a left on Bacon. It's three blocks down on your right."

CHAPTER 6

St. Joseph's Hospital
Delia Parker, patient (noun, not adjective)
11705 Mercy Boulevard
Savannah, Georgia
Monday, May 17, 1999

When Emma returned from checking in at the nurses' station, a frenzy of barely contained panic, the orderly had won the battle and Delia was now clad in the "hideous monstrosity" of a hospital gown. She did, however, manage to keep her three strands of pearls, which she clutched as a nurse gave her an injection.

"You were wearing pearls to your yoga class, Mama?"

"Don't be ridiculous, sweetie. I always have an extra set in my purse, just in case."

Emma glanced at the carpet bag of a purse and thought *it* seemed much more of a "hideous monstrosity" to her. The exterior changed with the season—now lime green with brass handles—but the size remained colossal. She was just remembering a time when her mother got a flat tire on a back road and was able to get help by setting off a flare that she kept in her purse (just in case), when the doctor, a harried man with glasses buried in a cloud of white curls, entered the room.

"Mr. Martinez?" he asked, squinting to look at his clipboard and patting his pockets.

"They're on your head," Emma said dryly, noticing that the doctor himself, sweating profusely, seemed unwell.

Looking a little chagrinned, the discombobulated physician patted his head, retrieved his glasses, adjusted them and looked back at the clipboard, then at Delia. "Not, Mr. Martinez."

Delia lifted the eyebrow that had brought many in Gadson to task.

"No, no, of course not." He riffled through the other papers. "Parker?"

Delia nodded, not unlike a queen staying her executioner.

"Pleasure to meet you, Mrs. Parker. I'm Dr. Corbin It looks from the prelims like a pulled hamstring, but we'll set you up for an x-ray this week to be sure there is no tendon avulsion. It says here you were doing yoga?"

"Hot yoga," Delia corrected.

"Hot yoga," Dr. Corbin murmured, patting his pocket again.

"Your ear," Emma directed.

Dr. Corbin retrieved the pen from behind his ear and made a note on the chart. "Hot yoga," he murmured as he wrote. "Huh," he grunted. "What will they think of next? Was this some kind of Jane Fonda video?"

Before Delia could answer, which probably would just have been another raised eyebrow, The Furies arrived in a tizzy of perfume and feigned fretfulness. Emma noticed they weren't so worried that it had prevented them from changing their outfits.

"Delia, look at you!" cried Chantilly.

"Just look at you," added June.

"You look terrible," finished Adelaide.

They crowded around her, jostling and flustering Dr. Corbin. The Beauregards plied Delia with chocolates, flowers, a balloon and a teddy bear. Adelaide handed Delia a carton of apple juice that looked suspiciously like it had been picked off the food tray of another patient.

Emma, who had little tolerance for The Furies under normal circumstances, used their arrival as an excuse. "Mama, I'm going to make a quick phone call."

"Oh, Emma? Get me a tabloid or something."

Emma nodded, knowing that her mother's version of "or something" really meant, "if you can't find that exact thing, don't bother coming back." She remembered the time Delia had sent her husband for concessions at the movie theater with instructions to get "Goobers or something." Mr. Parker had returned with Junior Mints and Emma was pretty sure he spent the rest of the weekend sleeping on the couch.

Emma stepped into the hall and dodged her way among hastening employees until she reached the payphone next to the staff room. She couldn't remember it being so busy the last time she'd been here, which was when Willadeene had gone into labor with the twins, but that had been in the early morning.

Grant answered on the second ring.

"Hey," she greeted.

"How's Delia?"

"Pulled hamstring. I don't know if the pain medication has kicked in yet, but they sure seemed to give her plenty of it. She's holding court at the moment."

"Should I head over?"

"I wouldn't. The Furies are here. You'd just be one more butt to pinch. I swear, those ladies are going to get sued one of these days."

"And how's the sheriff?" Grant's tone dripped with innuendos.

"I haven't the faintest. And don't think I didn't notice the tone."

"I'm just saying, that is one fine-looking woman the universe just dropped in your lap."

"A fine-looking *young* woman."

"I can't help thinking of all the trouble you could cause."

"I'm hanging up now."

"Not to mention the handcuffs."

Emma rolled her eyes and hung up.

"Dr. Parker? Is that you?"

Emma looked over to see a former student of hers, who was visibly pregnant and wearing a nurse's uniform. "Harlene Marshall! How are you?"

The nurse bustled over. "*Ellis* now, Dr. Parker. I'm doing well, doing well."

"Gavin Ellis?"

Harlene laughed. "Nope. Everyone always thinks that, though. Gavin's up in Atlanta. I married his brother, Calvin." Seeing Emma's expression, Harlene added. "I know, I know. We didn't really run in the same circles in high school."

Emma thought that was an understatement. To her recollection, Harlene ran in every circle and Calvin in none.

"Congratulations, and how's Calvin?"

"He's doing well. He's over with IBM. It's long hours, but good money." She patted her belly. "Which is a good thing since this is the third one. Due in July. It'll probably be a Cancer, which isn't great, since I'm a Leo and Calvin's a Scorpio. I was hoping for something more mellow, like a Sagittarius, or something." Harlene shrugged. "But what can you do?"

Emma could think of plenty of things one could "do" and couldn't help but wonder how Harlene had fared in nursing school.

"And Marshall?"

"Dad's fine. He's still at Mother's Bakery. We don't see him much. I'm trying to get him to move in with us, but I think the kids scare him. Plus, he still has all those cats and Calvin's allergic." She looked around. "Did you come with someone? Are you okay?"

"I'm fine," Emma assured. "My mother is—"

"Oh, my Lord! Is Miss Delia alright? Why, she is just the most precious thing."

"She's fine. Just a pulled—"

Emma was cut off when another nurse rushed up to them. "Harlene! We have another two down. I put them in room 312. Will you set up the IVs? I need to head back to the cafeteria."

Harlene nodded patiently. "Sure thing, Mirna. I'll be right there."

"Thank you!" The woman heaved a sigh before dashing away.

Harlene rubbed her lower back. "So, you said Miss Delia pulled something?"

Bemused, Emma said, "Her hamstring. What's going on?"

Harlene rolled her eyes. "Salmon. We're in Georgia, people. Salmon is, like, from Alaska. That's a whole different country. It's hardly going to be in great condition when it arrives. Plus, those cafeteria ladies. I never eat there. The doctors are so rude to them. I bet they spit in the food. *I* would." She sighed. "Anyway, there was this fancy doctor lunch today and now a whole bunch of them have food poisoning." She raised her voice. "Serves them right, if you ask me."

"Oh, well, uh...I should get back to my mother, actually. I just hopped out to get her something to read. Do you know where I can find a magazine?"

"Sure do," Harlene said brightly, and Emma had a sudden memory of how Harlene had always made sure Emma's pencils were sharp enough to wound somebody. "Right here in the break room." She motioned to a nearby door marked "Staff Only" and continued, "There's a whole stack of reading materials in there. I should probably get back to work." She leaned in conspiratorially. "With doctors as patients, it's always fun to pretend you can't find a vein."

Perhaps it was serendipity or simply the universe being bored, but just as Emma entered the break room, Harlene hollered back, "It was nice to see you, Dr. Parker!"

"Doctor?" exclaimed the sole occupant of the room, a small man grasping a manila folder in one hand and a half-eaten powdered donut in his other. There was a frantic look on his face, along with residual evidence of the donut. "Thank goodness!" He shoved the folder into Emma's hand. "I need a signature on this." He rushed out the door, grumbling, "Just because my patients are already dead doesn't mean that I'm not just as busy."

Emma stared at the folder, then jumped as the man popped back in. "I'll be back in just a minute. I left something in the morgue." He eyed the donuts, put his half eaten one in the pocket of his white lab coat and grabbed a second one. It looked jelly-filled to Emma and she could just imagine what folks might think of the red stains sure to appear.

Emma considered herself to be an ethical person. She considered herself to be a law-abiding citizen. Above that, she considered herself to be a woman who minded her own business. At the same time, half her chromosomes came from Delia Parker née Mobley, a woman who could never leave well enough alone. Emma opened the folder.

Having a doctorate in literature prepared her for a number of things, and if the folder's contents had been a literary analysis juxtaposing *A Room of One's Own* and *The Well of Loneliness,* she would have been well prepared to understand it. Unsurprisingly, it was not. Trying to access a part of her brain only visited when she was making half a recipe calling for three-quarters of something, Emma mentally slogged her way through the medical jargon. A number of items didn't need any slogging to understand. Underneath the heading "Official Coroner's Report" read, "Name of Deceased," and next to it read, "Everett Andrew Roach."

The right side of her brain couldn't help but note that The Roach's initials were perfect for his tendency to be listening in on everyone's business. Acknowledging the hypocrisy evident in her current activity, she promptly slid the thought back into the recesses of her mind and continued to scan. Snippets of information emerged.

Cause of death, asphyxiation. Red plastic sphere, two centimeters in diameter, with white numbers. Dangerously high levels of isradipine. Not enough to be the cause of death, but enough to be a contributing factor.

Just as the coroner returned, predictably with red goo in his beard, Emma gleaned one last piece of information. *Bruising in torso, possibly from being beaten or kicked posthumously.*

The coroner reached for the folder. "Thank you, Doctor."

Without hesitation, Emma made use of the excuse that had gotten her out of countless gym classes and awkward conversations. Bringing her hand and a panicked expression to her face, she mumbled something about a bloody nose and raced out the door.

When she returned to her mother's room, The Furies were still in full form. They had helped Delia back into her yoga clothes, and she was now sitting, ever regal, in the discharge wheelchair. The doctor had left, and Sheriff Walker had arrived.

Emma tried to calm her wobbling heart. "You ready, Mama?"

"Right as rain, Emma Jean," assured Delia. She patted the sheriff's hand. "The sheriff here needs to talk with a coroner about all that murder nonsense from this weekend."

The Furies gasped in mirrored disgust.

"Awful," said Chantilly.

"Just awful," added June.

"But totally deserved," finished Adelaide.

Delia nodded. "So, Chantilly is going to take us home."

"Sounds good," Emma said, knowing that with Chantilly Beauregard's driving record, they could likely all end up back here within the hour. Still, Emma, who had lost every single hand of poker she had ever played, feared an hour-long car ride with the sheriff would just add fuel to the fire of Emma's attraction as well as give plenty of time for her face to proclaim it.

Emma reached for the wheelchair and proceeded to move down the hallway.

"Not so fast, Emma!" her mother reprimanded.

Emma noticed that The Furies, who had been flanking her, had dropped back and were clutching their chests. Emma doubted she'd been going that fast, but stopped impatiently, fighting the urge to turn around, as the women caught up. When she finally gave in and looked back, she saw Sheriff Walker staring at her with an inscrutable look on her face.

Emma figured her own expression was likely one of panic, so she quickly turned away, silently cursing her mother for both her risky behavior and her DNA.

"Maybe lukewarm yoga next time, Mama," Emma grumbled.

Delia chuckled. "Lukewarm yoga, lukewarm men, sweetie."

CHAPTER 7

High Ground Café
Dr. Emma Jean Parker, occasional proprietress
104 Main Street
Gadson Township, Georgia
Monday, May 17, 1999

When Emma returned to the café, Corliss and her descendants had left. Now, it was Zion Jones, captain of the Gadson football team, who manned the counter, with Malik Jones, his best friend (and slightly younger half-uncle), keeping him company. Also, Emma's poetry team had arrived.

The poetry craze had hit Gadson in the summer of 1963, when Hollywood Briggs had bought up ten hectares of land just southeast of town. The income had been a financial boon for the community, and the purchase had provided years of grist for the rumor mill as residents shook their heads at all the razzle-dazzle Hollywood was putting into his Roundtree Ranch. The idea of a spa with mud baths could still get folks howling. Two years later, the construction was complete, and before the first guests arrived, Hollywood had hosted a week-long open house, with free food and free services for all. A handful of brave souls had tried the hot stone massage, and Mother Coburn had even tried the acid peel. The most popular attractions were *trying out* the gun range and *checking out* the mud baths. The week culminated in the much anticipated and first annual "Poetry under the Stars." While hitherto, citizens of Gadson hadn't had any particular inclination toward (nor aversion to) poetry, Hollywood, who was a dead ringer for Paul Newman, had a contagious passion for it—so much so that at each of the monthly town meetings, he would open his update on the ranch's progress with a recitation. Mesmerized by his charisma and dimples, a public enthusiasm was ignited. Before long, Kitty and Blade Abernathy—of Blade's Books—could barely keep up with the demand.

The following year, the citizens of Gadson, with pageantry in their veins, transformed Poetry under the Stars, which continued to be hosted in the open-air theatre at Roundtree Ranch, into a contest. Although people competed in teams, there was unanimous agreement that an individual contestant would still be crowned "Poet of the Year," a title that came with nearly as many obligations as "Miss Gadson." Up until recently, Emma had been the youngest member of her mother's team—the teams generally following bloodlines—but when a group of former students had approached Emma, even going so far as to write an *Ode to Dr. Parker,* she didn't have the heart not to "become a traitor to her family," as her mother had called it, which was just as well since the Parkers were short-lived and by now had been replaced with The Furies.

"Dr. Parker!" exclaimed Dixie Wilson, the fifth and shockingly unexpected daughter of Connie and Ridge. "We'd almost given up hope. How's Miss Delia?"

After giving assurance that her mother would be fine, Emma got down to business. "So, what did I miss?"

Curtis Edwards, captain of the poetry team, said, "We only just started." He glowered at Faye Greene, whose father made clocks for a living.

"Sorry. I lost—"

"Track of time," chorused the other team members.

Shaking off the irritation, Curtis expertly and efficiently facilitated the meeting. Over the next hour, the group finalized the set list and finished curating the poems based in part on the elaborate spreadsheet Wade Dixon had made analyzing which poems had garnered the highest scores from the judges—each of whom held lifetime appointments. Understudies were chosen, inspired by the debacle faced by the Sonnet Sisters a few years earlier, when Clarice Anderson, had started taking nips of Brandy to mitigate her stage fright and ended up being too inebriated to perform.

The meeting ended with each member reciting their piece for the handful of café patrons, beginning with Tabitha Wise reciting *Still I Rise,* basking in the hard-won lines that Dixie was convinced would disqualify them, "Does my sexiness upset you? Does it come as a surprise that I dance like I've got diamonds at the meeting of my thighs?" The impromptu salon finished with Emma's recitation of *The Highwayman.*

She was just reaching the final stanzas, performed to a rapt audience, when she noticed Sheriff Walker standing near the door. Only the fact that she'd recited the poem a hundred times prevented Emma from stumbling over the words, but she couldn't help blushing as she described the posthumous romance that brought the story to a close with, "Plaiting a dark red love-knot into her long black hair."

Applause erupted and Emma heard Sheriff Walker clapping the loudest of all. Emma smiled her appreciation, and, having a sneaking suspicion as to the reason for the sheriff's visit, tried to avoid eye contact with her. After thanking Zion and relieving him from his post, Emma tried to look for a task to occupy her. Noticing a new tip jar had been created and filled, she removed it, and knowing that Zion—like everyone else—would refuse it, put the money in an envelope on which she wrote "Corliss and Zion" before adding it to the growing pile.

At a clearing of a throat, Emma looked up to see the sheriff. "Oh, I didn't see you there," she prevaricated.

Sheriff Walker smiled, an action that surely belied the scolding to come. "That was quite a performance, Dr. Parker."

Flustered by the sound of the woman's voice as much as the compliment, Emma, renowned orator, mumbled, "Thank you. How can I help you, Sheriff? Tea? Oolong."

"No." The sheriff sat down on the stool Malik had vacated. "Say, there was a funny thing that happened at the medical examiner's office earlier today. Darndest thing."

Emma hoped it wasn't obvious that her hands were shaking as she plugged in the electric kettle. "Is that so? I can't imagine anything funny about the morgue."

"Well, not so much funny like ha ha, as much as breaking the law by impersonating a doctor."

Emma was silent, pretending to look for the unrequested tea.

"You wouldn't happen to know anything about that now, *Dr.* Parker?"

Emma sighed. "Okay, yes," she confessed. "But there is something you should know—"

"What I *should* know and *do* know, Dr. Parker, is that it is illegal to impersonate a physician and that it is also against the law to meddle in a murder investigation." The woman's voice remained at a low volume, even as the intensity of it increased. "Now, fortunate for you, Gadson's jail only has two cells and they're both occupied at the moment."

Emma did some quick calculations, then gasped. "Principal Simmons."

For the first time in her life, Emma was on the receiving end of the same look she had given to students who, despite the fact she had provided the instructions in writing and in person each day for a week, appeared mystified to learn that their project was due.

"Dr. Parker," Sheriff Walker continued, her tone coated in manufactured patience. "I'll tell you, *again*, leave this to the professionals." Almost as an afterthought, she continued, "I'm new in this position, you understand. Gadson residents don't know me." She motioned to the café. "But they definitely know you, and they clearly hold you in high regard."

Well, I sure recognize this speech, Emma thought, wondering in hindsight if it was just as transparent to her students when she issued the others-see-you-as-a-leader-and-you-have-the-opportunity-to-use-your-power-for-good speech.

Arms akimbo, Emma found herself channeling a truculent teenager. "You're trying to handle me," she accused.

Sheriff Walker took a deep breath. "What I'm handling, Dr. Parker, is a murder investigation, and unless you want to be considered an impediment to justice, you'll stay out of it." She tipped her hat in respectful dismissal.

"And what if I have information?" Emma blurted.

"Such as?"

Emma didn't hesitate. "The report referred to 'dangerously high doses of isradipine,' which is what my grandmother takes for her high blood pressure."

Sheriff Walker checked her watch. "Yes?"

"Which was impossible. The Roach—Mr. Roach— bragged constantly about not needing any kind of medication, not even to prevent a fourth heart attack, not even for his stupid allergies."

"He could have been lying," came the reasonable response.

Emma shook her head. "Not even the remotest possibility. He was blackmailing half this town. There is no way on earth that he would ever leave himself exposed to derision."

Sheriff Walker considered this before shifting topics. "There is *something* related to the investigation where I could use your help."

Emma tried to raise one skeptical eyebrow, but it was a facial expression she still hadn't mastered, so she lifted both, which she hoped at least showed surprise. "Is that so?"

The consummate professional, Sheriff Walker explained, "We'd like you to come back to the school and walk us through what you found yesterday. There are a number of things about that classroom that are...disconcerting."

"Happy to."

"Are you free later today?"

Emma considered that normally she'd close in an hour. Simultaneously, she considered that she had yet to actually man her own counter today. Reminding herself that she was not a charity case, no matter the overflowing tip jar that kept finding its way onto the counter or the outpouring of support she'd received from former students and their families, she decided she should stay open a little longer. "I'll be closed at 7:00, if that suits you."

The sheriff glanced at the sign in the window displaying the store hours but kept her expression implacable. "Fine. I'll pick you up then."

Somehow, the universe took over Emma's brain at that exact moment, because instead of something in the realm of *No need—I'll meet you there,* she found herself saying, "It's a date." *Let the mortification begin,* she thought, feeling her face redden. "I mean...uh...well, that is."

Sheriff Walker put Emma out of her misery with a merciful, "I'll pick you up at 7:00." With another tip of her hat and a look of suppressed amusement, the sheriff left the café.

With speed born of humiliation, Emma rushed to the restroom and splashed cold water on her face. When she returned, her poetry team was engaged in an animated assessment of that year's teachers.

"And Mr. Singleton, too," said Tabitha. "All you had to say was that you had female problems and he'd let you get away with anything."

Emma couldn't help but insert, "Well, Mr. Singleton had plenty of excuses when he was my student."

Tabitha laughed. "I forgot, Dr. Parker. You've taught *everyone.*"

"Was Mr. Singleton a good student?" Wade asked, rolling up his spreadsheet.

Emma gave them the oh-I-love-this-number-one-teacher-mug smile. "One of my favorites."

Dixie gushed. "Well, I'm not surprised. You know, he got the Chickering Scholarship. You only get that if you are really really smart." Considering her superlatives, she decided to add, "Like, *really.* He had a 4.0. You have to. That means that you need to get an 'A' in *every* single class." She leaned in to emphasize, "Like, *every.*"

The group nodded in grave amazement and understanding, before Faye piped in with, "That's the same scholarship Tucker Culverhouse received."

"Wow," Curtis said. "I didn't even know he was smart."

"You know who else Dr. Parker taught?" Dixie asked as if the answer was some delicious piece of gossip.

"Who?" the others chimed.

"You know the weatherman who does the evening news on channel three?"

The group nodded eagerly and in unison.

Dixie gave a self-satisfied smile. "His cousin."

CHAPTER 8

2000 Chevrolet Tahoe
Sheriff Jada Walker, driver
Gadson Township, Georgia
Monday, May 17, 1999

One's vehicle says a lot about a person, which is what Emma was considering as she stepped into the 2000 Chevy Tahoe. Although it was her second time in the vehicle, that morning she'd been too focused on her mother to notice the leather interior, tinted windows and a state-of-the-art sound system. "Where's the partridge in the pear tree?" she asked.

Sheriff Walker, who *was* able to raise a single eyebrow, did so. "Dr. Parker, I've been to your café three times, and I've yet to find you behind the counter."

This wasn't a question and Emma didn't much care for the direction of the conversation, so she ignored the comment and silently waved back to two men, whose youthful faces hadn't quite caught up with their height. One, Ayden Ward, the estranged son of Reverend Jimmy Junior and presumed father of Willadeene's twins, was holding a guitar case. The other, Riley Young, was holding a book, *Anna Karenina,* which he'd insisted on struggling through ever since Emma had started teaching him how to read back in January.

Sheriff Walker put the vehicle in gear and drove down toward Myrtle Avenue, where she took a right to head over Big Bridge, the middle of the three bridges that straddled Mill Creek, which divided the town in two. Unlike most communities, the division was not racial or economic. The majority of residences were on the north side. Beech-Byrd, Penelope and Heaven-Blessed, the three largest farms, were on the south side, along with Ledbetter Dairy, the canning factory and Mother's Bakery, a multi-million-dollar business employing nearly 200 people. It had started in the kitchen of Mother Coburn, but then a business tycoon staying at Roundtree Ranch tasted her pecan pie and now one could find Mother's Pies in the freezer section of any store in the country.

"So why is it that you're not teaching anymore?" The question broke through Emma's worries over Avery, who clearly loved Willadeene and, just as clearly, at twenty-two, did not have the emotional wherewithal to help parent her four children.

"I can't stand kids," Emma deadpanned.

"Or maybe because this is rural Georgia, and you're gay?"

Emma gasped audibly, began to bluster an indignant denial, then sighed in exhaustion. "It's a small town and people love their Jesus."

Sheriff Walker flashed her a winsome grin. "Not too small for a gay sheriff."

Emma looked at the woman's holster. "Well, it's a lot easier to be gay if you have a gun."

A boom of a laugh filled the car and Emma couldn't help but smile.

"And Black too," the sheriff added.

After a moment's hesitation, they both finished with, "And a woman."

The silence that comes with introspection was cut short, when Emma said, "I think there's something you should know."

Sheriff Walker smiled warmly, not taking her eyes off the road. Using her turn signal, she made her way onto Bridge Road, past Mill Creek Park, where several teenagers were hanging out at the swings, smoking. "And what's that?"

Out of habit, Emma made a mental note of the teens. "The ideal place to access a large amount of blood pressure medication at once would be Magnolia Manor."

"Ah, safe ground," the other woman assessed. "Probably, although someone could have stolen it from the pharmacy."

Now it was Emma's turn to let out a booming laugh. "First of all, Junior Freeman keeps that place locked down like Fort Stewart. He watches Dateline like it's church and he's convinced the only thing separating the residents of Gadson from becoming a cult of Satan-worshipping meth addicts is his adherence to protocol. Can you believe he's known my mother for over fifty years and he still makes her show him her ID?"

"And you think The—Mr. Roach wasn't using the drug for medicinal purposes?"

"Absolutely. He never stopped bragging about how great he was under pressure. Ask his doctor, Mason Dixon."

"Mason Dixon? I thought Dr. Williams was the only GP in town."

Emma scoffed. "Nope. The residents of Gadson fall into two medical camps. If you believe that AIDS is a punishment from God and teenage depression is just vying for attention, you go to Dr. Dixon."

Sheriff Walker mulled this over as they approached the school. The front door was propped open, and Deputy Levi Phillips was there to greet them.

"Evening, Sheriff. Evening, Dr. Parker."

"Levi Phillips," Emma exclaimed. "It's so good to see you. How's Genesis?"

"Mama's as cantankerous as always."

"Still trying to give Jimmy Junior a run for his money?" Emma asked.

Levi laughed. "Still trying. Revival season is starting up soon, and that always increases the fold."

"The woman can sure put on a show. I'll give her that. And your sister?"

"Grace is okay. Still over at Jill's Grill, which seems to make her happy."

"Good for her. I keep meaning to make it over, but with the café, I never seem to have the time."

Sheriff Walker tried to cover her laugh with a cough.

Emma continued, "Tell her I'll try to come this week, will you?"

"Sure will, Dr. Parker," said the deputy as he held the door open for the two women. He patted his front pocket. "Sheriff, I left the camera in the cruiser. I'll be right in."

Sheriff Walker nodded, then followed Emma down the lighted hallway. At the end, the sheriff reached into her pocket and took out two pairs of rubber gloves, handing one pair to Emma. "After you," she said.

• • • ● ●• ● ● • • •

Gadson High School
Sheriff Jada Walker, investigator
301 Jenkins Lane
Gadson Township, Georgia
Monday, May 17, 1999

The sheriff turned on the fluorescent lights. "Dr. Parker, why don't you walk me through the series of events?"

"Of course." Emma recalled the previous night. "I was here helping Grant Michael—one of the science teachers."

"Yes, we met this morning."

"Right, of course. So, I was helping him move classrooms and I kept walking past The—Mr. Roach's room, and I'll admit, I had no reason to come in. And, I shouldn't have. I understand that."

"Dr. Parker, I think it's safe to assume that I know and agree to all of these precursors. Please just explain what you did upon entering. Did you turn on the light?"

Emma shook her head. "There was enough moonlight, and I didn't want to touch anything. I was just wandering around the room." She indicated the shards on the floor. Now that the lights were on, she recognized its original shape. "I noticed this bust of Mussolini had broken, but I was more preoccupied by the memories of this horrible person and the idea that I was finally free."

"Free?" the sheriff asked.

"Well, *we* were all free. I mean *people* were free. The people he'd been hurting for all those years."

"Dr. Parker, had Everett Roach caused you to stop teaching by threatening to tell—"

Darting her eyes toward the door, Emma quickly cut her off. "Which was when I found myself closer to the desk and I heard the footsteps."

As if mirroring the story, Deputy Phillips' footsteps neared and he entered the room.

"So, I ducked underneath the desk. I told you about Principal Simmons."

"Indeed," Sheriff Walker agreed. "And that's when you heard the snake?"

Emma stood next to the desk, looked down at the trash can and wondered why she hadn't noticed the bright pink bakery box yesterday. "Yes," she muttered vaguely, thinking of dim lighting and how she had been focused on getting out of sight.

"Dr. Parker?"

Jarred out of her inadvertent gumshoeing, Emma smiled triumphantly. "The Roach had a weekly delivery of baked goods. This box is from Carla Nesmith's bakery, Merciful Savior Cakes & Cookies. It was delivered each week by Blakely Ward."

Deputy Phillips had a well-I'll-be expression. "Blakely Ward? The wife of Reverend Jimmy?"

"Yes, and—" Emma was unable to restrain her glee, but mentally chastised herself for being more excited about solving a puzzle than remorseful for the potential ramifications for a pillar in the Gadson community. "She is a resident of Magnolia Manor."

Sheriff Walker took all of this in, including, Emma suspected, the zeal that she had apparently failed to contain. "We'd like you to fill out a statement, Dr. Parker."

Deputy Phillips handed Emma a form and a pen, then joined the sheriff in the task of measuring the trajectory of the shards, to determine the point where the bust had shattered. As much as Emma loathed doing so, she sat down at The Roach's desk and began to fill out the paperwork. When she flipped the form over, her eye spotted the manila folder on the desk, where she had set it down after hearing the snake.

"Uh, Sheriff? There's something else."

"Yes, Dr. Parker?"

"Two somethings actually," Emma amended. "First, I found these blank official report cards and school stationery taped underneath the desk. Presumably The Roach was selling grades as an additional nefarious revenue stream."

"And second?" the sheriff asked.

Emma motioned up to a beam directly above the podium from which The Roach issued his diatribes. "If I were trying to brain him with a heavy object and I knew him well, I'd put it directly above where he spent most of the day."

Deputy Phillips, who, like most people between the ages of fifteen and forty in the town, had been taught by The Roach, seemed to cringe with the memory. "His voice had such a strong resonance and he'd get louder as the day progressed. If this bust was placed in the right spot, the reverberations from his lectures could have caused it to fall and knock him out—or even kill him—right in the middle of one of his rants." He took an evidence bag out of his pocket and began collecting the largest shards. "I don't know if we'll be able to get any full prints, but we should run it through the database at least to check."

"You could start with the school staff," Emma suggested. "We all have to get fingerprinted, since we work with children."

Hunkered down, the deputy nodded, before stopping to gaze up at the beam. "That's pretty impressive," he marveled. "I mean, you'd practically need a doctorate in physics to line that up."

"Or maybe just a bachelor's," Emma mused aloud.

Sheriff Walker cleared her throat and Emma looked up to meet another raised eyebrow.

"Singleton," she clarified. "His degree is in physics."

"Jesus," the sheriff muttered, the first crack in her professional demeanor. "How many people were trying to kill this man? We've got two kinds of poisoning, something lodged in his throat, a snake, and a bust of..."

"Mussolini," Emma finished.

"Thank you. That's five!"

Thinking of the bust reminded Emma of the faded Mussolini quotation that had been on the far wall for all the thirty years The Roach had taught in Gadson. She looked at it. It read, *Youth is a malady, of which one becomes cured a little every day.* How had she not noticed the misplaced comma for all these years? As she approached, it quickly became clear that it was not a comma at all.

"Make that six," she said, pointing to the bullet lodged in the wall.

The others joined her, and then all of them turned to look at the window in the opposite wall. The sheriff walked toward it, held out her fingers, squinted, measured, seemed to do some internal cyphering, before conjecturing, "It's not lodged deeply enough to have come from this room. It must have come through the open window." She looked outside. "What's the building directly across from here?"

Having spent her entire life in Gadson, Emma didn't need to look out the window, but she found herself joining the sheriff anyway, before answering, "Jolene's Jamboree."

"The childcare center," the sheriff confirmed.

Emma nodded. "It's owned by Jolene Dunn. She was Everett Roach's second wife."

Sheriff Walker considered this as she tapped softly on the glass. Emma noticed the woman's fingernails were neatly trimmed.

"I can give you a time frame for when the window would have been open," Emma offered.

Surprised, Sheriff Walker said, "Please."

"The window would have been closed in the morning, trying to keep in the cool from the night. And it would have been closed at 3:15, which is when school gets out." She pointed outside. "This is where the bus picks up the students. We're not a huge school, but freshly-liberated teenagers make a lot of noise. He would have had the window closed then, which gives you about a three-hour... uh...window, so to speak."

"How sure are you that it would have been open during that time?"

"Absolutely sure."

At the look requesting more evidence, Emma added, "I taught teenage boys in May for twenty-seven years. By noon, the room is no longer cool, and the air is life-threatening."

A crackling emanated from the radios of both law officials. "We have a...darn...what's the number for," the dispatcher, Jaclyn Hunter, was murmuring to herself. "187 is murder. I think there's one if it's a cat."

"Ms. Hunter," Sheriff Walker snapped. "Just tell us what happened."

Through the crackles—and what sounded to Emma like chewing gum—Jaclyn responded, "What's the one for robbery?"

"211," Deputy Phillips answered just as the sheriff said, "Where?"

"We have a 211 at the bank, Sheriff! A whole bunch of the safety deposit boxes have been looted. The bank has been robbed, Sheriff Walker! The bank has been robbed!"

Sheriff Walker rolled her eyes and shook her head.

"Welcome to your first week on the job, Sheriff," said the deputy. "If you want to head over, I can drop Dr. Parker off."

The sheriff nodded. "Yes, Deputy. Thank you. Do that and then head back to the station." She motioned to the shards. "I'll take care of the bank. These fingerprints are your top priority. Let's get those off to the lab." She looked at Emma, then at the trash can. "Deputy, you might as well take the bakery box as well."

CHAPTER 9

High Ground Café
Dr. Emma Jean Parker, beleaguered proprietress
104 Main Street
Gadson Township, Georgia
Tuesday, May 18, 1999

"It's all I have left of him," sobbed Delia.

"It's not all you have left of him, Mama. You have a whole house filled with his stuff."

Delia sniffled, and Emma noticed in bewilderment that her mother was actually crying. "Mama," she began, with more honey and less vinegar in her tone. "Father's watch is fine."

"That's not the point, Emma Jean. Bee Collins said twenty-two of those safety deposit boxes had been emptied. Ours *could* have been one of them! And it's practically all I have left of him."

"Mama, will you shush? I'm not exactly running a thriving business here, but I *would* like to keep the few customers I do have."

One of those customers—although Emma wasn't planning on charging him—was Waylon Pinckney, the fourth son of Heaven-Blessed farms, and local carpenter. He was measuring for the bookshelves he was constructing for Emma out of reclaimed lumber. As always, his niece, Clarabelle, clad in well-worn overalls, was at his side.

Emma had gone to school with Waylon and had taught
Clarabelle and hadn't heard much more than "Yes, ma'am"
and "That'll do" out of either of them in all that time.
Claire Roach, third wife and now delighted widow, lounged
on the faded purple chaise, basking in the late morning
sunlight, not unlike a well-fed cat. At another table, Lillian
Washington and Dolly Anderson, both "twice-overs," were
sifting through three stacks of boxes marked "book
donations for Dr. Parker." Emma had coined the term
twice-over nearly ten years ago when she began teaching
the children of her former students. Almost like an
overexposed picture, she could imagine Lillian and Dolly
as young girls in the classroom at the same time as she'd
seen their daughters, Lacey and Willow, whom she'd
taught twenty years later.

In the largest klatch, gathering for their bi-weekly game
of Dungeons and Dragons, were Malik Jones, his friend
from church, Chloé Williams, *her* fellow cheerleader,
Harper Coburn, *her* best friend, Gunner Wright, and *his*
after-school coworker from the peach factory, Kayden
Ward. They sat around a large, intricately carved and glass-
topped coffee table. It had been a gift from Jeb Harding,
whom everyone referred to as "the woodcarver of the
stars" since he started selling his handmade furniture to
celebrities for exorbitant prices. Despite the fact that
Emma had begged her mother not to, she had looked up
what a Harding table was worth and when Emma said if it
was over ten thousand dollars, she didn't want to hear
about it, Delia had just mimed zipping her lips. Jeb, who
had asked Emma to the prom a million years ago, was now
one of her dearest friends. When she was in high school,
she used to pray that she would wake up a different person,
not gay, and fall in love with someone like Jeb, someone
kind and thoughtful. When Emma had lied about having
to go to Savannah with her grandmother, to avoid the
senior prom, Jeb had ended up taking Charlene Bakeman,
and later marrying her. The couple's only son, John, had
died in Afghanistan just three years ago, mourned by all of
Gadson. Sadly, his mother had died a few months earlier
from Lou Gehrig's disease. Delia thought that Jeb still held
a tendre for Emma, but she felt it was more a kinship

they'd formed from dashed hopes that gave Jeb a special place in Emma's heart.

Delia took a deep breath, straightened her posture and took a sip of her signature drink, which consisted of coffee, cream and sugar, but in entirely swapped proportions. "Well, I'm going to go over to the bank this afternoon and take Hiram's watch out of there."

Emma waited for the comment she was sure would follow.

"I might as well take my gun out of the safety deposit box while I'm at it," Delia mumbled into her drink.

Now it was Emma's turn to sigh. "That's fine, Mama, but then you need to put your other one in. We've discussed this."

"Emma Jean, I told you. I like to have an upstairs gun and a downstairs gun."

"Well, Dad nearly lost his *downstairs* toe with your *upstairs* gun."

Delia's eyes darted to her purse.

"What? Oh, Mama. Give me your purse."

The petulant look, which never strayed very far, returned to Delia's face. "A woman's purse is her sanctuary, Emma Jean Parker."

"Your concealed carry permit got revoked, Mama. Give me your bag."

Unladylike grumbling accompanied the handing over of the oversized purse and Emma set it on the counter to begin rifling. "Mama!"

"That other stuff in there is not germane to this conversation, young lady."

Emma looked to heaven, withdrew the gun and made a point of slowly removing what looked like a Mento mint from the end of the barrel. She placed the gun in her apron pocket and tossed the candy into the rubbish bin before returning the bag to its rightful (if untrustworthy) owner. "I'm almost fifty years old, Mama."

"Fine. Fine. Keep the gun. There's something else I wanted to talk to you about anyway. I was thinking you should invite Sheriff Walker over for dinner."

"Over for dinner?"

"Yes. As a thank you for helping me to the hospital."

"So, then *we* or even *you* should invite her over. Still, I'm sure she's busy, and it would be weird. I mean, because she's so busy."

"Well, no one's too busy to eat, Emma Jean. Besides, she's such a strapping woman. I imagine she works up a good appetite with all that...sheriffing."

"Strapping? Mama, are you on drugs?"

"Emma Jean!"

Emma raised both eyebrows. "What are you up to, Mama?"

"How could I be up to anything? I don't even know anything."

"She's too busy. I'm not inviting her."

"Okay, okay. I'll make some of your brownies and you can bring those by instead."

"*You'll* make *my* brownies?"

Delia flashed her pageant grin. "Good point, sweetie. Better that you make them."

A bell ringing announced a young woman who could have been John Wayne's granddaughter.

"Talk about guns!" Delia called. "Brooklyn Wells, as I live and breathe, are you still working over at the gun range?"

"Sure am, Miss Delia. You should come over and I can give you a lesson. We have a senior discount on the first Friday of the month. It's a real hootenanny over there." Brooklyn propped her sunglasses on her head and scanned the room. "Claire! Good to see you! I saw your paper from Saturday. Nice shooting."

Claire raised her coffee cup in salute. "Thanks for the lessons. They did the trick."

Delia leaned over and asked, conspiratorially, "And Brooklyn, how many guns do you personally own?"

"Well, ma'am, that a good question." The young woman sat down on the bar stool next to Delia and Emma could picture two gunslingers about to talk shop in a saloon.

"Brooklyn, I'll be right with you." Emma gave her mother a baleful look. "I just need a minute."

Emma sidled among the customers in the hopes that no one would notice she was packing heat. The café was a large square with a hallway at the end that led to two restrooms, the utilities closet and a large pantry. Taking off her wrist coil key ring, she unlocked the padlock to the pantry, leaving the keys dangling as she stepped inside.

Emma did not survive twenty-seven years as a teacher without becoming an exceedingly organized person. As such, she had arranged the pantry alphabetically. After filing the weapon, Emma returned to her station, where she saw that Brooklyn had paused in her litany to call over to her younger sister, Londyn, one of the role players.

"Londyn, you got about five more minutes."

"Five?" Londyn wailed. "I can't do anything in five minutes! We're trying to attack Minderhall!"

"Not my problem."

Angry mumbling and stomping brewed as Londyn threw her belongings into her backpack, which she slammed down on the floor as she took her tiny velvet pouch and began collecting her dice. "Oh no!" she wailed again. "My d20! Where is it?"

Immediately, the other players were up, looking behind couch cushions and under tables. Harper looked down her shirt, which spoke volumes, but Emma wasn't sure about what, and Gunner, who had lost probably a hundred of Emma's pencils, looked in his pockets.

Emma went over to the group. "What are you trying to find?"

Londyn sighed with her entire body. "Ugh. Dr. Parker, I can't find my d20." She bent over to retrieve a camouflaged die about two centimeters in diameter, vaguely sphere-like and covered in numbers.

With a sense of impending dread, Emma asked, "What color?"

"Claret," Londyn answered immediately. "Well, maybe more of a merlot, or burgundy."

Emma quickly discarded a wonderment about how much wine was being imbibed at the Wells household. "Where did you last play?"

"In Mr. Singleton's classroom, oh—oh no! It's probably there! And now if I go back there, Mr. Singleton will think I'm a dork because I play Dungeons and Dragons." She turned to her fellow players. "No offense."

In quick succession came three responses of "offense taken" accompanied by Chloé, who said. "I could cast *Pass without a Trace*!"

Emma cleared her throat. "I was just heading over to see Mr. Singleton, Londyn. I'll let him know that *a* student was looking for it."

"Oh, thank you so much Dr. Parker!"

"Time's up, sis," Brooklyn bellowed from the bar.

"Coming!"

After the door closed behind them, Emma turned to the remaining players. Trying to keep a casual tone, she asked, "Did anyone come in to see Mr. Singleton while you were there?"

The teenagers looked at one another.

"Spit it out," Emma ordered, but when she saw all of them take a deep breath, she clarified, "Malik, you go."

"It was The Roach, Dr. Parker. He came in and started to yell at Mr. Singleton, who told us to head outside for a minute."

"Which you did?"

"Yes, ma'am, but we could still hear the yelling, so we went to the side entrance to wait."

"And how long were you there?"

The group conferred with one another. "Maybe like twenty minutes or so."

"There was a lot of yelling. Then no yelling. Then a lot a lot of yelling," added Kayden.

Chloé gasped. "Dr. Parker, do you think Mr. Singleton killed The Roach?"

Gunner began jumping up and down. "Please let me be the one to tell Londyn!"

"I wonder how he did it," mused Harper.

Kayden wiggled his fingers. "I would have cast *Finger of Death*."

"You can't," Gunner argued. "*Finger of Death* is a seventh-level spell."

"I *am* seventh level, Gunner!"

"*You're* seventh level, but that doesn't mean you can do seventh-level spells yet."

"That makes no sense!"

Gunner shrugged. "Ask Malik."

Kayden turned to his Dungeon Master, who nodded. "It's true."

"But why?" Kayden wailed.

Emma cleared her throat again. "May I borrow one of the...uh...d20s? To show Mr. Singleton."

Malik, who had a mason jar filled with dice of every size, color and facet, handed her one and Emma quickly excused herself. She grabbed her messenger bag from behind the counter. "Mama, do you mind keeping an eye on the café for a bit?"

"I suppose. Oh, and this was outside for you." Delia handed her a white business envelope with Emma's name on it.

"Outside?" Emma asked.

Delia shrugged. "I guess. When the Wells girls left, they said it was stuck in the door jamb."

"And you didn't notice anyone put it there?"

"I am not a machine, Emma Jean."

Emma tore open the envelope. "I'm just asking, Mama."

She read the opening lines and immediately felt her face blanch. "Oh Lord," she gasped.

"Emma! What is it?" Delia reached for the paper, but Emma instinctively recoiled, folding up the paper and sticking it in her bag.

Emma's brain began to spin. "Mama, you've spent most of the morning talking with your friends about the bank robbery, right?"

"Emma, sweetie, what's happening? You're scaring me."

"Just answer the question, Mama. Please."

"Alright, alright. Yes, after I talked with Bee from the bank, I called over to Glenda and she had talked with some folks."

"And have you talked to anyone who had something stolen who *wasn't* living at Magnolia Manor?"

Delia tilted her head in consideration. "Darndest thing. All of them."

"And Paisley Culverhouse. She cleans there."

"You know she does, Emma. Please, tell me what's going on. You're going to give me a heart attack."

"I'm fine, Mama." Emma considered under which circumstances someone would have access to so many safety deposit keys. At the same time, she thought of where The Roach might store all of his evidence for safe keeping. "Do you know if she cleans anywhere else?"

"No, just the manor, and maybe a few of the businesses—Oh! Someone told me—I forget who—"

"Mama!"

"Right. Someone told me she also cleans—well, cleaned, I suppose—for The Roach. Who knows what he had on her, but it must have been good, because according to all three of his wives, the man was filthy—and I don't mean—"

"I know what you mean, Mama. Thank you. I'm fine. Don't worry. I'll be back in bit." Emma knew she'd pay for her rudeness later with having to endure hours of her mother's sulking, but she knew just as well that if she told her mother what was in the letter, it would be so much worse.

CHAPTER 10

Yaupon Apartments
Asher Singleton, resident
517 Yaupon Avenue
Gadson Township, Georgia
Tuesday, May 18, 1999

Having seen its heyday in the swinging seventies, the liveliness of the Yaupon Apartments had faded in the following decades. Emma drove around potholes and past the buzzing vacancy sign to park in the shade of a southern live oak. At the front gate, when she scanned the list, she found Singleton's name next to the cleanest button. She pressed it. When no response came, she pressed it a second and a third time, holding it.

"Hello?" came a thready voice.

"Singleton, it's Dr. Parker."

"Dr. Parker?"

"Yes. Press the button."

"Oh, right."

The sound of the buzzer aligned with a heavy unlocking of the gate and Emma entered, maneuvering her way down begrimed hallways and up carpeted stairs the color of vomited mustard. When she turned the corner to Singleton's section, he had the door open.

He was wearing a gray bathrobe and his hair, normally slicked with product, was doing its best to point in as many different directions as possible. "Dr. Parker, it's so nice to see you?"

Emma bit back the urge to retort with the classic pedagogical rejoinder "Are you asking me or telling me?" Instead, she simply said, "Indeed." She entered his home. "This won't take long."

"Have a seat." Asher indicated the sole piece of furniture in the living room, a faded and duct-taped La-Z-Boy recliner, which sat underneath a creased poster of the Millennium Falcon.

Emma raised both of her eyebrows. "This is fine. She picked up a stack of magazines from a folding chair at the kitchen table and set them on the floor, indicating for him to take the opposite chair. As she took in the surroundings, she tried not to feel pity and when she did, she tried to keep it to herself. Still, it was impossible for her not to see him as the sniveling student he had once been.

"I know The Roach was killed in your classroom," she began, figuring it was the easiest way to get what she needed and get out of this cesspool of sadness.

"I didn't kill him!"

Well into teacher-mode now, Emma clasped her hands, leaned forward and said in a calm, rational tone, "Tell me what happened."

"I was in my classroom and Everett just came in and started attacking me for no reason."

Emma gritted her teeth. "For no reason?"

"I swear! He was just—"

"Good Lord, Singleton. Snap out of it! The Roach was blackmailing you and you know it. I don't care why and I almost don't even care what he had you doing for him." She took a deep breath and recentered herself. "You were in your room. He entered. He yelled at you. Then what?"

"Well, Londyn and some of her friends were there. I think you know them."

Emma nodded although she didn't like the way his voice seemed to linger on the girl's name.

"So, Everett told them to leave. Then he yelled at me some more. Then I left and—"

"You left and he was still there?"

"Yes. I went out for a cigarette. I was so upset," he whined.

Emma gave him a doleful look. "Keep it together, Singleton. You're an adult."

"I know!" he snapped, and Emma could see the lack of sleep in his eyes, and she could smell his sour breath. "And when I got back, he was just lying there on the floor, dead."

"But you didn't call the police?"

"I panicked, okay?"

"So, you just dragged him into the supplies closet?"

Singleton rested his head in his hands and began to sob.

"Singleton, do you remember what grade you got in my class?"

The crying immediately ceased. "It was so long ago, Dr. Parker."

"Not *that* long ago. There was a paper, as I recall. Something about the book, *Kindred*."

"Uh huh?"

"And you plagiarized it. Do you remember?"

"Plagiarized? Are you—"

"Asher Singleton, I have had just about enough of this nonsense."

"Yes, I remember the paper. Are you still mad at me about a stupid essay?"

"Singleton, I was not *mad* at you then. I am not *mad* at you now. I'm just trying to—"

Singleton leapt up. "Green jacket!"

"Green jacket?"

"I'd forgotten until just now. There was a man—a man wearing one of those bright green jackets—*he* must have killed Everett. *He* must have been on his way to Everett's room, passed mine, saw him there, killed him and then left the body there so I would be blamed. *He's* the one! *He's* the one!"

"What man? Singleton, what...man?

"Big guy, really angry, muttering. I don't even know if he saw me. Shit. What if he *did* see me? What if he's wondering why I'm not in jail?" He paced the room in a manic flurry. "What if he decided he needs to clean up the loose ends?" He scanned the room in a panic. "I need to get out of here. I need to leave town."

Up until this point, Emma had taken pride in the fact that she'd never seriously wanted to slap a student. She wasn't sure if this necessarily counted, but even so, she was closer than she had ever been.

There was a sudden pounding on the door. Emma jumped and Singleton peed his...robe.

Deputy Phillips' voice blasted through. "Asher Singleton. This is the Bacon County Sheriff's Department. Open up."

"Sheriff?" Singleton stared at the door. "Police?"

Emma could see the brain wheels beginning to move, and sure enough, a moment later, Asher Singleton was ushering himself out and into the arms of a nonplussed deputy.

"He's worried the real killer is after *him* now," Emma told the deputy as he handcuffed the third school employee in as many days.

"Well, good day, Dr. Parker," said Deputy Phillips.

"Hello, Levi. I'm assuming you found prints?"

The deputy nodded. "I'm not at liberty to share that information, Dr. Parker."

"I see. Well, Singleton will have lots of good information for you on the man who *did* kill The Roach."

Emma returned to her car, a gray Ford sedan. She had wanted a Toyota, but her mother had said if Emma bought anything other than American, she should also plan to live in it. Emma had left her bag on the passenger seat and she could see the corner of the white envelope peeking out. Enervated and adrift, she unlocked the car, took out the letter, re-read it, tossed it aside and rested her head on the steering wheel. She closed her eyes. The mid-day sun had turned the car into an oven, even though she'd parked in the shade and left all the windows cracked. She imagined the light bleaching everything away, leaving her clean and unfettered. A crunching of gravel preceded a tap on the passenger side window. Emma didn't look up.

"Emma?" It was Sheriff Walker.

"I'm kind of having a moment here, Sheriff. And before you ask what I was doing, I'll tell you, straight up, that I was meddling."

"It's not about that."

Emma followed the sheriff's line of sight and gasped, reaching for the letter that had been face-up on the seat.

The sheriff took off her hat and opened the car door. Stepping inside, she set her hat on the dash and turned to face Emma, who couldn't meet her eyes.

"Emma," she started to reach out.

"Sheriff, I really...I—"

"Jada."

"Huh?"

Jada laughed. "Call me Jada, and I'll call you Emma. This isn't about 'The Roach' or the reason you're running a café into the grounds."

Emma couldn't help but laugh at the pun. "That's horrible."

"You laughed."

"Barely," Emma grumbled.

Jada sighed. "It looks like maybe someone found Roach's cache of blackmailing materials in a safety deposit box and is now trying to pick up where he left off."

Emma looked at her, imploring her to let the subject go. "You want to get back to talking about murders, Sheriff?"

Jada shook her head. "Look, I'm not going to tell you anything you don't already know."

Emma turned to stare out the window.

"I'm just saying, closets can get lonely. So, I hope you have someone you can be yourself with. Maybe, your mama?

Emma squawked. "Mama and I have a strict please-Jesus-don't-ask and please-Jesus-don't-tell arrangement."

"I had that arrangement with my great-grandmother, but we didn't live in the same house."

"I do have Grant—Mr. Michael. He knows."

"Yes, you two make quite a team—the Yankee Casanova and the—"

"Old, southern prude?" Emma's laughs quickly turned to tears.

Jada reached out and wiped one away. "Not old," she said softly. "Maybe, the distinguished, southern heroine."

Emma snorted. "Shows how little you know me."

Jada smiled. "That's *one* thing we can fix."

Commotion outside the car announced the arrival of Deputy Phillips and Asher Singleton, who seemed to be having a change of heart about how well the police could protect him.

"Where will you put him?" Emma asked.

"Oh, we'll make room."

"And the pastry box?"

Jada shrugged. "You were right." Retrieving her hat, she stepped out of the car and back on duty. "We arrested Carla Nesmith and Blakely Ward this morning."

CHAPTER 11

Michael Residence
Grant Michael, owner
2307 Sweetgum Avenue
Gadson Township, Georgia
Tuesday, May 18, 1999

Grant Michael, of the Hartford Michaels, lived in a gabled-wing cottage at the edge of town. The porch light was off, but Sade singing about "minimum waste and maximum joy" radiated out, and, as Emma approached, she heard the tinkling laughter of a woman—no, make that *two* women. Emma, who was glad that someone in Gadson was living life to the highest, was reluctant to knock, but she was even more reluctant to ignore her hunch.

The door was opened by Isabella Green, the town librarian, who sported a martini in her hand and a look of contentment on her face.

"Who is it, Izzy?" called the voice of one of the Wilson sisters. Emma wasn't sure which one, but based on how well-attended Grant's landscaping looked, she was betting on it being Shelby.

"Why, it's Dr. Parker," crooned Isabella, her voice slick with invitation. "Come in, Dr. Parker. We're just getting started."

Emma didn't want to imagine what they were starting, but she was absolutely certain that she didn't want any part of it.

Fortunately, Grant soon arrived. "What's up?"

Emma glanced at the librarian, who took the hint. "I'll just get the camera set up, professor." She sashayed away.

Emma raised both of her eyebrows.

Grant chuckled. "Life is short."

Emma coughed and flushed simultaneously. "Please, no additional information required."

"Will Dr. Parker be joining us?" came the second female voice.

Grant called back, "She's on an important mission, Shelby." He winked at her. "I'm assuming."

"Yes. How do you feel about breaking the law?"

Without hesitation, he said, "I'm definitely in favor of it."

"I was hoping you'd say that. May I borrow your keys to the school?" She glanced inside. "I'd invite you to join, but you clearly have a full agenda."

"How long will it take?"

Emma considered this. "With two of us, maybe an hour?"

"Perfect. It'll give the ladies a little time to warm up and stretch. I'll just go let them know."

Emma shrugged. "If you say so. Also, grab a hammer and flat-head screwdriver."

With low murmuring fading into the background, Emma returned to her car. Moments later, Grant exited, carrying a large bundle. As he approached, she saw that it was the costume for the school mascot.

"I needed to return this anyway," he said, tossing it into the back seat.

"And your guests won't mind you leaving them?"

"Not at all. Those two love being left to their own devices."

· · • •· • •· · ·

Gadson High School
Dr. Emma Jean Parker, burglar
301 Jenkins Lane
Gadson Township, Georgia
Tuesday, May 18, 1999

Emma reminded herself that she didn't believe in ghosts as Grant unlocked the side door and held it open for her. The large windows along the hallway and her own muscle memory meant she didn't need the lights to make her way to the principal's office.

The administrative suite was always locked, but Emma checked just in case. She didn't want to take off the entire door, just to find out they could have turned the knob. She crouched down and reached into her bag to retrieve her pair of tools, lining up the edge of the screwdriver with the bolt in the door hinge. Lightly, she began tapping the head of the screwdriver with the hammer. Grant mirrored her actions with the top hinge and in quick succession, their tapping, which sounding like drunk woodpeckers on a streetlight, freed the bolts and they were able to maneuver the door open.

"Here," Emma said, grabbing a phone book and tucking it underneath the door. There were just enough residents and businesses in Bacon County to keep it in alignment.

After Grant retrieved the two chairs that sulked outside Sheila Simmons' office and used them to prop up the first door, he and Emma deftly removed the principal's door as well. They entered her spacious office, lined on the back wall with a series of filing cabinets.

"What next?" Grant asked.

"I found official report cards and stationery hidden underneath The Roach's desk. I suspect he'd been selling grades among other nefarious shenanigans."

"I can't imagine it made him much money. It's not like there are a whole lot of people around here who really care all that much."

"He may have sold them for favors instead. Who knows, but I remembered a few years ago, you told me about Beau Culverhouse just phoning in the final exam."

Grant laughed. "What a punk, although I have to admire his style. I still remember he answered the question 'What is the formula for magnesium chlorate' with 'Wouldn't you like to know.'"

"Do you remember what grade you gave him at the end of the year?"

Grant shook his head. "I could look it up."

"Was it an A?"

"Definitely, not an A. The highest possible grade would have been a B– or even a C. The final, which he bombed splendidly, was worth twenty percent of his grade."

Emma nodded, then motioned to the filing cabinets. "They're organized by date. His will be all the way on the right." Even before Grant could comment, she added, "I know there's a more efficient way of organizing them. It gives Victoria Roberts something to do each year."

"Understood."

Emma moved to the filing cabinet drawer marked 1990-1992. She found the most recent section and looked for Singleton's report card. She withdrew it and instantly saw one A after another and the glowing 4.0 in the corner.

"That bastard," Grant mumbled, staring at a similar rectangle of paper. "Hey! That scholarship—the one that pays for all four years, all expenses and requires a 4.0—what's it called?"

"It's the Chickering Scholarship, but there's no Chickering family. It's probably something else The Roach concocted, with siphoned-off money from who knows where." Emma closed the filing cabinet and put the folded report card in her pocket, where she felt the die she had borrowed from Malik.

Grant handed her Beau Culverhouse's report card before proceeding to sit at Sheila Simmons' desk and slightly alter the meticulous arrangement of papers, gewgaws and supplies.

Fidgeting with the die and pacing the office, Emma walked herself through the process. "So, Singleton, who wouldn't have been able to afford college, agrees to come back and teach here if The Roach secures the scholarship for him."

"And once Singleton is here, he's indebted and pretty much at The Roach's beck and call for his entire career," said Grant.

"Then Tucker Culverhouse gets the scholarship this year. So, was The Roach planning the same thing for him?" Emma asked.

Grant scoffed. "I can't imagine Tucker having much interest in teaching."

"So bribed with something else then. It makes sense. Otherwise, The Roach would have a bunch of teachers beholden to him in the same way. He would want to diversify. He was probably blackmailing or wheedling or bribing everyone on the faculty except you."

Grant began breaking the tips off all the exquisitely sharpened pencils. "Ah yes, the perks of being a flagrant reprobate with a trust fund."

"So, maybe he wanted something from Tucker's parents."

"Mr. Culverhouse has the trucking company. The Roach was probably planning to start running drugs."

"I wouldn't put it past him." Emma stared at Grant. "Are you almost finished? I want to run these over to the sheriff."

That got Grant's attention. "Ooh, the sheriff. I like her! And she sure liked the look of you. Maybe—"

"She's too young."

"That's getting old," Grant scolded. "Also, I bet she's great in bed—all that top energy." He shifted to his slow southern drawl. "I bet she'd tie you up if'n you asked nicely."

"I'm not interested in being tied up by the sheriff!"

"You say that now," he teased.

In embarrassed frustration, Emma hurled the die at him.

Grant caught it with an audible smack. "Whoa! Take it easy, slugger."

Emma froze, her mental cylinders clicking. "Maybe that's it," she marveled. "Maybe he was arguing with the man in the green jacket, who then picked up the die in anger and threw it. Could that have worked?"

Grant, distracted by science, his first love, considered this. "If the angle was right. If The Roach had his mouth open—maybe, taking a big breath to start yelling again—it could work." He paused before adding, "But it would have to be someone with a great arm. Otherwise, The Roach would just have been able to cough it out. He could try administering the Heimlich on himself, but he was a big guy and that would be a lot of mass to get through." Grant tossed the die, underhanded, back to her. "And what's with the green jacket?"

Emma updated Grant on her visit with Asher Singleton and the most recent arrests, then continued her thinking. "Which meant Green Jacket would have either watched him die or left him to die."

Grant stood. "Either way, he has my thanks. Ready?"

Putting the doors back in place was more challenging, and as Grant was fine-tuning the alignment, Emma roamed the halls, scanning posters advertising the gymnastic team, guitar lessons and the riflery club. She stopped at the large trophy case augmented with old photos of former champions where she saw the faded picture of Wynona Dawson, captain of the softball team and Emma's default high school sweetheart. Their love had been more fumbling and panting than wooing and swooning, but she had made Emma's senior year bearable.

She and Wynona had lost touch after college, both recognizing that, with a larger dating pool, there wasn't much that connected them. Thinking of Mount Holyoke furthered Emma's nostalgia. She remembered her mother pleading with her and threatening that everyone in town would think Emma was—she couldn't remember the exact euphemism for "gay," but she had a vague recollection that her mother had said "manly." Emma confirmed the memory as she thought of her father. He had been reading the paper at the breakfast table and muttered behind it, "I think it's fine if you're...manly." Mulling over those words again, Emma was halfway convinced that her father had known and was telling her that he loved her unconditionally in the only way he knew how.

Wiping her eyes at the thought, Emma smiled at the picture. The last she'd heard from Wynona, she and her girlfriend had moved to Massachusetts, which was rumored to be close to becoming the first state to legalize gay marriage. Emma imagined that Georgia, having only abolished its sodomy laws a year earlier, was light years behind. She also imagined that for most people, Georgia's laws would always be trumped by God's laws, and any legal developments certainly wouldn't do her much good in Gadson. *Maybe after Mama dies, I can move to Massachusetts.* Emma wondered if she had more Mobley than Parker in her DNA. Considering Meemaw was still alive, Emma could likely be eighty-years-old before she'd be able to leave Gadson and the closet.

To avoid the oncoming bout of melancholy, Emma made herself look at something else, finding the next picture over, which was one of Wyatt Culverhouse,

Tucker's father and award-winning pitcher. This further depressed her as she thought of his wife, Paisley. When Emma had begun teaching, in the early 70's, only half of the students were turning in typed papers. Like most teachers, Emma had developed not only the skill of reading cryptic and barely legible handwriting, but also the ability to recognize its author by the style, including the little circles which many of the girls had used to top their *i*'s and *j*'s. Emma had broken all but one student of the goofy habit.

She thought back to the hateful letter from the morning. Such vitriolic threats of malicious exposure, and all written with those same stupid little circles.

"Evening, Dr. Parker."

Emma yelped, then clutched her chest, turning to stare at the janitor. "Maverick, you startled me." Raising her voice in a warning to Grant, she said. "You're...you're here awfully late."

"I know. Fell behind in my projects, what with being in jail for kicking that son of a bitch, Roach."

"Yes. I heard."

The janitor smiled. "I tell you, Dr. Parker. It was worth it."

"I bet. Oh, Grant, here you are. I was just coming to see if you needed any more help moving rooms."

Grant looked at his watch. "I do, frankly, Emma, but it's nearly midnight and I have two lovely ladies waiting for me to make sweet love to them." He turned to the awestruck janitor. "Life is short, Mr. Hall."

The janitor sighed in admiration. "Ain't it the truth."

CHAPTER 12

Bacon County Sheriff's Office
Jaclyn Hunter, Dispatcher
211 Main Street
Gadson Township, Georgia
Wednesday, May 19, 1999

The Bacon County Sheriff's Office was located inside the Gadson Town Hall, which was across the street and a block away from the High Ground Café. Even though it was now past midnight and there was never enough crime around town to warrant more than a handful of employees at any time of the day, Emma saw that the lights were on. Out of habit, she parked at the café and walked over, immediately noticing the Culverhouse Enterprises truck parked in front of her destination. She entered the building and found Jaclyn Hunter, dispatcher, freshening her lipstick and making googly eyes at Wyatt Culverhouse. As usual, he was wearing his bright green company jacket.

He gave Emma a lupine grin. "Evening, Emma. What are you doing up so late?"

"Well, hello Dr. Parker!" exclaimed Jaclyn. "Are you here with more evidence? Wyatt, it's the darndest thing. Our own Dr. Parker is solely responsible for all the folks we've been arresting lately."

Wyatt eyed Emma, which made her want to bathe with industrial-grade cleaner. In feigned confusion, he said,

"You think our new lady sheriff can't handle the job, Emma?"

Jaclyn smacked Wyatt on the knee. "Don't you mind him, Dr. Parker."

Wyatt shook his head. "*Doctor*. Now that's a word that just sticks in my craw. Doctor Dixon is a *doctor*. Someone breaks a leg and he can fix them right quick. Doctor Williams is a doctor. I expect she can probably do just as well. Jasmine Johnson, she's a dentist, and we call *her* Dr. Johnson. But you're a different kind of doctor, Emma. Ain't that right? What is it exactly? Is it a foot doctor? A blood doctor? Maybe a lady parts doctor?"

Jaclyn tittered nervously. "Oh, Wyatt, stop giving Emma a hard time. Now Emma, Sheriff Walker is out on a call and Levi needed to have a talk with his no-good nephew. Lord knows, that family has seen enough trouble. Do you want me to leave the Sheriff a message? Have you solved the murder, yet? You know, you've got our sheriff madder than a wet hen with all your poking around."

Emma tried not to look at Wyatt, tried to ignore his baiting and bullying, but when Jaclyn said "murder," Emma's eyes locked on his and she was reminded of all the times her friends and colleagues had teased her about not having a poker face.

Jaclyn continued to prattle. "You're just about solving this case for her, Emma. We had to let Maverick go." She tsked. "On his own recognizance, as if he has a lick of that. Same with Carla, which makes sense. She wouldn't hurt a fly. We tried to let Mr. Singleton go, but he insisted on staying."

Emma could see Wyatt stiffen at hearing the teacher's name.

"Now, Mrs. Ward, I know she's a God-fearing woman and all, being the wife of Reverend Jimmy, but there's a coldness in that woman. You ever notice that? A *coldness*. But you know who Judge Chisholm did set bail for?" Jaclyn lowered her voice. "Sheila Simmons." Lowering her voice further, she added, "Set the bail at a quarter of a million dollars! Can you believe that? And she paid it!"

Wyatt stared unblinkingly at Emma. "You don't say."

"I do." Jaclyn giggled. "I *shouldn't*, but I do." As if reminding herself of her professional responsibilities, she asked, "Emma, what should I tell the sheriff?"

Emma, who had always been a straight shooter, struggled to come up with something plausible. "Delia just wanted to invite the sheriff over for dinner...to thank her for the ride to the hospital."

"Oh, and wasn't that such a scare! Is she okay?"

"Right as rain." Emma chided herself for the quaver in her voice as she turned to leave. "I should get going." On instinct, she added, "I've got people waiting for me."

Wyatt stood. "Let me walk you to your car, *Doctor Parker*."

"I'm fine, thanks."

"Wyatt," Jaclyn pouted. "You said you'd help me...*lock up*."

Emma shuddered to think of what the innuendo might mean.

"Quit your bellyaching, Jackie. I'll be right back."

"I'm fine," Emma repeated, but realizing that Wyatt wouldn't be put off, turned to the dispatcher. "In fact, please call Sheriff Walker and tell her that I'll be at my café in a few minutes and that Wyatt Culverhouse is with me." She glared at Wyatt. "What with all the murdering going on lately, I want to make sure folks know where I am and who is with me."

There was a crack in Wyatt's slimy façade, but he still didn't hesitate to accompany her out the door, down the stairs and across the street.

"Now, Emma, honey," he cajoled. "There's no need to get all hot and bothered."

"Wyatt, I am neither hot nor am I bothered. I am just heading to my café."

"Hey, I'm not sure what you think you know, but—"

"I don't think and I don't know. I'm just heading to my café."

"Damn it, woman! Look at me!"

A few months earlier, Emmeline Burns, a former student, had gifted Emma a series of self-defense classes. Emmeline, who had consistently showed more glitter than substance in her assignments, had made out the certificate by hand on heavy paper with inked violets in the corners and Emma's name written in calligraphy. When Wyatt reached for her shoulder, spun her around and shoved her against the brick wall of Raelynn's Emporium and Gifts,

Emma thought of that paper. When he pressed his forearm against her windpipe, she pictured the corner of the certificate tucked behind the edge of her vanity mirror. *In the morning,* she thought. *First thing in the morning, I'm going to call Emmeline at Might-As-Well and say, "Yes, thank you, Emmeline, I accept. I'd love to have some of those self-defense classes just in case some old bully tries to strangle me half a block from my own damn café."*

"Wyatt Culverhouse!" The screech of annoyance reverberated along Main Street, jarring Emma back to her senses and causing Wyatt to step away. "Stop haranguing Emma and come help me *lock up!*" Jaclyn followed her order with a prolonged whine. "Wyatt, c'mon. I've been waiting all day."

Someone who was *not* going to wait all day, or even a second longer, was Dr. Emma Jean Parker, who bolted down the block, keys at the ready. Once inside her café, it took her a moment to realize the heavy thumping was in her chest and not the sound of approaching footsteps.

· · · ● · ● · · ·

High Ground Café
Dr. Emma Jean Parker, jittery proprietress
104 Main Street
Gadson Township, Georgia
Wednesday, May 19, 1999

Cleaning had long been Emma's recourse in times of stress. She didn't know if Jada would arrive or Wyatt return, but she did know that as much as she resented what the café represented, it felt like a haven to her now. Making herself whistle, she began to wipe down tables. When she realized she was whistling *The Ride of the Valkyries,* which was more bolstering than soothing, she shifted to something lighter. At the same time, feeling too exposed next to the large windows, she set aside the cleaning supplies and decided to organize the pantry instead. As usual, she unlocked the padlock and left the keys dangling as she stepped inside. She was whistling the theme song to *The Andy Griffith Show,* when the door slammed shut behind her. Over the aroma of coffee, Emma smelled gasoline. Then, she smelled smoke.

It took no time at all for the large pantry to fill with the acrid tang of fumes and, after her feeble attempts at escaping had failed, all Emma could think of was how dying from smoke inhalation would be painful and the idea of dying in her own pantry would be embarrassing. Like generations of gay southerners before her, Emma was not a stranger to thoughts of her own demise. Not so much recently, but there had been plenty of dark times when she'd been a teenager. Every day had been coated in misery as she struggled to stifle her attraction to other girls. Every evening had included advice from her mother on how to catch a boy and, once caught, how to handle him. Sundays at First Baptist, without fail, would reference how people like her were an abomination. And every night, she'd pray for the gay to go away.

It didn't, and her emotional pendulum would swing from fantasies of escaping to Provincetown on one extreme to killing herself on the other. She had thought of drowning herself in Mill Pond, but she'd been too strong a swimmer. She'd thought of cutting her wrists or taking her mother's pills, but she couldn't stomach the image of her parents finding her or the mortification she'd feel if she survived. They didn't have a garage and hanging herself in the deep south seemed inappropriate, not to mention painful. In the end, she'd settled on shooting herself. It would be quick and if she did it outside, there would be less of a mess to clean. Plus, she knew where her father kept the keys to the gun safe and frequently, her mother would insist on keeping her gun in the drawer of her bedside table.

Lying on the floor with her shirt covering her mouth and smoke filling the room, Emma marveled that this was how it would end. She felt something tickle the back of her brain. Something about her mother and her—gun! She had her mother's gun! She leapt up, smoke immediately stinging her eyes. Shutting them, she felt her way toward the G section of the pantry. Stretching past the glasses, gloves and grande cups, her hands clasped at—nothing. *I know it's here. I put it here. Why isn't it—revolver!* Coughing and wheezing, Emma ran her hands along the shelves until she found the box of replacement parts and stack of rubber mats. Behind them, was also nothing. She racked her brain for where she'd filed that stupid Colt revolver.

And there it was, behind bags and bags of coffee. She retrieved it, squinted one eye open, tried to gauge the location of the padlock and pulled the trigger.

CHAPTER 13

St. Joseph's Hospital
Dr. Emma Jean Parker, patient (noun and adjective)
11705 Mercy Boulevard
Savannah, Georgia
Saturday, May 22, 1999

When Emma first regained consciousness, there was a tube chafing her throat and her mother was in an audible panic. Neither of those held any interest for Emma and even though she knew there was something important for her to do, her brain was too much in a drugged haze to think.

The second time she woke, the haze had lifted, her body was crowded with pain and Delia was out of the room. This time Emma *did* remember the important thing she needed to do, but nothing was as important as finding her way back into the absence of pain.

The third and fourth times featured other configurations of haziness, pain, tubing and mothers, one of which included a chorus line of inch-tall Delia Parkers, all dressed in carnation pink with pillbox hats. Emma told herself to make a mental note to ask about the dosage and the drug, but her mental note became an *actual* note—a syncopated eighth-note—that bounced along the row of hats.

The fifth time was the charm. Her mother was gone. The tube was gone. The haze and the pain were both minimal.

Most noteworthy, and something that brought a quick, sweet sting to her heart, was the presence of Jada Walker.

"My jeans," Emma croaked.

Jada moved to the bed and leaned in. "Come again?"

Emma thought of how her breath must smell, so she tried repeating herself through barely opened lips. "My jeans. Look in the pocket."

Jada smiled and took her hand. "Emma, we can worry about that later. How are you feeling?"

Emma frowned.

"Okay, okay. Jeans and pocket." Jada pulled open the built-in drawers until she found a pair of faded Levis.

There was a sound of paper unfolding and something plastic dropping. Jada stooped, then looked at Emma, raising the die and one eyebrow. "You play Dungeons and Dragons?"

"Students of mine. They play at the café, but on Saturday they played in Singleton's room."

Through fits and starts and sips of water—Emma's hands worked fine, but apparently, she and Jada were both pretending otherwise—she relayed all she had learned.

Jada nodded, as if what she'd surmised was in alignment. "We've taken Culverhouse to Reidsville. Along with his attempt to kill you, there's a long list of nonsense he's been up to with those trucks of his. Fortunately, my dispatcher was generous with all kinds of information, including where we could find you."

"He killed The Roach."

Jada closed her eyes and sighed. "I understand." She leaned against the bed and Emma found herself moving her legs to make room. Jada took the unspoken invitation and sat. "How about you take a break from doing my job— just for today—and focus on getting better." She held her hands up in mock defense. "Just an idea."

Emma smiled, half-raised her eyebrows and changed the subject. "Did I miss the salon?"

Jada nodded. "You did. And I had been looking forward to your recitation. One of the young women on your team recited *The Highwayman*, but I think she delivered it with a smidge too much drama and way more 'riding, riding, riding.'"

Emma grinned. "That would be Dixie. Once she mellows, she'll be a deft performer. She just needs to get it out of her system. How'd we do?"

"Fifth place."

"Oh. Did we at least beat The Furies?"

"The who?"

"My mother's frenemies—the Beauregard sisters and Adelaide Cook."

"I see. I guess, in a way. They were disqualified for reciting off-color limericks."

"I'll take it," Emma grunted. "My mother too?"

"No. Strangely enough, she must be the level head that keeps them reined in. She was here with you. Has been the whole time, I imagine."

Emma snorted and winced.

"Do you want to know how your café is?"

"Is it dead?"

Jada laughed. "You know how a tragedy will bring people together to support someone they love?"

"Yes?"

"And you know how that café was already being heavily underwritten by the grateful citizenry of Gadson?"

"I suppose," came Emma's truculent response.

"Well, they've redoubled their efforts and I imagine you're going to have one of the finest cafés in the state by the time they've finished with it." Jada reached for Emma's hand. "You, dear Emma, are the beloved pet project of an entire town."

A bitter pang hit Emma as she thought of how different those people might feel if they knew the truth. Just then, the scheduled dosage of pain relief was released into her IV. But even the combination of pain in her heart and pain relief in her veins could not overpower the euphoria she felt in holding the hand of Sheriff Jada Walker.

Epilogue
Parker Home
Delia Parker, hostess
501 Strickland Street
Gadson Township, Georgia
Wednesday, May 26, 1999

Emma and her mother lived in a large Queen Anne house built at the turn of the century by Emma's paternal grandfather, Ewell, for his bride, Geraldine. Festooned with all the trimmings a young wife could imagine—including balustrades, patterned shingles, second-story balconies and a polygonal tower—the house was primarily the color called rosewood, a deep pink that perfectly matched the blushes of Dr. Emma Jean Parker as she endured what was, to date, the most uncomfortable dinner of her life.

Over a meal of grilled bass—courtesy of Jeb Harding—Delia fussed over Sheriff Walker like she was an upcoming pageant judge. It unnerved Emma, evoking feelings that were exacerbated by the cheeky covert looks from Grant. Emma had tried repeatedly to veer the conversation toward local murder and mayhem, but Delia was having none of it.

This was probably just as well, since Emma had surmised the culprits behind all the other murder attempts and had decided to keep that information to herself. Claire Roach had clearly been the shooter, and the combination of bears, snakes and almost being buried alive was so Shakespearean in design that it had surely been fueled by Floyd Wiggins' thirst for revenge. But with The Roach gone and their attempts having failed, Emma felt no moral imperative to disrupt the happiness each victim had been able to salvage. Emma had considered ratting out Paisley Culverhouse, but since all of the items stolen from the safety deposit boxes had been mysteriously returned to their owners at Magnolia Manor, Emma had decided against it. At least, she tried to tell herself this was the reason. In reality, she and Paisley had settled into an uneasy stalemate, which meant Paisley's freedom and Emma's secret were both secure. It also meant that she wouldn't be returning to the classroom any time soon.

"Life is short," Grant said, and his oft-repeated taunt brought Emma back to the dinner conversation.

She checked the clock. Only minutes had passed since she'd last looked and she made a mental note to take it over to Tom Greene. Surely it was broken.

"I think May-December romances are beautiful." Delia rested her chin in a palm and fluttered her eyelashes. "Don't you, Sheriff Walker?"

Grant pseudo-scolded, "Why Miss Delia, are you flirting with the sheriff right in front of Em—of all of us?"

"Bless your heart and shut your mouth, Grant Michael. As I live and breathe, I'm not flirting with the sheriff. I'm flirting with the uniform. I can't help it. It's how I was raised."

"Mama, she's not even wearing her uniform," Emma mumbled, forgetting that her plan had been to say as little as possible.

"Sweetie, an officer of the law is always wearing their uniform. It's in the eyes. Can't you see it? Sheriff Walker, do show my daughter your stalwart eyes."

"Mama!" Emma snapped.

"Oh hush, Emma Jean." Delia's attention was riveted on their guest. "So, exactly how old are you, Sheriff Walker?"

Jada smiled. "Old enough to know who I am," she told Delia, before turning to Emma. "Old enough to know what I want."

Emma nearly spit out her latest of many sips of chardonnay.

Jada finished by telling all of them, "and old enough to know the value of others' opinions."

"So, mid-thirties," Delia confirmed.

Jada released a bark of laughter. "34, Miss Delia."

"Hmm." Delia flashed her pageant grin. "Grant Michael, why don't you and I take care of these dishes and Emma can show Sheriff Walker the back veranda. There's a lovely porch swing out there. In fact, I had my first kiss on that swing."

"You grew up in this house?" Jada asked.

"My no. Meemaw Mobley raised me and my sister, Dahlia, in a tin roof shack over near Beech-Byrd orchard. I grew up picking those damn peaches." She shifted from the memories of labor to the reveries of young love. "No, this is where Emma's *father* grew up."

"You told me you first kissed Dad under the bleachers."

Delia rolled her eyes. "I didn't say that was my *first* kiss. My *first* kiss was with his older brother, your Uncle Clifford. Or was it Sullivan? Darn it, now I don't remember. He had three brothers and I needed to work my way through to make sure I had the right one for me."

"Lord, Mama. Please tell me you didn't date all of my uncles before Dad."

"Not before, no."

"Miss Delia," Grant hollered from the kitchen. "I'd love to hear about your sordid past."

Delia released a miffed huff, grabbed a plate and sauntered into the kitchen, bellowing, "Well, at least someone cares about history."

Emma gave Jada a nervous glance.

"It's just a veranda, Emma," Jada said softly. "Show me."

They stepped out into the warm May evening, with the katydids chirping and the scent of azaleas heavy in the air. Emma sat down on one end of the porch swing, grabbing a faded India-print pillow and clutching it to her. Forgoing the other end of the swing, Jada, leaned against the opposite railing. She wore herringbone slacks and a thin sweater with a wide neck, exposing the most beautiful collar bones Emma had ever seen. She imagined trailing kisses along them.

"Emma?"

"Huh?" Emma flushed.

"Darlin', you are wound up like a top. What's going on?"

Emma let her head fall to the pillow. "I'm too embarrassed to say."

Jada hummed her understanding and leaned forward. "And what would you say if you *weren't* too embarrassed?"

Later, Emma would decide that it must have been the chardonnay that made her say, "Well, it's just my mother seems to have some sort of romantic agenda here, which must be wrong because it's completely bizarre, and Grant keeps making these comments about life being short—"

"Which it is."

"I know. Of course, I know, and then you show up with your collar bones and you smell so nice and you arrested all the right people and it's been so long, and I was just planning to, you know, hang up my spurs, so to speak, because it would just be easier and I have the café to think about and the poetry salon next year and what I'm going to recite and there's just a lot on my plate right now and... and...and I'm much too old for you."

Emma felt like she died of embarrassment a thousand times before Jada, in her authoritative caramel voice said,

"Come here."

Emma had never been ordered around by someone she respected, and a frisson of desire zipped through her, fortifying her spine. She set aside the pillow and approached the sheriff until their feet were nearly touching.

Jada leaned forward and whispered in Emma's ear, "I like your collar bones, too."

About the Author

Robin Russell lives, writes, kvetches and teaches in Seattle. Visit www.robinrussell.net to learn more about her books and check out her author page on Amazon.

ACKNOWLEDGEMENTS

This project was a lot of fun! Thanks to our readers, families, and friends for giving us their support and patience while we percolated our plots and brewed our stories late into the evenings.

We wish to thank Mariah Sinclair for the coffee-themed book cover and the various editors who helped refine each story.

Made in the USA
Las Vegas, NV
20 February 2022